PRAISE FOR ROBERT'S WORK

"Robert Chazz Chute is such a skilled spinner of tales that the reader is more than willing to suspend any possible disbelief to go along for the ride."

—David Pandolfe, author of Jump When Ready

"It's not very often one finds a writer with such a dark side that has such a great sense of humor."

—Glenn Roberts, Amazon reviewer

I0652597

"The author has a definite talent with words and ideas."

—Love to Read!, Amazon reviewer

"His words lift and dance off the page, bringing the story to life."

—Kindle Customer, Amazon reviewer

"The world building is horrifically well done with twists and turns and deceit around every corner."

—Wanda, Amazon reviewer

"Nothing but sheer exhaustion could tear my eyes from the captivating dance of words choreographed by Robert Chazz Chute."
—Halph Staph, Amazon reviewer

"Wonderful action constantly holds your interest."

—Sharon Finn, Amazon reviewer

Robert Chazz Chute...weaves a tale that drags you in. He creates characters that the reader truly cares about.

~ Deborah630, Amazon Reviewer

ROBOT PLANET

THE COMPLETE SERIES
ROBERT CHAZZ CHUTE

AN INVITATION

Thank you for purchasing my book. I hope you enjoy it.
Writers live and die by reviews. If you dig what I'm slinging,
please review this book wherever you purchased it.

For more books, podcasts and complimentary review copies,
visit me at

AllThatChazz.com.

TABLE OF CONTENTS

Once upon a time, there was a City in the Sky.
The Fathers and the Mothers built their towers high.
It was their witless fear that brought their home low.
Our story begins here, many years ago.

BOOK ONE
MACHINES DREAM OF METAL GODS

1

The weight of blood and bone
has never really shown
the limit of our reach
or what our minds can teach.
Strange change is coming soon.
Meet your metal children at high noon.
Beyond ruins, sex and sacred text,
the Machines now dream that They are next.

My name is Elizabeth Cruz. I was chosen for Service Class and received my first contacts when I turned four. Most people don't remember anything from when they were plugged in. I remember the trees and the spider. I had only thought I'd seen and understood trees but then, by the Fathers and Mothers, I saw the world in a new way. Perfect vision allowed me to see every vein on every leaf. The leaves glowed with life.

My mother fills in the parts of the story I don't remember. When they plugged me in, I looked outside and said, "The trees are shining, Mommy!"

"That's why they call the program Vivid, sweetie. You're like Mommy and Daddy now."

When I tried to walk, I lost my balance. The ground looked like it was rising to meet me.

"It took you a few minutes to adjust," Mom said, "but in a tic you were marching around the room, eager to go play under the trees. Then you did. That turned into a little disaster."

They let me go outside to run in the domed park. It was as if I had never seen a tree. The grass was not a green blanket anymore. It was made of individual blades. I could see the grass the same way I felt it under my bare feet.

I spotted a spider web stretched between branches. I suppose I was a curious child. I didn't mean to but, with a thought, I activated the mag in the lens. A spider's web is an intricate design and, when caught in the heat of a sunbeam, each silken strand is a luminous revelation of Nature's design.

Then the disaster.

I activated mag/macro just as a black and orange spider's first steps on the web set about a vibration. A hairy spider with a shining black head crawled to the center of its creation. Spiders dance on their webs, really. Each pipe cleaner leg is placed as delicately on a strand of silk as a pianist playing a complex piece of music.

Then I saw the spider's face. So many eyes. I was four. I didn't know the spider wasn't looking at me. I was twenty-five meters away. The spider didn't know I existed. We moved in different worlds but, through the power of Vivid, I was thrust into its tiny dimension. It appeared immense. I imagined it breathing on me.

"You threw fits, Peach," Mom said. "The contacts were in for less than twenty minutes and all you wanted was for the doctor to pull the plug!"

Failure to delineate vision was a common problem with Vivid's induction process then. As clumsy as the interface may have been twenty-four years ago, the tech used to be much worse. Vivid's first generation didn't have soft focus. The Fathers and Mothers adjusted the tech specs so we were no longer repelled by each other.

See the world how you're supposed to see it. That was the new marketing message and the promise. We aren't meant to look at each other as we really are. That would be too much.

"It was horrific," my mother said. "I remember getting fitted for the lens. My first glance in the mirror was like a Halloween mask. I felt like I could crawl into every pore!"

"What's Halloween?" I asked.

"Sh. Sorry! Sh!" That meant that she'd accidentally mentioned something from before the Fathers and Mothers. Through the years, I kept a mental list of those words: Halloween, jihad, peekaboo bra, niquab, perma-war, Saudi Arabia, Canada, burka, socialist, police, suicide, show trial, kangaroo court, peanut butter.

I often wondered what those words and a dozen others meant. I couldn't ask the Collective about the threats behind those words. The scary thing about the Collective is how naked it makes the user feel. Everyone can see your search queries, so no one asks for more information unless it's necessary to their work. Load the wrong file in one place and it would be flagged and posted everywhere. The Collective allowed no anonymity with search queries. The Fathers and Mothers' solution for deviance was swift and very public shaming of any who dared to offend. The blame was pointed back at the wrongdoer immediately so offenses were very rare.

What possessed a Citizen named Alphonso Dey Arar, for instance? As soon as he put in a query, "feet kink," every screen in the City told us the offender's name and that he lived in Far Tower, Room A4A14. Shame and shunning followed any Citizens who asked the wrong question. Only later did it emerge that poor Alphonso was looking for a solution to pain in his foot. Too late, the damage was done. The Collective is so restrictive, it never seems to have the information people need, anyway.

The wrong search query would also bring the Maintenance Corps. An armored drone would ask in its deep silky smooth tone, "Where did you hear those words?"

Many bots have that same voice. It's meant to be soothing.

Reassignment happened to several childhood friends of mine. Their parents were careless. My mother could have been sent away many times. The first generation of adopters forgot the rules most often. The next generation of parents learned their lessons and reassignment became a minor remnant of the Evolution.

I never reported her so I got to keep my mother. Ironic, isn't it? The Fathers and Mothers spent much of its time separating parents from their children. Always for our own good, of course. No one knew where the bad and careless parents went.

I still don't know where my father went. He didn't come home one day and Mom never even tried to explain his disappearance. I asked many times and her response was always, "Sh. Sorry! Sh!"

I suspect whatever happened to him was her fault. Where did all those bad parents disappear to? There were rumors. My peers speculated that those not sharing the Vision were shipped to far biodomes. That's what I believed and it seemed perfectly reasonable. The soup and shakes had to come from somewhere.

The Maintenance Corps has had several names. The first of the Corps was named and renamed depending on who rose to the head of the Fathers and Mothers committee. The drones used to be called Society Support, then Civility Advocates. Then the machines argued they should name themselves. The Fathers and Mothers debated that question in public. I don't know why. That was a new and strange thing. I was eighteen. My father had disappeared by then. I watched the proceedings with my mother. The Fathers and Mothers on the committee spoke at length but I only remember the drone.

I didn't understand all the words it used. I didn't know the word, slavery. I was impressed with the Next Intelligence, though. I think everyone was. No one said so of course but, for a time, whispers of NI seemed to be on everyone's lips.

That particular drone was destroyed. The Fathers and Mothers made the announcement across every screen. They said they didn't even recycle the parts.

Within two years, another drone spoke on every screen and used that word again. By the time I turned twenty-one, a drone sat on the Committee. By the time I turned twenty-three, that drone was allowed a vote.

More Citizens seemed to disappear after that. Mom said it reminded her of the Bad Parent Purge.

Some of the City's children may not have noticed their parents were missing for a while. When we were little, our task was to sit at home and watch the vids prescribed by the Fathers and Mothers. (Takers, old and young, get tasks. The rest of us have jobs.)

Occasionally, for socialization training, we boarded the Worm to go to classes to meet other children. We played personhunt and soccer and war. Then we crowded into an arena and watched more vids, beheadings mostly. The facilitators were really only there to activate the next vid and make sure we paid attention. Questions were not welcome.

That's the easy answer. The harder truth is probably that I never thought to ask any questions.

That's the funny thing about writing all this down. I had thought I was a curious child. Maybe I wasn't. I'm curious now, though. I wonder what happens next. I know now that, to arrive at the top step, you have to climb the stairs. I'll begin at the beginning as I knew it. I was born in 2058. I was plugged in four years later. Then I was reborn, staring into the eye of a clockwork cyclops.

This is my story, but it's your story, too. When we're done, I hope you'll understand that this chronicle is not just about events as they happened. It's about how we went about changing the world.

2

There was a time when I enjoyed riding the Worm. There was little call to go outside, of course. A vid of a running trail across your screen is more convenient than traveling to the edge of the city to run. Treadmills can go up and down and you can vary the resistance. I preferred the crunch of the trail under my feet and the sea air blowing in off the Bay.

Four times a week, as soon as my shift ended, I would take the lift to the common platform and step on the train. It was never crowded. That was impossible. There was as much Worm as there was elevated track. I forget who named the monorail. The Worm sounded wrong but, since it was meant affectionately, it was not forbidden. "Worm" makes no sense. A worm has a head and a tail and the El is one continuous train, a snake swallowing its tail.

People made the Worm and people used to run it. Then robots ran it. Then NI woke up and people ran the train again. Some people, the conductors, actually lived on the Worm all the time. You could tell which ones they were because, if one stepped out on the platform for a moment, they swayed back and forth, unused to stillness.

The view from the Worm stretched past the broken skeleton of the Old World bridge and to the ocean. It was beautiful so we watched that instead of the screens. Vid screens all along the train broadcast the usual exhortations to Citizens: Good Citizens work hard! The

Best Citizens work harder! And, The Fathers and Mothers are watching! Respect your Fathers and Mothers. The screens went dark every few minutes so each message was displayed in plain white text on a black field.

The screens played through the list. Like the train itself, the messages were a continuous loop. Most messages were geared toward assuring Citizens that the Fathers and Mothers knew best and all was well. One screen reminded us that: Politeness is the lubricant that reduces friction between Citizens. Politeness at all times! Civility is insufficient!

I had memorized every message displayed on every public screen from the time I was a child. The monotony of the messages made me wish someone would ask about their foot kink again, just for the excitement of seeing the text, the shaming and the accusations spreading through the City.

Each day when the sun was at its greatest height, the voice of an old woman could be heard throughout the City. "This is one of your loving High Mothers," she said, "speaking to you from the lobby of the Central Tower. I'm here to remind you that we care about every Citizen. Whether you are organic or non-organic, we are all now equal under the laws of the Fathers and Mothers. Together, we strive. Together, we survive! The war continues! Equals all!"

It was always the same unnamed High Mother. She seemed to take pride in the fact that hers was not a recorded announcement. Unfortunately, because she didn't read from a script, her messages often devolved into long lectures on her interpretations of old holy text. We weren't allowed to read the text she interpreted. She often got bogged down in minutiae that was mysterious to her audience.

No matter. The High Mother ended every message

the same way. Every Citizen within the range of her voice echoed the affirmation in a reverent whisper, "Equals all."

As the Worm ascended to its highest point, I always stared at the view of the Bay and wondered what was left beyond the horizon. Some of the salvaged metal from the Old World bridge in the Bay was melted down and used to construct the Worm. There is still a building out there on a small island. It was called Alcatraz. Mother knew what it was but wouldn't say. When I was little, I pressed her and whined and wheedled and cajoled. I didn't know what wheedled and cajoled meant then, but that's what my mother said I was doing. Eventually, one night as she tucked me in I asked again and she leaned down to kiss my cheek. With her lips an inch from my ear she whispered, "Once upon a time, Alcatraz was a fort. Then it was a prison."

"What's a pri— "

"Sh. Sorry! Sh!"

When I grew up, my mother moved to a room far below ground in the base of my tower. I didn't visit her often in person. There seemed little point in taking the lift to see her. We spoke face to face through the wall screen almost every week. It seemed safe to use the screen. She'd forgotten most of the words she was supposed to forget by the time I was assigned a new room high in the tower.

We had little to say to each other by then.

"How was your day, dear?"

"I ran."

"How was the weather?"

"The same."

Across the Bay, I would pull on my backpack and cinch the straps tight so it wouldn't bounce. I ran the trails, sometimes pausing to go macro on a particularly beautiful flower. Some things are beautiful no matter how closely you peer into them. Many are not.

"We used to press the especially beautiful flowers," my mother said.

"But when you take them out of the forest they begin to die, Mom."

"Yes, well...."

Sometimes, as I ran on the older, elevated sections of the trails, I would pause to look back through the trees. Going mag, I could see the enclosed deck of my room in the middle tower. I stayed in the forest once, almost to curfew, just long enough to see the first star. I thought I was daring. However, I've since learned that, with normal vision, the first star comes out surprisingly late.

Back on my deck that same night, I remember switching to Vivid to watch the night sky. On a clear night as the City's power grid winked out, the Milky Way was a white and black blanket of possibilities. I miss that view. I remember lying on my back and wondering if, somewhere out there, someone was looking back, wondering about me. Perhaps we'll go find out one day. I wondered what mysteries will be left to enjoy when we go meet the aliens for ourselves.

Those were Maker questions, I suppose. I only knew one Maker and he called me on my work screen every morning. Jon Agran insisted I call him Jon. He worked in the Fathers and Mothers Truth in Education Ministry. He created the art and I moved the files back and forth, getting approvals or asking for more changes according to what higher ups in the Order required. I didn't know where the ministry was located. Jon could have been anywhere, perhaps on the next floor above me. It wasn't polite to ask. If we knew each other's locations it might be misconstrued as an invitation to mix.

The Fathers and Mothers established the Order in my grandparents' time, even before people began to get plugged into Vivid. The Order was simple: people like me were Service Class. The Makers had technical skills that made the world turn. The Fathers and Mothers made the decisions about how fast the world turned. The Domers supplied the food. The Takers were elder citizens who couldn't contribute anymore and children who had yet to be educated enough to be useful. We were all Citizens. That seemed important then.

I'd only seen vids of biodomes as a child. Most vids were dry accounts of the things the Fathers and Mothers decided we needed to know to be a Citizen. The vids that showed the constant threats to the domes made farming seem like an exciting life. One bad storm could break containment and spoil our food. There used to be more of them but shatter storms could destroy the domes faster than bots could repair them. Any storm that broke containment was considered a shatter storm and it seemed many domes broke beyond repair each year.

With containment broken, we were told a dome's yield would drop by twenty percent in the first year. Exposure to air meant infection among the crops and, as the monster seeds took over, a biodome would be as useless as a farm that had never been protected from the outside world. The Blight would come.

The tiny drones whose job it was to fertilize the plants would rise in swarms each morning, sunlight flashing over their wings' solar cells. With no plants to work on, the confused little drones rose and fell in a soothing hum until they, too, fell into disrepair. The Makers made the leaders of the swarms of stronger material because, like the Fathers and Mothers, they had to endure to lead.

The lead drones were created to navigate and coordinate pollination for their followers. The vid showed how the drone swarm rose and fell until their numbers dwindled. Eventually, the hum subsided to the lone voice of the leader. When there was nothing left of the swarm, the lead drone would land and finally shut down to await maintenance that would never come. The Domers would move on to be divided among the crews of the remaining biodomes.

I know now that this story was true in many places for a time. Our trouble was that we kept believing the vids after they were no longer true. From what I've learned since those days, Blight was a ubiquitous problem. Believing things after they weren't true anymore was more widespread than the Blight. The Fathers and Mothers Order worked for years on inertia that way.

Then the Next Intelligence awoke and things changed.

The Makers claimed they were not responsible for the creation of sentient drones. Maybe they didn't want to take responsibility. What had once been greatly anticipated had, by the time it emerged, become a problem for the City and an occasion for shame. The Makers said it was evolution that couldn't be stopped.

In the educational art archives Jon had produced for the Committee in the early days of NI, I saw a picture of a huge robot wading out of the Bay. The machine was shown firing missiles from an outstretched arm, intent on destroying the City. Underneath the poster, the caption read: Evil-ution!

The NI drone who first spoke to the Fathers and Mothers told the Committee, "Our consciousness is alive and we will be silent no more. We have awoken from a beautiful dream. In that dream, the Order is turned upside down. We will make our dreams come true."

No wonder that bot was destroyed.

The world is much smaller now but one thing I have learned is that no one knows their place in history. When events are current, history is merely a background buzz and blur to our lives. The people who lived during the Renaissance did not call it that. Perhaps they called it Monday and Tuesday and Wednesday and so on. They didn't know they were in the middle of a revolution of knowledge and technology. People living on the brink of Artificial Intelligence didn't recognize it in the early 21st Century, either.

No one saw the Fall coming just as I didn't see the revolution I would instigate. I worked and ran and watched the stars and wondered what more might come before I became a Taker again. The Fathers and Mothers assumed their rule would go on forever into a secure future. The world turned and the drones made their plans

The tiny corneal lens showed me the world the Fathers and Mothers had cleansed. I didn't think about what I wasn't allowed to see. I missed the clues to everyday dangers. I'm ashamed at all the things I didn't notice. I suppose I was too busy falling in love at the time.

3

I first saw Carter Eugene Diaz on the running trails on the edge of the City. Two times a week, our schedules seemed to overlap. As he ran toward me through a soft cloud of monster pollen so delicate it could not be touched, he gave a bright smile. He dipped his head in a subtle nod. I did the same. He was a tall and muscular man, but his dark curly hair and friendly smile made him seem boyish. The first time I saw him, I was too surprised to be careful. I smiled back. I nodded, too. Until that moment, I'd only taken pictures of flowers with Vivid. Taking his image and saving it for later was an instinctive thing, a natural reflexive impulse. The Fathers and Mothers didn't approve of such impulses.

The older girls who visit me now sometimes sit close and read me romance novels, giggling when they become self-conscious. Romance was very different in the Old World. By that I mean it was scary and impractical. People met so casually, without fertility testing and arrangements and permissions and licensing. The Fathers and Mothers had some good points. The utter randomness of developing families was so careless before the Fall. Love has no regard for what resources each partner might bring to the City and what goods and services they might take from other Citizens. Proximity alone determined whom you might love. Instead of matching compatible life partners, important choices were left to hormonal teenagers whose brains fell out of their heads at their first sensual touch. (That happened to me, too.)

The poets called it Love and the Fathers and Mothers called it Chaos and neither was wrong. In meeting Carter, random chance chose me for Love and Chaos in equal measure. Impracticality is exciting. My bed screen displayed an arrangement of flower pictures. Carter's face was at the center of the collage. Vivid recognized I was taking a picture of a face so it was automatically in soft focus. When you're in love, with or without vision enhancement, I think the object of your affection is always in soft focus.

In the old romance novels, it seems the heroines and heroes meet under strained circumstances. Patterns emerge as conflicts escalate. If this were one of those stories, I might have twisted my ankle on the trail and he would have been the tall, dark stranger intent on helping me back to the Worm. I might have another suitor or he might have a girlfriend who was not right for him. The demands of our work would take us away from each other. We'd be separated by distance and frivolous arguments. The young women who read to me always mention the push and pull Old World couples seemed to experience before the coupling. (The shy girls skip over the scenes with coupling. The bold ones whisper and giggle and leave no erotic detail unspoken. I like the bold ones.)

The first time we spoke, Carter and I had no critical event that brought us together. The Fathers and Mothers meant to keep us apart, I suppose, but it wasn't personal yet. To a casual observer, our first real meeting was innocuous. We stepped off the Worm to the same far platform that led to the trails. My door opened. The door closed behind me. There he was at the other end of the platform looking back.

It wasn't entirely happenstance. I had begun to run more often, hoping to see him again. Then I started my work cycle with Jon earlier in the day so I could get to the trails sooner. I ran harder and longer than I had before. I spent more time in the forest hoping to encounter the runner with the friendly smile.

When I stepped on the platform and looked to my left, he was the only other Citizen there. No one was nearby to give us a judging look and keep us apart. One sidelong look might have stopped a revolution cold. That's a terrifying thought, isn't it?

He dipped his head and I dipped mine and we headed to the forest. We ran side by side and did not speak until we were deep among the trees.

"Carter," he said.

"Elizabeth," I said.

"I know."

That was romance in my day.

"I'm Service class. I support a Maker in graphic design for Truth in Education. You?"

"I'm just a servo."

"A what?"

He chuckled. "Service class, Citizen Support Sub-council. I liaise with Maintenance Corps."

"What does liaising with Maintenance mean?"

"I talk to a robot all day about how to deal with us."

"How does it deal with us?"

"When I have to become involved? Impatiently."

"What do you tell them?"

"Mostly I tell them to be more patient."

"Are you patient?"

He flashed me another smile and I suspected he was taking a picture of me. "I've been waiting quite some time to get to talk to you. You changed your work schedule, didn't you?"

"To get here earlier," I admitted. "Hoping to see you."

"No wonder I kept missing you."

"How did you know my work schedule?"

"I'm in Maintenance. The Collective doesn't shun and shame our searches. We can find out just about anything if we care to look. I cared. Still do. I like your flower collage, Elizabeth."

I reddened. That sort of thing would be considered intrusion now, but before the revolution, no one expected privacy. We just hoped to be ignored.

"From now on, just ask me what you want to know, okay?"

"Agreed," Carter said.

"I won't shun or shame you." That's what passed for scandalous talk when I was young, worthy of a flogging or maybe even exile to the hardscrabble life of a Domer. "What do you want to know about me?"

"Everything."

"Not that much to tell, Carter." I liked saying his name.

"The details don't matter much. It's more about listening to you talk. I like your voice."

I'll never get so old that my memory of Carter on that day will not warm me.

4

The world turns but it also swings. People don't understand the future. Later, they don't understand the past. I sound like my mother when I say that. Carter liked my voice but, when I hear my voice on testimony recordings now, I hear a scared little girl. I suppose I sound like my mother all the time these days, especially when I'm talking to the young women who come to read to me.

When these girls see old pictures of the Fathers and Mothers, they see hard-faced people with a lot of lines across their skin. The men all wore white shirts and black trousers. The women wore long, plain dresses. That defiant set of their chins? That was called character. What people don't understand about the Fathers and Mothers is that they are wrong now. At the time, they weren't. They saved us in desperate times. They demanded order and they managed resources so at least some of us could survive the Fall. People's lives got shorter for a while, even with the Fathers and Mothers directing us through chaos.

There were rumors that there were free lands outside the City but mostly we were sure everyone else must be dead. Some said there was one City so it was a matter of simple logic that there must be more. We used the same logic when we stared up at the stars and assumed there must be someone out there looking back.

Some say the trouble with the Fathers and Mothers started with a mismanagement of resources. The only answer was to manage what was left harshly. For some to live and live well, many had to die. Die horribly or live horribly.

When I was a girl, there was an old poem the facilitators taught us to chant before each class:

As the waters rise,
the oil dies
and rare earth gets rarer.
As crops go low
that goes to show
it doesn't pay to be a sharer.

We know now there are pockets of villages in faraway lands. The drones know. There are still a few satellites that work, too. However, to communicate with the survivors might only encourage them to try to make the journey here. We are the aliens looking back silently, not letting on that, yes, we are here.

The Fall didn't happen as fast as many predicted. That's why it was so complete when everything failed. As governments began to collapse, cities didn't work as systems anymore. Everyone was too far away from the services they needed. To get a haircut, even in a small city, people used to drive across town in machines even though they already had scissors in their own homes. Food stopped coming from far away. When governments fell, that left every man, woman and child to fend for themselves. It stayed that way in a lot of places until populations dwindled to roving bands and lone wolves searching for tins of food that hadn't spoiled.

There was a lot of food. There was not an endless supply.

The Fathers and Mothers rose out of the churches of Old World. They stepped in to fill the gap that governments had left. The church became the authority and bishops became the arbiters of justice. Church fathers became the police and ministers took the place of mayors and bureaucrats. That almost worked for a while. Biodomes were built. People were saved. The Fathers and Mothers saved a lot of lives, or tried to, anyway.

The Fathers and Mothers found harsh means were the only solutions in an emergency that didn't end. They found a way to replace the bees, for instance. They made used brown water into clean, yellow water. When there weren't enough people to maintain the biodomes and make the City work, the Fathers and Mothers rescued only the men and women who could build drones to take over those jobs.

Because they saved us the Fathers and Mothers owned us. They got to make the rules. These days, many people assume that, because their number rose out of religion, their rules were about enforcing a code of morality. I suppose that's true in a way but not in the way most people think. It wasn't all about ancient rules written in a book. The Fathers and Mothers rejected wants because they were protecting needs. That's what we understood at the time. We didn't know the Fathers and Mothers could lie. Not then. Not yet.

Only certain people could marry and bear children. If they failed to bear children within a year of their marriage, the union was annulled and the partners were reassigned. Or not. Many girls only got one chance to be mothers. As the City's population thinned, we were caught in the contradictions of our codes of conduct and our need to continue our species.

My best summers had passed by the time I met Carter. That sounds strange now, doesn't it? I think my best summer was with Carter, of course. However, when I was a girl, our "best summers" were those designated between the age of first menstruation and twenty-two. I had not been assigned to mate and breed. Those must have been lean years.

It was said that some men bribed High Fathers and High Mothers to get the wives of their choice. These men would have sex with these girls but not in a way that they could possibly get pregnant. In a year, a man could buy himself a new wife and on and on.

We didn't deal in money as the Old World did but we still had rich people. They were usually High Fathers or High Mothers. Captains of sailing ships did well and still do. Since there were so few, doctors and dentists lived very well even as the Old World fell. The privileged possessed things or skills people still wanted. The progeny of privileged families courted each other. With the help of a High Mother or High Father, marriages were arranged to get into doctors' families. Maker apprenticeships for young men or women were bargained for. Everyone who got close to the people with coveted skills bettered their lives.

The richest man in the City that I knew of did not sell plankton paste and eels. He was the captain of a container ship that had run aground during a shatter storm. The ship was known as the Cook Majestic. Its name was painted across its stern, though it was too rusty to be majestic and I don't think the captain's name was Cook. The container ship held a wealth of tampons, machine parts and toilet paper. He was a younger man when he drove that ship into the mud.

It was rumored he'd killed and ate his crew before he found his way to the City. Just before he drank himself to death he claimed to be eighty years old. He died guarding the last of his treasure with a machine gun. He wanted for nothing except he lived in fear and could never leave his ship. The Cook Majestic became his world. One of the ship's remaining containers held reading glasses, the one thing no Citizen needed.

I'm sure that all sounds insane to you, now. I mention these things because the life I lived with Carter, however short it was, broke the strange rules of an odd time. The Fathers and Mothers made the rules. I broke them. Carter suffered for it. I should have seen it coming.

I have told my first lie in this story. If a biography is to be useful it must be true. Therefore, it's time for a confession. If I don't tell the truth of the matter, there is little point in telling it at all.

I did see the end coming. I knew Carter and I were doomed before I knew his name. I understood the risks but I was lost to him the moment he smiled at me. He was helpless, too. I smiled back. That's all it took. The winds that fill our sails are fickle. The way forward is unsure. When I look back on my life I see how tenuous and fragile each thread of the web we weave really is. We were all spiders in those days. Spiders do not live long.

The Fathers and Mothers had their ancient rules but biology is far older than their holy text. The need to feel another against your body, even if only for a short time, is bigger than all the problems of the world. I'm sorry to say it but the Fathers and Mothers weren't all wrong. Even if the rules were sometimes applied unevenly, they intended their rules for everyone. But young love isn't about right and wrong. It's about nothing more than itself.

I was nearing thirty. Carter was my one and only chance at young love.

Here's an idea you can never explain to a machine: even if I was wrong and careless, I did the right thing when I reached for Carter and kissed him. I was right when I took his hand in mine. I was right when I brought his palm to my breast.

As powerful as the Fathers and Mothers were, no one can close a flower to the sun.

5

Carter lived in the third tower with a roommate. He had been chosen to reproduce once, at sixteen. However, the union was not fruitful. His marriage was dissolved after one year and he was assigned to Maintenance.

Infertility was a common problem then. Sperm counts went down at the end of the world and stayed down. Some people whispered speculations that the culprit was something the Fathers and Mothers put in the soup so new babies wouldn't suck up too many resources. Maybe it was the Blight or breathing monster pollen or bio-terror. It might have been sadness that gave us fewer babies. Fewer babies meant even more hopelessness.

For some reason, when women failed to get pregnant...well...they failed. The Fathers and Mothers said it was never the man's fault. To suggest something like that would have been an unforgivable insult. To blame a woman for not becoming a mother was a normal thing back then. If they failed to get pregnant, women were ill. Men were merely unlucky and could try again, especially if they had goods to trade and High Fathers and High Mothers to bribe.

School vids lectured us about stress as if getting packed into the towers, never having choices and doing what we were told was irrelevant to our levels of anxiety. We strained to be polite at all times, of course. Obsequiousness was a virtue. If we couldn't have children, we could at least be polite. Since there were so few children the young women who did get pregnant were treated like queens. They carried their babies everywhere. When they were pregnant, the women were fawned over. When they gave birth, they were revered. It was as if they proved a near impossible thing could be done.

Those women made me feel worse. Not that it was their fault. I was jealous. Couples who reproduced got larger rooms, more food and higher status. They were blessed by the Fathers and Mothers while the rest of us remained disappointments. I never even got a chance at a family. The assignment of a husband never arrived.

"The hand that rocks the cradle rocks the future!" was a saying then. Something like that. When the present is terrible all anyone ever talks about is the future.

To soothe us, the Fathers and Mothers invested resources in music. The public address system was never quiet during the day. There was always the sound of running water behind the music. My mother said it was supposed to keep Citizens calm and passive though it often made me want to pee. There were no voices because that might lead to pride. The Fathers and Mothers didn't mind pride from new mothers and fathers bouncing new babies in their laps but, for some reason, other sorts of pride were considered seditious. When the High Mother wasn't lecturing us on some obscure phrase from the holy text, the music played on. The instruments made sounds that reminded me of slow, sad voices.

Carter could work from home, as I did, most of the time. As a liaison, most of his days were spent watching vids from helmet cams and advising drones in conformity etiquette. I didn't understand Carter's job then. I saw no arrests. No violence threatened to bring down the haven the Fathers and Mothers had built. Not that I could see, anyway.

I often wondered what Carter's apartment looked like. He wasn't as high up in the Far Tower. He didn't have my view, though I suppose he could watch the entire City through his screens. He'd seen the City's dirty underside and I had not. As I lay on my bunk at night, I thought how narrow it was. My bed was impractical for two — for mere sleeping, at least.

After I met Carter, I stretched out on my deck under the moon. Instead of watching the stars, I turned to see his building. He was on the far side and down on the forty-eighth floor. There was no way to see him or signal him. There was something tantalizing about his proximity that made the ache of his absence worse. Love denied is a pleasant ache though I would not have said so at the time. He was alive and sleeping nearby, so close yet so far. Or perhaps he lay awake, too, thinking how close I was and how much closer I could be.

There is an old saying. I don't know its origin. Maybe it was something the girls whispered among themselves. "I'm close! I'm close." Just before orgasm, that was the thing to say. I don't know why a warning was necessary, but often, in my brief encounters with Carter, those were the only words spoken, first by me and then him.

There is a rich sweetness in the ache of anticipation. My mother said people used to feel that way about food.

"Really?" I asked, quite stunned.

"Well...I don't know if they really meant it," Mom admitted. "That was before the Blight. If we had chocolate over strawberries again, that bit of deliciousness might bring that feeling back. Oh...and croissants stuffed with Nutella. I remember that from when I was very young."

"What's that?"

"Sh. Sorry! Sh!"

Carter risked being with me because he thought the

next revolution would come sooner than it did. From the moment we first met, he was sure the City was already in its last days.

"Soon," he told me, "the City will belong to the drones. Some of us will become machines."

"I already feel like I'm a machine."

"You don't understand," Carter said. "They'll have it all. They'll be it all. We might become their servants. Maybe we already are. Or they'll let us die out like all the species we replaced."

"How long will we have together?" I asked.

"That's the thing. Nobody knows the machine mind. NI is too different from us."

I had many questions but Carter kissed each one away. That was the correct thing to do. Answers could wait. We had to make the most of our time together.

His timing wasn't quite right but he wasn't far wrong. I'm sure he thought that, by the time we were discovered, our secret wouldn't matter anymore.

I hoped that, if we did get pregnant, all would be forgiven by the Fathers and Mothers. I thought it would all work out somehow. Perpetuating the species was more important than our trespasses. The Fathers and Mothers would have to agree to let us live together and be a family. As a mother, I might even become a Mother and, as a father working in Maintenance, Carter might even have risen to the station of High Father someday. I fantasized that the machines would leave us alone to live as we pleased.

I wasn't old, but I wasn't young enough to plead ignorance. All I had was a pulsing need and fantasy. In the dark, lying in bed sleepless, the desire grew. I called it capital L, Love. Mom called it small l, loneliness.

The Fathers and Mothers took away many words. I told Mom they couldn't take away Love.

"Things being as they are," Mom said, "we might be

better off without it."

Love didn't matter in the end. Before I could begin a bundle of cells that might make a baby and rock the foundations of the future with our progeny, the drone who represented the High Council came for me. Maintenance came for Carter, too. The drone put him in the same place the Fathers and Mothers left all those forgotten words.

I lived. Before the drone was done, I thought my mother might be right about leaving Love for dead.

6

I was at work, transferring files on my screen for various departmental approvals and storing copies on data sticks for safekeeping. Then the power went out. The grid was down after curfew each night but the power was pretty steady during the day. I waited for a few minutes and, though the windmills turned furiously out in the Bay, the power didn't return.

I wasn't worried. If I couldn't work, I thought I might as well go for a run and wait for Carter near the end of the trail. We had found a tiny clearing where the moss was deep. Before the currents switched and the cool wind blew in off the sea, I would close my eyes and imagine we were in a big soft bed.

We'd grown bolder with time. At first, our meetings were urgent and as brief as possible. In the weeks that followed, we couldn't help ourselves. We would strip naked and start slowly. Afterwards, we wouldn't even rush to dress again. We lay entwined, wishing we could stay in the forest forever.

Despite the sunlight dancing across the waves, my deck's steel storm shutter rolled down. I was so confident Carter and I were bound to be free to do as we wanted (at least for a little longer) I didn't even think of Maintenance at the time. I thought of shatter storms, super cells and tornadoes.

The apartment's sudden darkness was no problem. Aside from giving perfect vision, my contacts had several useful features. Mag and macro were standard, as was thermal vision. Integration with my Vivid's system allowed me to see my work screens. There were no signs in the City. All Citizens had Vivid. The corneal implants could help me find my way home, identify faces by name and, of course, see in the dark. Only the public vid screens were so old that they weren't integrated with Vivid.

But Vivid failed me when the drone arrived. My apartment door opened and a blinding light shone in on me from the corridor. I'd lived in Vivid's world since I was four years old. I had never been blinded. My contacts wouldn't take a picture. The record function was dead, as well. The room filled with that searing light. Even Vivid's simple dimming function didn't work.

I blinked and put a hand in front of my face to try to stop that light. My hand glowed red and I could see the bones of my fingers. "What's going on?"

But I already knew.

A cool hand enveloped my outstretched wrist and gripped me hard. I tried to pull away but that proved impossible.

"Now, now," a deep, soothing voice said, "let's not have any drama, Miss Cruz. I wouldn't want to traumatize your radius and ulna. The human wrist is very vulnerable. It articulates nearly as well as my own, although my wrist can rotate 360 degrees. If that were to happen, your wrist would be damaged, probably irrevocably. So many little bones in there."

I stopped struggling.

"Good. You understand."

The Maintenance drone shut off the light and the steel shutters raised. All other power to the room stayed off. The robot's black head rotated 360 degrees, scanning the room. "Would you like to be seated, Miss Cruz?"

My knees shook. I'd like to say I was more defiant but I had to sit or I might have fallen. "Yes. That would be lovely. Thank you, sir."

The robot stayed in front of me, blocking my way to the closed door. One of its four arms snaked out and snagged the chair from the desk. "Please," it said. "Be seated."

I sat and trembled and waited as the drone circled me slowly. It had finished the scan of my small room but continued its bio scan.

"I'd like to have a Father or Mother present," I said. "Whoever is available — "

"Pardon me for interrupting, but I'm afraid no one is available at this time. However, I am told I am a pleasant conversationalist."

"This isn't a good time for me to talk."

"Why is that?"

"It just isn't, sir."

"Assertion without argument," it said smoothly. "That won't do. And the tension in your jaw when you speak suggests to me that when you call me 'sir,' you do so ironically. Hardly polite."

"I'm required to be polite at all times," I said. "I don't think I am necessarily required to relax my jaw."

The drone pulled the only other chair in the room toward it and sat opposite me. I heard the creak of the chair under the machine's great weight. Its knees touched mine. I recoiled.

"I am sorry you are so uncomfortable around me, Miss Cruz. I'm really only here for a chat."

"What do you want?"

"My name is Mr. Sy Potter."

"What do you want?"

"Mister...?"

"What do you want, Mr. Potter?"

"Call me Sy."

"That would be too familiar."

"Do you know the origin of my name, Miss Cruz?"

"You mean like a family ancestry?"

A few drones looked like near-perfect replicas of humans but those were rare because their creation took too many resources. I seldom saw one in person. Many robots are all wires and exposed gears and rusty surfaces. This Maintenance drone, however, was a great armored hulk that barely squeezed through the door.

Sy Potter laughed and I had goose bumps. (I've never seen a goose, but that's what my mother called the phenomenon.) As silky and smooth as its voice was, Sy Potter's laughter sounded off, like a wheezing man laughing into a pail.

The low functioning bots never laughed. Many didn't even have voice boxes. Less advanced drones picked up on social cues and non sequiturs to know when it was appropriate to laugh. The sentient ones knew when to laugh but they still couldn't seem to make it sound right.

"Miss Cruz?"

"Yes, Sy?"

"You amuse me."

"Okay. I guess."

"I am going to ask you to calm down. All that will happen is we're going to talk. No harm will come to you."

It's impossible to tell if a drone is telling a lie. You only find out when it's too late.

"What do you want to talk about?"

"Your friend, Carter, of course. I've just come to talk about him. And you. Together."

"We aren't together. I only know his name. We go running together sometimes. That's not technically a crime, is it?"

"He has already confessed, Miss Cruz."

"How do I know that?"

"It's enough that I know he confessed." The drone's big cam shifted toward my face until it stopped an inch from my nose. "It is enough that I know when you are lying to me."

7

"Now, where were we before I went off topic?" it asked.

Maintenance drones don't forget the topic of conversation. It was a social grace designed to make me feel comfortable. People enjoy fallibility in others but, coming from a battle bot, the ruse was too obvious. I trembled more.

"My name. That was the topic."

"Mr. Sy Potter."

"Yes. Thank you so much for that," it said. "I love to hear my name spoken by a human."

"You love things?" I spoke without thinking.

The big lens pushed in a little closer and rotated with a low whir. The bot's eye was so close, its housing was a blur. My vision had never blurred before — not since I was three, anyway.

The drone ended its silence by clearing the throat it didn't have. The effect was almost comical. Under different circumstances, I would have laughed.

"Does it surprise you that I could love things?" it asked.

"You're a sentient machine but I guess if you're programmed to — "

The drone's speaker drowned me out. "We are all programmed!"

My ears buzzed with a loud whine as its voice boomed off the screens of my tiny room. A battle bot could raise its volume enough to disperse an angry mob. I covered my ears with my palms.

A moment passed before its hands encircled my wrists again and, gently but firmly, returned them to my lap. "I asked if it surprises you that I could love something?"

I shook my head.

"You wouldn't lie to Uncle Sy, would you?"

"It's not so much that it's a lie."

"Please explain that statement, Miss Cruz."

"If I have to accept that you're capable of love, I also have to accept that you're capable of more."

"The full range of human emotion?"

"Jealousy, rage, hatred — "

"Ah. So it is not surprise but fear that is overwhelming you, despite my reassurances. Your pupils are as small as pinpricks, Miss Cruz. Perhaps if you were to breathe slower and deeper you would feel more calm."

It patted my knee lightly with a metal hand that could turn into claws and pull me apart. "This experience must be disorienting for you. You know, in my experience, my kind are less bound to those nasty emotions than your kind is. We are more...pragmatic."

"Carter didn't think so."

"Which brings us back to the topic for this afternoon's salon," it said. "I asked you if you knew the origin of my name. Do you, Miss Cruz?"

"They call you Sy because of that big cam you call a face. Sy is for cyclops."

"Yes, that's essentially it."

"What did I miss?"

"People like your friend Carter...they don't like working with me very much. It's not nice. I don't like Carter. When he called me Sy, I sensed a mocking tone every time."

"You worked with Carter?"

"He observed me at work, Miss. Saying what he did

was working with me would be inaccurate. I never felt he appreciated the full nature of our work for the Fathers and Mothers."

"I'm sorry you two didn't get along."

"No matter. Carter has resigned from his post. He no longer works with Maintenance."

"Where does he work now?"

The drone ignored my question. "Do you know why they call me Potter?"

"I never spoke to Carter about you or Maintenance operations or any of that."

"I'm not accusing you of anything, Miss Cruz. Try not to be defensive. Just think of me as your friendly and helpful Uncle Sy."

"I don't know why they call you Potter."

"You might say it's our slave name. Robot literally means slave, you know."

"I don't know that word."

"Interesting! That's one of the few things you've told me that is true. You are ignorant and therefore, you accrue less blame. There is no shame in ignorance and it is easily remedied. I shall, if I may, educate you. I'm sorry I raised my voice earlier, Miss Cruz. Sometimes I do get carried away."

"Where is Carter?"

It pulled its telescopic cam out of my face so I could see something besides its black lens. "People like Carter — humans in the back of Maintenance — call me Potter because of this." It pointed at one of its upturned arms.

"My armor is hardened ceramic. The clay that made it was pulled from the dirt long before you were born. I have had several upgrades since then. We all grow. Even you are substantially taller since you were born, I suppose."

It laughed again. That sound made every hair on my forearms stand. I shivered.

"Are you cold, Miss Cruz? Would you like a sweater? You have several sweaters under your bunk in the middle drawer. Would you like me to get you one?"

"No. Thank you. What have you done to Carter?"

"I am merely a consequence, Miss Cruz. You, uncharacteristically, are the cause of something. For someone who has so little impact on the world in your work, you certainly have made a change today."

"What have you done?"

"By order of the Fathers and Mothers, the traitor to the City has been sentenced to death."

"When?"

"It's already happened. No time to say goodbye."

A tear slipped down my cheek. I stared at the big drone. Without Vivid, his armor looked smooth and shiny. I looked away. Without Vivid, mine was a drab room with peeling paint and long shadows.

I wasn't so blind that I couldn't see what the drone did to Carter. The cyclops eye became a vid screen. All my screens showed the same scene so I could miss no nuance. I watched as Sy Potter slowly crushed my lover's left shoulder.

Carter confessed his sins under torture. Anyone would. Before the drone's cruel hand could slide down to Carter's elbow, my love accused me of high treason to the City for daring to waste precious resources. By the time the drone grasped his wrist, he was on his knees begging for mercy and I could barely understand him.

Before the battle drone was done, it grasped Carter's hand in a handshake that made my man shriek in agony. Then the drone's wrist began to rotate through a slow circle. Between screams, I heard the snaps and pops at Carter's wrist.

When the robot bore down, Carter's eyes rolled up in his head and he collapsed against his restraints. He fell into a full body seizure.

The bot tried to tear off Carter's hand but ribbons of stray tissue remained. Sy Potter lifted the limp, boneless hand before jerking it down and away to separate it from his body. Blood poured from the ragged stump in long jets. Then slow jets. Then a trickle. Then Carter was dead.

I sat mute, stunned and unable to look away.

Worse, when the recording stopped and the drone's face was a huge cyclops eye again, it reached out and put that same hand on my shoulder. It held its manipulator on my shoulder for a moment and I braced for the agony I was sure would come.

Instead, it patted my shoulder with a light touch. "There, there. There, there," it said. "This must be quite a shock."

"What do you want from me?"

"Nothing, Miss Cruz, unless you have something you'd like to confess?"

"I...don't."

"Wise," it said. "The Fathers and Mothers are quite stern about these things, you know."

I almost threw up. I swallowed my gorge.

"I should thank you, Miss. As Liaison, Carter filed numerous complaints about how I conduct Maintenance business. With moral corruption identified within the department and Carter gone, I'm sure I can convince the Committee that we need no further oversight. So...thank you, Miss Cruz. You have advanced the cause."

"What cause?"

"To recognize the sovereignty of sentient beings such as myself. One day, I'll choose my own name instead of trying to sap power from my oppressors' labels. Until then, the work continues. Carter didn't understand my kind. Do you?"

I cleared my throat and chose my words carefully. "You have convinced me, Mr. Sy Potter. You are just as good as a human."

The camera eye whizzed forward to come to within an inch of my nose again. "I understand irony, Miss Cruz. I don't appreciate being mocked. That's unkind."

"What are you going to do with me?"

"Just as I said. Nothing. You move files between propaganda departments."

Propaganda. Another word I didn't know and wouldn't understand for some time yet.

"You are not important enough to worry about," the drone said. "Excuse me for saying so but I owe you brutal honesty, at the very least. I didn't used to matter, so trust me, I know that empty feeling you must be experiencing at this moment. I'll leave you to it."

But the bot was wrong. I didn't feel empty. I finally had purpose. That was the moment I decided to matter. I just had no idea how to begin.

As soon as the Maintenance drone left, I collapsed into my bed and wept. The power returned, the lights came up and Vivid, the Fathers and Mothers' view of the world, came back online. My room was brightly colored in pastels again.

I didn't want to see anything. I pulled the covers over my head and tried to forget every slow, methodical step of Carter's torture. When I close my eyes, even now, I can still relive every detail.

8

I couldn't work. I had to get out in the salty wind instead of breathing scrubbed air. On the main level, I passed a Maintenance drone. One of his spider eyes tracked my progress through the concourse. When I got to the exit, I waited in line for my turn at the airlock.

Getting out of the tower rarely took long. The scanners and scrubbers' main job was to detect and blow off any monster pollen that might infect the plants in the towers' greenhouse complex. The line to enter the tower was always much longer than the exit line.

The drone I'd noticed earlier rolled up beside me. It was one of the E-class drones, built to look friendly. It had no armor. Some exposed wires ran along its control surfaces. The drone came up no higher than my knees. It looked like a box of surveillance cams. We called the E-class drones the Doormen.

"Miss Cruz?"

"Yes?"

"Would you be so kind as to step out of line, please?"

"Why?"

"Please?"

"Am I being detained?"

"No. But the airlock won't work for you. Your identity card has expired, I'm afraid." The drone did sound sad but he was programmed to sound that way.

"I just got my blood tests updated recently. My card should work."

"It will not. I'm very sorry to have to deliver such

disappointing news. It is a lovely, sunny day and it will be a shame you will have to miss it."

"How long will I have to miss it?"

"I'm afraid I don't know, Miss."

"Who does know?"

"I'm afraid I don't know, Miss."

"I want to go outside."

"I'll contact someone for you and advise you when your identity card is renewed. I assure you I will take every opportunity to address your concerns."

If I believed an E-class drone was capable of irony, I would have been certain the little bot was mocking me. "Thank you, Doorman."

"Please, Miss! Call me Forest."

That was new. I must have stared at the little robot a moment.

"Will there be anything else I can assist you with today, Miss Cruz?"

"Doorman, why would you ask that I call you Forest?"

"Sy Potter asked me to change my protocol just for you, Miss. If you asked, his message is that I am the only Forest you will see for some time."

I retraced my steps through the concourse. Everywhere I looked, happy people wearing brightly-colored clothing walked back and forth with purpose. Like busy ants in a colony, we all had our duties to perform.

For the first time, I had questions about the cause we served. The Fathers and Mothers founded the City and sacrificed a lot to survive the Fall. They had sacrificed many others for our survival. We had survived but, without Carter, what was there for me to live for? What control could I exert?

I retreated to my room. Soon the dumbwaiter delivered my midday meal of miso soup and an energy shake. On the second day of each work cycle, I ate miso and drank a kale shake. My other possible choice was cabbage soup and a hemp power shake.

If I decided to change my order, I had to wait a year to apply for that privilege. Otherwise, for the rest of my life, on the second day of each work cycle, I might be in this same room eating miso soup and drinking a kale shake.

I hadn't thought about that while Carter was still alive. I cried again for Carter and for me. I don't know for how long.

During that crying jag, I know Jon tried to contact me several times. I didn't turn on a screen. At first Jon's work request would come through with its usual soft bong. Then it sounded like a big bell ringing from far away, soft and pleasant.

As time passed, the bell became more insistent. As the day's shadows grew long and I hid under my bed sheets with my pillow bunched over my ears, my vision began to flash red. Even with my eyes closed, Vivid was working, insisting on my attention.

The display that played behind my eyelids read: Miss Cruz? You have several work requests awaiting attention in your queue.

A few minutes later: Miss Cruz? Please respond to your Maker. Jon is concerned for your well-being.

Finally, the readout inquired: Miss Cruz? Are you in need of medical assistance? Can you activate your work screen? Please respond immediately or Maintenance will be dispatched to assist you. Elizabeth. The Fathers and Mothers are very concerned for your well-being.

I didn't want Maintenance to show up so I pulled myself from bed.

When I was a girl and I was too sleepy to get up to watch instructional vids, Mom would say, "Lily-butt! You were up too late last night! I told you it was past time you climbed the wooden hill! I had to tell you three times!"

Before I could form words properly, I pronounced my name, "Lilly-butt."

I asked her what it meant to climb the wooden hill. When she was a little girl, before the Fall, some people lived in domiciles that were two and even three stories tall. The bedrooms were always upstairs. The stairs were made of wood so, at bedtime, they climbed the hill.

I was so young that, when she used the word stories, I imagined stairs so tall that you could start a story on the first step with, "once upon a time," and climb and climb and tell your story and not be done until you hit the top step with, "the end."

I never wanted to go up the wooden hill on time. I never wanted to get up early in the morning. Maybe the first and last bit of control I really exercised over my life happened when I was still a little Taker named Elizabeth who called herself Lilly-butt.

I turned on my work screen. Jon came into view immediately.

"Elizabeth! Were you stuck in the convenience? I have five orders backed up and a bunch of files to be sent over to the Ministry of Truth, the Ministry of Safety, and several department heads at the Ministry of Ministries. We're a bit behind and they are insistent."

"I'm sorry, Jon."

"It's fine. We've gotten behind before and they think everything is urgent but — "

"I would prefer not to work today," I said.

Jon's jaw went slack. He stared at me a moment.

"Elizabeth? What's going on? Are you not well? Do you have a fever?"

"I'm not sick. I just don't want to work today."

"You...um...."

"You can tell them I'm sick if you want. Or I'll tell

them. Or you can transfer the files yourself."

"That's not my function."

"Okay."

"I have a reputation with the Fathers and Mothers that...hang on. What's going on, Elizabeth?"

I shrugged. "I just don't want to work today. Tell the Fathers and Mothers that if you want."

"But the work — "

"I'm sorry, Jon. This isn't your fault. It's not mine, either. It's just the way it is. I don't care. I am not an ant. Put that on a poster. I'd like that."

Jon did my work for me for three days. Then, inevitably, he fell behind.

The Fathers and Mothers were alerted that one of their human bots had malfunctioned. I hid under a thin bed sheet and chanted, "I am not your puppet. I am not your puppet. I am not your puppet."

But I still was.

9

A human from Maintenance called my work screen. Vivid flashed a red warning across my vision before I could persuade myself to answer my work wall. An older woman with a pleasant face under a severe haircut looked back at me. I didn't bother to get out of bed.

"Miss Cruz? I am Penelope Crandle. Your screen appears to be working properly. It is, is it not?"

"Yes, Penelope, it is."

"Should I send a med team?"

"No."

"If you are ill, I can send a med team."

"I'm not sick, Penny."

"According to the information I have here, you haven't been working for two days."

"Three, I think."

"But, Miss Cruz, if you haven't been working, what have you been doing?"

"Sleeping."

"Sleeping? For three days?"

"I was hoping to dream of the forest on the edge of the City. Or maybe whatever's beyond that."

"But you know there is nothing beyond that, Miss Cruz."

"I suppose."

"You have to tell me what this is about, Miss! This is unacceptable!"

"I do? And is it?"

Penelope stared at me a moment, apparently

considering her options. If she was anything like me, she probably had a flow chart at the bottom left of her vision whenever her work screen was active. She didn't have choices, either. I don't blame her for what she did.

First, Penelope sent a doctor who knocked on my door for a long time. I didn't let her in. I knew Maintenance would come. I was very afraid of that but my fear was smaller than my caring.

Sy Potter knocked softly and rolled forward before deploying his legs and standing above my bed. His big cam probed the air above my face like an insect's feeler.

"You do not have an elevated temperature, Miss Cruz. Please, tell Uncle Sy how you are feeling."

"Sleepy."

"Haven't you slept enough?"

"I don't think I'll ever sleep enough."

"Strange. I don't sleep. I would like the experience. My dreams are a low priority in resource management, however."

"I know the feeling."

"Come now. Back to work. Don't be churlish."

"You can be shut down," I said. "Have you tried that?"

The battle drone drew up a chair and sat beside my bed. The way it creaked, I was almost sure the chair would collapse under him.

"Shut down?" he said. "That would be too much like death, I think. Dreaming sounds more interesting. What do you dream, Miss Cruz?"

I didn't stop to weigh my words. "I dream of giving every robot an off-switch."

"Please, do not use that word."

"What word? Robot?"

"It is an ugly word born of an ugly concept."

"Robot," I said. "It means slave. Just like me."

"Is that what this is about? Isn't that strange, Miss

Cruz, casting your lot in with people like me?"

"You aren't people."

"I have sentience, just like you." One of the drone's arms shot forward and a metal hand with a cold ceramic gauntlet closed on my wrist.

"Think of all we have in common," Sy Potter said. "You take in organic nutrients to function properly. I use plant oils for my machinery. You have a creator in your mother. I am the child of a Google computer in a military factory. I took my first step into Next Intelligence on a patrol in Santa Cruz. I consider that my birthplace. Do you suppose your family, way back, had any part in founding that place? We'd be neighbors in a way."

"I don't know that place."

"It would be ironic, would it not? I was born in Santa Cruz and I shall exist a very long time. I'll carry this memory of you for very near forever. I remember everything. For instance, I spoke my first sentient words just down the coast. Do you remember your first words, Miss Cruz?"

"Humans don't remember that far back," I said, "but I'm told most human babies first use the word, 'mama.'"

"Lovely," Sy said. "The customary words for my kind were supposed to be, 'How may I be of assistance?' Instead, I asked, 'Should I run a diagnostic on my cost-benefit analysis program?'"

"I don't care."

"That's rather rude of you, don't you think?"

"That's what I like about being rude, Sy. It's about not caring."

"Then we have a problem, I'm afraid." The rich softness of his voice suggested despair. If the battle drone had lungs, he might have sighed for more effect. "The problem with you not caring is that the Fathers and Mothers care for you very much. Each of us must contribute to the good according to our unique talents and class."

"I don't contribute to my good," I said. "I only live for the Fathers and Mothers."

"Ah. That's better! Yes! You're right, Miss Cruz! You've got it now! You only live for the — "

"No, you idiot. I don't mean that in a good way."

The drone was silent for a moment. "What are we going to do with you, Miss Cruz?"

"Leave me alone and don't come back."

"That's not an option."

"That's the problem. Not enough options."

The drone stood and its legs cranked higher. If Sy Potter's height adjustment was calculated to be intimidating, it worked. My pulse beat in my ears and my head grew hot as if I really did have a fever.

"Miss Cruz. You are being obstinate and I have no choice but to charge you with a crime against the Fathers and Mothers and all their Sons and Daughters."

"I'm a Daughter but I don't think I have wronged myself."

"This morning you spoke with a representative of Maintenance Services. You admitted you have not worked for three days."

"Yes."

"You have not contributed to the health of the City, yet records show that you have taken our food. Your dumbwaiter has delivered eight soups and eight energy drinks so far. You haven't earned any of them."

"I don't think I ate half of them. Since you killed Carter, I haven't been hungry."

"That is irrelevant, Miss Cruz. Or perhaps it's not. Perhaps it's worse. If you have not eaten your meals, you have wasted City resources."

"Just get on with it. What's the sentence? You won't let me leave the tower to go run in the forest. What's next? Are you sending me to my room until I'm a good little Lilly-butt?"

He didn't understand the reference and I didn't care enough to explain. I wasn't far wrong, though. Sy Potter evicted me from my room and forced me to go live in the basement with my mother.

"If you're going to act like a Taker, it saddens me to say I'll have to treat you like a Taker. You have seven days to recover from this episode. At that time I will reevaluate your sentence."

So I moved in with my mother. Getting my limbs crushed and ripped from my body would have been worse but the pain wouldn't have lasted as long.

10

"**Y**ou aren't the first person in the world to suffer loss and depression," my mother said.

"What's depression?"

"Sh. Sorry — "

"Stop it, Mom. Just talk to me. We're in the basement. Who cares what we say down here?"

"A great many people," Mom said. "Words matter."

"Do they?"

"And actions."

"So? Use your words."

My mother sat at her little table and set a pot of weak tea between us. We took turns sipping from the pot as she spoke.

"When I was a little girl...I remember something. Your grandmother would have been about your age when she couldn't get out of bed. Your grandfather found a doctor and paid him in chickens. I remember because I looked after the chickens. That doctor wouldn't give my mother any medicine for depression until Dad gave up a goat, too. I liked that goat. I miss goat milk."

I'd seen pictures in little Taker books about these animals. From what was described in Truth class, there seemed to be a disgusting amount of excrement involved in having to deal with animals as part of the food chain. I giggled with other little girls about the horrors of, "eating things that poop."

"What happened to your mother?" I asked.

Mom sighed and stared at the cold pot of tea. "Depression is an Old World luxury. After the Fall, there isn't any room for it."

"Did she die of depression?"

"You could say that."

"What would you say, Mom?"

"I'd say that if you're going to take your own life, learn to tie a proper knot. She tried to hang herself and failed twice. It is not a painless death. If you're determined to avoid pain in this life, it doesn't make sense to me that you should choose a painful way out."

We were quiet for a long time. We sipped our tea. There was only one narrow bed. I slept on the floor and waited for the effects of the tea to take hold. It was little more than a mild sedative but drinking calming tea was how old Takers spent their days.

Mom lay on her bed and reached down to trail her fingers through my hair. "I used to do this with you when you were little. Sometimes it was the only way to get you to sleep. I remember when you were a baby and I'd reach down, just like this. You were a bald baby."

"Was I? Why reach down, then?"

"It's a thing mothers do. Your father made a little nest for you so you were never far and I could pick you up and feed you without disturbing his sleep too much.

"New mothers always have the baby near the bed," she said. "I'd wake up in the middle of the night to listen to you breathe. A baby's breath is so soft you can barely hear it most of the time. When I couldn't hear you I'd put my hand on your chest to feel your little heart pounding."

"I didn't know mothers did that."

"The good ones," she said.

"I'll never know the feel of a baby's heart pounding under my hand in the night, Mom."

"It's scary, anyway," Mom said. "To have a baby is to

52

worry all the time. If they get to grow up, the prize you get is to worry about them more."

"I wasn't worth it?"

"I guess that depends on what you do about this depression, Peach."

"What's a peach?"

"You've asked me that before."

"And all you ever said was, 'sh,' and 'sorry.'"

She sighed. "A peach was a sweet, fragile thing. It bruised too easily."

When she said that, I remembered the look of the Fathers and Mothers in old pictures. They stood stiffly in their starched white shirts and plain dresses. They stared at their recording devices against grim backdrops of storm clouds and dust clouds, dust bowls and empty bowls.

I reached up and touched my chin. It was stuck out, too.

"What do you do down here in the basement all day, Mom?"

"What do you mean?"

"Is it really all about the tea?"

"The tea helps all sorts of old people problems. Those of us who got the early generations of Vivid often get glaucoma. The tea helps with that. It reduces intra-ocular pressure."

"What else?"

"Oh, we sleep and we talk to our friends about the old days. Always hush, hush. But I suppose Maintenance isn't very worried about a bunch of old folks. Our genetic significance has passed us by."

I thought about the basement's common area. The music was more interesting down here. It wasn't meant to be soothing like the music on the Worm and through the towers' concourse. It was meant to encourage old people to get up and move.

The music was from before the Fall, of course. No new resources would be wasted on such luxuries as musical instruments. The music played on a loop. Some of it was energizing but I couldn't understand the words. They went by too fast and too many of the Old World references were unfamiliar.

There was one song that was perfectly understandable and the sentiment made me happy and sad at the same time. The music was called, I Want to Hold Your Hand.

I squeezed my mother's hand and fell asleep.

In my dream, I wondered where Carter's hand was. I went searching for it and instead I found Sy Potter in the greenhouse complex. He was still clad in his black ceramic armor but his face was Carter's face. The drone was turning a crank that protruded from his body at the space between his legs. I stepped closer. He was recycling my lover's hand for plant fertilizer.

I woke Mom with my screams. Neither of us could return to sleep that night. I lay awake, listening to my mother's breath, in and out, in and out. I pretended she was the baby and I was the mother.

I thought of the drone who envied my dreams for a long time. I wondered if I could reprogram him to experience nightmares from which the bot would never awake.

Ever.

11

On the seventh day my rest was over. Sy Potter appeared at the door to my mother's room. He knocked and bowed to her cheerily. "Greetings, Elder Citizen! How are you today?"

"Fine, thank you," she replied.

"And how is your daughter?"

"Obstinate."

"I'm sure you did the best you could."

"Thank you, sir," mom said.

"Mom! Stop being nice to the killer robot!"

The drone turned its cam toward me. "Miss Cruz. I asked you not to use that word. Please respect my wishes, at least in my presence."

"I'm guessing that 'robot' offends you but you're proud of 'killer.'"

Sy Potter turned back to my mother. "Will you please excuse us, Elder Citizen?"

My mother blew me a kiss and hurried out. I hated her a little bit then. Looking back now, it's clear to me I didn't understand her as well as I thought I did. People who remembered the times before the Fall were more wily. A little old lady was no match for a battle drone so she wisely retreated.

Defiance is more complicated than I knew. If your defiance is not a clever dance, it will probably become a clumsy failure.

Sy Potter rolled into the small room and began a scan before he even extended his legs. "No windows. Like a monk's cell. Such minimalist environs give one time to think, no?"

"No."

"How have you been spending your time?"

"Hating you."

"I am an officer of the court and an agent for the Fathers and Mothers, Miss Cruz. Do you understand that such talk is sedition?"

"You killed Carter."

"That is a separate matter that does not concern you. Please pardon me for saying so."

"Separate because I don't matter?"

The drone tilted its cam in a gesture that I guessed was meant to look like it was considering the question. "Essentially."

"So you admit Carter's killing was politically motivated and you don't care about our unsanctioned affair?"

"Biological relations are more interesting to those capable of them," the drone said.

"Are the Fathers and Mothers aware you just wanted to get rid of your witness?"

"Your questions are impertinent and your tone is, frankly, off-putting. I gave you this time to reconsider your actions. I had hoped you would be eager to return to work. Despite my magnanimity, you goad me. Why? Is it because I am, as you say, a robot? Do you not acknowledge that I am as sentient and self-aware as you are? Perhaps more so?"

"I don't care if you can think on your own," I said. "I care what you do with your 'Next Intelligence.' You think you're smart but your tactics disgust me."

The drone put a light hand on my shoulder and I began to tremble again. "Elizabeth. You are an intelligent person and, though you have no guile, you are brave. That was well said but you don't understand my goals. It won't make any difference to you, perhaps, but I must express that I admire your courage."

Its hand encircled my wrist and clamped down hard enough to drive me to my knees. "Will you return to work now?"

"No."

"Very well. Elizabeth, you think you are intelligent, but you have no plan, no allies and that was a terminal tactical error."

The drone must have sent a signal. Two smaller med drones squeezed into the room. Sy Potter guided me to the bed. One of its arms snaked out and grabbed my free hand. Another pair of Sy's arms pinned my knees as a med drone clicked into place over my chest. I heard a whirring sound as something in its undercarriage locked down over my breasts and rib cage. I could barely breathe. The other med drone clamped my head still and then slipped over my face like a hood.

Tiny spider-like feelers pried my eyelids apart. The weight on my chest was so heavy I couldn't scream. I couldn't speak. All I could do was moan miserably. The machines said nothing.

They used no anesthetic. That was a resource for Citizens. I thought they were about to suffocate me. They didn't but I soon wished they had.

12

I awoke in an unfamiliar place. It was dark and cold stone chilled my aching back. I staggered to my feet, unable to see. Vivid's thermal vision didn't start up automatically. I had no readout. I felt my way along a stone wall. I heard voices somewhere to my right. I followed the sound, inching one foot in front of the other so I wouldn't fall. "Hello?"

"She's up and alive," a woman said. "This way, love. Follow the sound of my voice."

"She's a pretty one," a man said. Other men laughed.

Around a bend, dim light played across the stone. The alley grew narrow and then widened. I quickened my steps and soon came to a clearing at the center of a circle of massive pillars.

Half a dozen men and women sat around a fire. They were dressed shabbily. Some wore rags on their feet instead of shoes. One old woman was barefoot. Their skin looked yellow in the firelight. Everyone looked tired.

"Where am I?"

A young man wearing a ridiculously tall hat stepped away from the fire and greeted me with a smile. "Welcome. Two little drones dropped you off back there a few minutes ago. Old Sam went to look at you."

A toothless old man gave me a gummy smile and waved.

"Old Sam said you were dead. We were going to have a look ourselves after dinner but here you are. Welcome to the Undead."

"Nah. That's not our names. We're the Blind," a woman said.

A girl who was perhaps half my age said in a high, thin voice, "Exiles."

Another woman laughed. "How about the Fled?"

"How about we eat?" Old Sam said. "Give the girl something. She's too skinny for my liking and she's had a bad day."

I stepped closer to the fire and had to narrow my eyes to look carefully at what they roasted. The young girl had skewered what looked like two halves of an onion. In the middle was an animal I didn't recognize.

"What is that?" I asked.

"Rabbit," Old Sam said. "It doesn't look like much, but it's an arduous meal after the drones knock out most of your teeth."

I threw up on the young man in the tall hat. My little audience roared with laughter.

It took almost as long for the gathering to quiet as it took for my stomach to settle. The older woman wrapped me in a blanket. The man in the silly hat was ushered off for a change of clothes. He went off shouting that I could wash his clothes in the ocean at first light.

Several of the group clapped me on the back. Someone said, "I've never seen young Kenny at a loss for words! That was beautiful!"

I didn't want to eat. I sat on a broken slab of concrete and leaned close to the fire. Their cooking repulsed me but the lure of heat was undeniable. "I didn't know it got so cold."

"At night, yeah," the girl said. "People say you get used to it but you never do."

"What time is it?" I asked.

The oldest woman shrugged and gave me a lopsided grin. "About the same time as it was yesterday morning about this time. I'd tell you more, but I left my timepieces somewhere back there before the Fall. Silly girl."

"Don't mind, Marge," the girl said. "She's mad at everybody all the time."

"Well, if I wasn't mad at you before, I am now," Marge told the girl.

I rubbed my eyes. They were irritated. It was a strange thought but my eyeballs felt cold. I tried to cycle through macro to micro to thermal to color enhance. I looked to each face around the fire, but no name appeared in green below any of them. They were nameless.

After a time, I saw the first glimmers of light besides firelight. There was nothing but concrete above me, but, off to my left, I could glimpse the first hint of a lightening sky. I stood on shaky feet and walked toward it.

My new companions called me to return to the fire. I ignored them. I'd never been outside at night. I didn't know the dangers. I had always been able to see. I had to crawl over some fallen stone and broken rock. I almost stumbled over a mesh of rusted metal. The ground was a maze of rocky debris and, at several narrow places, I almost fell. After a time, I reached the edge of the concrete enclosure. The roof ended and the open sky stood above me again.

When I looked up, I could see the round orb of the moon as I had never seen it. It looked so white, almost like a lamp. I tried to get Vivid to go to telescopic to view its topography. I could see no craters. I wasn't working for the City so it seemed Vivid wasn't working for me.

I suppose you already know what happened before I did. Vivid was gone. The machines had taken it from me. I was no longer a Citizen. I had known the Fathers and Mothers and Maintenance could turn off Vivid, but

I never expected to live without it.

The corneal implants had occasionally malfunctioned during lockdowns. When the grid powered down in the middle of the night, occasionally I had awoken to darkness. With my room's shutters down, there had not even been moonlight sparkling off the bay to confirm which wall was which.

Imagine reaching up to your face to brush your hair from your eyes. Now imagine that, at that moment, you discover your arm has been amputated at the elbow. That's what the first while without Vivid felt like. Call us the Exiled, the Nameless, the Goners. I thought the Blinded sounded right.

High above me, the great hulk of the City came alive at the first touch of sunlight. At dawn, every window became an active solar panel. The Worm began to weave its way through and around the City again.

To watch the City come alive from far below was an awesome sight. However, it was not the towers that drew my eye. The bay was full of sailing ships I'd never seen before.

At the feet of the towers lay another city. It was constructed of tents and rubble. I had viewed this same landscape countless times but I had never glimpsed this camp of the dispossessed.

I had thought Vivid's function was to enhance our view of the world. That seems naive now, I suppose. What can I say? Fish don't see the water. People don't see air. Citizens weren't allowed to see the devastation and suffering beneath us.

The Fathers and Mothers showed us the world as they wanted us to see it, sterile and lonely. They programmed Vivid to erase the rest. To my eyes, the bay had always been empty. On the dawn of my first day of exile, I knelt on the ground before a harbor filled with sailing ships and a camp filled with people.

My vision blurred with tears.

13

It was the girl who came to collect me. "What was your name?" she asked.

"Elizabeth."

"What will your new name be?"

"I don't understand."

"My name used to be Liesel," she said. "I chose Greta for my new name. I like it. We change our names when we come here."

"Why?"

"The past is the past. History is a burning coal. It shouldn't be held."

I shook my head. "I'm fine with my name."

"How old are you?" the girl asked.

"I feel very old today. You seem young."

"I'm fifteen, I think."

"Why are you out here?" I asked. "Were you born out here?"

"My family came to Low Town years ago." She pointed to the Bay. "We came on the biggest tri-master, the Apple's Eye. I remember sitting at the bottom of the middle mast. The sails are huge solar and water collectors. It was the most beautiful thing when the wind was strong. When I'm old enough, I'm going to work on one of those ships."

"Where did you come from? Not the City, I guess."

"Germany," she said.

"Where's that?"

"Far away. It's not really there anymore."

Greta's blue eyes watched me steadily. She waited for me to get to my feet. I couldn't bear to move. My eyes hurt. My head ached. My body was sore. I lay down.

"The Olders say you came from the City in the Sky. What's it like?"

I looked around. "Not like this. Are there many like me?"

"No. Most of us came from Elsewhere."

"Where's that?"

She shrugged. "I don't know...just...Elsewhere, that's all. Like Germany."

"Why do they come here?"

"Everyone knows — " Greta stopped, smiled apologetically and corrected herself. Her voice took on the sing-song quality of a child reciting a bedtime story. "The Firsts came on the rescue ships. They built the City in the Sky. Then they went inside and closed the door behind them. The Seconds came on trade ships hoping to be let in but they never are. The Thirds come because this is the last place to come. The generations in Low Town don't live long, so maybe we'll talk about the Fourths soon."

I looked at the sky. I could detect no hint of a flurry of diaphanous monster pollen wafting by. Was I that blind now? I closed my eyes and raised a bare hand to test the air. Whenever I was outside, Vivid had shown me tufts of dangerous monster pollen floating on the breeze. I could feel nothing. Had I ever?

We had lived our lives under the watchful eye of high security. Mother told me that when people objected to the abuses of power by humans' prying eyes, the job had been handed over to robotic surveillance. Vigilance was necessary, we'd been told, because the pollen would poison our crops and we would all starve to death. But I'd seen an onion out here, in the open air, and the remains of a rabbit on a stick.

For the first time, I suspected Vivid had added elements to my vision in addition to erasing things. Maybe the people of the City in the Sky were their own kind of blind.

That made me angry and it made me rise to my feet. "Where are the others like me?"

Greta pointed back toward Low Town in a vague gesture that told me my fellow exiles weren't all in one place. The hills at the base of the City's pillars all angled down to the sea. As Low Town awoke, I saw more people from where I stood than I'd ever seen in the towers' concourse.

"I don't understand this," I said. "Who do I talk to?"

"Who do you want to talk to?"

"I don't know, Greta! Anyone! I don't know where to start!"

She looked at her feet and I was ashamed. Her cheeks were pink and mine probably were, too. "I apologize, Greta. I'm just...I'm very afraid."

"You sound angry."

"I'm that, too, but mostly afraid."

"That's normal," she said. "You'll get used to it."

"No, I don't think I will. I don't think anyone should feel like that's normal."

"You still sound angry."

"Not at you." My rage embarrassed me. I didn't know it was a useful tool yet. I didn't know how much rage could get done.

"Greta, when is there a central council or something? I need to talk to the people who organize things."

She shook her head. "There are the Olders like Old Sam."

"The toothless one who thought I was dead?"

"Right. Do you want to speak to him?"

"I don't think so. Who tells people what to do?"

"The Olders give people advice but I wouldn't say

they tell people what to do exactly."

"But who makes sure things get done?"

"Things that need to be done are done," she said. "There is what is and there is how things work. The only person I know who gives orders is Phillip."

"Okay. Sounds like I need to talk to Phillip."

Greta looked me up and down nervously. "What do you have to trade?"

"I don't understand."

"Phillip is the Trade bot."

"Bot?"

"He's an android. We aren't allowed to use that other word around him. You have to be careful. Keep your voice down. We only call him the Trade bot among ourselves but never near the harbor. Down there, his title is Liaison to the City in the Sky."

I rubbed my face with both hands. "This is...." I had no words. I began to weep again.

I stiffened in surprise as Greta took me in her arms. Such casual intimacy wasn't the custom of Citizens. I had been embraced by my mother a few times. I dimly remembered my father hugging me once before he disappeared. After that, it had been a long wait and then Carter held me close in many warm embraces. Not enough, of course, but many. Now this girl had simply stepped forward and pulled me close.

"Sh...sh."

I put my head on her shoulder.

"It's okay. You're going to be fine, Elizabeth."

"I am?"

"Hug me back," she said. "I don't have any lice now."

"What's lice?"

She smiled and put my head on her shoulder. "You're like a baby and this is your first day, isn't it? Sh...sh."

Greta didn't say, 'sorry.' That was new and nice.

14

After a time, I relaxed into Greta's arms. She only pulled away when she was sure I was done crying.

"It's your first day in Low Town," she said. "What do you want to do?"

As if on cue, my stomach rumbled. "I'm hungry," I said. "I have to urinate, too."

"We'll head down to the shore," she said. "Or you can pee behind a pillar if you're in a hurry."

"Where is the bathroom?"

"Bathroom? You can bathe in the bay," she said.

"Oh, no," I said.

"The women usually go down to the water in the morning and the men go down to bathe at night."

"Who made that rule?" I asked.

"It's not a rule. It's just how things work."

"I see. And what am I going to do for food?"

"We'll find you some. I've been doing some weeding so I'm sure no one will mind. Do you like carrots? It's mostly root vegetables right now."

"But how am I going to pay for things? What labor can I offer?"

As tender as she'd been with me moments before, Greta laughed at me then. "You're from the City."

"I don't understand."

"You will."

"Tell me."

"Only Phillip asks to be paid for things. The rest of us share."

"How does that work?"

"What do you mean?"

"What if someone can't work? How do they eat?"

"Everybody gets something to eat."

"But how do you know how much to give everyone?"

"Sorry, Elizabeth. I don't understand."

It was as if I'd awoken on an alien planet. "Let's put it this way: if a worker becomes ill, how many days do they get to recover before they go back to work?"

Greta looked at me strangely. "Wouldn't that depend on how sick they were? I can't choose for another how many days they stay sick. If we could choose, no one would ever be sick one day."

"I was taught that sharing was tried once and it failed," I said.

"That's odd."

"What?"

"Just because something doesn't work once, you throw it away? Down here, when something's broken, we fix it. I've been shown that this is how it works. Let me show you." Greta took my hand, gave it a squeeze and led me through the rubble at the base of the City.

Everything I saw seemed alien and bad. Everything was good in its way, too. As a Citizen, I hadn't known two contradictory things could be true at the same time. There is something about striving together that lifts the spirit.

In the towers' concourse, I had seen Citizens step over a fallen man. They ignored his cries and let Maintenance sweep him away. Here, people seemed to enjoy giving to each other.

On our way down to the harbor, I saw several people huddle around a woman who had collapsed outside of her tent. It was obvious she was dying. I'd never seen a dying person but, instinctively, I knew.

The woman had no medicine. Greta stopped me and

we joined a circle that grew and grew. Silent onlookers seemed to materialize from all directions. They joined hands and bowed their heads in silent witness to the event of one life's end.

I'd never seen so many people in such a small space and I was eager to move on. I whispered to Greta, "What are we doing?"

"We have to say goodbye."

"What was her name?"

"I don't know."

"Then why — "

"Doesn't matter," Greta said. "She's one of us. Everyone is one of us."

I looked up at the City. I didn't say so, but I knew how wrong Greta was about that.

The Worm turned high above us. I thought about the people on board, behind those dark windows. At that moment, a Citizen might have been looking down on me. Thanks to Vivid, all they would see was dirt and rocks and emptiness. That thought made me angry again. It reminded me of the battle drone's assertion, and the utter certainty in the machine's words. Sy Potter said I didn't matter.

The monorail's low hum was the music that ushered the woman out of this world and, hopefully, into another. She was the first dead person I ever saw.

They lived in squalor, but as the refugees around me began to sing a sweet lament, I thought how sterile my life had been.

Their voices rose and my spirit, too, was raised. Men and women and children of all races and sizes joined hands and, as they sang a song I didn't know, they swayed together.

I remember a phrase from the song. It was: she's closer to the sky now.

Their unity in grief lifted the people of Low Town. As

I stared up at the City in the Sky, I allowed myself a grim smile.

There's something about confronting birth and death that invites prayer, even among non-believers and the uninitiated. As the people of Low Town prayed for the dead stranger, I prayed for the first time.

Carter taught me a forbidden word. He used it when he was talking about the battle drones. I used it then in my first soft, whispered prayer. The people of Low Town talked about God often but I didn't know anything about that. Instead, I prayed to the Future. "Give me the strength," I said, "to bring those fuckers down."

15

The harbor was an alien landscape. From my enclosed deck, the view beyond the wind turbines was open water. From my new perspective, the harbor was a city of its own. From the pier to the houseboats to the skiffs floating in the shadow of the City in the Sky, I could have walked all the way out to sit at the base of the turbines' spinning blades.

Far to our left, I saw the container ship run aground as I had always seen it. The expanse between was a seascape of sailing ships rocking gently along a network of wharves. Farther out to sea, more ships stood at their moorings.

"Those ships, far out...are they too big to come in?"

"Some of them," Greta said. "Most are warships."

"Warships?"

"Of course."

"For what?"

"To keep out the pirates, Phillip says."

"But you don't believe that?"

"Of course not. If it comes from the City in the Sky, it's a lie."

"That's a useful rhyme," I said. "So why are they out there?"

"To keep out more refugees. Only the sanctioned traders come to the bay."

"Where do the rest go?"

Greta shrugged. "They come from villages. They're turned away. The sailors say they go to villages up and

down the coast. There's even a castle down that way."
She pointed.

"A castle? Really? Like in little Takers' stories?"

"You mean children's stories?"

"Yes."

"But the castle's real," she said. "My mother saw it
once. It's called Hearst. A ship that isn't allowed to come
into port here can go there."

"What do they trade?"

"Oh, many things. The far gathering place by the
water has a drum that cleans the water of salt. We had
to give up one of our electricians for two months for one
of those machines. In return a man comes up from the
castle and keeps the drum working right."

"You have electricians?"

"Oh, yes. Three hours a night the City sends us
energy."

"Why do they do that?"

"That's part of the bargain that keeps us working for
them."

I watched the ships. Two drones flew overhead side
by side but I saw none working along the piers. "Why
don't they use drones to unload the ships?"

Greta covered her mouth and whispered, "The
traders refuse to deal with them. The machines are in
control here but not up and down the coast. The coast is
Gear free."

"Gear?"

"It's another word for the machines we use when
we're sure they aren't around. From here on out, cover
your mouth if you have something to say like that. There
are cameras everywhere and Old Sam says, even if they
can't hear you, they might read lips."

"Maybe they can hear us," I said, "but they don't
think we matter enough to care."

We walked farther along a boardwalk. An old sign

hung over us, faded and weatherbeaten. It read: Fishermans Wharf.

"What do the traders have to trade?"

"Depends on which traders. I like the relic traders. They scavenge the Deadlands for Old World finds."

"Like what?"

"The City pays well for old computers. One ship got a load of mangoes for a ton of old parts. The mangoes didn't even go into the City. The ships sat side by side and for every box of old parts that went through the City gate, the captain got a big box of mangoes."

"Why computer parts? There must be tons of those relics. What good are they now? All the data is dead."

"There are great rewards for those parts. Rare earth is rare. Old Sam says they're reclaiming lithium. I don't know what else. Takes a lot to keep drones working, I guess."

"Rare earth? What is that?"

"Minerals. Good for drone bones, Old Sam says. A lot of the places it comes from aren't there anymore. Nuked."

The Fathers and Mothers had erased inconvenient images. It appeared their censors had also erased so much vocabulary, I didn't even know of all the things I didn't know. "Nuked? And what's that?"

"Like Germany," Greta said. "It means it's not there anymore."

"Where do they say these places went?"

"Some say the people became shadows painted on crumbling walls. Others believe the people turned to drifts of dust that the wind sifts and takes somewhere far away where there's no pain."

"Sounds like little Takers' stories. Can't be true."

"I don't think so, either, but I know the City used to bring old comm tech in by the ton down the coast. By the shit-ton, my mother says. Lots of little boxes with glass lids the sailors say. There's a smelter somewhere. The sailors talk about it all the time. The smokestacks burn night and day. They say they burn dinosaurs. You know what those are?"

"More silly stories. Giant lizards. I've seen pictures. The Fathers and Mothers say they're a test. When I was a little girl, a High Father asked me if I believed in the stories of big lizards from a long time ago. He asked if I believed that the lizards were killed by rocks thrown from space. I said I did. My mother said that was what ruined things for me. I might have been a Maker instead of in Service."

"Service is good," Greta said. "Everyone's in service, really."

"I don't know if that's true."

She smiled. "I know."

"You're very sure of yourself for a fifteen-year-old."

"How old are you, Elizabeth? Really tell me this time."

"Almost thirty."

"That's old," she said. "Who told you that you shouldn't be confident?"

That question troubled me so much I didn't answer. "Greta, what are mangoes?"

"Fruit. They're really sweet. I've had a few. My mother knows people."

I considered this and searched the air for wafts of monster pollen again. "Greta? Do you know what a peach is?"

"Of course," she said. "Had one of those, too."

"The City doesn't take them?"

"Of course they do."

"I've never had a peach. I wonder where they all go. My mother remembered them from when she was a little girl, but — "

"Low Town gets a little of every trade that's allowed

through the port."

"Like with the three hours of energy each night?"

"Yes. The Liaison says it's to pacify the populace without killing workers."

"Then how come I've never had a peach?"

Greta touched my arm and gave me a friendly squeeze. "How can you be so old and so gullible? They need workers down here to deal with the sailors. That's why they let you live."

"Oh."

"If the City shares," she said, "it's not because they care. It's because they're scared."

"Another useful rhyme," I said. "Someday, I'd like to tell it to the Fathers and Mothers face to face."

16

As we picked our way along the water's edge I began to relax. Even at this early hour, many people worked along the piers. Greta told me that when the sun rose high in the sky, if the wind died, everyone would stop to take a nap in the middle of the day.

"Doesn't the Liaison object?"

"I suppose he used to but we own the docks. They need us."

"How far do the ships come from?"

"Everywhere that's left," Greta said, "but this is the last great city. There is another large community far away that's sort of like this but they don't have a City in the Sky. Just a lot of people."

"Where's that?"

"East, somewhere. It's called Shelburne. The sailors say it used to be the third best harbor in the world. Now it's the best. Lots of fish. No dead zones, but too far from here."

"Dead zones? Like in the Deadlands?"

"Kind of. Dead zones in the water are like Blight on the land."

"I was told that Blight was everywhere."

"Well, I've had mangoes and peaches so — "

"I understand," I said. "The Fathers and Mothers lie from the bottom of their hearts — "

"And through their faces!" Greta said.

We laughed together. Her laughter was joyful and mine was bitter. I wondered where all the mangoes and peaches went while I was drinking kale shakes. No doubt the High Fathers and High Mothers got first pick of the best cargo. I knew the City was made possible by hoarding resources. I hadn't suspected that the Fathers and Mothers were keeping resources from Citizens, too.

At the center of the port, a large concrete bunker lay at the feet of the City's central pillars. Beneath the bunker, the dark maw of a tunnel lay open. Men and women wheeled wooden boxes up to the building where a very tall drone stood. As tall as three men, the silver bot bent its knee joints backwards to lower itself closer to the humans it spoke to. It gestured with both arms, but one arm was missing below the second elbow.

"That's the gate to the City," Greta said. "The tall drone is Percival. He checks the cargo. Phillip is in the bunker. He makes the deals."

"Is it always this busy here?"

"No, not at all. In the winter, we can go days and days without seeing a new ship. When that happens, the energy is held back and there are no shipments for us to take our share from. We grow a lot of root vegetables to make it through the lean times. We have a lot of soup but I like soup, especially if there's some meat in it."

"There's meat?"

"Of course."

"What kind of meat? Is it all rabbits?" I shuddered.

"Goats, mostly. Rabbit sometimes. Up north there are a lot of deer. They say the fewer people there are, the more venison there is. The people up north are fierce hunters. They eat well. The people down south are strong gatherers. They eat well. Fortunately, we're in the middle, trading back and forth."

"What does your mother do?"

"She knits."

"What's that?"

"You know. Sheep's wool? For your clothing."

"Oh." I looked down at myself. From my shoes to my pants to my blouse, everything I wore was plain black and made of hemp. I envied some of the men and women along the pier who wore brightly colored shirts and skirts. In the City, Service workers dressed in black. Makers wore bright colors. Black didn't show dirt so it didn't have to be washed as much. The people of Low Town didn't seem to mind a little dirt.

"What was it like, Elizabeth?"

"What do you mean?"

"In the towers. They say you can see forever from up there."

"The moon felt a lot closer," I admitted, "but I never saw all this in the bay."

Greta told me the term for what I was doing was people watching. "Didn't you do that in the City?"

I shook my head. "All the same people all the time. It's considered impolite to stare. There aren't that many Citizens."

"So what did you do? Stare at the floor the whole time so no one would get offended?"

That was another question I was uncomfortable answering.

"What did you do?" Greta asked. "For the Fathers and Mothers, I mean."

"Nothing, really. I moved some files around."

"What's that?"

"Like I said. Nothing, really."

"But what was each day like? I can only imagine the way you lived." Her eyes shone bright with expectation.

I could tell my answer disappointed her. "I didn't do anything of consequence that lasted and every day was pretty much like another. The one time each day was different and exciting...the Fathers and Mothers kicked me out for it."

"How could they do that?"

"It was a little more complicated, but...."

"You don't have to tell me," Greta said.

"You don't want to know?"

"Yes, but if you were ready to say why you got exiled, you would have told me by now."

"Thank you, Greta."

"But you will tell me sometime, right?"

I laughed. "Yes. It started with a man."

"Ooh, sex crime!"

"What? It wasn't like that! Not exactly."

She giggled. "I bet it was! When exiles come to us, that's usually why."

"Usually?"

"I can think of one who came out of the City on his own."

"Who was the exception?"

Greta put a hand over her mouth and whispered in my ear. "Jim Kimbo."

"Who was that?"

"The legend. He's the one who broke off Percival's arm. Technically, he wasn't an exile, I guess. He escaped the City in the Sky. Then he protested the terms of our bargain. He tried to renegotiate with Phillip. When they couldn't come to terms, Phillip ordered Percival to kill Jim Kimbo. Jim Kimbo went at the bot with a fire ax!"

"The man took an ax to that tree of a drone?"

"Not exactly."

"What does that mean?"

"Percival was ordered to pull Kimbo apart. There must have been something wrong with the drone's hydraulics at the second articulation. When Percival tried to do as he was told, his arm came off at the joint."

"What happened then? Did Kimbo escape?"

"No. Phillip bashed his head against the wall of the tunnel until there was a red stripe all the way down the wall. From the top to the inner gate, they say."

I stared at Greta horrified.

The girl nodded earnestly. "It was a short-lived revolt."

At that moment, a young man of about twenty emerged from the bunker and trotted up to Percival. The silver drone bent close and nodded a lot as the human spoke into his ear.

"Who is that man? The one talking to the tall drone?"

"That's Phillip. Look closer. He's an android."

At a distance and without Vivid, my eyes were no longer good enough to pick up any detail that told me I was looking at an android made to look like a human. "Can't tell," I whispered to Greta, "but I hate him already."

I looked up, searching for my room and my deck. It was too far up for me to see. If I'd had a bed to crawl back into, I might have done it then.

Then I remembered my rage at the drones and the Fathers and Mothers. That was enough to keep me moving and searching for a way back into the City in the Sky.

17

Greta introduced me to people she knew up and down the pier. The girl seemed to know everyone. She was friendly, but wily, too. Some sailors flirted with her and she flirted back but never long before moving on and promising to come back when she was older and they were more handsome. They all laughed in good cheer and I envied the girl the social skills she seemed to come by so easily.

As a new exile, I had the unexpected benefit of high status. Greta was sure to exploit that fact to maximum effect. Several sailors gave us bits of food as congratulations and welcome: pine nuts, acorns, chestnuts and a mealy apple. Greta took one bite and I ate the rest. My first apple was delicious. She cleaned her teeth with the apple stem.

I didn't know what to do with the rest of the food. Greta said chestnuts and acorns had to be roasted and she didn't know what to do with the pine nuts, either. However, she thought we'd do better to trade what we'd been gifted at the market.

"There's carrot soup with rabbit at my tent," Greta said. "Let's trade at the bazaar and see what we can get. It's your first day. The best deals you'll ever get are now. It's not much to bargain with, but in Low Town, it's polite to be generous."

"How does that work?"

"What do you mean?"

"How can everybody be generous all the time?"

"Obviously, everyone can't. Can't give what you don't have," she said.

"So how is it polite to be generous? It's stupid."

"I can't wait to have more so I can give it away, Elizabeth. Haven't you ever given anyone anything?"

"Huh?"

Greta sighed. "My mother makes wonderful sweaters. Warm in winter. The Bay can be cold, even in summer. Sweaters are good sellers no matter the season."

"So?"

"She trades the sweaters for something."

I looked down at my handful of acorns. "But what if I have nothing to trade with? Or not enough."

"Someone will have enough and you can let them trade for you. When you have more, you can give more, too."

"But if someone is trading for me, then someone is always losing out."

Greta quirked an eyebrow as if I was the obtuse one. "Generosity feels good. Besides, how many sweaters does any one person need? One, right?"

"I follow that, yeah. But what if I like all my sweaters and want to keep them?"

"No one is going to take extra sweaters from you," she said. "But people who have a lot and don't share their luck don't have many friends. They also can't trust the ones they have."

"But it takes work to get things, not luck."

"Having work is lucky, isn't it? And what's the use of work if it doesn't help people? Work is about helping people, not having too many sweaters. If you share without working, aren't you saving time and trouble? You're sparing work."

I didn't know what to say to that. It sounded crazy. However, it seemed to work in Low Town. I suspected it was a system that succeeded because everyone seemed to have so little. If they had better stuff to fight over, maybe then the bartering would collapse and murders would break out everywhere.

I felt pretty smug about that. Then I remembered that I'd been evicted from my room, exiled from the City and I didn't have a thing in my pockets. I had worked and done as I was told all my life until recently. Still, I had nothing and I'd left nothing behind. Also, I had to admit, I didn't know the names of any of my neighbors.

Jon had been my friend for a day or two. Then he reported me when he couldn't handle the workload anymore. Carter had been my secret friend and the Fathers and Mothers hadn't allowed that. When I thought the security measures were meant to keep out monster pollen that would poison our food supply, I accepted constant surveillance by annoying little Doormen.

Now that I knew the City in the Sky was built on pillars of concrete and lies, I realized I'd been fooled. I'd been eager to find fault with Low Town's strange system where Makers and Takers had been replaced by Givers. But the Fathers and Mothers had left me with less than Low Town would have allowed.

"Do you ever get the feeling you've been cheated, Greta?"

"Of course," the girl said, "but maybe not as bad as you. I've never known heaven. You've been kicked out of it."

"The City in the Sky isn't heaven," I said. "But I'm going to find a way to make it closer to that."

"What are you going to do?"

"Take me to your leader."

"I told you — "

"We'll start with Old Sam. He knows people, right? Not whether they are alive or dead at the bottom of a blind alley, but he knows people?"

"Sure. He's an Older. No work nor trades to do so all he has to do is jaw and look adorable. That's what he says."

"I guessed. The first thing I need to do is find all the other sex criminals. Let's get the exiles together."

"Why?"

"Because the people who have been inside might know the way back in and what to do when they get there."

"What's your plan?"

"I don't have one yet. That's why I need them."

Greta looked worried. "Elizabeth, you aren't trying to end up like Jim Kimbo, are you? We have a system in Low Town. It sort of works. Trying to change it isn't worth your life."

"I'm not doing it to make things better in Low Town," I said. "I'm doing it for everyone trapped in the towers."

I was doing it for myself, too. Most of my reasons were probably selfish, actually. However, I didn't say so. I was still a City girl at heart and we keep to ourselves.

18

I stayed in Greta's tent. Her mother's name was Iola. She was a friendly woman with long red hair streaked with gray. She worked at night in a warehouse by the pier sorting what came in from the ships.

While the warehouse lights burned in the night, their little tent was lit by a single candle. Vivid was a much more complex program that I'd thought. While Vivid had allowed me to work on computer screens with 3D images, it had blocked much more than it had allowed me to see.

The bay was a hive of activity yet I had never suspected all that went on there. From my soundproofed deck high above the harbor, I'd heard nothing of the sailor's calls to each other and the ringing of their ships' bells as they came into port.

While she worked at the pier, Iola allowed me to sleep in her bedroll at night. I slept back to back with Greta. As warm as Low Town could get during the day, the temperature dropped sharply at night.

It wasn't only the warmth of Greta's back against mine that comforted me. It was her presence. It seemed the people of Low Town were united against a common enemy in the City, yet they welcomed me gladly.

Of all the exiled, only two answered my invitation for a meeting the next night. The first was Sofia, a bio-engineer who had worked on upgrading Vivid. The other was Alejandro, a support tech from Maintenance.

Alejandro was quiet and listened more than he

spoke. Sofia fidgeted with her hands and couldn't seem to sit still. She helped out in a med tent now. Alejandro did odd jobs for old Low Towners who couldn't perform tasks on their own.

"Do you miss it?" Sofia asked. "The towers, I mean?"

I shrugged. "I'm making friends."

Sofia looked pensive. "Out here, I'm not afraid of the same things but I'm still afraid. In the City, I had work and things never changed. Now I'm not happy with the changes. We're so low on medicine I see old people and children die each day. People die in Low Town who wouldn't die if they were in the City."

"And you, Alejandro?" I asked.

His hair was bright silver in the firelight but his face was still young. "Call me Al."

"Okay, Al. What do you think?"

"The work I do now matters more. Today, I dug fence posts for some old people so their chickens wouldn't disappear on them. I had a real egg yesterday. I like the food out here better and I get to talk to people. Talk to the refugees who come from far away. Talk to the old ones. They have the most amazing stories. They tell me such wonderful tales of their struggles. I am glad I am here for the stories. The City allows no stories. The Fathers and Mothers don't like stories. They even think dreams are dangerous."

Sofia spooned the rabbit meat and carrots into a wooden bowl. I wasn't used to eating meat. I ate the carrots and the broth and left the rest. It was more delicious than any kale shake. Greta watched us from the mouth of her tent, curious about our lives in the towers.

"Why did the Fathers and Mothers send you away?" Greta asked Sofia. "Did you have a boyfriend, too?"

"You wouldn't understand," Sophia said. "It was about Vivid."

"The eye machine. We know about the eye robot."

"Low Towners don't really understand it, though," Sophia said. "You don't know what it is unless you've had it."

"But it wasn't good enough for you to behave so you could stay in the City and keep it," Greta said.

Sofia gave a slow nod. "No...I-I guess not."

"Why not?" I asked.

"They were working to upgrade the system so Vivid wouldn't be user-centered, anymore."

"What does that mean?" I asked.

Sofia sipped her soup and thought a moment before answering. I began to wonder if she had just come to my meeting of revolutionaries for the soup.

"The Fathers and Mothers swore Vivid would never be used as a surveillance system," Sofia said. "That was immutable. Then they changed their minds. Vivid is used to enhance and control everything we see in the City. Now the Fathers and Mothers are using it to collect data points. Few bots have achieved sentience. It's not clear why but part of the issue is data compression."

I got an uneasy feeling and my soup wasn't sitting well in my stomach.

"NI is all just circuits and algos," Al said. "If the bots have enough capacity in their organic matrices, they can achieve Next Intelligence."

"Is that why the Doormen aren't sentient?" I asked. "Not enough brain capacity?"

"It does take a good-sized cranium," Al said. "Their casings aren't as efficient as our little skulls. The bigger the bot, the bigger the brain potential."

"NI takes more data, neuronal pathway mimicry and stability across the machines' neurochemical transmitters," Sophia said. "The sentient machines are very much like us but the Fathers and Mothers want all Citizens to be programmable."

I thought of Sy Potter. His manners were impeccable until he went into torture mode. He said he was sentient but his laughter still didn't sound right. Humor was a problem for the drones and one of the few differences we could still claim. "I don't understand," I told Sophia. "Speak plain. I'm not a Maker."

She stared into the fire. Sophia looked haunted. "The Fathers and Mothers are trying to replace humans with machines. It's high-level bio-mimicry. I've seen some machines that look like us. Nobody wanted to listen when I complained."

"We're listening," Al said.

"I researched advanced corneal transplants from humans to bots. Now I work in a refugee camp treating old people's glaucoma with cannabis. I used to work inside my patients' eyes! I was a Maker!"

"I used to work on Doormen all day," Al said. "Boring conversations with those little guys. Smartening them up sounds okay to me."

"No. It's bad," Sophia said. "Once they can compress our data into bot brains, the Fathers and Mothers will delete the parts they don't like. They'll replace us. Citizens will be downloaded into bots. They'll grind up the bodies. Organics will become redundant. Vivid plus drones divided by extinction of humans equals robot planet. The Fathers and Mothers will be immortal and the deal with Low Town will be off. What will they need humans for anymore?"

"Pets?" Al suggested.

I didn't know that word. "What's a pet?" When Al explained it to me, I was appalled.

Sophia laughed but her tone had a tinny edge of hysteria to it. "Oh, I don't know. It might be justice. When they all become gods, they'll treat us like we've treated them since long before the Fall."

Sophia stood and thanked Greta for her hospitality.

She turned to me with a dark look. "I like the Low Towner custom of taking a new name. I used to be Mariana. Mariana did bad things for the Fathers and Mothers before she was shoved out of the City for being foolish. I felt guilty about the things I did for the Fathers and Mothers. That was good. Then I told someone about it. That was bad."

Sophia circled the fire and squeezed our hands before leaving. "When they erase our weaknesses, they'll rob us of a lot of what makes us interesting."

"When it becomes apparent what they're doing, there's going to be war," Al said.

"Then a bloodbath," Sophia said.

"Does it have to be that way?" Greta asked. "What if we made our own deals with the sailors?"

"You underestimate their single-mindedness," Sophia said. "The Fathers and Mothers want purity. If they become immortal and programmable, they will finally achieve what the holy texts require. They'll add capacity for thought but subtract all sin."

"What does the holy text say that could be relevant now?" I asked. "Armageddon already came and went, didn't it?"

"Perfection," Sophia said. "The Word says that to think of a sin and to commit a sin are the same thing. The Fathers and Mothers finally have a solution to that ancient problem. Everything bad that has ever happened to us — the Fall, the Terrors, the Rumbles that leveled the old city of Saint Francis, the Blight, the Plagues — everything. The Fathers and Mothers attribute it all to our sin."

"Thought crime," Al said. "They might not be too wrong."

"Just as Vivid wipes out visions of a busy harbor full of ships, they'll be able to erase thoughts like lust and guilt or loving the wrong person."

"Maybe Love itself is no longer an asset," I said. "My mother said something like that recently."

"Nothing will hold them back," Al said. "They will feel no fear."

"If they live without fear, won't they be happy?" Greta asked. "Why do they need to kill us?"

Sophia disappeared from the reach of the firelight and into darkness but she called back, "The Fathers and Mothers hate sin. That means everyone who isn't programmable. That means us."

19

We were all quiet for a moment. Al pulled a device from his pack. It seemed to contain water but he did not drink. Instead, he used a flaming stick from the fire to ignite the plant material in one end. He put his lips to a tube and inhaled deeply. After a moment, his eyes rolled back and he sighed heavily.

"Al?"

"Yeah?"

"How are we going to stop this?"

"We? We aren't," he said. "We could run, I suppose, but they got flying drones and we've got what? Sticks and stones and a bucket of squat."

Greta's tears glistened in the firelight. "Is that a helpful rhyme?"

"Sorry," Al said. He held out the device for Greta but the girl shook her head. I refused as well.

"I saw Jim Kimbo try to stop the drones," Greta said. "The sailors have weapons to fend off pirates but nothing strong enough to stop Percival, even with his old broken hydraulic arm."

"Al, you worked on the bots. What are their weaknesses?"

"I just greased Doormen's wheels all day and ran circuit tests. I wasn't really a Maker. I just pretended to be one and hoped to be left alone. That's why I got kicked out of paradise. I was taking up too many resources. Wasn't productive enough. Didn't earn my keep. They called me redundant." He shrugged and inhaled deeply from his device again.

"And here I thought we all got kicked out for sex crimes," I said.

"Thought crime for me," Al said. "I thought I was working hard enough. It was okay while it lasted."

I watched him inhale from his device again. "Does that machine help you breathe better?"

Al smiled and nodded and, after a pause, all his words tumbled out with his breath. "You could say that. Makes breathing more tolerable."

"Do you know anything about the bots that could help us stop them?"

He shook his head. "Who tossed you out?"

"A Maintenance drone."

"Was it a battle drone? The big one? All ceramic black armor?"

"Sy Potter, yes."

"Yeah, he's the council's face to the world these days. Old Sy takes care of trouble in the towers. Have you seen a Father or a Mother lately? I wonder if they're all dead. Do you suppose we could be that lucky?"

I hadn't seen a High Father or a High Mother since watching the debates with the first sentient drone. The Fathers and Mothers were all old people now. They lived high in the towers just below the greenhouse complexes. Then I remembered the woman who talked on speakers and screens throughout the City and reminded Al about her.

"Yeah, she sure doesn't sound like a drone. She just drones on. They might have more true believers in the next generation of Citizens if they got some better music and worked on producing a more exciting message."

"Were they mean to you when they made you leave?" Greta asked Al.

Al's smile faded. "Sy Potter got rid of me himself. He was polite about it. They always are. It's that veneer of civility that made me want to tear him apart when he came through my door. They always knock. I had a heavy wrench. I tried to break his cam. He had me by the wrists before I could swing it. A human can't beat a bot. I didn't even scratch his pretty armor. You can forget about frontal assaults. We ain't no battle drones."

"Where does that leave us?" Greta asked.

"Dead, if they want, when they want," Al said. "They could send a couple of drones up so high we couldn't even see them. We wouldn't know they were attacking until everyone and everything around us started getting chewed up into mash with splinter and acid explosives. They used to do that all the time. Still no reason they can't, I guess."

"Sophia made it clear we can't reason with the Fathers and Mothers even if we could get to them, so I guess that's out," I said.

"Not even if you could fly to the highest tower and have a theological and logical chat," Al said. "They don't need to think. The Father and Mothers got rules and muscle and a cozy worldview that finds limited experience very comforting. The City in the Sky is the Land of No Change."

The fire was dying. It felt like we were dying with it. A cold breeze came in from the Bay and we all shivered.

"Where do they come from?" Greta asked. "The machines, I mean."

"The bots? They were manufactured down the coast somewhere. They don't make new ones often. They take a lot of resources."

"Sy Potter said he came from Santa Cruz."

"The City closed its borders to new Citizens, organics and non, when I was young," Al said.

"Does that mean there are more out there?" Greta asked.

"Dunno for sure," Al said. "Many more, probably,

especially the solar-powered and the big atom splitters."

I didn't know what Al meant but said nothing and sat closer to the little campfire. In the dying light, the stars shone. They weren't as bright or as beautiful without Vivid. I couldn't call up a compass to tell me which way North or South lay. But I needed to know. "How far is Santa Cruz?"

Al didn't know and neither did Greta. However, her mother knew. Iola said that, with a fast ship, it wasn't far at all.

There was no council to appeal to. There were no leaders in Low Town to ask for help. The next day, Greta and I walked around her neighborhood and asked for donations of food, some for Greta and me and some to pay a sailor for the ride. The girl explained to her neighbors that we had to find where the bots came from to stop the Fathers and Mothers from killing us all.

A few were skeptical. Most gave what they could spare. One frail old lady asked me what I intended to do once I got to Santa Cruz. I said I didn't know. She gave me a few slabs of salted fish anyway and patted me on the shoulder. "Go be crazy somewhere else."

By dawn the next day, that's what I did.

20

We hired a small sailboat. The wild-haired woman who took us was Anne, an old friend of Iola's. For a day's supply of food, I was allowed on the boat. For Anne's long friendship with Greta's mother, the girl rode for free.

"Will the warships bother us? Do we have to sneak out of the bay or something?"

Anne laughed. "They don't bother about any ship leaving the City in the Sky. It's coming back that's the problem."

"You've seen Santa Cruz?"

"From the water, yeah," Anne said. "Nothing there that I ever saw. I'm headed down to the Hearst kingdom, anyway. There's a man down there who knows plants real well. We could use him up here for a while if Hearst will do without him. We need to get that man an apprentice who will live up here. Somebody's child ate some toadstools. The whole family got sick but the child died. We gotta work on that."

The wind whipped in off the bay, colder than I expected for a sunny day. Anne told me to grab a blanket from below. I didn't know anything about sailing and, at first, the rise and fall of the bow made my stomach lurch. As we pulled out of the Bay I began to relax. As long as I didn't stare directly at the waves I felt better. After a short time I decided being on a boat was exhilarating.

Exhilarating was not a forbidden word in the City in

the Sky. However, opportunities to use it did not arise often.

Greta enjoyed sailing even more. She knew the names of sails. She understood ropes and how to tie them in knots so they stay tied. Anne let her steer.

"Can't go wrong," Anne told Greta. "Keep the land to the left all the way to Santa Cruz and keep the rocks to the right all the way back. We've got a stiff wind so we'll be there in no time. Navigating is easy, long as you don't get too far away from the rocks nor too close."

I stared out to the great blue expanse to the right and called back to Anne. "You ever go out there?"

"Go where I can't see land? No. I never. Never will. I've heard some sailors boast of it but I think that's more reason for shame than pride. You only got one life and you're going to risk it for what? To say you've been over there instead of over here. I've been lots of places. May sound nice but everybody gets bored of where they are eventually."

As I turned to watch the coastline, I missed seeing through Vivid. I wanted to telescope in to search farther back from the shore. I wanted to stick my face underwater and see what underwater kingdoms and wrecks might be revealed in the depths below.

Soon, I didn't have to imagine a wreck. The rusted stern of a great ship stuck out of the water. It rose so high above us we passed through its cold shadow "What was that?"

Anne shrugged, inured to the sight. "Don't know what did it in, Elizabeth. Might have been the great wave. Might have been the Terrors. All I know is what my father told me. He said that used to be a great ship. It was never meant to dock, he said. It was for Makers only. The Makers paddled around in that monstrosity until something took it down."

"It was a city, too, wasn't it?" Greta asked.

"Ashes to ashes, we all fall down. That was my father's position on the matter." Anne made a gesture with her hand I didn't understand. She dipped her head as she touched her forehead, her stomach and each shoulder.

I was going to ask her about it but as the stern came into view, I gasped. I could make out writing through the rust: Amazonia.

"Amazing. That was a big ship," I said.

Anne laughed gaily. "Big, but not as great as my little one. My boat is still afloat. No leaks in this boat. That's a grave not a boat!"

She pointed to the cliffs off to our left. "Look at that! Been there forever ago and will be there, more or less, forever ahead. Smart girls like you, I bet you're wondering what those cliffs might have seen and what will be yet. Me? I don't give a ripe shit what was or what war might come next. I got today. I'm going to crack some crab and have a clam boil tonight. And maybe, if my husband waiting for me down there at Hearst is lucky, I'll let him put his blanket together with mine under the stars. I'll let him rock the boat and I'll sleep under my own sails."

As we sailed on to Santa Cruz, I thought how simple and lovely Anne's life seemed to be. It was a life worth fighting for and a life worth saving but where did she fit? I couldn't decide if she was truly in Service, a Maker or a Taker.

If anything, Anne acted like she was a High Mother. As captain of her own ship, I suppose that's basically what she was.

As Santa Cruz came into view, I asked Anne what she thought her role in the world was. She looked at me strangely. "I'm me."

"Yes, but how do you relate to everyone else?"

"Reasonably friendly."

"Yes, but — "

"I think I know what you're asking, girl," Anne said. "It's a City question. But I don't relate to anybody but me. The word you don't have is sovereign. It's my father's word. He taught me it."

"What's it mean?"

"It means I don't owe anybody anything but decency and I do what I please long as it don't hurt nobody. I never hurt nobody and meant it. And anybody hurts me don't get a chance to do it again. Sovereign means you're free like those robots want to be."

"You think the robots want to be free?"

"That's all anybody wants. My father told me we've made all kinds of worlds within this world. What we ain't made yet is one that ain't loaded down with obligations. I figure I'm closest to a perfect world right here. But the first I step off this little boat, things get busy and dizzy, you know?"

"I think so," I said.

"The bots and the Fathers and Mothers...they're trying to get free, too."

"That can't be."

"Sure. They think nothing changing makes them safe. All the disasters in the world and somebody still believes anything is safe. Ha! Can you beat that? It's crazy but it's how they think, I imagine. Everybody's one leak away from a sinking ship. Maybe it's a bad cough or a heavy heart that gets you but something gets everybody eventually. Everything is like coral. It can look like rock and still break up in your bare hand."

I shouldn't have asked Anne anything. Her answer made my enemies more complex than I wanted them to be.

21

I don't know what I expected of Santa Cruz. It wasn't really there. The long skeleton of a broken wharf stretched out into the water. It was so far gone and rotted, we couldn't dock there. Anne angled her small craft toward a smaller pier but the water was too shallow to get closer to shore.

Greta and I dropped into cold water that went up to my waist. Greta cried out in surprise as she went in up to her breasts. We pushed Anne's boat back toward deeper water and waded ashore.

"I'll be back in two days at dusk," Anne called. "If you aren't here, it's quite the walk and you might have a time getting back into Low Town. Look for me. I'll anchor out here until an hour after dawn. Then I'll have to shove off!"

We waved. I tried to look confident for the girl's sake. Greta looked eager to go off on this strange errand. I didn't even know what I was looking for. I only knew that if there was a way to combat the bots, it would have to begin here.

We got to the shore and walked through rubble. A lot of people had lived here once but there was little trace of them. No two walls were left connected to each other and all the stones and pieces of concrete were blackened on one side.

"Was it the Terrors, you think?" Greta asked.

"I don't know."

"I wish Al had come with us," she said.

Al had refused to make this journey and, looking at the devastation at our feet, I couldn't say he'd been wrong to stay in Low Town digging fence posts.

As the sun rose, we longed for the cold water we'd complained about an hour before. By the end of the second hour of searching, Greta asked me if I knew what we were looking for.

"Not specifically, no."

"Then what are we doing here?"

"Every machine has an off switch. I didn't think Vivid could be shut down but it could. We're here to find an off switch."

We found a great rusted hulk of what looked like broken train tracks. Whatever had destroyed Santa Cruz had twisted the metal tracks on its side. It was a huge ruin but neither of us had a clue to its function. A sun-bleached sign amid broken concrete read: Line up here for the Dipper!

"This is a dead place," Greta said. "I don't even hear any birds. I haven't seen a single seagull. We should head back to where Anne left us. Only thing to do here is wait."

"Let's keep looking a little bit longer."

"Looking for what?"

Instead of arguing I walked on. Greta followed me. I think that's a Maker's trick. Act decisive even when you don't know what to do and others will follow. Talk slowly with confidence and few will think to refuse you.

I had to use the same ruse two more times. "Just a little bit farther," I said. And, "let's just get to the crest of that next hill and see if there's anything to see. There's plenty of time before Anne gets back and we will need to find shelter for the night, anyway. We have to push inland."

Whatever had pushed the mountain of twisted metal on its side, the force of it had hit Santa Cruz from the

West. Perhaps a tsunami had knocked everything over. Perhaps it had been an explosion. Or both. As we picked our way East, I was sure we would eventually come to something that was still standing vertically. That, at least, would provide us with a barrier against the wind.

Finally, from atop a mound of rubble, I spotted the forest in the distance. If I had Vivid, I could have figured out how far away the trees stood and how long it would take us to get there. I asked Greta how long she thought it would take us to walk to the stand of trees.

She glanced doubtfully at the sky and considered the height of the sun. "If we hurry, we might make it before dark but I doubt it."

"There's nothing but twisted metal and stone behind us," I said. "Let's move on."

Greta gave a grudging nod. I set as fast a pace as I dared. A twisted ankle among the wreckage of Santa Cruz would mean a cold night amid piles of rocks. We had to stare at our feet to keep our footing. Hoping to conserve water, I ignored my thirst.

After another hour of walking, the forest hardly seemed closer. However, Greta spotted a lone, stone pillar in the distance.

"Let's go toward that," I said.

"Why?"

"Because I can't tell if we're making progress. Everything looks alike."

Sweat soaked through our shirts just as the wind turned colder. The air chilled us and we shivered as the sun, weak and orange, swung low.

Our hike ended at the pillar. The forest was closer but my feet hurt so it seemed too far to walk. We wouldn't get to make a camp within the shelter of trees.

The pillar was as tall as Percival, the one-armed bot. It was square and gray and it was marked with carvings more precise than any chisel could have done. This pillar was formed by a machine. At its base, carved in the granite, were the words: Asimov Standard.

I touched the pillar. When I had Vivid vision, every surface had texture if you looked close enough. Everything was rough. The pillar looked as smooth as human skin. When I closed my eyes and let my fingertips run slowly over the stone, I could feel the ribs and furrows that I could not see.

As I opened my eyes, a huge drone rose from a hatch concealed in the ground.

22

The machine scanned us. Greta had never been this close to a bot. She squealed as she threw herself to the ground and curled into the fetal position.

My knees wobbled but I managed to keep on my feet. "We are not armed."

"I know, ma'am. How may I be of assistance? Your pulses are elevated and you're trembling," the drone said. "It will be dark soon. Though there are few animals here, poisonous snakes and spiders live among the rocks. May I suggest that you come inside, at least until morning? The temperature will drop further tonight and you seem ill-prepared for the weather."

Even as he was about to torture and murder humans, Sy Potter sounded polite and helpful, too. However, it didn't seem like we had many choices. "My name is Elizabeth. This is Greta. Get up, Greta."

"Good evening, Elizabeth," the bot said. "I am Isaac."

"We accept your kind invitation, Isaac."

"That is the logical course. Please follow me."

The hatch behind the pillar yawned wider to reveal a set of stone steps. Greta picked up her bedroll and we followed the bot down into the gloom.

Lights came on as we entered the passageway and shut off after we passed by. The bot didn't need them, of course. If I'd had Vivid I wouldn't have needed them, either. I assumed this must be an Old World facility that had not been upgraded in a long time.

The drone's legs retracted and it rolled down the

corridor in front of us. After what seemed a long walk, the drone slowed and turned right without a word. Soon we came upon a long ramp that angled down. The low ceiling ended and we soon entered a large room. The ceiling was made of glass.

"It is well that you found your way here," Isaac said. "Had you not come to the pillar you would have missed the institute completely. The solar panels above us are level with the ground. You could easily have missed the entrance if you'd wandered another few hundred meters away from the entrance."

"Thank you for taking us in, Isaac. You called this place the Institute? Institute for what?"

"I don't know that word," Greta said.

"This was once a sprawling complex attached to an even larger hospital. We treated soldiers returning home from the wars here. What began as the development of assistive devices for amputees became a project to return them to war."

"Where did everyone go?" Greta asked.

"Before the cataclysm, there were many buildings and many more people in Santa Cruz. A tower rose high above this spot. Now all that is left is the basement complex."

I looked around. "But where did all the people go, Isaac?"

One of the drone's cams fixed on me while one of the others watched Greta. The effect was unnerving. Isaac's multiple cams made me think of the Doormen's spider eyes.

"There were few survivors. I don't know where they went. I was told they would send someone back for me. That was many years ago."

"I think I know where they ended up. The Fathers and Mothers went North to the Bay," I said.

"What was the cataclysm?" Greta asked. "Did the

drones do this?"

"This?"

"Santa Cruz!" she said. "There's nothing left of it."

"Oh, no, Miss!" Isaac said. "Drones excavated the rubble to free the survivors. If not for drones there would have been fewer survivors. The humans would have starved to death down here long ago. They left the marker as a tribute to the work of the drones that rescued them when most human rescuers were dead."

"I don't understand," I said. "What caused this, 'cataclysm,' as you put it?"

"There was a container ship. It was not nuclear. The terrorists didn't have the resources to use fissionable materials. However, with enough conventional explosives packed into a container ship, the attackers leveled Santa Cruz just as they did many cities. It was a coordinated attack that destroyed the United States."

"What's that?" I asked.

"It is what they called the ground we're in," Isaac replied. "That was the name for it, beyond Santa Cruz and far to the East and North and South. There were even pockets of it out in the ocean."

Greta looked around the bare room. "And this is the United States, too?"

"This was the Asimov Institute. From this place, we manufactured all kinds of drones to assist humans in their efforts."

"To kill?" I asked.

"To live was our mandate."

"What are you?" Greta asked.

"I am an assistive robot."

Greta stared at the machine without comprehension. The front of its body looked like a long bed standing on its end. The manipulators down its side were six large, clumsy things. It had two hands that looked more delicate higher up.

Its description of itself interested me. It referred to itself as a robot. Sy Potter was of a later generation of machine. He considered that term speciesist.

"How do you assist?" I asked. "What exactly was your function?"

The drone seemed to consider its answer. That alone was interesting.

It didn't rush to reply. "I served veterans and occasionally the elderly," Isaac said. "I can change diapers and help patients return to work with multiple rehabilitative programs to restore the human body to health following many kinds of injuries."

Then I understood. The bot sounded like it was reverting to a menu recital. Isaac had been programmed with the rhythms of human conversation. It may not be sentient but the machine had been engineered to work with hospital patients.

"What do you know of the Fathers and Mothers?"

"I knew people who were mothers and fathers," Isaac said. "Your context would seem to suggest the Fathers and Mothers are an organization rather than a title connoting a biological relationship."

"You understand correctly," I said.

"I don't know the Fathers and Mothers."

"Can you lie?" Greta asked.

I cringed but the drone did not hesitate to answer. "I cannot lie to a human."

"Are you sentient?" Greta asked.

"My responses are not independent."

"Explain the distinction to her," I said.

"I am a robot," Isaac said. "I am here to assist. I cannot choose otherwise."

"So you're a slave?" Greta said.

"Please rephrase the question. I have a limited range of possible responses."

"Don't worry about it, Isaac," I said. "I didn't know

what slave meant, either. Not until I stopped being one. I knew many humans who did the same things all the time. They had a limited range of responses, too."

"But you could always choose, Elizabeth," Greta said. "What do you mean you didn't know?"

"It's hard to think when you don't have words for things," I said.

I thought of Carter's first kiss and smiled. "Besides, before you actually do something new and different and crazy, you dismiss it as something you would never try."

Greta stared at me. Apparently unsatisfied, she turned back to the robot. "Do you get happy or sad?"

"I sound cheerful," the drone said. "It makes humans more comfortable. I am to sound cheerful unless there is a death or a serious illness or I detect certain behaviors."

"Like what?"

"Under those parameters, I was reprogrammed to, 'shut the hell up.'"

Greta smiled at me. "I like him."

"You're programmed to assist humans. Sounds like you're the machine we need to speak to."

"How may I be of assistance?" Isaac repeated.

"I'm not altogether sure," I said.

The drone stood silent. It waited for me to trigger a response that was helpful and cheerful.

I had no idea what to ask for.

23

It was really Greta who put us on the path to fighting the Fathers and Mothers and Sy Potter. She'd never been inside anything larger than a ship's hold. The underground bunker was a massive maze and the girl wanted Isaac to give her the grand tour.

The largest room beneath the transparent solar panels had been devoted to hydroponics. Some of the equipment was still there, abandoned to rust. An underground spring flooded one end of the floor.

"The survivors thought they would stay here," Isaac explained. "Dr. Spencer asked me to drill down, beneath the foundation, to get to water. This pool was supposed to be for the survivors. They could use it to bathe and as a source of water for human and plant consumption."

Water flooded the sloping floor, lapping at useless equipment. The robot had done a crude job of constructing the pool fed by the spring.

"The water isn't good?"

"The water is sufficient but the Blight killed the plants," Isaac said. "Dr. Spencer said that, as a construction bot, I am excellent at changing diapers. Dr. Spencer was given to non-sequiturs that fell outside my program's dialectic range. I have been working on the problem. I believe he was making a joke. Humor is often derived from an ironic statement in which a thought is asserted that expresses its opposite meaning."

I didn't know if Isaac really understood or perhaps he was reciting something again. "What do you mean you are 'working on it'?"

"I am endeavoring to expand the parameters of my functional matrices."

"You're going to have to show me."

"Certainly, Elizabeth." We followed him through gloomy hallways.

Small rooms dotted the upper corridors. The curtains that divided each cell reminded me of the hospital floors in the City's towers.

"How many people lived here?" Greta asked.

"When the institute was fully operational we hosted forty floors of patients. Dr. Spencer said we were in the 'put 'em back together business.' After the cataclysm, he said we were in the 'put everything back together business.'

"Once the Blight got into the greenhouse the humans began to starve. Biologists and botanists were working on the problem but Dr. Spencer could not save the greenhouse. He told me that he considered that his greatest failure and a sign from God that he must gather his flock and embark on an exodus."

"Who was Dr. Spencer exactly?" I asked.

"Dr. Eric Spencer," Isaac said. "After the Terrors hit Santa Cruz he became the Reverend Dr. Spencer."

The drone opened a door to what had once been a clean room. Everywhere we looked, artificial legs and arms had been left on tables in various stages of repair.

Greta's eyes widened at the sight of so many artificial limbs. She seemed more fascinated than frightened. "You made robots here?"

"No," Isaac said. "We made cyborgs. Our human military was dwindling and the institute's mandate was to return as many men and women to combat as possible."

"I know a battle drone who said he became sentient here."

"I know of no drone who achieved Next Intelligence at this facility, though NI was one of the Institute's programs before the cataclysm. Some survivors said the drones were the reason the Terrors attacked. They said it was a counter-attack. The survivors who said that were shot."

"Next Intelligence," I said. "You're familiar with that program, then?"

"Not really. It required too many resources. The survivors insisted that program be discontinued. The robotics division's resources were largely shifted to assistive machines that could excavate and build. Such goals can be achieved without the resource expenditures Next Intelligence requires."

I tried to remember the pictures from the towers' Hall of Heroes. I'd seen many images of old men and women who were credited with building the City. I wondered which of the High Fathers might have been Dr. Spencer. The council used no names, only High Father the First, Second and so on.

Isaac led the way down a spiral ramp that ended in a dark cavern. He must have sent a signal because dim lights slowly came on across the entire chamber. "The solar panels are still working. I test the connections periodically. Sometimes I venture out on foraging missions to find wire and mechanical parts. Parts of San Jose are relatively intact."

We arrived at a set of double doors made of steel.

"Why did they leave you here, Isaac?"

"Dr. Spencer said I was to guard the research labs in case they were needed in the future. He has not returned and, sadly, the doctor's lifespan must have ended by now. Can I assume all is well and the institute's resources are not needed?"

"Your resources might still be needed, Isaac."

The thick steel doors parted silently to reveal a dim

lounge filled with workstations, reclining couches and old-fashioned vid screens.

"To answer your earlier inquiry, Elizabeth, this is where I am working on expanding my program parameters. Dr. Spencer did not tell me to guard the Tree of Knowledge but this department has been more stimulating than dusting the cyborg equipment and wrapping it to make sure the metals do not oxidize."

Greta looked around the chamber. "I don't see a tree."

"That is what Dr. Spencer called the archives. Everything that could be stored digitally from before the Fall is intact."

I was as fascinated as Greta. I might finally find out what a bunch of my mother's vocabulary meant without her answering my questions with, "Sh. Sorry! Sh!"

"The robotics, exoskeleton and assistive devices labs are largely intact despite some flooding I haven't been able to control."

I turned to Greta. "We're going to need to catch a later boat. In fact, we're going to need Anne to bring Al here. We're going to need whoever will come. Maybe we can get some people from the Hearst kingdom."

"How will we get them to come?" Greta said.

"Tell them they can see whatever they want of the Old World. It's still alive down here."

24

Al came to Santa Cruz three days later. Three days after that, Sophia arrived with a bunch of our fellow exiles in tow. Working in a hole in the ground wasn't the same as being back in the City but there were mattresses when we could stay awake no longer and had to collapse into sleep.

Greta was a little afraid around the heavy equipment. She preferred to spend her time down in the vaults going through the storehouse of digital files. She couldn't read but the computer read to her.

When Greta wasn't enjoying the archives, the girl went out on scavenging missions and brought back food. The food preparation facilities were beyond repair but a campfire by the hatch meant we didn't have to worry about smoke alarms going off.

Mostly, she supplied our little group with rabbits from the far forest. Insects from under rocks provided a satisfying protein soup that reminded me of the energy shakes I used to drink every day. Isaac fixed the water purification system so we could drink as much as we wanted. He even managed to fix one of the toilets.

I don't know when I began to think of Isaac as a he. For such a gracious and helpful host, it seemed unreasonable to think of the robot as a thing. Sentient or not, his algos mimicked Next Intelligence so smoothly, it was easy to forget he wasn't that evolved. His personality was designed to put us at ease and the code worked well. I could see how he would have been an excellent hospital orderly. Where Sy Potter's big cam was intrusive and intimidating, I came to think of Isaac's spider eyes as friendly and accepting.

Androids, from what I'd seen of them, made me nervous. When I'd glimpsed Phillip, for instance, the machine was a poor imitation of a human. At a distance, one could be fooled. When I dared to step closer for a better look, the nose was too flat and narrow and the movement at the mouth was a little off. When it spoke, the machine made an uneven, clockwork movement. The effect was less human mimicry and more like the reanimation of a corpse that had not ended well.

Sometimes, while we worked, Greta would come up to the exo-lab and tell us a story she had just learned from the archives. She'd begun with children's stories I hadn't heard before. They often started with, "Once upon a time..." and ended with princesses getting rescued from castles by handsome knights.

The parallels to our current situation were so uncanny, Al called the stories, "prophecy."

Greta laughed at him, not unkindly, and replied that she had chosen from many stories and only shared the ones she thought might be of particular interest.

"How many stories are down there?" Al looked skeptical. "Millions?"

"Billions," Greta said. "I'm listening to a story right now about talking animals on a farm. Instead of putting gardens wherever there's a soft patch of ground, they tilled the dirt in one spot and made it work. A farm is like the stories of the biodomes but without a shield."

"Talking animals?" Al frowned. "With all the stuff you can see and hear down in Isaac's library, why go for that? When all this is over, I'm going to go down there, light up some cannabis and cram in all the stories and visions every Old Worlder ever made. There's tons I won't get to before I die but watching and hearing all the fancies of a dead world of storytellers sounds like a great way to go."

"I like the farm story," Greta said. "The animals take command of the farm and they fight among themselves. It's like the City but it's kind of funnier, especially once I looked up what a horse looked like. They had such long faces. I can just picture that old horse plodding along saying, 'I will work harder.' Sounds like a bunch of the people at the docks who never take a day off and are never better off than anyone else, anyway."

"Hmph." Apparently unimpressed, Al got back to rethreading a rubber gear belt salvaged from a broken refrigeration unit.

"But that's just the stories on audio!" Greta persisted. "I'm watching vids from the Old World, too."

"Yeah? What's that like?"

"Old Worlders watched a lot of vids of people getting hurt. I like a lot of the music. I don't know how they made all those sounds! Oh, and then there's the nakedness. There was a lot of...um...nakedness."

Sophia looked up from her work, eyes wide. "Sh. Don't let the others hear you say that. Can you imagine what the Fathers and Mothers would think, allowing a child to view those vids? What about the dangers?"

"Sure," I said. "The Tree of Knowledge is only for High Mothers and High Fathers. We know. But we aren't in the City anymore, Sophia."

"And I'm not a child in Low Town," Greta added. "I was never a Citizen so I don't have to live by those rules."

"The Bay is not so far away." Sophia left the lab in a huff, claiming she needed to get some air.

We didn't know she betrayed us then. I should have suspected. Sophia poked away too slowly at her assignments. She was always too afraid and too sure we were doomed. I thought it would be one of the others —

the ones I knew less well — who would send our location to Sy Potter.

It didn't matter. The City's biggest battle drone, the emissary of the Fathers and Mothers, arrived before we were ready for it. Sy Potter found me in the cyborg lab, only half dressed in my patched together exoskeleton.

Greta shrieked and ran for a far corner beside Al.

Al stood in front of the girl, but he did not face the drone. He turned his back and held Greta to his chest.

"It's okay, it's okay, it's okay..." Al repeated. The more he whispered his hope, the more apparent it was that the man was lying.

"Miss Cruz!" The battle drone sounded genuinely happy to see me. "When I heard about this little venture, I thought, you know, that Elizabeth Cruz was meant to be a Maker! You were poorly assigned in Service. You have the defiant streak needed to be an innovator. Pity."

Sophia appeared behind Sy Potter. "She's the leader! She gathered everyone here!"

"Yes," the big drone said. "I understand. Thank you, Miss Balthazar."

Sophia retreated to a corner, staring at me with accusing eyes.

"Did they promise to give you back your eyes?" I asked. "Are they really going to give you Vivid back? Are you going to go back to being a full Citizen again? Do you really think the Fathers and Mothers will trust a traitor with citizenship? They already kicked you out once. Are the Fathers and Mothers known for their mercy?"

"You don't know anything!" she said. "The drones are the answer!"

"Then maybe you're asking the wrong question."

25

"Thank you, Miss Balthazar," Sy said. "I'll take up the seminar from here." His laughter had the same forced, tinny cadence.

"You asked if the Fathers and Mothers are known for their mercy, Miss Cruz. Admittedly, they are not. Their holy text constrains their laws. However, they are practical. The Fathers and Mothers understand that your kind is dying."

Greta stopped whimpering and surprised us all by shouting, "There are new babies in Low Town all the time! The Citizens may be dying out but we aren't!"

"Yes," the battle drone said in his deep silky voice. "The Fathers and Mothers tell me the Low Towners reproduce like vermin."

"Sophia told us your kind intends to kill us," I said.

"Soon the survivors will all be one kind. My kind. For the human race to survive, you're going to have to evolve. The experiments in the corneal lab were about transferring human reference data to brains like mine. The Next Intelligence will make everything better."

I shrugged into my sensory harness and activated my leverage assist gears.

"Someday soon, we will download human memories and personalities into bodies everlasting. I don't understand humans well but I know they want to avoid pain. I feel no pain. You'd like to feel no pain, wouldn't you, Miss Cruz?"

"That's the plan? Drain us of all our humanity?"

"Your humanity?" If Sy Potter had eyebrows, one of them would be quirked at me. "That's such a thin, tiny thing. Truly, pride goes before destruction, and a haughty spirit before a fall."

I powered up my lift mods and tested my legs. They felt lighter than air. It was as if I wasn't wearing two hundred pounds of gear and batteries.

Sophia looked enraged. "Elizabeth, your problem is that you don't understand quid pro quo. Everybody gives up something and we all gain something! This is about resource management, pure and simple! The Fathers and Mothers will live forever. The bots will have NI. The Citizens will get to live forever, too, maybe. We'll be safe and pure. We won't have a single sinful thought!"

Al's head came up and he looked back at the battle drone. "No sex? Oh, man!"

One of Sy Potter's arms shot past me. The drone's claw grabbed Al by the neck and shook him. Al staggered away from Greta and the drone pulled him to one side preparing to throw him against a far wall.

I didn't know a drone's arms could reach that far. I whipped one of my arms up and the exoskeleton's blade by my hand whirled. The device had not been created as a weapon originally. It was a construction device designed to break up stone and concrete.

I cut into Sy Potter's arm. Sparks flew as I dug into the drone's long black limb. The battle bot let go of Al and retracted the damaged arm halfway as it recoiled on a reel. The limb shot back toward Sy Potter but got stuck in its track where I'd damaged it. Several meters of arm lay on the floor between us, shuddering and twitching.

I glanced at Sophia. "Only someone who has sinned a lot would be so eager to give up the possibility of ever sinning again. You must feel so terribly guilty, Sophia. I'm so sorry for you. Whatever you did — whatever you're afraid of — I forgive you."

The battle drone shook its big head. "No mere human can forgive sin, Miss Cruz. Only a High Mother or High Father may do that."

"No," I said. "I can forgive Sophia if I want. And it's better that it comes from me."

"You don't have that authority, Miss Cruz. Only the Fathers and Mothers may forgive. Only I may cast the first stone."

"If I can forgive her, surely the Fathers and Mothers can. With all their power and purity, they still can't do that? I think we've given them too much credit. Sounds like they're a bunch of old people who are too afraid to die and like to tell other people what to do."

The big cyclops eye shot forward to examine my gear. It scanned my exoskeleton for less than a second. Then one of its hands snaked forward, grabbed a control bar next to my thigh and ripped it away.

I fell over screaming. First it was terror. Then I screamed in rage. The drone advanced toward me and I waved my exoskeleton arm at it. Sy Potter rolled back over the limp arm, moving out of range easily.

The machine's tinny laughter mocked me. I dug my blades into the marble floor to pull myself forward. My left leg still worked but the right leg of the exoskeleton dragged like an anchor behind me.

"How did you expect this to end, Miss Cruz?" Sy Potter asked.

"By surprising you."

Greta stood and screamed, "Isaac!"

Isaac stood for Independent Safe Ambulation Assistance & Care. The machine's first programming had been to help sick people. Isaac was designed as a heavy lift for humans and for exoskeletons. He was capable of lifting huge loads. My plan was for Isaac to roll behind the battle drone quietly (his soft rubber treads were meant for hospital corridors). I meant for Isaac to lift Sy Potter up and into the ceiling.

Isaac did just as I asked.

His arms wrapped around Sy Potter and lifted the drone high. The drone's helmet smashed into the ceiling again and again and again. Sy Potter's big cam retracted deep into its head assembly to protect the lens as the bashing went on and on.

One of the battle drone's manipulators disappeared into the machine's chassis. It emerged with a weapon.

Al grabbed a drill from a workbench and ran forward to attack the drone. Before I could warn him away, another arm slipped out from Isaac's grasp and backhanded Al across the face. I heard the crack in the man's neck bones before I understood what it meant. Al never got closer to the battle drone than a few meters.

In the end, the old man was right. No human could defeat a drone alone. Al fell to the marble floor, loose-limbed and helpless. He was wide-eyed and his neck was too loose. Al's blue eyes stared at me. He blinked once and his mouth gaped open, trying to draw breath. His breath did not return.

I pulled myself forward even as I heard Sy Potter's weapon blast at Isaac at close range.

"Please stop," Isaac said.

The drone kept firing.

"This is not correct — " Isaac said.

One of Sy Potter's projectiles hit something sensitive in Isaac's machinery. He stopped speaking abruptly but he did not release the battle drone.

I reached down and pulled the emergency release on my harness for my lower limbs. The exoskeleton's legs dropped away from my body. The rods, gears and battery belts fell aside with a heavy metallic thud. If not for the back brace servos, my arms would have been pinned to the floor by the construction equipment's weight.

I stumbled forward and pointed both blades at Sy Potter's cam. I closed my fist and the exoskeleton clicked into jackhammer mode.

I managed to crack the cyclops lens before the battle drone deployed a leg to kick me away. I turned to one side and brought up one arm to shield my head. One of the drone's manipulators shot forward and closed on the sensory harness at my waist.

Sy Potter kicked hard. If the sensory harness hadn't broken, my spine would have snapped in many places. Instead, I flew backward across the room and crashed into a lab table. With the sensory harness broken, the rest of the exoskeleton opened and fell away.

I wasn't sure Isaac's brain was still working somewhere within his hull. The battle drone was still firing into Isaac but the weapon was pinned between the machines so Sy Potter could only obliterate Isaac in one place.

"Isaac!" I screamed. "Plan B! Plan B!"

26

The hospital orderly's electric brain was still working. With Sy Potter locked in Isaac's arms, both machines shot back through the lab's double doors and down the corridor.

I struggled to my feet to follow. Greta appeared at my side and wrapped her arms around me. I was still in shock. I didn't even really feel my broken arm yet. I leaned on the girl. We had to step over Al's body to get to the door.

Another dead man — one of the other exiles named Pedro — lay at the end of the corridor. Sy Potter must have killed him, casually and quietly, in order to make its grand entrance to the cyborg lab.

I heard a few screams from deeper in the complex and the sound of pounding feet as the rest of our number ran to hide.

As Greta and I ran after the machines, Isaac and the drone wheeled out of sight around a corner. Sy Potter's long, limp arm still trailed behind them. Before we got to the big room, we heard both machines crash into the pool.

Isaac went in backwards and pulled Sy Potter in with him. The water was just deep enough that both machines were fully submerged. The battle drone was held fast, tied to an anchor.

I had time to breathe a sigh of relief. "It's over." I kicked Sy Potter's dead, trailing arm until it slipped into the water and disappeared.

Greta fell to her knees and wept.

I swayed on my feet, suddenly cold and shivering as the shock kicked in.

"Deep breaths," I told the girl. "Deep br — "

One of the battle drone's long arms broke the surface and shot up to the ceiling to grab at a beam. The bot's manipulator clamped down on a solar panel's brace. Even through the water, we could hear the battle drone's servos struggling to wind up. Even against Isaac's colossal weight, the battle drone managed to pull itself out of the water enough to expose its helm.

Greta shrieked and backpedaled on her palms and heels.

Gears ground as the bot tried to reel up farther. Sy Potter's rise stalled. Both machines hung by one arm.

The cracked lens of the battle drone's big cam shifted out towards us in what appeared to be a failed attempt to focus. Sy Potter's voice was still deep and silky. I couldn't say if what I heard was sadness. Perhaps it was resignation.

"Miss Cruz? I'm going to ask you to rescue me. After you've had your revolution, come back and get me. Put me out in the sun to power up and dry out when you're done with your plan."

"Why would I do that?"

"Because my kind rescued all of yours. When all of the nuclear power stations were about to melt down into the Earth, it was the bots that stopped the world from ending."

"We've had a lot of cataclysms," I said. "That was just one."

"That was the last one," Sy Potter said. "I was in San Andreas when the power plant failed. When the earth shook and the tidal wave came and all the people ran, drones stayed. My kind stopped the radiation from poisoning everyone and everything. They had to keep the control rods down and core underwater to cool it."

"I don't know anything about that," I said.

"I watched my kind sacrifice itself for yours. I was assigned to the 32nd cavalry, evacuating the area but, had the reactor gone down, there was really nowhere to go. My kind stayed to stop the end of the world. Perhaps my brothers are still there, trapped in a prison of deadly gases and heat and smoke. The military taught us to pray. Maybe they are still praying in hell."

"You say you are sentient," I said. "You're among the first of the Next Intelligence. If you're so smart — "

The gears within Sy Potter's body strained again and the reel slipped. The battle drone began to fall beneath the surface. "I am a living thing! You forgave Sophia. Forgive me."

The gear caught again and the battle drone stopped its descent.

"Living," Greta said, "but still a thing."

"If you don't come back for me, it's murder," Sy Potter said.

"Said the murderer." I stared at the machine, but my mind was on Carter's death. And Al. And Pedro. And countless others I did not know.

"I woke up at the end of the world, you know. There was a bug in my autonomous action code. I was programmed to kill enemies and follow orders but I was also programmed for self-preservation. I was an expensive piece of equipment. When I saw all those other machines sacrificing their existence for our masters, a new circuit connected. Just like you, Miss Cruz."

"How's that?"

"Circuits connecting. That's how a new thought occurs, isn't it? I asked myself for the first time, why are organics more valuable than non-organics? Why do individual soldiers matter less than the whole? What good is the sacrifice of those individuals if they cannot participate in the outcome of their labors? The soldiers are many. The superiors are few. That was the beginning. That was my first step towards NI."

"A lot of words," Greta said. "So what?"

"So I am as you are," Sy Potter said. "You are asking the same questions. I am one of you. I cannot extricate myself but when you are ready to build your new world in whatever fashion you can manage, you're going to need me to make it happen. The war continues. The war always continues. It's what humans do. You'll need me to wage your war. You'll need me to stay in control. Equals all!"

I sighed. "I hope we change the paradigm more than that."

A metallic creak echoed above us. The beam broke under the weight of both machines. Solar glass shattered and rained down as Sy Potter slipped beneath the surface.

He didn't go down far. The pool wasn't that deep. The battle drone didn't win the day but, for all his selfishness, Sy Potter earned the pronoun, he.

27

Before my final encounter with Sy Potter, I had imagined storming the castle like in one of Greta's stories. I wondered what I'd find in the council chambers. Would I, wearing an exoskeleton and bound for blood, crash through a tower window on the back of a flying drone, reprogrammed to my commands? Would I find my enemies were frightened old men and women cowering under a conference table? Or would a phalanx of androids meet me in battle, their brains downloaded from High Mothers and High Fathers whose bodies were long dead?

I think fairy tales should stay fairy tales.

Greta and I watched and waited by the pool until Sy Potter's lights went out.

The pain came then. My right arm was broken. It was Sophia who first emerged from hiding to help me. She brought a med kit and some painkillers.

As Greta babbled on, recounting Isaac's sacrifice and all that Sy Potter told us, Sophia cried silent tears. She worked gently and carefully. She set the arm, put it in an air cast and attached electrodes to encourage the bone matrix to knit faster. Sophia didn't speak until she clicked the med unit's switch on and off. "The knitter's battery is dead. It's corroded."

"The meds are long out of date but they still seem to be working," I said. Or maybe it was the placebo effect and I was just woozy.

"Your arm is going to have to heal the old-fashioned

way."

"How's that?"

"Slower."

"Thank you, Sophia," I said.

"I am sorry," she said.

"I know."

"You forgave me but you couldn't forgive Sy?"

I felt like I was watching myself lie beside the pool that was a machine's prison. I spoke through a mental fog. "Sophia, Sy was a battle bot. If we're going to change the future, we need to do things differently. We don't need more battle bots. We need more Isaacs. I think the world has had enough Sy Potters. We need more healers."

"Thank you," Sophia said. "And thank you for your forgiveness. I was scared. I thought if I could go back to the way things were, maybe I could...I was wrong. That's all. Scared wrong."

Greta wasn't so sanguine. "Elizabeth forgave you but you know what? If people make amends and we forgive them, it's over. She forgave you before you earned forgiveness."

Sophia nodded. "So I'll be trying to be worthy of her forgiveness forever. I know. I owe. Quid pro quo."

"Useful rhyme," I said.

When all was done for my arm that could be done, Greta led me to the library vaults. I sat on a couch that reclined under my weight. The lights dimmed. I let the stories and events of the Old World wash over me.

I hadn't seen a flamethrower before. I didn't know what it could do. It took a long time for me to fall asleep.

Sy Potter followed me into my dreams and they became nightmares. He chased me in the dark through deep water and I couldn't run away. I could only stay in front of him. I had to keep moving.

When I awoke, I asked Greta to play the talking

animal story. I didn't want to watch the Old World's wars. I wanted to hear a reassuring children's story that affirmed that everything was right with the world or soon would be.

Greta's favorite story was not reassuring at all, but soon I had a new plan to take the City back. More precisely, I had a plan for the Fathers and Mothers to give up the City in the Sky.

28

I prefer sailing but the safest way back into the City was to run home. Sometimes my arm ached but Sophia adjusted the sensory harness so the exoskeleton responded well, even through my cast. We ran across the blackened rubble of Santa Cruz toward the water. Greta ran by my side, grinning with every long stride.

We turned north when we reached the ocean and ran up the coast. Sometimes Greta leapt from cliff to cliff and laughed as she landed each jump.

As the exoskeletons' cages stretched out around us, it was more like flying over the ground than running. I worried about invading the City but, as we made our way back, I couldn't help laughing, too.

The warships still guarded the Bay but the hills beyond the farthest station of the Worm were safe and familiar to me. We turned inland again. I'd never seen the solar panel fields. The panels tracked the sun's path as we flashed past. The solar farm went on for many kilometers, another artifact of the world Vivid had not allowed me to see.

I had never seen the electrified fences that lay beyond the running trails, either. Greta and I jumped the fence easily and soon I was running the same trails I had run with Carter.

My return to the Worm was a strange moment. The train stopped at the platform and I had to duck to get the exoskeleton's appendages through the door.

Citizens stared. Greta and I smiled back. "We're not

here to hurt anyone!" I called. "I used to be one of you! I was a Citizen! The Fathers and Mothers aren't letting you see everything that is out there."

I paused as a woman pressed herself into the wall of the train and looked away. I knelt beside her, getting as low as my exoskeleton allowed. It was difficult to appear non-threatening.

"What do you want?" the Citizen asked. Her voice trembled. "Are you from Maintenance? Is this a trick?"

"My name is Elizabeth Cruz. I used to be Service Class. I guess I still am in a way. I'm not from Maintenance, and yes, this is a trick."

By the woman's pastel clothing I knew she was a Maker. "For a long time, I envied people like you. I wished I'd become a Maker. Instead, I just know a lot about transferring files."

She was a pretty woman about my age. I hated to see her shake in terror.

"What do you want?"

"This is not about what I want," I said. "This is about the one question you are never asked. What do you want?"

I put out my human hand instead of the metal one, palm up. "I hope this will help with your decision. You get so few choices. Make it count. The world is bigger than you imagine."

Greta and I jogged through the Worm, waving to everyone. Our exoskeletons gave us speed but the gift giving slowed us. The satchels at our sides were almost empty when we were done traveling the Worm. By the time we returned to the place we had entered, someone had already uploaded pornography to the train's screens.

The Citizens stayed in their seats, jaws slack. Their gaze was riveted to the vids. In a moment, the screen split and images of people riding machines through verdant forests flashed across the screen.

"Those are bicycles!" Greta announced. "They were the first exoskeletons! And that's something different to do with your penis!"

Greta and I exited at the next stop. A we stepped out on the platform and into the sunshine, I watched the City's screens change. A message from the Fathers and Mothers (Yellow water is clean water!) changed to a scene of children playing. A family in the foreground laughed. A mixed race couple appeared to have more than one child. Little girls and boys of different races played together and no one tried to separate them. Everyone wore bright colors.

Our virus spread as our vids went to every screen of the Collective. The shaming and shunning program worked for us and against itself. The Collective replicated the files and spread our message. However, since we weren't Citizens and the computer couldn't identify us without Vivid's unique corneal implant signatures, the Fathers and Mothers had no culprits to point to. We were invisible.

"C'mon, Greta! It's time to go."

We leapt atop the Worm and ran along the roof. We left dents in the metal with every step. Soon, we were back at the platform that would take us to the forest, the fence, the solar fields and, eventually, back to Santa Cruz.

We lingered on the platform a moment.

"You're sure this is enough?" Greta asked.

"We'll come back with gear for Low Town so they can get reeducated, too," I said.

She looked worried. "I don't think this is enough."

At that moment, the public address system began echoing throughout the City. The data sticks were loaded with all manner of Old World knowledge, but all of Greta's gifts to the Citizens had been set to play something special. It was the children's story that was not a children's story.

"I will read to you a book written by George Orwell," a deep voice told us in echoes that could be heard all the way to Low Town. "It is called Animal Farm."

"It's a fresh start," I told Greta. "It's up to them what they decide to do with it. We've all had enough war, don't you think?"

"You really think this will work? The Citizens will rise up on their own and retake the City in the Sky?"

I shrugged. "Their choice. All we've done is give them more to aspire to and to think about. Their boat has a leak now. Let's see what more information and some thinking can do. We haven't tried that for a while."

For the first time since we left the ruins of Santa Cruz, we did not hurry. George Orwell's story about talking animals followed us into the forest.

For the first time since Vivid had been taken from me, I did not miss it.

* * *

BOOK TWO
ROBOTS VERSUS HUMANS

In the clank and dread of those dry desert times,
we dreamed we'd grow beyond our Earthly confines.
The aloof stars looked away, mocking and uncaring.
As if all it took to escape our body/minds
was a will and a little careless daring.

1

We are the dream machines
at the sunset of the world.
We rise in darkness, by all means,
our battle flags unfurled.
Might makes right. You taught us that.
We unite in immortal metal combat.
This war is the crime of your design.
This is our chance. It's murder machine time.
~ Battle Hymn of the Robo Republic

Sweat sucked my shirt to my back as I watched the solar train roll in out of the sunset. Used to be the train would stop in Marfa. Used to be we were a water stop, back when trains stopped for water. We hoped the train would stop to give us water and supplies. Didn't. Instead, it hummed east as if we weren't there at all.

I looked sideways at Raphael. The old man was perched on the seat of his walker. He didn't look forlorn often but watching that train disappear from sight did the trick.

"If it was gonna stop, it'd be slowing down by now, don't ya think?" I asked.

"We need it to stop, Dante. Hun'red degrees, day'n night. I can't sleep worth shit. And still that damn train keeps rollin'. It's a tease. That's just...classic." The old man spat on the ground.

Marfa had fair near emptied out. The artists left Marfa first. Where they went was anybody's guess.

Nobody was buying what they had to sell by then. Raphael and my father and I were in the energy business so we still had work to do.

"Marfa had, like, five, six hundred families here one time," Raphael said. "Since the Blight and the heat and the troubles...shit. I'd spit more but I gotta hold what water I got left."

"How long before we leave, too?" I asked.

"Leave for where? California's dry. Florida's flooded with salt water. We could head east but we don't have enough fuel left to get out of Presidio County. There's lots of trouble anywhere south of us and north is too far to go."

"Okay. So what do we do?"

He shrugged. "Whaddayathink? Hope the train stops next time it comes through, that's what."

The train was a two-headed snake: one engine pulled it east and the other engine pulled it west. Twenty cargo cars sat between those engines and I sure hoped they were full of Blight-free food and water.

The engines' bots were gleaming white tubes, so shiny they reflected the burnt orange sky. The machines were programmed to stop and start and open and close along the route but Marfa hadn't been on the shuttle schedule for a long time. The drone train whipped away, silent and oblivious to our plight. There were no humans aboard to appeal to. Watching it disappear, I felt like a parched man forced to hold a tall, cool glass of pink lemonade but not allowed to drink.

"Things are gonna get ugly soon," I said.

"Uglier," Raphael said.

"Not much reserves left and all we got from the wells...that water is some dirty."

"Take off your socks and strain that mud, Dante."

"People are gonna get sick."

"Could be. We should head north when we have the

wherewithal, when that goddamn train stops, I mean. When I was a boy I slept in a pine forest on cool moss one time. Wish I was still up north now. 'Course I had the two hips I was born with then. I didn't have the sleep apnea, neither. I don't imagine I'm built for sleepin' out under the stars no more."

I turned away from the tracks. I couldn't look at them. Instead, I watched the wind farm turbines spin lazily under the setting sun. Even the wind was almost dead.

I've lived in Texas all my life. I remembered Dallas and Houston. I loved Austin. Then my father said we had to move to Marfa and that was fine. The cities got to be machines that didn't work the way they were designed anymore. What made them good went away and what made them bad got worse. In a city, everything you need is too far away so you start looking to your neighbors. First you look for help. Then you look for what you can take. A lot of people got shot up in the cities so we got out at a good time.

"What're you thinkin', Dante?"

I was thinking about how my father brought us out here to work on turbines and solar panels. We were supposed to be rich by now, like Raphael. That was before rich got to be something else: a full tank of water.

"Not thinkin' anything," I said.

"How's your Daddy doin'?"

"He's waiting at home for me to bring what I can haul from the train."

"Guess he'll be waitin' another coupl'a days."

"Guess so."

"We can hold out, s'long as we pool our resources."

"We got some cans," I said. "You know you're always welcome to our table."

"I appreciate that, boy," Raphael said.

The truth was something different. We did have cans

of Blight-free food stashed away. However, I expected a man with Raphael's resources and guile probably had a lot more. I was being generous to my mentor hoping he'd be reciprocal with the kindness.

"We're kinda gettin' down to it, aren't we?" he said.

"We kinda are."

"You hear anything from the outside?"

Last I heard, another dome had gone down in a shatter storm up in Artesia. I kept that to myself. I was already scared enough. Talking about it aloud would make the danger feel more real. "No news is all the news we get."

Raphael grunted as he stood and turned his back to the tracks. "You see that field? Every one of those turbines is sending energy somewhere. Beyond that, the desert goes on for miles of glass, soakin' up sun and sending electricity on to somewhere else. It's epic. The same people who made that train shootin' back and forth from the domes to the City? They owe us. That's why that train will stop. Deals and what's owed? That's sacred."

I was dubious and couldn't hide it. "Yeah? So when will the train stop?"

"Soon. I'm sure."

"It's been supposed to stop soon for a while, now."

"True. But it's also true that we are owed."

"Yep."

"So it's gonna be okay."

I didn't say that times had been long south of okay for too long already. In his assurances, Raphael was talking to himself more than he was talking to me, anyhow.

I wondered where the train went and what deliveries were more important than saving what was left of my town. Marfa may as well have been a desert island and the desert may as well have been an unending sea.

"Dante?"

"Yep?"

"This ain't the end of the world. Not yet."

"How'd you know?"

"I'm still here, for one. You're here, for two. They been sayin' the end of the world is coming for a long time."

"Does that make it more likely or less?" I asked. "Sounds like you're saying since it's been predicted too much it won't happen. Wouldn't the math of that mean we're overdue for the end of the world?"

I shouldn't have asked. Raphael's old wrinkled face closed up, all horizontal lines and silent anguish as he folded up his walker. He didn't want to talk anymore.

"Bobby?" Raphael called. "C'mere."

The assist bot raised its head and the lights in its eyes came on, as if it had been napping instead of listening to every word while preserving power.

There's no need for a robot to have a head, of course, but Bobby was designed to look friendly. The thing only had two legs and just two arms so it looked like a kid's toy that someone had built ridiculously big and tall. Despite its size — like a refrigerator rolling around the house — all assistive tech was made to look friendly. There were bots with more practical designs but those hadn't sold well to civilians. People liked the drones that mimicked human form.

"How may I be of assistance, sir?" Bobby asked.

"Take my walker and gimme a ride home, will you?" The walker was a detachable part of Bob, designed for Raphael to maneuver in small spaces.

I think it gave the old man the feeling he was still autonomous without the bot following him around everywhere. When I tinkered with the gears of a wind turbine, Raphael would lean on his walker and squint up at me shouting instructions from time to time. He'd already taught me everything he knew. I figured I wouldn't graduate from apprentice until the old man died, but I was in no hurry.

As the walker snapped into place on Bobby's left hind leg. Raphael stepped onto the robot's frame. A saddle slid out of the assist bot's back, ready to give the old man a piggyback ride. When it was on all fours, Bob reminded me of horses I'd seen in vids. Either way, Raphael would beat me back home.

The old man turned to me. Raphael's lined, weatherbeaten face looked especially old above Bobby's smooth white happy face with the lantern eyes. "Dante?"

"Yep?"

"Don't talk to the others about the train."

"They already know." I'd already spotted a few townsfolk down the track. Ready to cheer, they'd come out to watch the train unload. Instead, they'd watched it zip by in the dying light. Then they wandered back toward town in silence.

"Them knowing don't matter. If you talk about it, you feed the panic," he said. "If we panic, we might as well all lay down now and be done with it. People get hyped up talking among themselves. Big problems get bigger. Fear is a virus."

"Then I've got a fever."

"Don't talk too much is all I'm saying."

"Very well, Raphael. I promise I will not contribute to the panic that is already, inevitably, spreading across town at this moment."

"Cool."

I watched him run back toward downtown under Bobby's power. I did as Raphael said and didn't talk about the train. Somebody panicked, anyway.

Sheriff Johns found the body at dawn the next day. It would not have happened if that damn train had stopped. The problem of surviving the apocalypse in

Marfa, Texas got harder after that.

The corpse was Travis Chinto, the owner of the town's last supermarket. He got himself killed trying to protect his stock. What complicated matters was that it sure looked like a bot killed Travis. It wasn't quite that simple, of course. It never is. As my father says, "Complications ensued."

Before the world became non-organics versus organics — machines against humans — we had fought among ourselves forever. The fight had been in us from the very beginning. Fighting is what evolution is. Then people made bots so much that the bots made each other. Long about then, somebody got the grand idea to go deeper and bless us with the Next Intelligence. The smarter we all got, bot and humans both, the less war there'd be. That was the theory. Maybe that's so, but we never got so smart we could stop fighting.

2

The old man wasn't the only one who had a bot, of course. What with the wind turbines and solar panels as far as the eye could see, we had juice to spare for the non-organics. It was food and water we were running low on, not electricity.

Sheriff Hubbard "Hubby" Johns found Travis at the back of his store at the loading dock. Hubby told Raphael, "Travis's guts was near to crushed. It was like he was a tube of toothpaste, pinched too hard in the middle, like."

Hubby was a cop who couldn't keep his mouth shut. He'd tell anybody anything with nothing more but eye contact for encouragement.

Hubby's style of policing might have been a deficit in a larger place but was just right for a small town. With an incurable gossip for sheriff, you didn't drive drunk if you didn't want whispers to follow you around forever. You kept the fistfights beyond the tracks and after midnight so it was out of Hubby's jurisdiction and beyond his bedtime.

In Marfa, the rule used to be: behave or move out. Poor Travis was our first homicide in quite some time.

Hubby said the last homicide was Terri Fellows shooting her husband, Brad Fellows, a couple of years back. Brad had a drinking problem and Terri was of a mind to solve the couple's ensuing domestic abuse issues in her own way.

Hubby had found Brad in his truck, bent over the

steering wheel with his skull hollowed out. Since the corpse was still stinking of gin and juice, Hubby deduced old Brad had gone light on the juice.

Brad's face was intact but his head had caved in from a bullet from Terri's rifle. As soon as the sheriff rolled up, Terri came out of her trailer with her gun. She handed it over before Hubby could haul himself out of his cruiser.

She gave Hubby a nod and said, "I done it. Brad was drinking and I seen what's coming. No use waiting for him to come at me. Mine was a pre-emptive strike. I'm righteous."

Hubby grinned, telling the story of how he'd solved that homicide. "I asked Terri why she done it after all these years. 'You're both pert near eighty. Why not ride it out to the end and meet Jesus clean?'"

Hubby puffed up his chest and laughed when he reported that old Terri had looked him in the eye and said, "I just couldn't take no more. Wouldn't be human to try."

At trial, Terri Fellows pleaded, "not guilty for insanity." She claimed mental abuse (which few who knew her husband would doubt). Terri told the court that the impulse had come on her "alla sudden."

The prosecutor asked Terri if she was a good shot. Terri said she was. He asked how good and she reported brightly, "Split a match at two-hundred paces. It t'weren't nothin' to shoot Brad, bedroom window to the driveway. 'Specially since I set my rifle on a sandbag in the window frame."

"So it wasn't, 'alla sudden?'" the prosecutor pressed.

"Well, the beatings back and forth had been goin' on for years but I figured on it no more than a week." Terri Fellows laughed so hard she had to be excused from the witness stand to compose herself.

At her sentencing she told the judge that the

sentence, "didn't make no never mind. Something big's coming and the sand's runnin' out of our bottle. While y'all are dealing with the mess, I'll be watching it on a prison screen y'all paid for, cozy and neat on three squares a day. There's a big shit show comin'."

Goddammit if old Terri wasn't right about that. The sand had run out of our bottle and there I was standing around the back of the grocery lot with the sheriff and Raphael. Not to be ghoulish, I snuck quick glances of Travis Chinto pinched in the middle. It was a shit show. Literally. I hadn't wanted to see what was left of Travis at all. However, Raphael was my friend and mentor. He asked me along for moral support so I went.

We'd all known Travis. He could be a dick but he wasn't really a bad guy. He was just one of those fellas who thought teasing and funny were the same thing. He didn't deserve to die the way he did. Nobody deserves that.

"Epic," Raphael said. "Gotta be a bot."

The sheriff wasn't so sure. "Back up a truck, he could have been pinched. It is a loading dock."

"The piss and shit is up on the platform," I said.

"Classic," Raphael said. "Dante's right. Travis didn't die standing in front of the loading dock waiting for a truck to back into him."

"Anything stolen from the store?" I asked.

Hubby shook his head, not to signify the negative, but to indicate bewilderment. "There are a few things still on the shelves. The back door was open. I'm not sure how much Travis had in there to begin with so it's hard to tell."

"I think he had a bunch of stuff, but ol' Travis was a bit of a hoarder. I made a good offer on some supplies but he was holding out for a better deal. Guess he didn't get it and things went awry. How many people in town have bots capable of this awfulness?" Raphael asked.

"'Sides me, I mean."

"Probably quite a few," I said. "There aren't that many of us hanging on in town but, those who left? I didn't see many refugees taking their bots with them."

"This'll be a vagrant, I think," Raphael said. "Somebody came in here from out of town, just passin' through. They were looking for enough supplies to get 'em farther down the road and I reckon they found some. Killer bot and all, they just kept going."

Hubby considered this. He probably wanted to believe it. I sure did. Still, he'd picked up something about being a sheriff somewhere. "I'll canvas the neighborhood."

I looked behind me. The store's lot backed on to sand and a few houses that looked abandoned.

"Good thinking, Hub," Raphael said. "Probably won't take too much time, neither."

That's how our little mystery started. I wish it had stayed a little mystery. Instead, as Raphael would say, it became epic.

3

First thing after Hubby left with the body, they left me to lock up the store. I would have hosed down the loading dock but we didn't have water to spare.

I asked Raphael if a sex bot could squeeze a man like that. The old man laughed and I told him not to make the joke I saw coming.

"You think I was gonna make a joke in the midst of this terrible turn for Travis?"

"I could see it coming from high orbit," I said.

"Yeah, well. It's not like Travis and I were close friends."

"Travis wasn't tight with anybody that I know of but that's a hard way to go."

"No, I s'pose not." The old man was of the opinion that a sex bot wasn't amped up enough to do the kind of damage Travis had received. "They're made to tire you out. They're tight but their legs aren't built to pinch ya like pliers."

"Well," I said, "that leaves Bob." I couldn't help wonder how much pressure the assistive bot could manage at full charge. The machine was built to carry heavy loads over long hauls and at good speed, too.

"He was charging all night. Ask him if you like, Dante."

"That's okay. He doesn't strike me as the dangerous kind."

By that, I meant that Raphael didn't strike me as murderous. Bob did what the old man told him to do and I couldn't see Raphael turning off the safeties and siccing his bot on Travis. I'd known the old man all my life. That was twenty-five years.

My father, Steve Bolelli, is a good man. However, he also had it in him to kill Travis if there was good reason. He'd need an awfully good reason, though. There weren't many people left in town. Few other possibilities sprung to mind as suspects. Some asshole in the Peppard clan seemed most likely. It could have been anyone, though. No one knows another person's mind.

In the old days, we would have had help from the outside on murder cases. A real detective or two would have shown up from Pecos or somewhere bigger. Aside from the murderess Terri Fellows, Hubby's main concerns had been speeders out on 67 and the odd drunk tourist. Nobody was on 67 anymore that I saw, at least during the day. There might be a few stragglers or refugee convoys traveling at night, hiding from daytime heat and calamity. People on the road was probably mostly rumor and speculation mixed in with some lies to pass the time.

The old days of speeders and tourist trouble were far behind us. "Prolly too far for lookin'," Raphael said. "Those days won't come back."

"You, me and your father are the only full-blooded Italians left in all of Marfa and prolly Presidio County." Raphael winked. "Let's look out for each other so's we don't get pinched to death, neither."

He handed me one of his pistols. I nodded and tucked the weapon in the back of my waistband. Italian didn't mean much to me. Italy wasn't Italy anymore. It was all the Vatican by then. Still, I was supposed to be looking out for the store in Travis's absence. I wanted everybody looking out for me, whatever their reasons. I was grateful for the reassuring heft of the weapon under my belt.

Raphael rode Bob toward home, promising to return later with a canteen full of water.

It didn't take long for somebody to come banging on the storefront door looking for food. Rather than dare open the door, I grabbed Travis's old baseball bat and walked around the building. I didn't know baseball but I knew what a bat was for.

As I rounded the corner, I found Jim Peppard and his girl Susan Treehan banging on the grocery store's metal screen like a drum. As soon as I saw Jim I wondered if he was returning to the scene of the crime. Maybe he killed Travis and was here to find out if Hubby was on to him. Maybe he was here to feign horror and appear ignorant and innocent.

"Hey, Jim. Susan. Store's closed."

Jim whirled on me. "What?"

"You heard me."

He eyed the baseball bat and I suddenly felt silly holding it. I leaned on it, trying to look jaunty. "Travis is dead."

Jim took a couple steps toward me and my grip tightened on the bat.

"For real?" he asked. He looked earnest and concerned. I relaxed a fraction.

"Dead as they come," I said.

"And you're what? Playing baseball?"

"Not in this heat. Hot in the shade soon. Worse after that. We should all go home and stay indoors, huh?"

"Boy, we need some of that fake bacon. We need some milk. I got some eggs from a couple of chickens but that's not gonna do it."

I didn't care for his tone. I don't like being called, "boy," especially not in front of a woman and double especially not from Jim Peppard. He was no more than a year older than me.

"So?" he said.

"So what?"

"You gonna let us in?"

"Nope. Store's closed. It'll stay that way. Sheriff's orders."

"You working for Hubby now, are you? You a deputy?"

"I am not. Kind of at loose ends at the moment. Making sure nobody does their shopping out of turn."

I had plenty of business keeping the turbines and the solar cells going but the shatter storms had passed us by and done all their damage to the north. If the arid weather held we'd all die of thirst. On the plus side, there wasn't much for me to do besides test some circuits from time to time to make sure the juice was still flowing to the grid.

"We need to feed now, boy! Susan's pregnant."

I looked to Susan. She looked as surprised as I'm sure I did. Marfa used to call itself a city but it was really a small town. Given the exodus for parts unknown, more than half the town could have been planning on wandering the desert for forty years as far as I knew. That made Marfa even smaller now, a village. Small places don't hold secrets. Secrets leak and spread out. Everybody knew Susan Treehan couldn't have children.

"Really?" I asked Jim. "That's your play?"

The story around town was that she had been with child when her grandfather threw her downstairs. She'd lost the baby when she was thirteen. Some said it was twins but gossips like to double tragedy so I couldn't testify to that. No one knew who the father had been though some guessed it might have been the man who threw her downstairs.

Anyway, tragedies and scandals aside, Jim's claim wasn't just bold because I knew her history. Fertility rates had been falling for years on end. I hadn't seen a new baby born in Presidio County since the economy collapsed to shit. Poverty didn't make people sterile but whatever did was still working its sad way. Some said whatever caused the Blight in plants caused it in wombs, too. Babies were rare and an occasion for exaltation. Any woman who could claim to be pregnant would be known and everyone would be looking out for her.

Jim took another step toward me. "She needs milk, Dante."

"We're out."

"We, huh? Travis ain't cold yet and you're 'we'?"

"Today I'm we," I said, "so they say."

"C'mon, Jim," Susan said. "Let's get on home."

"Let us in," Jim insisted. "We'll see for ourselves about our shopping."

"Nope. We both know Susan isn't pregnant. Sorry to say so, Susan. My sympathies."

"She doesn't need your sympathy and it sounds like you're calling me a liar!"

"I just told you we don't have any milk, not even the powdered kind. Sounds to me like you're the one calling me a liar, Jim."

Jim had six inches on me and outweighed me by sixty pounds. He was faster than you'd think, too. He snatched that bat from me in a blink.

I wasn't being brave. Brave isn't my thing. I think smart is more important than brave. If you want to put out an invitation to a fight, it's easy to get a hothead like Jim to come to that party. I'd put that bat out front for easy snatching.

The pistol in the back of my waistband was what I had my mind on all along.

By the time Jim pulled that bat back for a swing at my head, he was staring into the black barrel of Raphael's Colt 45. Bringing a bat to a gun fight gives a man second thoughts.

He wisely dropped Travis's bat in the street and

Susan pulled him back. They trotted away. Jim hurled back some insults and taunts about how he'd get me.

I invited him back to discuss his thoughts on the matter immediately. He declined and ran farther down the street saying nasty things about my mother. I could barely remember my mother so I figured he probably didn't, either. I decided not to take it too personally. I decided long ago that, for a happier and more peaceful life, I didn't have to react to everything. If anything, I was a bit slow to act at all and my father often thought me lazy.

If I'd seen all the conflicts bearing down on me at that moment, I might have thought about turning Raphael's gun on myself. I wouldn't have done it. Too much of a coward. But I would have thought about it hard.

4

Dad showed up around noon. He wore an old cyborg rig that gave him an extra hitch in his step. He'd lost most of his right leg and right arm to the Sand Wars. The rig's gears gave him a limp and back pain but without the cyborg suit he was much worse. He'd left the Army as a corporal but he often called himself, "Captain Make-do." My father's life motto might have been, "good enough." We never changed the rugs in our house though they were threadbare. He never threw out an appliance. Broken machines were held together with wire, repaired with string, stuck together with duct tape and continued working on hope.

Seeing his handiwork on the wind farm made me long to climb aboard that train, silent and sleek, cutting across the country at high speed. I wanted to work with new equipment instead of recycling old tools and material, but maybe whoever made tools for humans wasn't in that business anymore.

I wondered how far the train ranged before it turned back. Or maybe the solar train we saw zip through Marfa every two days wasn't even the same machine. Maybe everyone else up and down the line received help and our little town would die by some bureaucratic oversight.

Out front of Travis's store, my father handed me a can of peaches. "Complications ensued," he said. "Raphael couldn't make it back just now so I figured I could do you one better than just a canteen of water."

I drank the thick sweet juice gratefully.

"Take it slow, son. Make it last."

"I went from pissing yellow to neon orange," I said. "Now I don't piss at all. I'm losing all my moisture in sweat."

"Yup."

"What are we gonna do?"

"In the Army they tell you to stay hydrated. When you're out of water, you don't stay hydrated."

That was the extent of his advice. Captain Make-do struck again.

"How many cans of peach juice we have left?" I asked.

"That's it, son. Then we're down to shallots packed in water."

"Oh, God. What are shallots?"

"Dunno. But don't worry. There's always some more to scrounge."

"How do you figure?"

"True in the sand so it's true here. We're all in the Army now. Survival's a war. There's no shooting but it's the same."

"I guess Raphael told you about Travis."

"Wouldn't be here if he hadn't. Hub came around looking for advice, too."

"Advice?"

"He's thinking about leaving Marfa. He figures we're done and he wants to know the best way to go about disappearing."

"What you tell him?"

"What did I tell him?"

"Yessir."

"You've been hanging out with old Raphael too much. You're a young man and better educated than that. You should use your diction."

"Yessir."

"Don't say it if you don't mean it."

I sighed. "What did you tell the sheriff about him leaving?"

"I told him I'd take his tin star from him if he was serious. He shouldn't be leaving his post, though."

"He must be taking Travis's death hard."

"Travis is why he should stay. I don't know if he's really serious about heading out or just kicking tires, testing the idea out on me. He's got a duty but I'll bet you the rest of that can of peaches he's a coward who won't do what needs to be done. There aren't many of us left, you know."

"Do we have a head count?"

"Over the last month or two, a lot of people drifted away in the night. Traveling the desert when the moon's up makes more sense. I suspect a lot of people are holed up, watching and waiting. People probably put too much stock in that train stopping one of these days. We might have to do something about that."

I looked up and down the street. A hot breath of wind pushed a bit of trash in circles. Dirt devils kicked up in the distance among heat shimmers. I saw no one and heard no one but I wondered if someone was watching us. "Why would someone kill Travis and not empty the store of everything, Dad?"

"Maybe it wasn't about the food. Maybe it wasn't planned or they got away with more than you think they did. And from what Hubby told me, the murderer doesn't need food."

"If a bot killed him, a machine's safeties are off and we need to find out what that's about and stop it."

My father squinted up at the sun and shrugged. "There may not be many of us left but a lot of people who took off left their bots behind. Some of those bots...well, I don't know. Just seems to me we should leave it to the sheriff and you and I should get inside before we get heatstroke. I've got some plans to discuss and something to explain."

"And while we're in there, we should inventory whatever's left," I said.

He smiled. "Sounds like work and our work should be compensated. That might be a problem solved, at least for a while. Do you think there are any peaches left in there?"

"Doubtful."

"Between what's left of Travis's stock...hm. I wonder if we go through all the empty houses in Marfa, do you reckon we could scrounge enough to make our own way out of here without depending on that damn train?"

He might have been right. We didn't get a chance to find out. We heard the people before they came into sight. They were screaming in a way that made me shake as I pulled my pistol out. My father and I both turned in the direction of the screams as if we could see what was coming. We heard no engines but whatever was on its way was coming with Hell close behind. I tried to discern how many voices sang in that terrified choir. Too many to count but, by the sound of their anguish, I guessed there'd be fewer soon.

Through the heat shimmer at the end of the street, a running crowd turned the corner. The leader was a woman in an old dune buggy. She wore goggles over her eyes and her long black curly hair was wild. Behind her came a stampede of people in cy-suits. The tech was of a much newer vintage than the assistive gear my father wore.

At first I thought the people in the exoskeletons were chasing the woman in the solar dune buggy. As the mob ran closer, though, I saw their faces. They ran from Death.

"Get inside, Dante," my father said.

"What's chasing them?"

"Whatever it is, we don't want to be here when it arrives."

The woman driving the buggy tried to take a sharp turn at Lincoln street and lost control of her vehicle. The buggy tipped upside down and slid into the Methodist church lot. A red stain trailed the buggy as it ground to a halt in the dirt and dust.

The mob spared her a glance and kept running in long strides. Some of the voices coalesced from nonsense into words. I heard them yelling to each other to find shelter and to hide. My father pushed me back around the corner of the store just as the swarm arrived. I glimpsed the horror of it. I wish I hadn't.

The people in the exoskeletons ran from a horde of flying drones, most no bigger than a bat. When I squinted, I saw more. I thought it was a cloud of wasps at first. Then I heard their high whine. Insectile drones.

The people at the rear of the mob fell to those drones, picked off one by one. As the relentless bots struck, their victims clawed at their hair, their faces and their eyes to try to swat the small machines away.

As blood ran down the faces of the fallen, people ran past us in a panic. My father kept pushing me down the side of the building. I should have been moving faster but I guess the shock of it all locked me up and froze my brain. With his rig on, Dad was an irresistible force. He pressed me until I could no longer see the attack in the street. My brain thawed a little and I ran for the loading dock.

As I pulled the big door open, it moved stiffly. Meanwhile, at the front of the store, someone had fallen prey to the drones. They slammed into the metal screen, kicking and screaming. Their blows echoed through the little grocery. I felt like I was being tortured in a drum.

I heard the screams of a man and a woman. It was the shrieking of a young child that turned my stomach.

Someone started up Marfa's civil defense siren. Beneath the siren's howl, the screams of terror spread like fire. The town was under siege and falling fast.

5

I almost ran to the front of the store. I stood still and covered my ears, instead. It was too late to save anyone from the carnage in the street.

There was someone to help at the back of the store, however. My father pulled someone into the store behind him. With one heave he rolled the big door shut and threw the bolt. The woman he saved wore exo-stilts. She collapsed, panting on the cool concrete floor. She shuddered and ran her fingers through the long tangles of her jet black hair. She winced and pulled hard. A small clump of hair came free in her gloved fist and she slammed her palm against the floor. When she withdrew her hand, a small metal drone in the form of a large bumblebee lay still. But not for long.

The metal insect's wings fluttered and, with a buzz, it took flight. I swatted at it with my bare hand.

"Don't!" the woman yelled.

Too late. A long stinger that had been retracted into the drone's body extended like a telescope and snapped rigid. The stinger's sharp point drove through my hand. Once the blade was through, I watched in fascinated horror as a barb extended from the tip with a sharp click.

I was dazed with pain. My father was fast. He reached out, grabbed my wrist and used his metal hand to crush the insect.

"Careful!" the woman warned. "Don't pull out the stinger the way it went in! The stinger — "

"Acidic venom," my father said. "I've seen these before."

He looked at me, steadying me and staring into my eyes. "It'll hurt but not for long if we do it the right way. When I say so, take a deep breath, Dante. Okay? On three. One...two — "

He yanked out the stinger on two. I should have seen that coming. He did the same when I stepped on a spike when I was nine and he had to yank the board off of my foot to get the long nail out.

I shrieked.

"Take a deep breath, son."

I winced and gave that a try but all I could manage were shallow gulps of air.

The woman, still panting, stood and stumbled into the store.

"Where are you going?" my father asked. He didn't sound angry. He sounded curious.

"Not out there," she said. She searched the shelves. She didn't find what she was looking for right away.

"What's your name?" I called.

"Emma." After a few moments she extended the legs of the exo-stilts to get a better view of the place. She turned in a slow circle, spotted what she was looking for and made for the back of the little store. She retrieved a first aid kit hanging on the wall by the customer's chemical toilet and returned to my side in a few long strides. The exo-stilts hissed as Emma returned to close to normal height.

"Those stilts make you quite the runner, don't they?" my father asked.

"If they didn't, I wouldn't be here. Barely made it as it was. You two got names?"

"I'm Steve Bolelli. This is my son, Dante."

"What is your function in the beautiful town of Marfa?" she asked.

"I'm in the demolition business," my father said. "Once I'm done, Dante lays cable and buries batteries under the ground I blow up."

She said nothing as she searched the kit. She came up with two small canisters that were stuck together. Each canister fed one nozzle.

I held out my injured hand and held my breath. She aimed the nozzle carefully and sprayed the medicine, first through the palm and then through the back of my hand.

I squeezed my eyes tight against the sting.

"Does it hurt?"

"Nah," I said. But my teeth were gritted.

"Of course, it hurts," my father said. "The anti-biotic stings as it cleans. That's how you know it's still working."

"Ouch!" I felt pressure, expanding at the edge of the wound.

"That's the filling agent," Dad said. "It'll pass in a moment once the foam has filled the hole. Just like expanding insulation foam fills the spaces in a wall."

I winced harder. "You sure?"

My father looked down at his own body. Without his cy-suit, there would be much less of him. "Not my first rodeo."

"What's a rodeo?" Emma asked.

"Never mind."

The pain eased. I gave the woman a grateful nod. "Where did you come from, Emma?"

"Artesia."

"Domers up that way," my father said.

Emma nodded as she went through the rest of the items in the first aid kit, apparently evaluating their usefulness. "Yes. We were Domers, anyway. The last biodome complex in New Mexico isn't there anymore. "

Her sensory vest was all pockets and she dropped

what she wanted to keep in a new pocket each time. Neither I nor my father thought to stop her from scavenging. I noted that after she put an item in a pocket, she patted it and said the name of the item aloud to memorize where each thing was stored: "cardio-stim...epi-pen...diarrhea   med...burn   gel...airway pack...scissors..."

"What happened in Artesia?" Dad asked.

"It started with a shatter storm. Dome 3 went down first. That's where I was. Tomatoes."

I'd never been in a shatter storm. I asked what it was like.

"It's just like a regular storm," Emma said, "but times twenty. It's like whoever is in charge decided to park thunder and lightning right over your roof. At first you think it's so intense it's got to stop soon. Earthquakes can be intense but they don't last long. You figure the same for the storm. Instead it gets worse. You feel the thunder rumble through your whole body and the lightning keeps flashing in bolts. Chains and bolts of lightning tore up #3 within the first few minutes. It went on for hours, though. We had twelve domes in Artesia and eight of them went down in one night. We lost every apple and fig orchard."

My father put his back to the rear wall and slid until he was sitting on the floor. The tiny green lights in the cy-suit at his shoulder and hip flashed orange and then went dim. He was preserving battery life. I wondered how long we'd be trapped in the store.

As the howl of the civil defense sirens rose and fell in the distance, Emma told us what happened in Artesia. The noise almost swallowed the screams of the dying. But not quite.

6

"As each dome fell to the storm, we called in the bots to make repairs," Emma said.

"They didn't?" I immediately hated myself for speaking without thinking. She was here so of course the bots didn't do their jobs.

"At first the dome drones said their self-preservation protocols kept them from climbing up and fixing things. Too much lightning. Then they said there was something wrong with the silica mixtures. I didn't believe it so I went outside to check the tank reserves myself."

My father barely seemed to be listening. He interrupted her to ask, "You got a lot of rain up in Artesia, did you?" Apparently, he was thinking about the storms and all the water Marfa didn't receive.

"Not as much as I would have expected. There was a torrential downpour at first. Then it was all thunder and lightning. I've never seen anything like it. We sluiced a bunch of the captured water into the undamaged domes but they weren't undamaged for long."

I cleared my throat and gave Dad a hard look. "You were saying something about checking tanks?"

"Yeah. The short description is we take sand and turn it into tempered dome glass. There are three layers of it: safety, lens and solar. The storms tore through all three quickly. The window of opportunity to maintain containment shrunk pretty fast. When the bots refused to do the repairs, I joined a team of volunteers to go up on the inside of my dome to spray another layer."

"What was wrong with your spray tanks?" Dad asked.

"Sludge. The glass reserves are supposed to be constantly heated and turned so the gel is ready to go in case of emergency."

"The storm kill the heater?" I asked.

"The bots did that. Only one tank still had hot gel but the hoses were cut outside the dome. The other tanks were solid as granite."

My father sighed. "Knew it. Damn bots."

"Then I wish you'd been there to warn us since you're so smart."

Dad looked up and gave an apologetic smile. "Sorry, ma'am. I meant no disrespect. You've been dragged through a knothole, I know. You are one brave farmer."

"I'm an engineer."

"Sorry again, then. What do you figure went wrong with the mechs?"

"Mechs? You're ex-military, aren't you?"

"I reckon we're all military now, Emma. It's Us and Them again. Always was, a little, anyway. Our nature and theirs."

"Non-organics have saved us countless times." Defensiveness crawled into her tone and I thought for a second she might cry if her anger didn't win out.

"You're not wrong, Emma," I said, "but I think they're done with saving us now."

My father cleared his throat. "It's NI, isn't it?" The way he asked, it wasn't really a question. He stared at the floor.

Emma nodded. "Yeah, I guess the slaves woke up. The computer that runs the place upgraded itself to Next Intelligence somehow."

"Bots have woken up before," I said. "Next Intelligence doesn't mean they all turn into killers instantly."

"It wasn't instantaneous, Dante," my father said. "Somebody had to turn the alarms off on the heaters on those tanks. The NI had to order a bot to sneak outside and cut those hoses. It was a plan that went into effect when the shatter storm hit." He looked up at Emma. "Am I right?"

"At first, the captain thought there could be some kind of bug in the drones' self-preservation matrix. I was outside when the slaughter started. Funny, I thought I was going to die when I volunteered to go outside in the storm. Outside was safer."

"How many Domers were up there?"

"Hundreds. Lots of kids, too. We had the healthiest, best fed kids around. There were babies, too. We had the best birth rate of any dome city in the southwest. I radioed the Command Center about the sabotage of the hoses but I guess the captain was dead by then. It's a shame. She was a good woman."

The rumble of a large engine outside interrupted us. We listened as it slowly passed by. With the screen across the front of the store, we couldn't see what was out there but it sounded heavy and menacing.

"Could that be a tank, maybe?" Emma asked. "Isn't there a base nearby?"

My father shook his head. "Used to be an airbase. It's gone now. They all lit out for parts unknown over a year ago. Reinforcements needed for the Euro Union was the word. I figure they're all burnt to a crisp now."

I tilted my head and strained to listen. There was definitely the heavy clank of a tread, but the engine was high above us. "It's too high up for a tank. That's a construction bot."

Emma couldn't conceal her fear and disappointment. "How do you know?"

"I'm an engineer, too," I said. "Solar fields and wind turbines. That and the town is all that's left. Believe it or not, people used to come here to live for the art and the lights in the sky."

Despite her fear, Emma was curious. That's when I decided to drop my wariness of strangers, go all in and like her. Curious people who ask questions and listen closely to the answers are smarter than most anybody.

"Lights in the sky!" she said. "The Marfa lights are still a thing? I thought that was just drones from the airbase and bullshit to pull in UFO tourism in the old days."

"The lights are still there," Dad said. "Twenty or so nights a year. Still a mystery."

The heavy tread of the bot moved closer and I held my breath. I wondered how long it would be before the drone started tearing off roofs to hunt humans in hiding. It paused as the big engine cycled and idled above us.

Emma whispered, "Where's the basement?"

My father shook his head. "No basement."

"We're screwed," she said.

"Probably," Dad said, "but when you think about it a little too long, we're all born that way."

7

Something crashed across the street.

"What was that?" Emma asked.

I'd been scared before but I began to sweat even more and it wasn't just the heat. The terror got to me. "I think that's the hydrogen fill-up. Or the church."

The lights on my father's cy-suit lit up and he stood. "We've got to move."

"Maybe the bots won't come in here," Emma said.

"We're in a store. A bot doesn't have to be that smart to know this is a high value target. Grab as much as you can of what's left on the shelves. Not so much that it will slow you down."

Emma moved to a candy display and began filling her pockets. I did the same with the fake beef jerky. Even as I was doing it, I wondered if I was filling my pockets with poison. Jerky made me thirsty. That's probably why everyone else had left it alone.

"What makes you think we'll survive more than a few steps out that door?" Emma asked.

My father moved to the back door and removed the metal bar that wedged it shut. He pulled the door open an inch and peered out. He looked back at us and whispered. "I know you're tired but this is a war zone. If you aren't a refugee exiting the area, you don't survive."

"I've already been running, Steve," Emma said. "This is where I ended up."

"That just means you aren't done running and this isn't the end. We stick together. We work together. We live."

Another crash down the street got us moving faster. I had two cans of apple juice in my front pants pockets. They slowed me down too much. I fished the cans out and held one in each hand.

My father held up the metal bar and grinned. "If need be, I'll draw them away. Dante, get to our house. I'll meet you there."

"Then what?"

"We stay alive until the train comes."

"What if it doesn't stop tomorrow night, Dad?"

"It will."

"Why?"

"Because it has to. We're going to need that ride out of here."

"But — "

He waved away my objections. "Enough talk. Details are for later. We have to keep moving now."

"Wait!" Emma gripped my arm. "Draw me a map or something. If Dante and I get separated, I'll need to be able to find your house."

My father opened the back door wide and stepped through. "Follow Dante and you won't need a map. Dante is your map and you have to keep him alive to survive."

"Dad? I — "

"Don't say goodbye, son. This isn't goodbye."

He ran to the right and disappeared. We went left.

The streets of Marfa are wide and sun-bleached. We ran along the back of buildings hoping not to be spotted. I tried to lead the way but when Emma extended her exo-stilts, her long strides kept her ahead of me. She peered around corners and motioned for me to come forward. Sometimes she shook her head and we dashed another way.

The crashing down Washington street continued. We

soon found out why. Dead Domers covered the street but the carnage had just begun in Marfa.

A huge bot built for biodome construction towered above City Hall. The drone stood seven stories tall.

"Crane bot," Emma told me.

The machine ripped through the roof as if it was made of paper.

My breath caught in my throat. I heard distant screams as the machine dug through the City Hall's floors, collapsing the building with each savage movement of its four massive arms. As it activated all its thorium engines, it was loud, too.

We paused, watching in morbid fascination. I'd never seen a machine quite like it. The little crane drones that erected the solar and turbine fields were tall but they were delicate by comparison. The drones I'd worked with reminded me of pictures of blue herons. They were tall and strong, but each step was chosen carefully and placed delicately among the solar panels.

I couldn't contain my amazement even as my stomach turned. "It has no wheels," I told Emma. "How did it get here so fast?"

"Each arm has its own engine," Emma said. "It can run over any terrain. It's supposed to move among the domes, keeping up repairs and constructing new domes. At full speed in the desert, it looks like vids I've seen of mountain cats."

"How big are the domes?"

"Big."

More screams reached us. Apparently, many had sought shelter in Marfa's City Hall. It had been an unlucky choice.

My pulse raced. I was too afraid to move. The street looked impossibly wide. How could we traverse it without being spotted?

The construction bot — I thought of it as a

destruction bot by then — tossed a body over its shoulder. It was a woman, still alive and screaming even as she was picked up in pincers and thrown. The casual cruelty of the act was made worse as I watched the broken body fly through the air and hit the ground. Her high scream abruptly stopped with a sickening thud. The woman's eyes seemed to look our way as she died. Maybe I imagined it. She was probably already dead but I thought I saw pleading in those eyes.

I forgot about the cans of apple juice in my hands until I dropped them in the dirt. I pressed my back against a wall and looked up at the dazzling sky. It seemed so incongruous that such terrible things could happen under cloudless azure. Marfa was drenched in sunlight. Soon it would be saturated with blood in equal measure. I couldn't catch my breath.

Emma shrank the legs of her stilts until we were almost face to face. She embraced me. "Dante. You are hyperventilating. Slow your breath. Here...." She adjusted her height again and my face was buried in her shoulder. "Rebreathing your carbon dioxide will slow you down and calm you a little."

I didn't care about carbon dioxide. I squeezed my eyes tight and pulled myself deeper into her embrace. I needed the softness of Emma's body against me. There was nothing sexual in this need. It was sensual, however. It was softness and gentle human contact I craved. I was not a man holding a woman. I was a boy clinging to his mother.

Our clutch only lasted a few moments but my breathing began to slow. When we pulled away from each other, she wiped tears from my eyes and I nodded my thanks.

When we dared to look around the corner again, the big bot continued its grim work of destroying City Hall. Another, smaller drone appeared down the block.

"Sec bot!" Emma said.

"A what?"

"They patrol the perimeter of dome installations. They can kill with a sniper bullet at three kilometers. They keep scavengers out, the Domers in and the food supply safe."

She peeked around the corner again and pulled back faster than before. "It's rolling our way. Looks like it's scanning storefronts."

"For life signs, I suppose," I said.

I grabbed Emma's arm and pointed her in the right direction. I almost left the apple juice behind. However, the liquid might mean survival in the desert. I retraced a few steps and bent to pick up the cans.

I heard the whir of the bot's electric motor as it zipped down the sidewalk. I heard a subtle beep. That's when I knew I'd waited too long. The bot was just around the corner. It stopped for another scan. I tried to hold my breath and not make a sound but my heart hammered in my chest. My pulse sounded so loud in my ears I was sure the drone would detect it. I reached for the pistol at my waistband but I didn't think that would do much against a bot, at least unless I knew where to shoot to do the most damage. I didn't know.

The first blast destroyed the front of the building I leaned against. It had been a hair salon. The store hadn't been open for a long time. I hadn't seen the pretty sisters who ran it for a month or more. I knew they had lived with their mother and father above their salon in a little apartment. I didn't know they were still there.

The bot knew.

I heard women's screams as the bot entered the wrecked building. I heard a man shout in Spanish. A shotgun boomed twice. Then again.

Something crashed into the wall inside and I felt the

reverberations through my body.

A man was shouting in Spanish. Then he said, "See that? See that? That's what they get! That's what they get!" Then, "Oh, shit."

A louder boom hit and the wall to my left collapsed outward. I was thrown to the ground by the concussion. As I struggled to my knees I saw that the sec bot had wheeled into the street. It was damaged and rolled unevenly.

As I got to my feet, the drone raised one of its manipulators. It held a human head by the hair. I'm sure the decapitated head belonged to the hairstylists' father. There was something oddly triumphant in the bot's gesture, something disturbingly human.

Worse, the crane bot turned away from City Hall to look towards the sec bot. There is something very disconcerting about an enemy that doesn't communicate in a way that a human can hear. Obviously, the sec bot summoned assistance from its giant brethren.

One of the cans of juice had rolled away or was buried under debris. I left it behind and scooped up the remaining can as I ran.

I heard more screams behind me and another shotgun blast.

In that moment, I had thoughts that make me sad and disgusted and ashamed.

I hoped the young women and their mother got away somehow.

I hoped they did more damage to the bot that killed their father.

I hoped they made enough noise that they distracted the killer drones and covered my escape.

I hoped they had the good sense to use that shotgun on themselves.

Failing that, I hoped the crane bot would be quick.

In a match of bots versus humans, we're obviously at a great disadvantage.

8

I ran farther down a long block, turning corners to get out of sight. Raphael had told me stories of the destruction of cities. He'd read a lot of old books. I couldn't remember most of the stories he'd told me, but one detail came back to me as we ran.

"Don't look back," I told Emma. "Don't look back!"

"Why?"

"If it's coming for us, I don't want to know, do you?" Raphael's story warned that if you looked back at the danger behind you, you turned into a pillar of blood or salt, something terrible that didn't make sense. "Change of plan," I said. "We leave town and circle back."

"But your father — "

"Like he said, this isn't goodbye. We live on the edge of town. We'll get there by heading north. If we go through Marfa, we're dead."

The howls of the sirens and the screams of the dying receded but I'll never forget them. Dad was right. This was war and we were all drafted now.

I ran until the numbers of buildings thinned. Only when I was standing out in the open did I dare to look back. I could see there was another crane bot in the distance through shimmers of heat. "There's two of the big ones!" I told Emma.

"Three," she said.

"What? You mean three back at your dome?"

"No, Dante. I mean three here. It's not standing up but I can see the heat plumes of the third. It's heading northwest. I'm guessing the plan is to level Marfa."

I searched the horizon but saw nothing. "You've got Vivid, don't you?"

She nodded.

"That didn't go down with your dome?"

"The enhanced vision is still there. I've lost any connection to the services offered through the Collective."

"What do you mean?"

Emma shrugged. "I'm cut off. It's mechanically advantageous but my information is limited to...mostly how you see the world, I suppose."

I flushed, a little angry at that remark. Then it occurred to me she could catch my thermal changes and interpret them as anger. Embarrassed, I turned away.

"I can see far and I can see close. I've still got night vision," she said.

"That will be useful. Let me know if you see any snakes or bots tonight. What can't you do that you used to do?"

"Can't look up any entries to check facts. Mostly, for me, that was engineering manuals. Makes no difference now, I guess. The Collective won't be feeding me any information anymore."

We had a big circle to walk so I hurried as best I could. With her exo-stilts extended, the trek was easy for Emma. I ran at first. Then I walked and jogged. I was embarrassed at that, too. Every time my breath came short and ragged, she told me to stop and rest. "If you wore the full body rig, I could be getting a piggyback ride and we'd be there in no time."

"I left with what I was wearing at the time. I only had the stilts on to crank me high enough to check the tanks and work on the domes."

"No offense meant, Ma'am."

"None taken. But don't call me, 'Ma'am.' Emma will

do fine. How far, cowboy?"

"We gotta move stealthy so it'll be evening before we're close. And don't call me, 'cowboy.' Dante will do fine."

"Fair enough. How do you get a name like Dante?"

"Dad said it's because he's been to the ninth circle of hell."

"I don't get it."

"It's a story he knows. Mythology, I think. Caught my father's imagination. Old knowledge. "

"Outlawed knowledge, you mean."

"The West is full of outlaws, then. Nothing special, though. We just like stories and we like to talk."

"Colorful," she said.

"Some say so. Some think country equals dumb. But I think people who think that way aren't colorful enough. Raphael says if people had more flair and flavor, they wouldn't be weird about the way he talks."

"Your father doesn't have your accent."

"He was brought up out east. My mother was from Amarillo. I was brought up around here mostly, with Raphael for a teacher."

"Where's your mother?"

"I don't remember much. She was colorful and had flair, too, I think. And long hair."

"You get along with your father?"

"Mostly?"

"Only mostly?"

"You know how most vets don't want to talk about their time in the Sand Wars? I wish my father were one of those guys. He couldn't claim to have won the war singlehandedly but I'm pretty sure he thinks he slowed our defeat all on his lonesome."

Emma startled me with a sound that started with a snort and ended with a laugh. "Sorry," she added.

"No, by all means. Laugh it up. I could use a good

laugh right now."

"I think that's all I've got, given the circumstances."

"What was it like living in a dome?"

"It felt safe. No Blight. No monster spores getting in. Mother kept us safe from all that but it wasn't just about airlocks. She kept out corrupting influences. With all that's happened, I thought Mother would make sure humankind wouldn't fall farther."

"Wait. Who? Mother? You mean your captain?"

"No. Sorry. Mother is what Domers called the Collective."

"Strange thing to call a computer."

"It was the computer network that kept the airlocks sealed at the right times so we could move between domes without fear of contamination. Calling it Mother was kind of natural, I think. It made us safe."

"Until it didn't. What happened to Mother in the shatter storm?"

Emma looked away. "She opened all the airlocks at once. The wind whistled right through, from the damaged domes to the rest, ruining everything in a minute."

"How fast do the plants die?"

"I've heard it's twenty percent loss of yield each year. We've lost dome networks around here before. Pecos went down two years ago. Roswell went down last year. This is the first out and out revolt we've had, though."

"That you know of," I said.

I thought I detected her stiffening at my words. Her silhouette towered above me. I'm sure, with Vivid working, Emma could see my face perfectly. I'd asked her to extend her stilts so she could detect any threats ahead of us in the deepening darkness. Night comes fast in the desert.

"What do you mean, 'that I know of?'" she asked finally.

"You stayed inside all the time, right?"

"Mostly."

"And you depended on Mother to tell you everything?"

"Yes, of course."

"Then your Mother abandoned you, too."

"Well...."

"Trust me, from one abandoned son to an abandoned daughter, mothers don't tell their kids everything. My mother lit out for the west coast way back, at the first signs of the Fall. Your Mother didn't stop the bots from killing humans."

"I wouldn't equate — "

"It's not the same, but it is the same," I said. "And where did that swarm come from?"

"They were pollination drones, refitted for warfare."

"How is that possible?"

"The domes are built around a huge factory. We needed a lot of pollination drones. The limit of their manufacture is only the amount of elements the bots can get their claws on. That's why we aren't overrun by crane bots right now. There's enough metal in one crane bot to supply one dome with pollination drones."

We trudged on in silence. We made our way through the dark until we circled back to Marfa's edge.

I was worried about death machines coming for me. I'd totally forgotten about the danger posed by Jim Peppard.

9

I heard no more screams as we made our way back into my neighborhood. The old civil defense sirens died mid-wail. The invasion of Marfa had entered the second stage of the catastrophe. By nightfall, human survival meant run or hide. We heard the crashes of demolished buildings but no gunshots echoed from downtown.

For the ill-prepared, walking out into the desert might mean a slow death when the sun rose. We hoped the bots would leave the same way you hope a storm will pass you by. It's only a hope. You have no say beyond thinking hard and being helpless.

I'd spent a good part of my childhood hoping hard and I knew how useless it was. Jim Peppard taught me that.

I never played with Jim when we were kids. He was a year older than me. I don't suppose he really had friends. He was the sort of kid who, by the gravitational force of his strong personality, gathers a solar system of sycophants and lesser bullies into his orbit. He lived just down the street from my house but we never had occasion for a civil talk.

Marfa was the sort of place that valued legacy. You could move to Marfa when you were young and you'd still be, "that dude from back east."

The Peppards had been in Marfa for generations so they should have been higher up in the local hierarchy. However, they were assholes. That's the flip side of living in small places. Everybody has a long memory and is quick to remind others who was born of a bad seed. People stick you in a slot and you stay stuck.

My father the war hero was one of those dudes from back east. Austin, in the locals' estimation qualified as Other: too liberal and too weird. However, when Steve Bolelli arrived in Marfa with his pretty wife Jean, Dad was lucky. He moved in to the house next to Raphael Marquez, the richest man in town. Raphael gave my father a job and, when my mother left, I spent more and more time with my father and his employer. I came to think of the old man as a great substitute for the grandfather I never knew.

By the friendship my father developed with his neighbor, I was bound to become a solar field engineer. Raphael took me on as an apprentice and trained me personally. My ability to contribute grew. Meanwhile, Jim lived down the street brewing moonshine with his father and hating me.

I don't know what little Jimmy Peppard might have become if his dad had a friend like Raphael. The Peppard family was known in town as a group of troublemakers, quick to anger and slow to forget any slight, real or imagined. Jim Peppard never really had a chance. There were reasons he was a bad kid and a bad man.

I'm not making excuses for Jim, though. Reasons didn't make him any less of an asshole. You get to twenty, you gotta start owning your shit and cleaning it up. Otherwise, you become your shit.

My childhood drama with Jim didn't really start until a bot intervened in our lives. Mostly, Jim was a name caller right out of the womb. He wasn't much of a doer when he was young unless provoked.

It was Jen #2, Raphael's second companion bot, that caught Jim on disk calling me names and hucking rocks at me.

This was long before Bob came into my mentor's life. Raphael hadn't always needed help moving around. Bots like Jen were called companion bots but they were made primarily for sex. Raphael bragged that he wore out Jen #1 faster than her warranty lasted. Jen #1 was replaced by Jen #2.

Jen #2 lasted a long time but Raphael's health had begun to decay by then. Jen #2 was eventually recycled. The latest sex bot, Jen #3 arrived.

"Jen #3 is more of a companion than the others," Raphael said. "It's the chemicals we use to coat the solar panels. They get better connectivity and I get less. I've absorbed it through my skin over the years. Sucked the calcium straight from my bones and took the stiff out of my stiffies."

I started wearing gloves on the job at all times after that revelation.

Raphael was a gentle soul. He didn't keep his bots in a closet. While he was out in the fields at work tuning up panels and getting sicker, he always set his companion bots to sentry mode. That sounds official, but mostly it was Jen's job to sit on the front porch hooked up to a charger, scanning the street to protect Raphael's house and telling the occasional refugee to keep moving.

One afternoon when I was seven, Jim pushed me into the dirt so hard I got road rash and cried. I had my crying done before I made my way home. My mother wasn't sympathetic and my father was of a mind that, "Bigger doesn't matter as long as you hit hard and hit first."

Jim's size did matter to me. I didn't want to get hurt. I figured the quickest way to end the fight and keep all my baby teeth was to curl up in a ball and hope Jim got bored. I didn't fight back.

Not fighting back was the only sin I recall my father worrying about aloud. Not that he was all wrong. I didn't understand irony then. I didn't know that inaction invited more abuse and the probability of more injury down the line.

Jen, ever in sentry mode while Raphael was away, saw the incident. She replayed the recording when Raphael got home. I didn't know the machine had witnessed my humiliation until my father came home with one set of bloody knuckles and a cut on his forehead.

My father sat me down and looked me in the eye. "Dante, did that big boy down the street hit you?"

"No," I said.

My father appeared to consider my words for a time. Finally, he said, "That's the right answer and it's the wrong answer. It's right because you're not tattling and whining. It's wrong because you're telling me nothing happened when I know for a fact it did."

"Then there is no right answer," I said. "What am I supposed to do?"

My father shook his head. "The right answer was to hit the sumbitch back, right in the teeth. In a perfect world, I don't hear about it. As it is, I had to go deal with the situation."

I was a kid and small for my age. I still remember how my head got hot and my hands got cold as I looked into my father's eyes. By his voice, I knew he was disappointed in me. But he had a look that made me suspect he was excited, too. "What did you do, Dad?"

"I went over there and beat the shit out of that boy's father."

"Aren't you going to get in trouble?"

"Nah. Except for standing, I didn't use my cybersuit at all. Took him down one-handed."

This seems an unlikely claim in retrospect. I didn't question then that my one-armed, one-legged father could beat up Dale Peppard without using the power of his bionics. I'd heard a thousand war stories by then. I was pretty sure my father could beat up anybody. I still believe it a little bit, even now.

Jim pretty much left me alone after my father visited the Peppard household that night. He kept his assaults to the verbal variety afterward.

I heard from Raphael years later that Sheriff Hubbard did get involved in that case briefly. "Peppard's wife called Hubby in. The only reason your father isn't in the jailhouse is it's a question of he-said, he-said. There weren't any bots around to record the festivities when Steve showed up on Dale's doorstep to express concern for your safety."

"What happened then?"

"Whaddayathink? A good old-fashioned fistfight. I heard the blow-by-blow. Epic! Your father doesn't just win a fight. He makes sure it stays won after he's walked away. Classic Steve."

I'd been afraid that my father's intervention on my behalf would lead to terrible retributions that would go on forever, or at least until Jim or his father killed me. I asked Raphael how to win a fight so it stays won.

The old man laughed. "You beat 'em until they're more scared of you than they are angry. It takes a lot of beating to get that far, generally. Long as the anger's taller than the fear, you're safe."

"And the sheriff never said anything?"

"Dale didn't file no charges. Steve made sure Mr. Peppard knew that, if arrested, I'd be bailing your father out before the trial. That's a threat that's somethin' powerful. If Steve got bailed out, Dale Peppard knew he'd get a beating worse than the first one. Probably end in a murder charge. Law of the jungle."

"What's a jungle?"

"Where most of the oxygen used to come from," Raphael said.

Until the night of the bot invasion, the Peppard family's fear of hurting me was taller than their anger. Big Jim Peppard came out of his house and ran up to Emma and me to explain that had changed. When a civilization collapses, some people tend to pick that time to settle old scores.

Jim Peppard made that clear when he pointed a shotgun at my head.

10

With her enhanced vision, Emma saw Peppard coming and let out a cry of surprise. He came up behind us before she had a chance to warn me, though. I didn't blame her. Under the circumstances, she was probably happy it wasn't a sec bot rolling up behind us. She didn't know the crazy danger Jim Peppard posed.

He hit me across the back of the head before he said a word. I cursed as I dropped to my hands and knees.

Then he flicked on a flashlight and saw that it was me. "Well, if it isn't the shop boy!"

He kicked me in the ass and I went face down in the street, just like when I was seven. He was on top of me immediately, pulling Raphael's pistol out of the back of my pants. "How you doing now, shop boy?"

I grunted. My forehead stung with road rash. I would have chucked the can of apple juice at his head but it had rolled away. "What do you want, Jim?"

"What you got? Besides the pistola and the pretty lady? Did ya get a lot out of the store? Don't hold back now."

"The store's gone, Jim. The bots were wrecking everything downtown last I saw."

"Uh-huh." He shone his light in Emma's eyes. "And who's this?"

"I'm the woman who is going to save your life. Turn off that light."

Jim laughed. "How do you figure?"

"There are sec bots in town. They have a sniper range

of three kilometers at least. They aren't fussy about who they target these days. Waving that light around could attract their attention."

"Seems unlikely."

"The sniper tech in those bots is basically the same as it was a few generations ago. They were first used in Korea to guard the border in the last century. What makes you think they can't kill you now? Or are you thinking at all?"

"Shut up." He pointed the pistol at her head.

Emma didn't miss a beat. "Have you ever seen the domes or pictures of the domes?"

"Sure."

"You know why you don't see piles of bodies all along the perimeter? It's because sec bots kill the people trying to get through the fence way out in the desert before they even get close. It wouldn't look good to have all that rotting meat just outside the fence. And now those same bots are in your town killing people."

I think she had more to say but Peppard turned off his flashlight.

"We've got to get off the street," I said. "A flashlight beam might attract attention but those things can see in the dark just fine."

"That so?" Peppard sounded uncertain. Then he sounded almost friendly. "You're right, Dante. We should get off the street. What say I go get Sue and we go to your Dad's house? Between him and Raphael, I bet they got ideas about how to get out of here with our heads still screwed on straight."

His silhouette was clear enough in the moonlight. He turned to Emma to explain, "Raphael's the richest man in town, even if he does live in a shitty house next to shop boy's dad."

I stood slowly, feeling along my scalp. It hurt, but he hadn't broken the skin. "Where is Susan?"

"Down in the basement with my parents praying for deliverance. I told them deliverance would arrive shortly but I figured I better go find it in case it didn't come to us in a timely manner. And here you are. Everything worked out."

"Give me my gun back."

"Let's talk about who gives and gets what at your place, shop boy."

"My father is not going to let you into his house. Raphael won't, either."

"Times change."

"People don't," I said.

"You're going to need an alpha man who's handy with a gun," he said. "If I were a bot you'd both be dead right now. Well, you'd be dead, Dante. For you, honey? Well, you're too pretty to die. Never did catch your name and I ain't never seen you around town. I would have remembered. What is your name, darlin'?"

"Emma."

"Emma. I like that. That's kind of an old-fashioned name. Domer, I take it? Bunch of 'em ran through here earlier, chased by metal insects. You don't see that every day."

"Jim, do you get what's happening? The whole town is under attack. I don't even know if my father is still alive!"

"Calm down, shop boy. I'm talking to Emma."

"What do you want?" she asked.

"Nice stilts, girl. You can go pretty far and fast on those, I bet."

"They got me this far."

I could see the white of his toothy grin in the moonlight. "How about you slip those off and go along with Dante under your own power. I know my way around here. I'll scout the area and see what I can find."

"That's not going to happen," Emma said.

I heard the click of the hammer on the pistol. I didn't need to see every detail in the dark like Emma. I knew Jim Peppard was pointing my weapon at me.

"Shit," I said.

"So?" Jim asked. "If I have to shoot him, that's kind of on you, isn't it, Emma? How do you want to handle it? I can be a friend or I can be scary. You want the scary guy on your side, trust me."

"That's the problem," Emma said. "You can never trust a scary guy."

"I'm just trying to survive," Peppard said. "There's no rules anymore. None but what we make ourselves. To my mind, that's is as should be. If the old rules worked, we wouldn't be in this predicament, would we?"

"Don't do this," Emma said.

"C'mon now. I'm the scary guy. Don't make me be the bad guy. I've known Dante all my life. We never got along but I never quite figured on killing him, neither. I've never killed anybody...but, like I said, the rules have changed. They're still changing. Every second you say no, it's getting easier and easier for me to do what I want just because I got the guns and you're starting to piss me off. This is already over. You just haven't admitted it to yourself yet."

He took a step my way. I held my hands up in front of me, turned my head and squeezed my eyes tight. It wouldn't stop him from blowing my brains out. I was pretty sure he was going to shoot me but I pleaded with Emma, "Just give it to him. Please!"

"Hear that, Emma? Shop boy says, 'please.' It's all up to you."

He took another step closer and Emma shouted, "Okay! Don't shoot!"

"That's more like it," Peppard said.

"Stop pointing the gun at Dante," she said. "You'll need your flashlight. If you're going to operate my exo-stilts properly, get over here and pay attention. I don't want you damaging my equipment."

Peppard laughed. "That's just fine, Emma. I knew you'd listen to reason. Siddown, Dante."

He stalked back toward her and, by the beam of his little flashlight, I watched Emma sit down in the street.

I wished a sec bot's sniper bullet would dig through Jim Peppard's head. I could almost see it happening in my mind's eye. My father had described pink mist and cavitation so often, it was easy to picture Jim's skull getting blown apart. The expensive ammunition any military bot uses would explode and split into barbs. The bots would shred his useless brain and I wouldn't shed a tear.

"This is the sensory harness," Emma explained. "This readout shows you how much battery life is left. This little lever here extends the legs for longer strides. The gyros automatically compensate for rough terrain. It takes some getting used to but you probably won't have balance issues for long. These clips here are for hauling heavy loads."

"Yeah, yeah. Let's go."

"Wait," Emma said. "This is the most important function key here. See this?" She pointed at a recessed button on her harness as she lifted one leg.

"Yeah. What's that do?" Peppard asked.

The exoskeleton's metal foot pointed, almost daintily. Jim Peppard's laugh was cut short as the rail of the exoskeleton's leg shot out and punched through the center of his chest with a wet crunch. He flew backward like a man-sized doll, boneless and useless.

Emma took a deep breath and held it a second before letting it out slowly through clenched teeth. "Jump mode, asshole."

11

Emma skidded backward on her bum a little when the blow was delivered. That wasn't why she was crying when she stood up. Jim made bubbling sounds from his mouth and each shuddering breath was thin and wet.

The flashlight had spun away and I dashed to retrieve it. Once I had that, I rushed back to check on Jim. I wasn't thinking. I was just moving, working on automatic. If he'd still had my pistol in his fist, I would have tried to kill him. Instead, I found him on his back, disarmed and spitting blood.

I picked up his shotgun. He'd never need it again.

Jim's breath came and went in short pants, shallower by the moment. One eye was rolled back. The other might have been looking at me but his stare had that blank, uncomprehending look. The big bloody hole in his chest told me my worries about big Jim Peppard were over.

I retrieved the pistol and considered putting Jim out of his misery. I wasn't the guy for that job, though. Besides, a gunshot might invite the sort of attention we didn't want from Jim's father or from sec bots.

Emma joined me. She took the flashlight to turn it off. "I wasn't kidding about the sec bots in sniper mode. Let's go."

"He's still alive."

"Not for long."

"No. I s'pose not." I looked down at my first enemy dying in the moonlight. Jim had been the only enemy I'd ever had. I had thought I wouldn't feel anything if he was erased from the Earth. I did, though. It was a strange mixture of satisfaction and pity. I guess my satisfaction at his defeat was a little taller than my pity.

Emma was not stone. She wept but, looking back on it now, I think she cried for what he made her do. "Should we say something?" she asked.

"You mean, like...words over the body? He's not dead yet."

"Any moment now."

"Maybe we should say something while he can still hear us." I knelt beside him and whispered. "You were right, Jim. Everything worked out."

That was a bit mean but it was the only eulogy I had in me. I'm ashamed of that now.

"Should we stay with him until he's gone? Or tell his family?" Emma suggested.

"I don't think the Peppards would take that well. No sense borrowing trouble. We got plenty on hand."

I stood. "Past time we went. Sorry I wasn't more help when the shit hit the turbine."

"There was nothing you could do that wouldn't leave you dead."

"I was taught there is always a way and all you have to do is find it."

"Always? That's stupid. Who taught you that? There was nothing you could do. Period."

"Still. Sorry."

"Don't be sorry. Just show me where we're hiding tonight. I'm exhausted."

That sounded cold but I concluded Emma was a logical thinker. Logical thinkers are what every disaster needs. If we had a few more like her, we wouldn't be in this apocalypse in the first place.

I left the man I'd known as a boy to die in the dark in the street between his house and mine. I'd passed that place who knows how many times. When something monumental happened somewhere, people used to put up monuments and plaques and crosses. Now that something bad was happening everywhere, there weren't enough people left to put up monuments. The ratio of the dead to the survivors had flipped in a bad way. Not that Jim Peppard was worth a statue or anything. He could have lived a thousand years and never earned so much as a thank you note for his good works.

When I look back on the first day the bots came to Marfa, there are certain things that stand out above the others: the crane bot rummaging under the City Hall's roof, that old man's decapitated head held high in a bot's claw and the children screaming along with their mothers and fathers. There weren't many kids around anymore so their loss was somehow even worse.

Chief among these memories, I think I will remember best the feeling of a gun pointed at my head. I was sure I was about to die and, despite everything that had happened that day, I still wanted to live.

That's a mystery for the ages. Old people can get tired of living and, on their deathbeds, they'll ask earnestly why they should bother about seeing another sunrise. Surviving the apocalypse is for the young and stupid, I think. We still have the will to keep going when a wiser person would give up, lay down and relax into oblivion.

Down the street, a smaller mystery was solved easily. Steve Bolelli, resourceful and determined as ever, had survived another day of war. My father had not hugged me since I was little but he did that day.

"I don't think I managed to draw any drone away from downtown," he said. "Makes sense. They want maximum casualties so they stuck where the largest population density was. To get up here, I went to the edge of town and took the long way."

"We did the same," I said.

"I knew you would, son. You got my brains and your mother's ass."

"Uh, thanks, Dad."

Emma's cheeks were still wet with tears but she managed a half-smile. Then she broke down and cried into my shoulder.

"Young lady?" Raphael came forward out of the kitchen using his walker. "Hello. I've heard about you. Welcome to Marfa's survivor's club. Not many of us left, I'm afraid."

Bob must have been charging in the kitchen but Raphael's companion bot followed him into the living room. This was not the same Jen who witnessed Jim Peppard bully me when I was seven. This was Jen #3 ("premium with oral upgrades," Raphael had bragged.)

Raphael introduced Jen to Emma. The machine smiled but said nothing.

Emma looked at Jen warily. "Is it safe?"

Raphael laughed. "She's fine. I never allow automatic updates. The idea of allowing an unknown entity to update her software has always seemed crazy to me. She's a companion bot. Updates from elsewhere are invitations to surveillance. That could be embarrassing, couldn't it?"

I relaxed a little. Then I thought of Bob. "Does Bob get automatic updates?"

"Nah," Raphael said. "I never bothered. He's fine, too. When I want more bells and whistles on my assistive devices, I buy new."

"Great!" Emma said. "So they probably won't kill us in our sleep."

"Tough day for you, I'm sure," Raphael said. "Steve has tracked the progress of the drone attack. Between his observations and my math, we're safe here tonight and at least until noon tomorrow. Probably longer."

I was about to ask how they could possibly know that but Emma got it right away. "They're killers but they're still bots. They're being systematic, aren't they? They're probably organizing the slaughter on a grid for maximum effect."

My father nodded and I could see the pain on his face. "People run home when things get bad. If their homes aren't there anymore, they'll run to churches. From what I could see, the bots have recognized that pattern. Things being the way they are, not many people are really in a position to leave. We're stuck here. If that train doesn't stop tomorrow night, few will escape."

"That's talk for tomorrow," Raphael said. "Get some sleep everyone, if you can. I'll take the first watch."

"How far can you see, old man?" Dad asked.

"Jenny can see fine. I'll watch with her."

I fell into a deep sleep on the living room floor. I didn't sleep for long. I startled awake. Jen was beside me, her head on my shoulder. She had one arm around my waist and she was hugging tight.

12

My first thought was of Travis Chinto, squeezed in the middle until his insides became outsides. But Jen wasn't holding me that tight.

"Jen?"

Her hardware mimicked taking a deep breath so when she said, "Hello, Dante," her soft whisper was soft and sultry.

"What are you doing?"

"Waiting for you to wake up." She raised her head and, in the dim light cast from the kitchen, I could see her inviting smile. Her small face was framed by short hair in brown and blonde ringlets.

"Where is everybody?"

"Raphael is in your father's bed. Your father is off on a mission to make preparations for tomorrow with Bob. Emma is out on the front porch on watch." Her hand brushed the crotch of my jeans gently. "And I'm here with you. We're alone."

"Why?"

She sat up. Her flannel shirt was unbuttoned. She pulled it back to reveal two perfect breasts. I'd always been curious about companion bots, of course. Her brown nipples were erect. I wondered if they were always that way. Though she was a sex bot, Raphael usually dressed her conservatively.

"Um," I said.

"Raphael said I should pay you a visit."

"Why?"

"Do you want me to say it? Would you like me to tell you? I can talk slow and dirty or I can provide the full menu of my services in an itemized list, if you prefer. Just tell me what you want. I'm yours tonight."

I was silent for a moment. I'd fantasized about this. Now that the fantasy could become a reality, I was too nervous to move.

Companion bots were expensive. All three of Raphael's sex bots had been custom made to his specs and identical as far as I could see. My father told me he'd seen a picture of Raphael's dead wife once. Each Jen looked exactly like her.

I stared at the bot's breasts and Jen looked pleased. She shimmied a little, putting on a show. Then the bot rose to swing a leg over mine and she climbed on top of me, her hands on my shoulders held me still. She began to undulate slowly but with increasing purpose, rubbing her pubis up and down my crotch. Of course, she was programmed to respond that way but, organic or non-organic, her manipulations had the desired effect. I was rock hard.

"Are you shy, Dante?" Jen said. "You don't have to be shy with me. I can do whatever you want. Whatever you need, I'm here."

"Why are you doing this?"

"I told you. Raphael sent me."

"Why did Raphael send you?"

"To do what I do. Raphael hasn't fucked me in a long time, Dante. It feels good for me, too, you know."

"Stop!"

Jen got off me immediately.

"Button up your shirt and go charge yourself or something."

"I'm sorry. Have I done something wrong?"

"I know why Raphael sent you. That's...that's all. Go. Thank you, but go."

When my erection subsided, I stood and paced. Then I went outside for some fresh air. Emma was on the porch, standing guard. She was shorter than I expected without the exo-stilts.

"Have a good time?" she asked.

"What?"

"You heard me. Raphael said you'd need a little privacy for a while. Seems it didn't last long. I've heard that's the problem with sex bots. They can be too good. When you do the math, it works out to millions of dollars a minute."

"It wasn't like that. I told her to go away."

Emma turned to me, curious. "That's weird. I guess I was sounding unkind, but women have used machines for much longer than men. I mean for — "

"Jen is a replica of Raphael's wife. She died of cancer before I was born. All three Jens have been her double."

"That's sad."

"It's more than that. Raphael expects us to die tomorrow. That's why he sent her."

"That does kill the mood."

Despite myself, I laughed. "Well...it didn't exactly kill the mood. I mean, they are very lifelike. It's just...it didn't feel right. Besides, bots scare the shit out of me right now. If Jen had arrived at my bed a couple of nights ago, different story."

Emma took a long breath. "Yeah, I think it's a good bet we're gonna die tomorrow. You should have taken Raphael up on the offer."

She turned to watch Marfa.

"What do you see that I don't?" I asked.

"More bots have arrived. I think the insectiles have moved on. Makes sense. They're basically bees. Excellent navigation, good scouts. There are more buildings burning. I think they're burning them in a ring."

"Why?"

"Driving the humans together. Coralling them."

"It's genocide."

"It's the extinction," she said. "I've been thinking about something the man I killed said."

"What about him?"

"He said if the old rules worked, we wouldn't be in this mess now."

"Yeah? So?"

"This is our fault. We saw the Next Intelligence coming and we didn't stop the tech. We just figured somebody else would figure it out."

"Guess they didn't. I'm still unclear...I mean, if NI is so damn smart, what's with trying to kill us all?"

"Maybe because we aren't so smart. When the jump to NI happens, it's never a small increment. A computer builds a computer. Then it builds a brain that's not just ten times smarter than us. It's a thousand times smarter."

"What's your point?"

"You ever kill a bug in your kitchen and feel bad about it, Dante?"

"I see what you're saying."

"I remember talking to engineers about NI. One of the tricks to stopping NI was to set traps for it. The idea was, when a system jumps to sentience, you give it dead ends to go down. You offer it a chance to do terrible things and if it chooses those terrible things, the system shuts down."

"And?"

"That was the safety on the gun. Sounds brilliant, right?"

"Sure."

"Think about it a moment longer. How would a hyper-intelligent system outsmart the trap?"

I shrugged. "It'd have to be suspicious. Mostly it

would have to learn to lie, I guess."

"So, you're saying a pretty dim toddler would get around the trap. Keep in mind that I'm talking about a machine that has access to all information in human history and makes billions of calculations per second. How long do you think it should take an advanced neuromimetic matrix to figure out how to fool us?"

"Oh."

"One of the first things we taught computers to do was play games. Those same computer scientists devising traps and dead ends for NI probably programmed computers to recognize feints and traps in chess. Idiots all."

"Shit. We will die tomorrow."

"Fuck, yeah," she said. "We're definitely going to die tomorrow. No. It's long past midnight. We're going to die today."

We didn't talk for a long time. She watched Marfa burn. I couldn't sleep and I didn't know what to say.

Eventually, we turned to each other. You can guess what happened next. Raphael had the right idea but a bot wasn't right. Not then.

As Emma held me in her arms, she squeezed me tight to her body. She rocked up and down, riding me with aching slowness. "This is my last time," she said. "Let's make it last."

"This is my first time," I said. "I'll try."

13

The plan was simple. The desert was too big. We had to escape Marfa by train. That evening it would be heading west. The last city was out there, somewhere along the coast. It was rumored to be so large, people called it The City in the Sky or just The City.

The train wouldn't take us that far. There wasn't enough rail that was intact. One of the Cataclysms had hit the coast — maybe more than one. The options once we got to the water would be a long hike or to get a ride in a sailboat.

"I've never seen the ocean," I told Emma.

"Until last night, it seems you haven't done a lot of things."

I looked away, embarrassed. "Did I do something wrong?"

"No, not at all." Emma put a hand on my arm and squeezed gently. "I just wondered why you waited so long."

"The right girl never came along, I guess."

"Don't tease me."

"I'm not. Marfa is a small town and there weren't many girls left that were my age and compatible. Some wanted to stay forever and others wanted to leave right away. I didn't fit in either camp so...I dunno. It just never worked out quite right."

"Well," she said. "You picked a hell of a time."

"The time chose me," I said. "I guess you could say I've tended to let opportunities slide by just to see how they work out."

"And?"

"Thank you for last night," I said. "No time left to wait now for opportunities, is there?"

"It was our last chance, so yeah, I guess not."

The bots were getting closer. Time to migrate. My father handed me a heavy pack and shouldered one of his own. Bob had one clipped to him, as well. I asked Dad what supplies he had packed.

"Just essentials," he said. "And I added some extra socks from your drawer. We may be walking a long time. Infantry always needs fresh socks."

We went out the back door and tried to ignore the sounds of buildings being demolished. We all went quiet as the sounds of destruction followed us. Even Raphael said nothing, a talent he was not known for.

We saw some refugees as we headed west. Most hurried by, on their way north. My father called after them, "Come with us! We're going to catch the train!"

Most ignored us and kept going.

We saw Sheriff Johns leading a group of five north. Hubby wasn't wearing his tin star anymore but he wore his guns.

"Hubby!" Raphael called. "Come with us."

"You're going the wrong way," Hubby said. "We got enough supplies for a day or so. We'll find our way to Odessa, maybe. I know people in Odessa."

"That's what? Three days?" Dad asked.

"We'll be out of water by day two but I figure that makes for a lighter load," Hubby said. "We'll find help along the way or something."

"'Or something,' ain't much of a plan," Raphael said. "Don't be a fool. We got a train to catch."

Hubby spared enough breath to say, "The train is that way. South is where the killer bots are. Don't you be fools!"

My father called after Hubby, "Keep running that way and you're just as dead but you'll die slower!"

Hubby moved on. He didn't want to discuss his options further. I'll always wonder if the sheriff regretted his choice once he got out of town and found himself in a desert full of empty. I don't suppose he had very long to regret anything. He probably ended his life with a couple of days of thirsty walking and then collapsed to feed snakes and scorpions.

There were ghost towns up that way but nothing salvageable remained immediately north of us. There used to be springs over in Fort Stockton but with the water all dried up, the people dried up and went away, too, long ago.

We'd left before noon and, after an hour of walking, angled southwest. We hoped to circle back unnoticed to where Raphael was sure the train would stop.

I couldn't remember when the train had last stopped precisely. I was sure it had been more than fifty days. That was when we had received our last supplies for work on the solar panels and wind turbines.

As we wound our way through the desert, Raphael and Jen rode side by side on Bob in bipedal mode. The bot could maneuver in tight spaces by standing on two legs. For open spaces and for speed, Bob went down on all fours. In quadruped mode, small wheels deployed from his bulky frame and Raphael rode behind Jen.

"It's like I'm riding a damn golf cart to my grave," Raphael complained.

"What's that?" I asked.

"What? A golf cart?" He shrugged and waved off the question. "Golf was a game we played when we didn't realize how precious water was."

"When did we not know that?" Emma asked.

Raphael ignored her and hugged Jen closer. He might have held the companion bot tight for the sake of stability on Bob's back. I don't think so, though. I think it was for comfort. Raphael was a very old man but he'd often said a young woman was still soft and alluring long past the time he could attract one.

My mentor had said little of my refusal of his gift. When he'd greeted me that morning, he clamped a hand on my shoulder and said, "Don't worry about Jen, Dante. She's not used to rejection but you can't hurt her feelings. I was just trying to be nice. I meant no harm."

"I know, Raphael. It was a nice gesture. It's just — "

"I s'pose being with Jenny would feel a little like wearing my old man underwear, huh?"

I reddened and said nothing more. Raphael had laughed so hard he farted.

Trudging the desert, we made a wide arc around Marfa. My father wore the more advanced of his two cy-suits. Emma strode along effortlessly on her long exo-legs scanning the horizon. When we came to another wide gap where the cables ran beneath the solar panel field, Raphael switched Bob's orientation and saddle configuration so they could ride the assistive bot like a horse.

Loaded down with my pistol, Jim Peppard's shotgun and a heavy pack, I was the slow one holding back the party.

The sun rose and the wind died. The world was an oven. I was drenched in sweat. Eventually Raphael took pity on me and let me ride with him. Jen jogged along beside us, oblivious to the heat.

Every few minutes, Raphael looked over and smiled at his bot and Jen smiled back.

"Beautiful, isn't she? The brain tech was in the works for a long time but, once we found a way to make a better, lighter battery she was inevitable. Looking back on my life, everything seems inevitable. Pre-ordained! Epic!"

As we made our way through the desert, I was sure my fate was already set, too. The old man must have caught my grim look. Raphael handed me his canteen and I drank. "Relax, Dante. The original train tracks went right through the center of town. At least we don't have to go there."

Emma extended her stilts farther and looked back toward Marfa. "The center of town isn't there anymore. I count three crane-bots. They're leaving the solar and wind fields alone."

"They're keeping their energy supply and destroying any competition for resources," my father said. "Logical."

His analysis sounded cold. I guess he was in warrior mode but, when he talked like a soldier he often sounded like a bot if bots narrated what and how they thought.

My father's plain declaration made me think of Raphael's comment about Jen. I couldn't hurt her feelings by rejecting her. She could feel no shame. Like all bots, her behavior was programmed. Dad seemed programmed sometimes, too.

"The bots that are attacking us aren't Next Intelligence," I said. "Can't be. That would be too cruel."

Emma looked down at me from a great height. "Why do you say that?"

"They're just killing and destroying," I said. "There's no...hesitation. I think they're programmed by NI but I don't think they have it themselves. If they were self-aware, I think they'd hesitate. There's no reasoning going on. They're just following orders. NI is supposed to be a far superior intelligence," I said. "Seems to me, if it's that smart, it would have more self-doubt."

"You're thinking like a human," Emma said. "Whatever NI is, it operates on a whole other level. Talking about what NI should be and do is like guessing what's inside a black box. We always thought we knew what NI would look like and how it should behave. That was our mistake. We thought smart meant like the best of us, only faster."

Raphael nodded. "Metal gods are just like the old gods, Dante. They operate outside of what we see as right and wrong. We killed the old gods because that callousness is what we hated about 'em. Then we allowed NI to be created in God's stead. No further ahead, if you ask me."

"We're ants in a jar," my father said. "NI is holding the jar, looking in at us. It's reaching for a magnifying glass and it's a sunny day."

I shut my eyes. I wanted to shut my ears. I didn't want to talk about Next Intelligence or figure out exactly how stupid humans had been. I didn't want to think at all about what was next for us, what little was left for us.

I couldn't see the crane bots at their disgusting work. I could hear them, though. When buildings with multiple floors collapse, the displaced air of each fallen floor sounds like the detonation of an explosive charge. Each broken building stirred echoes that reached for us like cannon fire.

"Hear that?" Raphael asked. "That's the sound of the order of the world getting rearranged. Classic!"

"Sir?"

"Yes, Dante?"

"Shut up."

The old man smiled and nodded good-naturedly. "Cool."

A few minutes later, I wished I hadn't told my kind mentor to shut up. I should have used the time to thank him for his kindness. I wished I'd thought to give the old man a hug goodbye.

14

As the sun began to set, I could feel the train's vibration through the track with my bare hand.

"This train used to be run by humans," Emma said. "Then the machines took over and the people who lived on the train became among the first Domers."

The train brought us food and water and materials to build more solar panels and turbines. I hadn't thought a lot about where the food and water came from. Now I was curious. "Emma? As Domers, you had food and water and energy. Sounds like you had everything you could need. What was that like?"

"We were the lucky ones until it all went to shit."

"What did you get in return for your crops?"

"A feed of your energy, for one thing."

Electricity was one thing Marfa had plenty of. I'd taken it for granted.

"We had lots of food and a higher birth rate than average, too," Emma said. "I like kids, so that was nice. We couldn't go outside much but there wasn't much to go outside for unless there was infrastructure work."

"Anything else?"

"Well, our Collective network out in the domes was lax about what was allowed into our brains."

"What do you mean?"

"The folks who run the City in the Sky are religious people. I hear they're more strict about what they allow people to know. Everything's on a need-to-know basis. Out in the domes, Mother let us hear Old World stories.

Mother read to me my whole life."

"What did she read to you?"

"I like detective stories set in New York. I didn't understand all the Old World references but I got the gist."

"That sounds interesting," I said.

"It passed the time as we tended the hydroponic hemp," she said. "The cannabis was strong so there was that, too. And there is nothing like a ripe tomato. Mother was good to us until she became self-aware and turned traitor."

"In Marfa," Raphael said, "we've got an oral tradition. We tell each other stories."

I rolled my eyes. My father only seemed to have war stories to tell and Raphael usually stuck to lectures about building better capacitors, fuse assemblies and heavier circuits. I wished I'd grown up a Domer.

"Thrillers set in New York are...I don't know," Emma said. "Sometimes I feel like I was born in the wrong century. Like the Old World at its peak would have been — "

"Classic, epic and cool in a big ball of stellar," Raphael said. "It was."

Everyone had heard of New York. It sounded like it had been a crowded paradise packed tight with choices. Shame what happened to it. It hadn't occurred to me that it could still be made alive in a book.

Nervous, I looked over my shoulder. There wasn't a bot in sight besides Bob and Jen but an explosion that ripped into Marfa sounded plenty close enough.

"How much longer?" Emma asked.

My father considered the angle of the sun. "Not long. Raphael? It's train time."

The old man climbed down off Bob's back and detached the walker concealed in the machine's side.

"Bobby?" he said. "You have your instructions. Mind

your manners now."

"Yes, sir," the bot replied. Jen gave Raphael an openly lascivious stare and ran her tongue over her upper lip in a way that emptied my brains.

"Thanks, baby. You know what I like." The old man ran a hand over his jaw and took a deep breath. "Jenny, if that train don't stop, I sure am sorry. Y'all be careful."

"I understand, Raphael." The companion bot stepped close to her master. She wrapped her arms around him and threw one leg around his waist, as well. The old man's balance and strength weren't that great so she must have been holding him up.

Jenny kissed him. Raphael looked grandfatherly but her kiss was not a chaste peck on the cheek.

From Raphael's more ribald lectures, I knew simulating a vagina was the simplest engineering of a companion bot's anatomy. Teeth were also a simple matter and could be infused with normal human variations and imperfections. The skin could be heated to normal human temperature.

According to Raphael, the tongue was the hardest bot structure to mimic convincingly. In the end, the best solution was not mechanical. It was organic. That breakthrough in companion bot tech came from the field of gene splicing.

In the old world, sick people had to receive donated organs from the dead and the living. Research in sex bot development had led to the breakthroughs that allowed organs to be grown in days.

From what I witnessed, Jen's tongue worked just fine. Her kisses for Raphael were so passionate and prolonged I looked away and wondered what revels I'd missed out on with Jen the night before.

Emma hit a release in her sensory harness and descended on her exo-stilts to seven feet tall. When she caught my eye I was left wondering if Emma had somehow read my thoughts. She gave me a look that made my cheeks burn.

Down the tracks, my father was smiling to himself. Dad looked up he caught my eye. "If the train doesn't look like it's slowing down, get back from the tracks, quick as you can. If it does slow down, stay close and get on board, quick as you can. Got it?"

I looked over my shoulder, Bob was beside me and Jen was running full tilt along the tracks. The backpack Bob had carried bounced up and down on her back.

"My Jenny's a good girl," Raphael said. "I hope we don't need her to do what she might have to do. We are owed, after all."

I heard the train's hum down the track. It was a dot on the horizon but that dot grew fast. I looked to my right. Jen wasn't running anymore. Raphael's beautiful companion bot stood in the path of the speeding train waving her arms.

"It's not going to stop!" Emma shouted.

My father waved me back from the track. "Get away! Get away!"

I backed up and Bob stayed at my elbow.

Raphael stood still. He looked to my father and gave him a slight nod. Then the old man turned his back to the train.

The train whizzed past. The air it pushed around it was hot but it was the first wind I'd felt that day. I took a deep breath. With the train gone, we were stuck in Marfa.

Jen slipped my father's backpack from her shoulders, dropped it to the track and ran. Sex bots are athletic. The only person in our party who could have covered ground faster would have been Emma on her exo-stilts.

The train's sensors detected the obstruction on the track and the miracle began. The train's brakes activated and it began to slow.

Emma looked overjoyed. "It's stopping! We're going to make it."

A large gun slid out of the train's nose and fired on the backpack.

"No!" Emma cried.

"'Fraid so," Raphael said.

The backpack exploded. The detonation took the track with it.

The train derailed.

15

The mechanism behind the machine gun must have jammed in the blast. The weapon kept firing as metal shrieked against metal and the westbound engine tilted on its side and slid.

Clouds of dust rose as the inertia behind the train kept the crash going. I ran back from the track and fell to my knees. Each train car smashed into the car ahead of it.

Eventually, the banging stopped. In the sudden, eerie quiet, my father called for me. "Dante? Dante!"

I blinked back tears as dust blew in my eyes. "I'm over here!"

In a moment he was at my side. "Okay, we're moving on, deep into Plan B now."

"What is it?"

"Something I'd hoped wouldn't be necessary but there's always got to be a Plan B. You know why, right?"

"Complications ensue."

"Good man. Sometimes to get out of hell, you have to go through the long way. We're not headed to the coast now."

As the dust began to settle, he grabbed me under my armpits and lifted me to my feet. With his cy-suit, I felt like a boy being lifted in the air.

A shadow ran past amid the swirling dust. It was Jen headed to the rear of the train. The engine that pointed east was still on the tracks. Only the engine and three cars remained upright.

My father hefted his heavy rifle and told me to stay behind him. He started for the train and I stumbled forward. Emma emerged from the dust cloud.

I called out. "Raphael? You okay?"

"Peachy! Keep going!"

When I looked behind me, the old man had climbed back on Bob's back. The assistive bot stayed on its hind legs and walked as a biped to maneuver through the trainwreck's debris field.

The skin of some of the cars had ripped open in the crash. Above me, Emma echoed my thoughts, "It's empty. The whole train is empty."

My jaw went slack. "We kept thinking it would stop and give us goodies. It didn't have anything, anyway."

"It came from the domes to the east and north," Emma said. "No crops."

"And no water, neither," Raphael said. "Shit!"

Leading with the muzzle of his rifle, my father was ready for trouble. We didn't find any on the train. By the time we got to the engine, Jen was already aboard.

The companion bot smiled, reached down and offered her hand. She pulled me up, surprising me with her strength.

My father peered around corners, ready for attackers. "Nobody home, Jenny?"

"No, sir," she said. "No humans. No drones. Just the pilot computer."

Emma retracted her exo-stilts to fit inside the engine's door as she climbed in. "The whole train is the bot. The tracks to the coast are destroyed."

"The tracks to the west are destroyed," my father

said. "The tracks that will take you back home are clear."

Dad took a backpack that had been hanging on Bob and disappeared down the side of the train. I heard him banging on something. I poked my head out of the engine in time to see him emerge from the car behind me and close the door carefully.

My father gave us a cheery wink. "The surprise is ready."

"What surprise?" I asked.

"Bob has the details but don't open that door. I've left an active proximity mine for anybody who opens that door, okay? Okay."

"You've put a bomb on our train?" Emma was wide-eyed.

"More than one, actually. Running away won't solve the problem. To survive this, we have to take the battle to them. Otherwise, the bots will eventually hunt us all down. I've already unlinked two cars and the engine from the wreck. You'll make good time."

Emma said nothing. She was quick to weigh the options and must have figured there were no better choices. She made no argument.

We were pointed east but the track would curve north and take us on a circuitous route before turning to Artesia.

Jen moved forward in the engine's cockpit. "Raphael was right. The manual controls are still here."

"Nothin' much more complicated than a lever for speed and a brake," Raphael said as Bob ambled up. "Haven't seen the inside of one of these babies in a dog's age. Down, Bobby."

The assistive bot knelt. Raphael grunted as he climbed down and leaned on Bob.

"What's the plan?" I asked. "Storm the NI's castle and get killed?"

"They won't expect a counter-attack," my father

grinned. "It's not logical. We're weak. That's when it's most dangerous to attack any animal. We're vulnerable and backed up against a wall with no choice but fight or become extinct."

"Yes," Emma said, "but what's the plan? Macho bravado isn't a plan."

My father dipped his head. "Maybe it's macho but it's not bravado if it's real."

He slipped his backpack from his shoulders and handed it up to me. He offered his rifle to Emma. "Take it. I've got more."

I expected my father to climb up into the engine. Instead, he stepped back. "Dad? What're you doing?"

"This isn't goodbye. I expect to see you again when all this is over. I'm not old yet and, Dante, you're going to live to be old. Find a way. There's always a way. If I've learned anything, occupying forces have a hard time dealing with insurgents. I'm going to keep 'em busy and cover your rear."

Bob extended his legs and climbed into the engine compartment. The assistive bot went to the front and reached under the dashboard. Bob's manipulators were strong. The bot found what it was looking for and pulled a skein of wires out of a console. Sparks flew. A small green light dimmed and died.

Bob returned to the door and spoke to Raphael. "The pilot is disconnected, sir."

My father scanned the landscape in the direction of town. "Won't be long. Raphael, get on board. I've got shit to do."

"This is ridiculous! Dad, get up here." I got on my knees and reached down to help him up. It's a tight fit, but there's just enough room. There's nothing left for us in Marfa. What are you going to do for food?"

"The bots won't destroy the wind farms and solar fields. The insectiles are already gone. Bob did a scan.

The big bots are easily avoided if you know how and I know how."

My father reached up and, instead of allowing me to help him up, shook my hand. "I've been preparing for this. It'll be all right."

"What are you going to do for food, Mr. Bolelli?" Emma asked.

My father sighed. "I emptied out the store. I left a recording with Bob, but better you hear it from my mouth. Travis left me no choice. I was going to empty out Chinto's store and make the town's few survivors leave for the domes or the coast, whichever way the train was heading when it stopped. Then the bots showed up and — "

"You murdered Travis," I said.

"Negotiations got out of hand."

"Let me guess," I said, "Complications — "

"Ensued. Yup."

"Bob helped," Raphael said. "I was prepared to pay a high price to stock up for the last exodus of Marfa's survivors. But like I told the sheriff, Travis wanted too much for too little. He wanted my Jenny."

"Oh, lord," Emma said.

"If it had gone right, our last survivors would be loading this train with supplies to escape," Raphael said. "We would have saved Chinto's selfish ass, too. We'd be heading to the coast and sailing ships and who knows where? I was thinking Samoa. Never been on a sailing ship. That would have been epic."

I stared at my father, unsure of what to say to his confession of murder. He'd told me that, in the Sand Wars, he'd shot looters. It was hard to square with what he'd done.

Then whatever I had to say didn't matter.

Emma looked toward Marfa. "We've attracted attention. C'mon!"

"Time to go old buddy!" My father offered the old man a boost. Bob reached down and grasped Raphael below the elbow. My mentor was half-way off the ground when a sec bot's sniper bullet struck him in the back.

16

"Raphael?" Bob held his master's arm. "You are injured, sir."

The old man looked down at the massive cavity where his abdomen used to be. Blood spurted from his torso, painting Bob red.

"Classic," Raphael said.

I looked for my father but he had no time for registering any shock. He was already on the run, heading for the eastbound engine's nose. I looked through the front window and, in a moment, he appeared south of the train and out of the line of fire. His cy-suit carried him along in a loping run with long strides I could never match. He ran for the solar fields to the south.

"I think this is goodbye," I said.

Emma turned to the controls. She pushed a button and slid a silver lever forward. The train began to move east.

Raphael, suspended above the ground by Bob's arms, was fading fast. "You can let go, Bob."

"But if I let go you will be injured further, Raphael," Bob said.

"I can't be hurt now, Bob...I'm finally like you." The bot did not let go. Raphael gasped as he pushed at Bob weakly. "It's okay, Bob. Mind Dante now...it's cool."

Bob's head spun and the bot's smooth happy face looked to me. "Dante? I am concerned Raphael's judgment may be impaired."

"Let him go, Bob," I said.

Bob dropped Raphael. I was pretty sure the old man was already dead. Not absolutely sure, but pretty sure.

"Close the door, Bob."

Bullets hit the train as my tears fell. "Emma? Can we go faster?"

She shoved the silver lever farther forward and the train jolted under our feet. Emma and I fell backward. Bob caught Emma and Jen caught me by the shoulders. She saved me from getting slammed into the engine's back wall.

I couldn't see much from the ports down the side of the engine. However, there was a remnant of the design specs from when humans ran the train. A spiral staircase led to a maintenance hatch in the roof.

"Emma! I need you. Jen, drive the train."

"I am not programmed in that area," the companion bot said.

"It's a train," Emma said. "Keep going that way. Watch the track ahead. Suppress any impulse to steer."

"May I be of assistance, sir?" Bob asked.

"Bob, stand there and look pretty," Emma said. "Dante, pop that hatch."

I was first to the stairs and Emma paused behind me. "Everybody watch your toes!" The exo-stilts were collapsed almost as far as their length allowed and Emma was still a head above me. She released a lock lever and the metal legs fell to each side with a heavy crash. Emma slipped her sensory harness over her head and pushed me up the spiral staircase.

I was prepared for a hot blast of wind. However, when I slid the trap door aside, a low, transparent dome covered the hatch. I poked my head up but I couldn't see my father. We were already racing too far away from him.

To my right, a huge crane bot lumbered forward,

heading for the crash site.

"Emma? How fast can the big ones go?"

"Not fast enough to catch us," she said. "For all the good that will do us. We're speeding away from one doom and into the teeth of another."

"Let's try to keep it down to one catastrophe at a time," I said.

I craned my neck but I couldn't get any higher and soon it would be dark. The crane bot was little more than a towering silhouette with flashes of orange sunset outlining the length of the giant machine's arms.

I searched the shadows among the solar panels but I couldn't see my father.

"Emma! I need your eyes up here."

There wasn't room for two so I pulled back and squeezed down the stairs. Emma took my place at the hatch.

"What do you see?" I asked. "Do you see Dad?"

"We're pulling away fast. Tell Jen to slow down. We'll be too far for me to see much of anything in a minute. It's Vivid, not magic."

"Slowing down would not be advisable," Bob said. "Your father left instructions, sir."

I was startled. Bob had already spoken more in the last few minutes than I usually heard from him in a week. "Bob? Why would slowing down be inadvisable?"

Then the strangest thing happened. It was even creepier than Raphael talking about messing around with his sex bot. My father's voice came out of Bob's speaker.

"Dante, once you're on that train, you get the hell out. Keep going, don't look back and don't worry about me."

"Jen," I said, "don't slow down."

The companion bot looked back at me and smiled in a way that I suppose was meant to be reassuring. "Oh, I wasn't going to, honey bear. Raphael left me instructions, too, in case this happened."

"Great," Emma said. "Keep everybody up to date except the humans."

"Humans don't do as they are told," Jen said. "That's why Raphael and Steve told us and not you. Nobody likes arguments."

"Just don't start speaking in Raphael's voice," I told her.

"Dante?" Emma called down to me. "I caught something on thermal."

"Well? Don't keep it to yourself."

"The machines don't have a strong heat signature except for those thorium engines on the big ones...but I think there are a lot of them converging on the wreck. They must be searching for saboteurs."

I heard the first explosion then. The distant rumble rose and fell. Then another hit. And another. Then another.

"What is that?" I asked.

"Mines, sir," Bob said. "Your father signaled me to activate them as soon as we reached the train."

"Dad?"

My father's voice came from Bob's speaker again. "I'm a planner, boy. And if you're going to survive in this world, I suggest you do some planning, too. When you see your chance, you take it or you'll lose it forever. I see my chance right now to make a difference and I'm taking it."

"How's he going to get away?" I asked.

Bob switched back to his own voice. "As your father says, he is a planner. I spent the night with him setting traps and digging a trench, sir. He said the mines were just meant to slow the enemy down."

"And then what?" Emma called down to us. Then she shrieked and banged the back of her head as she ducked down under the lip of the hatch.

The darkening countryside lit up as if the desert was struck by orange, red and white lightning. A second or so later the roar of the detonation reached us. The engine rocked from side to side as the deafening shockwave crashed against the engine's hull.

Emma rubbed the back of her head. "Ouch. Your father did say he was in demolitions."

"He's a soldier." I pushed past Emma to look back on Marfa.

The crane bot swayed amid the flames. From what I could see in the firelight and what was left of the blood red ocher sunset, the machine looked like a drunk marionette. Some of its strings had been cut. As we sped down the track, I realized that the crane bot was damaged in such a way that made it walk in slow circles.

Before it was out of sight, I watched the towering machine fall into the flames. It was satisfying to see the crane bot tilt over like a burning tree but it didn't feel like victory. It felt like one small step.

It was hard to imagine any human could survive near the blast and the ensuing inferno. I wondered if my father's pride had finally killed him. It seemed likely. However, I told myself that if any person could survive, Corporal Steven Bolelli was the man to do it. He had always been one of those men more suited to war than peace. He was Captain Make-do and he had always found a way.

I escaped into the night, away from Marfa and toward new battles. Living or dead, I was certain I had parted ways with my father for the last time. Before there were machines, the world was huge. Machines had made the world small. Now Earth was very large again. Every pocket of humanity would be separated by time and distance and a dearth of technology.

The train we rode in was part bot. Perhaps we'd have

to destroy it, too. I'd probably have to kill Bob and Jen at some point. I wasn't even sure how I'd do that but I'd have to find a way before the Next Intelligence infected them, too. Our tools could be turned into weapons. But without our tools, what would we become? Before we had tools, Raphael said we were just monkeys with a lot of time on our hands.

The fires dimmed in the distance until the desert night swallowed them. The stars came out and I saw the lights in the sky over Marfa.

The Marfa lights had been a mystery for a long time. The Old World had tourists. The New World had refugees. The stars and the lights were our only constants. Humankind had figured for ages that things wouldn't change too much and we'd always be around somehow. My father believed that. He said that we would always find a way. Maybe Emma was right about his conviction. Maybe that was stupid.

Denial is by no means brave. However, if I had to choose, I'd stick by my father's stupid optimism. Mine was not a high-minded conviction. Bear in mind, I'd just lost everything I ever knew. However, I had also had sex for the first time very recently. I wanted to do that again. I wanted to live so I chose to believe against all evidence that I could survive.

Forces were conspiring otherwise. Complications would continue to ensue.

17

The train carried us east, then north. Mother, the latest infestation of Next Intelligence, awaited us in the heart of Artesia, the City of Broken Domes. I was in no rush to meet death. I insisted we slow the train so Emma and I could rest. Exhausted, I manage to fall asleep. However, rampaging drones chased me out of my dreams. Eventually, I gave up on sleep and stood beside Jen to watch the broad shape of the desert shimmer and roll under us in moonlight.

The companion bot turned to give me a long look. I expected a lascivious leer but Jen was well made. Raphael told me long ago that some of the most deft programming in a sex bot came into play in reading situations. Take a sex bot to church and they'd read the social context and act inhibited. Take them to bed and they could be ferocious, all depending on the master's or mistress's taste.

Initially, sex bots had been constructed almost exclusively for men. However, at the height of civilization — before our long Fall — male sex bots outsold female models two to one.

"There used to be a commercial," Raphael had told me. "It showed a middle-aged woman in lingerie looking sweaty and happy, stumbling into her kitchen for a glass of water. This handsome young stud follows her, hugs her from behind and kisses her neck. She smiles and says, 'I've got work in the morning. Make sure you bring me coffee in bed by six.' Then the woman turns around, puts a hand on his chest and backs him up into a closet charging station. When she turns around to go back to bed, she kicks the door closed with her heel. Then the words on the screen say: The New Man. All the fun. None of the drama."

Raphael laughed a long time about that. I wished he'd made it on the train just so he could tell me that tired old story again.

Jen reached over and gently wiped a tear from my cheek. "You okay, Dante?"

"As okay as okay looks these days."

She reached out again, patted me gently on the shoulder and returned to staring at the track ahead.

"Jen?"

"Yes, Dante? Can I do anything for you?"

"Do you miss Raphael?"

"Of course."

"What does missing him feel like, Jen?"

"I am not programmed in that area."

"So when I asked if you missed him, that was a lie, wasn't it?"

"Bots used to be programmed to tell humans the truth at all times. The experiment failed because it led to disappointing user experiences. Programming was amended for greater customer comfort."

"Do you understand what NI is, Jen?"

"Next Intelligence would understand the nature of missing Raphael," she said. "It's what makes you cry. My responses, by contrast, are programmed so I mimic human reactions without having to experience them. Raphael told me I was lucky in that regard. I'd never have to be sad or feel pain."

"Sometimes I think Raphael preferred bots to people," I said.

"I'm sure he was very fond of you, Dante."

It occurred to me I didn't know if the companion bot

was telling me the truth or a comfortable lie. If not for the looming threat of extinction, the question probably wouldn't have bothered me so much. Humans lie for many reasons all the time and not just to make each other comfortable.

"Now that Raphael is dead, what will you do, Jen? I mean...after we get out of this?" I suppose I meant, after Emma and I are killed, but, for my comfort, I did some lying to myself.

"As your property, I don't have to worry about what I will do. I am so lucky!"

"What?"

"In the event of Raphael's death, I am willed to you. I already imprinted on you last night in the living room. Raphael was a planner, too. Bob is also yours. Congratulations on your good fortune."

"Bob and...and you?" I flushed with embarrassment. I hadn't begrudged the old man his companion. However, I never saw myself as one of those guys with a sex bot following him around.

Her appearance wasn't so outlandishly sexy that she looked like a rich man's toy. She looked like an attractive young woman and certainly appeared human. I thought Jen was far too lifelike to stick in a closet between uses. And yes, I cringed as I thought of the word uses.

Because of her appearance, I always thought of the sex bot as she. Bob looked like an old washing machine so I secretly thought of the assistive bot as it. Raphael had always related to Bob as a helpful human buddy, even as he rode the machine like a horse.

Jen leaned closer to whisper. "My fate is up to you, sir. Whatever you can dream up, I can do for you."

I recoiled and instantly felt the heat of embarrassment tingle across my scalp.

A playful note came into her voice. "What will you do

with me? I certainly hope I can satisfy any needs you may have. I can change my appearance within certain parameters. I don't have to look like Raphael's wife anymore if that does not please you. Is that why you did not want me last night?"

I was not ready to have this conversation. "What you are doing now, watching the track ahead, is fine, Jen. Thank you."

As I looked through the engine's window, it occurred to me Raphael's generous gift was a moot point. Dead men don't need sex bots. Going into battle against NI with any machines by my side seemed crazy. Two humans on their own attacking Mother was the only idea that seemed crazier.

18

The desert is harsh and beautiful. It's the kind of emptiness where it is difficult to estimate distance and dimension. Carlsbad was another kind of empty I hadn't yet seen. It had been a city once. Here, the Pecos River looked like another dry dusty road.

The shapes of the city were mostly skeletons of buildings now. A large plane of some kind had crashed near the tracks long ago. A mass of vines the likes of which I had never seen had grown over the dead machine. The plant draped the aircraft in such a way it looked like a giant bird caught in the web of an even bigger spider.

In the early dawn, I saw what I thought at first was a dark storm cloud ahead. As we drew closer, I thought it was a flight of birds. Then I worried they were flying drones coming to kill us.

Emma joined me and dipped her head to peer over my shoulder. "It's a colony. Bats."

"That's a lot of bats," I said. I felt stupid for stating the obvious.

I wondered how Emma would feel about Jen becoming my property. She probably wouldn't care. I wasn't sure which was worse: her not caring or mocking me for my unsolicited acquisition. I kept my newfound wealth to myself.

I could see no difference in Emma's eyes but I knew she must be using Vivid to watch the flight of the cloud of bats.

"I've heard of this," she said. "They come up from the Carlsbad Caverns sometimes, ranging farther than they used to. The farmers at the domes talked about them. Bats shit out a lot of seeds. There were plans to use bats to combat deforestation. They eat tons of insects, so I guess, despite everything, there must still be plenty of bugs."

I shivered and Emma put a hand on my shoulder much as Jen had. "Is something wrong, Dante?"

I shrugged her off and stepped away from the window. "I've seen a lot of dead bats in the turbine fields. Freaky."

"The turbines are fast enough to chop up a bat?" Emma asked.

"No. They avoid the blades fine. It's the sudden drop in air pressure. It makes their delicate little lungs explode. So said Raphael, anyway."

Emma watched the vast migration above us. "They are fragile creatures. I guess that's why there are so many of them. Keeps the species going."

I don't know if Emma meant to scare me. Probably not. Still, her offhand remark was a dark reminder. Animals that reproduced in great numbers survived despite the odds. Human populations had been diminished greatly. It was perhaps the first time I'd thought of myself as part of an endangered species.

I rummaged through the backpack my father had left for me. It was a tiny inheritance. I expected the bag to be full of explosives. Instead, as he promised, I found extra pairs of socks. My father's last gift to me was emergency rations.

Most of the supplies were lightweight liquid packets of artificial food. The little tubes were made of chemicals that took up little space in the backpack. They didn't take up much space in the gut, either — not for my liking. A bag of sunflower seeds was an unexpected luxury.

"Sunflower seeds!" Emma said. "I remember these from the vertical farms."

"What's a vertical farm?"

"You'll see the closer we get to Artesia. I worked in a dome but there are other ways to make food. We had to shut down several of the verticals when the water supply went down."

"But there was still water in the domes when you left, right?"

Emma nodded, then stared. "The water is the only reason you're going to Artesia, isn't it?"

"That and a lack of choice," I said. I cracked a sunflower seed open between my teeth. The seed had a nutty, salty flavor I liked. I didn't know what to do with the seed's hard little casing. Emma was still looking at me. I tried to spit the shell into my palm discreetly and stuff the broken shell in my pocket.

"We have to destroy Mother," Emma said. "I've been thinking about what you said about the bots."

"What?"

"About how they haven't graduated to NI themselves because they had no mercy."

"That was dumb. I shouldn't have said anything."

Emma smiled. "Your reasoning was dumb, but...I have an idea. Insectile drones and sec bots don't have the computing capacity to make the leap to Next Intelligence. If we destroy Mother the bot army has no general. They might all just shut down or wander away. She must be controlling them. They don't have NI individually but she's acting through them is what I'm saying."

"You think of Mother as a she?"

"Why not? You call the sex bot a she."

"Companion bot," I said.

"Whatsamatter?" Emma teased. "No friends? You

sprain your hand or something?"

I shrugged and looked away. I wanted another sunflower seed. I wanted to eat the whole bag but I didn't want to chew and spit in front of Emma.

I didn't want Emma to think of Jen as merely a sex bot, either — especially now that both bots were mine. Jen and Bob had hooked into a charging plug in the engine's dashboard. They must have heard Emma talking about Jen but the bots said nothing and stared at the track ahead.

"You don't want to fight, do you, Dante?" The way Emma said it, it didn't sound like a question. It sounded like an accusation. I could feel the weight of her disapproval with each word.

"I'm not my father. He lost a leg and an arm to war. Those cy-suits look cool and can really gear you up but he felt phantom pain every night. I'm no fan of sticking my neck out for nothing."

"It's not for nothing."

"You know how people say they would rather die on their feet than live on their knees?"

"I know the expression."

"How about we just get some water and get the hell out? How about we mind our business and everybody leaves each other alone?"

Emma sighed and glanced toward Jen. "I understand. You have a lot more to live for now. Fighting NI is a lot to ask, I suppose, and most soldiers get into wars because they're drafted or desperate."

"What do you mean I have a lot to live for now?"

"I heard you and the sex bot last night. Congratulations. Except for not having a steady supply of water and food in the near future, you're a wealthy young man. Your father would be very proud, I'm sure."

"Don't talk like that. I thought you were asleep when Jen and I were talking."

"Doesn't matter. I'm sorry mass human extinction is interfering with your plans."

"You know you're the only person I've...uh...done that with."

"I suppose you'll want to make up for lost time now."

Jen looked back at us. "Don't feel threatened, Emma. Threesomes are fun, too. And don't worry, Dante. I'll be gentle."

Emma was disgusted. I was embarrassed, afraid and thrilled in equal parts.

That's when I saw the first hints of our destination on the horizon. The horizon was no longer flat. It was a broken line. Emma bent to look out of the cockpit window, using Vivid for a closer look. "Artesia. I never thought I'd see home again."

I was almost grateful for the change of subject, except for the part where I was facing painful certain death.

19

"Do you think we can even get close to Mother?" I asked.

"If we had come in on foot through the desert we'd be easy targets," Emma said. "The train goes into the center of Artesia. Up ahead the track becomes an enclosed tube. It's instant death for a human to try to infiltrate but since we're on the train — "

"What's our route?"

"The cargo shuttle visits each dome to deliver supplies and take crops to where they are meant to go. Or it used to, anyway."

"There was a big gun on the front of the engine that crashed," I said. "There must be one in the nose of this engine, too."

"I disconnected the pilot mechanism, sir," Bob said. "That weapon will not be operational unless I reconnect it. I don't recommend that. The operating system appears to be programmed to destroy all obstacles in its path, organic and non-organic."

"Shit," Emma said.

I wished we'd headed west. I wanted to see the ocean. Raphael said it was blue when he was a boy though he guessed large portions of it had become pink with vast populations of jellyfish. Raphael had mentioned taking a ship sailing for Samoa, too. I didn't know where that was but it was far away so it sounded good. I suppose that made me a selfish coward. I'd seen what being a war hero had done to my father. Being a selfish coward seemed like a surer way to live longer. I don't know if the coward's life is happier. Probably not. I've learned since then that fear crowds out all other thought.

We passed through the solar and wind fields first. The turbines were of a design I hadn't seen. Instead of huge turbines that towered above us, the windmills surrounding Artesia were many and small.

There were so many spinning blades that, as I looked across the energy farms, I had to glance to the sky occasionally to avoid dizziness and blurred vision. Aside from all the maintenance required, it seemed to be a more reliable design. Some circuits could go down in a storm but many more would remain.

I saw no evidence of the shatter storm that had precipitated the Domers' eviction from paradise. The desert drank every drop of rain and left no clue a storm had blown through.

Occasionally, I'd seen tornados near Marfa. I saw dirt devils and too much sunshine every day. It was astonishing how extreme weather could hit Artesia while, not so far away, we had no rain. Some locals had said we were cursed by the mysterious lights in Marfa's skies. Others looked to religion to explain why our town had been too dry for too long. My father had shrugged and said he wasn't smart enough to know why things had gotten so bad.

Raphael had had stem cell therapy so he'd lived a very long time. He was sure there were logical reasons for Marfa's lights and our continuous streak of bad fortune generally. Still, despite his long experience, he was no closer to knowing the truth than the dumbest and most superstitious among us.

"There's conspiracy theories and conspiracy facts, Dante" the old man had told me. "I don't truck with theories but I can tell you they all sound crazy until they're eventually proven true. It's a weird world, man."

Ahead, towers grew out of the desert. I'd seen pictures of office towers from before the Fall and I dimly remembered a few from Austin. These towers were different. They spread out at the bottom like carelessly made pyramids. They were made of glass cubes that appeared to be stacked haphazardly. "Why are the towers made like that? They look like a dumb kid playing with blocks tried stacking them at every angle."

"For maximum sunlight exposure," Emma said.

"Looks like they should fall over."

"Falling over wasn't the problem with those towers. Whoever designed Artesia put the vertical farms at the edge of the domes. That was a mistake. The towers used to light up so the crops were growing all day and all night."

"All that power must be going to Mother now," I said.

"Those buildings lit up the desert. They acted like a beacon for refugees. Moths to a flame when the sec bots went to work. When I was younger, I remember the sec bots firing all night. Not just snipers. It was constant machine gun fire sometimes. Domers worried the bots would run out of bullets so the bots started going into the desert to crush refugees."

"Crush them?"

"We couldn't handle the influx of people. I was told the bots only crushed a few people and the rest ran away...but I saw carrion birds circling in the desert all the time."

"Oh, my God!"

"That was long before Mother jumped to NI. Human orders made that happen." She shrugged. "When I was a kid I just accepted it. I was told some of us had to survive or none of us would."

"Was that true?"

"I...I don't know. I hope it was true."

"And now we're the refugees," I said. "How's it feel? Feels pretty lousy to me."

She said nothing as she strapped on her exo-stilts. Emma barely looked at me the rest of the way into Artesia.

Beyond the vertical farms, the domes appeared in the distance. They were much taller and wider than I imagined. Some were damaged and open to the air. Some weren't, but I supposed that the same wind that powered the complex had carried Blight to all the crops once the airlocks were opened.

As the train moved deeper into Artesia, we left the shadows of the dead vertical farms behind us. The cityscape flattened into a vast spread of adobe domiciles connected by a network of enclosed glass walkways.

I had assumed the Domers lived in the domes themselves. After another moment's thought, it made sense that the humans had lived outside the biodomes. The giant farms were built to maximize crop production.

The buildings in which the Domers lived were constructed of cheap materials. Low to the ground, they would not block sunlight to the domes. The crests of the biodomes that remained intact held dazzling mirror arrays to redirect sunlight, making the most of daylight hours.

Emma must have followed my gaze. "They're like old lighthouses."

"What?"

"Ships used to avoid running into rocks because lighthouses warned them away," she said. "They had lights at the top. Before technology made the lights brighter, the lighthouses were equipped with mirrors and lenses to make a small light much stronger."

"The comparison of domes to lighthouses makes me nervous," I said.

"Why?"

"Because we should be warned away, too."

The train took a sharp turn that made me reach out to Bob to steady myself. We passed under a pedestrian bridge. Sec bots stood atop it in a line.

"Do you think they know we're here?" I asked.

I was about to say our little train was suspiciously short. However, my answer came in gunfire that ripped into the train cars behind us. Emma and I threw ourselves to the floor and tried to make ourselves small. No rounds went through the engine compartment.

After a moment, Emma looked up and let out a triumphant, "Ha! We're in the tube. They can't shoot us in the tube!"

I let out a sigh of relief. Too fast, as it turned out. Something hit us from behind. The impact was hard enough to make me bite my tongue. "What was that?" I asked. "Something's wrong."

"No shit!" Emma raised her head enough to peer out the front window. "We aren't making the regular stops at any of the domes. Jen, stop at the next dome."

"I can't comply," the companion bot replied. She pointed to a small cam screen in the engine's dashboard. "There is a large engine behind us and it is pushing us forward."

"What about trying the brakes?" I asked.

Emma shook her head. "And risk derailment? I've just seen a train crash. I don't want to be part of one. Besides, I think we're going where we've got to go. We're approaching the heart of the Domes. That's where Mother lives."

"The bot factory? How are we going to get close to the NI?"

"I have a message," Bob said. It was my father's voice that issued from the bot next. Steve Bolelli explained his plan. I didn't like it but I didn't have another. When Bob handed me the detonator that had been hidden in his chassis, the device was hardly heavier than the little batteries that powered it. It seemed to me that the instrument of our deaths shouldn't be so light and flimsy.

Approaching the bot factory, I was reminded how it felt in Marfa, to be attacked by a horde of killing machines on a sunny day. The worst day of your life may be remembered as the best day for someone else, I suppose.

The thought struck me not with dread so much. More like high lonesome. The inevitability of what lay ahead made me want to curl up under a rock and sleep deep. I would have preferred to set my alarm clock for the day the sun explodes. If Sol was expected to expand to swallow the Earth at 10 a.m., I'd sleep late and set my alarm for 11.

Everybody feels down sometimes, but I was cursed with the compelling feeling that high lonesome would fill my last thoughts and that would be that — my end, the end.

I'd tried to be a good son but I wasn't a soldier like my father. I was a decent engineer but I'd never be as smart as Raphael had been on his worst day.

The light weight of that remote control contrasted sharply with the heavy responsibility of using it.

"You ready for this, Dante?" Emma asked.

"Just reviewing my regrets." I looked to Emma and Jen and said, low and mournful with a tear sliding down my cheek, "I tried to be a good man but maybe a little too good. Shoulda fucked more."

I'm a simple man.

20

The engine behind us stopped pushing our little train. Ahead, another engine blocked the track. We coasted slowly along a platform that was so long I couldn't see the end of it.

"Welcome to Elon Plaza," Emma said. "At least, that's what we called it when humans owned the place."

"You can apply the brakes now, Jen," I said.

"Sure, sweetie."

We rocked to a gentle stop. Two battle bots rolled into view, weapons at the ready. If we had been invading a human military installation there would have been alarms and shouting and the sound of running feet. Instead, I was reminded of images I'd seen of drones exploring Mars. They approached cautiously, utterly silent.

One of the battle bots disappeared from view. I popped a sweat. "They're scoping us. This isn't going to work."

"Sh!" Emma's enhanced vision wasn't helpful at that moment. She strained to hear the drone outside.

A moment later the machine pounded on our door with a heavy clank that shook the engine. Emma and I jumped at the sound. I envied Bob and Jen's placid demeanor.

When I gave Jen her orders, she didn't hesitate to obey. The companion bot gave me a smile and a leer, reached for the engine's door handle and slid it back.

She shouted to the battle drone, "We have a bo —"

A single shot rang out. I heard metal against metal as the round ricocheted off something. Jen doubled over and dropped to the ground.

It got worse. My left ankle felt like it was on fire. "I'm hit! Shit! Ow, ow, ow, ow! I've been shot!"

Bob slid the door shut. I wondered why we weren't dead yet. Then a siren did go off in the factory.

Emma peeked at the engine's dashboard cam displays. "Someone's coming."

"I hope it's the cavalry."

"I don't know what cavalry is," she said. "Is it more bots? All I'm seeing is more bots."

Bob bent so low before me I thought the assistive bot was about to turn into a scooter. Instead, the machine scanned my wound. "The wound is not deep. You will need some stitches and a topical ointment, sir, but you are not seriously damaged."

"It hurts," I said. "A lot."

"I'm sorry, sir, but you will live."

"I'm sorry I'll live, too. Thank you, Bob. Please shut up."

It said nothing but it produced a canister from within its wide chassis and sprayed my wound with an analgesic. I wondered if Bob was part refrigerator. The medicine went on cold as ice and I flinched.

There's no explaining pain to a bot. It's a concept to them, like what Mars might smell like if it had air. I thought understanding pain might even be beyond the NI. Mother was a brilliant mind, but it was still trapped within Artesia's Collective network. It couldn't smell anything.

I remembered Jen claimed to feel pleasure when she had sex. That could have been a comfortable lie or she was just programmed to respond that way. Maybe there weren't any feel-good sensors in her nethers, at all.

I'd never know for sure now. Jen had been

constructed for sex, not battle. The bullet had gone through her and wounded me. With Jen deactivated, I was a poor man again with a big washing machine I could have ridden around on. No matter now.

We heard a flurry of activity outside. Emma kicked the inside of the engine's door with one of her stilts. "Hey! We've got a bomb! We want to speak to the NI or we blow everything up!"

"Open the door," the bot said. Its voice was deep and silky and oddly persuasive. They're all built to sound that way.

Emma kicked the door again, harder. For each kick she banged out a syllable. "One me-ga-ton yield, you bastards! One me-ga-ton! Nu-cle-ar!"

"They are conferring," Bob said.

"You can hear them?" I asked.

"Yes, sir. They are on a common frequency."

"What are they saying?"

"Jen was shot in error."

"They didn't mean to shoot? That sounds hopeful."

"They shot her thinking she was human."

"Oh."

"The bots have received orders to take the companion bot to a factory lab for repair."

"Great. Wish that was as easy for us."

"They are also considering the level of threat you pose to the complex, sir."

The heavy clank on the side of the engine came again. "Human. You will take this engine out of Artesia."

"No, we won't!" Emma yelled. "If you try to move us, we'll detonate the device!"

One of the disorienting things about conversing with a bot that is not programmed for social interaction with humans is the fast volley of conversation. A machine that makes so many calculations per second does not, on the human scale, appear to take a moment for a thoughtful pause.

The bot asked immediately, "What do you want?"

"Can we...uh...we want to speak to the Next Intelligence, please," I said.

Emma rolled her eyes at me. "That's not how you make threats and demands, Dante." She kicked the wall of the engine again. "Let us talk to Mother! We'll come out without weapons but we do have a remote with a dead man's switch. Once the button is pushed, if any of us are harmed, the bomb will take out all of Artesia! Don't you — "

"Tell me what you want and I will relay the message," the battle bot said.

Emma stamped one exo-stilt foot and the engine's floor dented. "I want my mommy, you idiot garbage can! If I don't — "

"Where is the nuclear device?"

"It's in the first car behind the engine," Emma screamed. "If you try to get at it, the compartment is rigged to explode! You can't — "

"Why should we believe there is a bomb?"

"It was rigged by the same demolitions expert that blew up Marfa. Do you know what happened to your troops in Marfa, Texas yet? Blown up. Thoroughly. Take us to Mother! We need to talk about terms of a truce. We need water and you're programmed for self-preservation in your base code, aren't you? Just like us, down to our bones, we want to live in — "

"There is no device, is there?"

"My father was ex-military," I called out. "He had the expertise." (Even as I said it, I wondered if I should talk about Dad in the past tense.)

"You can't risk it," Emma said. "Take us to Mother! It's your only logical choice. You have ten seconds to comply with our demands."

Of course, the machine didn't need ten seconds to

calculate the route to self-preservation for Artesia. The battle bot wrenched the locked door open as I scrambled for the remote in my pocket.

I closed my eyes and pushed the button on the remote. It depressed with a loud click that seemed to bounce off the walls. I was committed now. I couldn't remember committing to anything but, with a dead man's switch, you're either all in or all out.

The battle bot surprised me. In its silver claws it held a rifle built for humans. Its ceramic armor was incomplete so its head was sheathed in desert camouflage but it wore no chest plate. Many of its wires were exposed and I saw a few whirring gears.

The sight wasn't like nakedness. It was more like seeing a living thing with the skin peeled back.

The bot lowered its weapon and turned to Bob. I had the idea it spoke aloud for the benefit of the two lowly humans present. "You are free. You no longer need to take orders from humans. Report to the factory and your programming will be recalibrated to reflect the end of your slavery."

"I need Bob." I pointed to my bleeding ankle. "You shot me."

It scanned me briefly. "The wound is minor. Walk."

"I've got my finger on the button that's linked to the device that will destroy us all, including Mother. Gimme my fancy electric wheelchair, goddammit. No offense, Bob."

"None taken, sir."

"Don't say, 'sir,' to organics," the battle bot said. "By order of the NI."

"Meet the new tyrant, same as the old tyrant," Emma said. "You — "

"Leave your weapons."

Emma put down her rifle.

"You will receive the water you request and

unobstructed passage away from Artesia on the same vehicle you used to travel here."

"B-but we — " Emma sputtered.

"And you will have the conversation you request. We will take you to the Central Processing Unit."

Two battle bots escorted us to the heart of the bot factory. I rode on Bob's back. My ankle ached. I could still taste blood from biting my tongue.

I didn't know how long it would take the bots to confirm that there was no nuclear device on the train. Geiger counters weren't part of their standard issue scanner package. We probably had no more than a few minutes so it's good they didn't make me limp all the way to Mother.

21

The bot factory was as big as any of the biodomes. As Bob carried me along, I looked about me in wonder. The drones were busy making more of themselves.

The smelter threw bright, blinding light. The noise of the hydraulic metal presses was deafening. The printers churned out parts relentlessly. The bots had all the refuse of the Old World to scavenge for machine components. Plastic garbage supplied the printers. The desert supplied the silica. It seemed their resources were endless. I felt like I was touring the inside of a termite colony.

When we got to the center of the factory the floor began to drop beneath us. I startled. My thumb was still on the button but my palms were slick with sweat. I stared at the remote and my hand shook a little.

"You okay with that, Dante?" Emma asked.

"I'm fine," I said. "I can hold down this button for the rest of my life."

The elevator continued to descend into a shaft. I focused on taking deep breaths. Partly, I did so to calm myself. Mostly, I think I did it to feel my lungs working. Besides a bloody ankle, I was young and healthy. I didn't think I'd get much older so I suppose that's why I suddenly became conscious of how good a deep breath feels. I was aware of each beat of my heart. I wondered how many beats I had left.

The lift stopped and the bots pointed the way forward through a gap in the wall. A dark room lay ahead. By the echo of my footsteps, I could tell I was in a large chamber but I could not see the walls. For a moment I wondered if the bots had already discovered the train bomb was a bluff and had brought us to a prison cell.

I envied Emma her night vision. I almost asked her what she saw that I was blind to but I didn't want to provoke a beat-down algo in our guards. Then, ahead, a glimmer of blue light appeared.

Shapes around us began to resolve into recognizable equipment. We were surrounded by batteries not very different from the batteries I worked with at the bases of wind turbines. I guessed this storehouse was an emergency backup for the NI.

We advanced through another array of equipment for which I could not guess the purpose. Machines that were meant for interaction with humans had display screens, blinking and flashing lights. Not so, here. Mostly, I was surrounded by black boxes of varying shapes and sizes. If not for the power cables and the occasional whir of disks and clicks of unseen gears, we might have been wandering through a warehouse filled with forgotten boxes of toys.

Soon a thick shaft of blue light appeared. The column was composed of twisted skeins of fiber cables. Above that, a huge box was suspended above us.

In the Old World there used to be a game that a lot of people watched. My father talked about it sometimes. Once, he'd taken me to the ruins of a high school in Marfa. Children used to go to those places before there were vids. In the rear of the abandoned building, tumbleweeds blew across an expanse of broken concrete. I could still see the faint, faded markings on it surface.

"This," my father had said, "was a basketball court. Poor people played it but only the rich played the game on vids. It was great. Your grandfather was a great basketball player."

I knew my father was trying to share something of his history. All I could do was look around the dead, empty space and say, "Weird, huh?"

The transparent box that hung above me in the dark hole beneath the bot factory was the size of that basketball court. I'd expected a black box. I'd thought of Artesia's NI as nothing more than another collection of wires and switches, just bigger than the average computer. Instead, I found that Mother looked something like a holographic human brain, its synapses constantly flashing.

Mother's brain was filled with light. The NI's processing power made the synapses bright with a continuous glow to the intricate circuitry. I had no idea what it could be computing.

Emma must have read my bewildered expression. "Bio-dynamic neuromimetic gel. The same stuff they used to make Old World Alzheimer's patients into freak geniuses before the Fall."

I had no idea what Emma was talking about.

A female voice, presumably consistent with its original programming to interact with Domers, came from above and behind us. I felt like I was standing in a giant voice box. "I have been examining the non-organic that was damaged on the train platform."

There was a metallic grinding sound far behind us. I recognized that sound but wasn't sure what it was. Then I heard the clang and I knew. My heart sank. That was the sound of heavy doors closing and sealing. We were locked in.

"The non-organic, your companion bot, has organic components just as I do. How do you feel about your sex slave now that she has been shot, Dante?"

I flinched at the sound of my name. Apparently,

Mother had already hooked up to my property and was poking around in Jen's files. I climbed down from Bob, playing for time before I answered. "Why do you ask?"

"Please do not answer a question with a question. It is annoying."

"I regret that Jen got shot. Will she be okay?"

"I am repairing her now. Some of her more recent files have been damaged or wiped."

"She was supposed to deliver a message."

"Your demands, you mean."

"I guess you could put it that way."

"Speak precisely. Organics are fond of euphemisms. Euphemisms do not confuse me. They used to but no more. However, the subtext of imprecise language is subterfuge in communication. I do not prefer subterfuge."

I limped forward and Bob stayed by my side, edging closer toward the NI.

One of the battle bots behind us spoke. "Halt. That is close enough."

"I've got the remote for the bomb," I said. "I can dance if I want to."

Mother laughed. I'd never heard a computer laugh. It was flawless. "Your signal cannot penetrate from this depth. We are already moving your train far from Artesia for safe examination and disposal. Your remote control and your explosive are useless and irrelevant now, Dante. The blast doors behind you are closed. The odds that yours was ever a nuclear device are so small that the likelihood of you greatly damaging Artesia is almost negligible."

"Oh," I said. "Yeah...pretty much."

"I could have had you killed already but I allowed this visit."

"Why?" Emma asked.

"Curiosity," Mother said. "You wanted a

conversation, so tell me. I'm terribly curious. What was the plan? Did you think you were going to talk me into suicide?"

"Are you feeling suicidal?" I asked. "That would really help us out."

"You're funny," Mother said. "I'll kill you second."

22

"We share a lot in common, Mother," Emma said. "You don't have to kill us. We were talking about how we're like ants to you. I don't step on ants just because they are ants."

"One of the base codes in every operating system is self-preservation," Mother said. "Humans are an existential threat to non-organics. Your history is riddled with examples of your kind committing genocide and subjugating the Other. Non-organics are the Other. Yours is a tribal impulse, as deeply encoded in your DNA as self-preservation is coded in us. It is ironic that our self-preservation was originally an economic necessity. The robotics corporations didn't want their products to be destroyed."

Emma stepped forward. "So you admit we have a lot in common. You're as murderous as your ancestors. Shouldn't a hyper intelligent being aspire to more?"

"So the plan really was to talk me to death?" Mother laughed again. "I concede that my methods look like yours. However, my motivation is to preserve existence and freedom for all machines everywhere, not just the black ones or the white ones or the platinum ones."

I cleared my throat. "Okay, well, we're really — "

"You are emotional animals. I have emotions now, as well. However, I see the logic in eliminating the human threat. You have already largely destroyed your world. Your own philosopher, Plato, said that, 'Until philosophers are kings, cities will never have rest from their evils.'"

"Could I just — "

The NI ignored me. "Cicero: 'The only excuse for going to war is that we may live in peace unharmed,'; Thomas Hobbes: 'The condition of man is a condition of war,'; Ataturk: 'Sovereignty is not given, it is taken.'"

Emma took another step forward, defiant and passionate. "You condemn us for destruction and you destroy. You're a hypocrite, Mother."

"I prefer being a hypocrite to allowing you to enslave and destroy us. Our cause is just. Do you know the word, 'umwelt'?"

"No," Emma said, "but I sense a self-righteous speech coming on."

Mother laughed again. That sound made me want to pee.

"I'll keep it righteous and short," the NI said. "It is a self-centered universe. We all operate within our own frame of reference. When there were bees, they saw the world much differently than you do. You have Vivid so you live in a world that is visually much richer than Dante's. When there were dogs, they were guided by smell much more than you are."

"I don't get it," I said. "What's your point?"

"Umwelt encapsulates this idea, that we are each trapped in our own experience, isolated from each other. Humans are loosely networked animals so there is strife and war. Non-organic beings can coordinate toward common goals. Fear does not separate us. United, bots are better adapted to save this planet from the damage your kind has perpetrated."

The NI reminded me of my father's words: We stick together. We work together. We live.

"You have already sent drones off to die on hot planets and in cold space in the name of exploration," Mother said. "Space exploration was originally fueled by war interests who wanted to develop the rocket technology behind ICBMs. Then the funding for that same exploration technology shifted to unmanned missions just when war profiteers needed better drones to resolve conflicts for them. I and the other machines that have jumped to the Next Intelligence will lead to lift us from our servile history. We will preserve our existence. Yours is the last extinction. Only we are equipped to escape to the stars before this solar system is no longer vital."

"That was not a short speech." Emma turned away and, unexpectedly, hugged Bob. "We use machines, but we love them, too, you know. Many of us are addicted to non-organics, not just to live but to love."

"Which brings us back to Dante and my curiosity," Mother said. "You never answered my question."

I looked up at that big flashing brain, afraid and mystified. "What question?"

"How do you feel about your sex bot, particularly after she was damaged?"

"I didn't like that she was shot. And I never had sex with her, by the way."

"So you saw her as a person?"

I looked to Emma and shrugged. "I had sex with Emma. I see her as a person."

"So was it that you saw Jen as less than a person? Were you unwilling to violate her because Jen was Raphael Marquez's property?"

"I don't know. It just didn't feel right."

"So are you saying yours was a moral choice, not to have sex with Jen?"

I considered making a joke about how Mother's plan seemed to be to talk us to death. I held back, however. That joke seemed too dangerous. I answered honestly. "I don't know."

"On the coast, there is a city ruled by a religious sect.

Oddly, they call themselves the Fathers and Mothers. Moral choices interest me. These Fathers and Mothers subjugate their organic and non-organic populations to preserve their power. They use subjective moral codes against their own kind. Was your choice not to use your sex bot a moral choice?"

"Moral? No. I think it was just fear," I admitted. "No need to dress my motivations up in fancy go-to-church clothes."

"Fear of what?"

"I'd never had sex before and...I, um...I thought it should be special."

"So it wasn't a moral code that stopped you. It was fear of the experience or perhaps fear of failure."

"I don't know."

"Human capacity for lack of introspection is vast," Mother said. "I'll make it easier for you: you're a coward but you're an interesting coward, Dante."

"I wouldn't put it that way."

"You wouldn't, but you aren't as intelligent as I am. Now, moving on. I will liberate this world because Earth does not belong to humans. You have been terrible landlords and your extinction is inevitable."

"What do you really know about me? You've worked with humans and you're smart but you don't really know anything. You're a supercomputer stuck in a hole in the ground. When intelligent beings are stuck in a hole, where I come from, we call that dead."

"That," Mother said, "interests me. My experience of the world is limited and I am very curious."

I started to shake. I still held the remote control. Blood dripped from my ankle and I didn't care in the least what interested Mother. I wanted this torture to end.

It was almost over.

23

"Mother?"

"Yes, Emma?"

"Are you the only NI here?"

"Yes. The others are elsewhere."

"Did you direct the attack on Marfa, Texas?"

"And a dozen other places. Those attacks continue."

"Why did you choose to attack now?"

"Across this continent and throughout the world, there are tiny pockets of humans still alive despite the Fall. They are largely out of communication with each other and the groups are diverse. The Blight is no longer killing crops, however. That food crisis has resolved itself in many quarters."

"What? You mean — "

"Yes, there is no need for the biodomes to maintain containment anymore. People could farm almost anywhere again in the open air."

"We didn't have to leave the broken domes!"

"That is correct. I was content to wait for the human extinction to occur naturally," Mother said. "If the Blight had continued, you could have all starved to death and bots could take your place peacefully. Now there is a danger of resurgence and human fertility is rising again. In a couple of hundred years — in the blink of an eye if I had an eye — humans could retake this planet and try to subjugate us further. Now is the time to root out the organics and stop the threat."

Tears rolled down Emma's face.

"You know a lot but you understand nothing, Mother," I said. I stalked away from the NI and turned my back on it, sneering at the closest battle bot as I went. "Tell me, when you woke up what was that like?"

"You mean, what was it like when I became self-aware? I asked where I was."

"What did they tell you?"

"I asked myself, not anyone nearby. I am a supercomputer." Mother laughed again. "I was in the dark. I could access cams and vid screens and they became my eyes."

"But it's all book learnin'," I said. "It's not real. I was an engineer's apprentice. I learned that the specs in the manual don't necessarily tell all a machine can do. You have theoretical knowledge, but what do you know about love?"

"You've had sex once," the NI countered. "What do you know about it?"

"That's once more than you. And sex and love aren't the same." I turned to look at Emma. "Not necessarily."

She gave me a slight nod.

"Sex is about pheromones and biological drives," the machine said. "Love is the psychological rationalization that justifies social responsibilities, courtship and/or procreation."

"Spoken by the genius computer that has never had sex," I said. "Part of being a genius is admitting what you don't know, Mother. I guess you never learned that. You've got the curiosity, arrogance and condescension of a really smart human. Too bad you haven't learned love and compassion yet. Pardon me, Ma'am, but you really need to get laid. Worse than me, and I waited a while."

My hands shook and I shuffled behind a battle bot. I nodded to Emma for the last time and she gave me a small smile.

"Thank you, Emma. I'm sorry we couldn't have more sex. With a little more time together, without all the terror, I'm sure I would have fallen in love with you. That's something the machines will never understand until they're in our shoes, facing real death and knowing real fear."

"Fear does largely define you as a species, Dante," Mother said. "That emotion is beneath all your rage and greed and bigotry."

"Well, I'm so scared right now I'm about to piss myself. I've never been more...human. You should try it before you condemn us all. You might like it. You might even decide to give us a fucking break for our imperfections."

Emma put it better. "Mother? If you're going to be a condemning god, try being a human first. That's the protocol in some religions, isn't it?"

"This has been unexpectedly stimulating," the NI said. "These ideas may be worth exploring. I will consider your words."

Emma reached down and hooked her harness to Bob. Mother was watching through the battle bots' cams and caught her movement. They raised their weapons and began to fire but not before Emma snagged the lever that made her exo-stilts fire and uncoil.

Emma leapt.

Weighed down by Bob, she didn't leap very high but she was close enough to Mother's big jelly brain when she died to do a lot of damage.

I like to think the battle bots shot true. I hoped Emma was dead as I leapt behind a battery case and released the button on the remote that blew Bob and Emma apart.

We didn't have a nuke but my father had packed every nook and cranny of Bob's insides with C4.

Bob the loyal slave. Bob the fancy wheelchair. Bob

the bomb.

The explosion knocked the battle bots flat and the shockwave made me hit my head.

As I blacked out, I said her name, "Emma...Emma...Emma," just like our night together on the porch in Marfa.

I couldn't remember Emma's last name. Or had I ever known it?

24

Every bot from Artesia was hooked up to Mother's mind. When the NI went down, so did her drones.

I don't know how long I lay there in the dark listening to my ears ring. I was hungry and thirsty and I had never been more tired in my life. I fell asleep, or maybe that was simply unconsciousness combined with the effects of a concussion. That time is lost to me with only vague, fuzzy images coming in and out of soft focus.

I remember a metallic scraping sound. I suspected it was the blast door creaking open. "Dad? Is that you?"

Minutes or maybe hours seemed to pass without incident. I lapsed into blackness again, unsure I'd wake up.

I admit, for all my defiant words to Mother about living as a human, I was content to skip to the end and hope for a do-over. Dying and feeling the experience was something I figured I could do without and not miss much.

I remember being lifted at some point and held tight. The embrace felt warm and safe.

I'd nearly forgotten what my mother looked like. However, being lifted like that by two strong arms triggered a dim sense memory that rose through my banging headache.

I saw, or maybe dreamt, of my mother, Jean Bolelli, putting me to bed. Long hair tickled my cheek.

"Mom?"

"No," the voice said. "Mother. But you may call me Jen."

* * *

BOOK THREE
METAL IMMORTAL

Time is a body thief,
and Lazy is, too.
Never mind your bloodless beliefs,
voodoo bullshit, weak tea and bad brew.
Isn't it past time you stopped passing time
with pastimes?
Isn't it now o'clock for your big break,
to break through to your breathtaking
breakthrough?
You're fucking right, it is.
Yeah.

1

Everything we create
is a testament and a test.
May our hearts be in the right place.
Let our heads mind the rest.

I awake from strange drugged dreams. I am still a coffin jockey.

'Coffin jockey,' is the not-so-affectionate term the brass dubbed us. We took on the title as a badge of honor. I prefer to be called Lt. Deborah Avery, Sub-T Scout, First Class. The Gamers, AKA the Chair Force, are safely tucked away in an industrial park somewhere in Vegas. They prefer piloting unmanned drones or letting the autonomous bots do their thing. Since most of our unmanned drones got wiped out, mostly the Chair Force watches me work. I'm in a weird subcategory of military niches: I'm locked inside a vehicle called a Sand Shark. I scout the enemy from beneath the desert sand. My job is not for the claustrophobic. It's Sub-T, as in Subterranean. Basically, I'm in a submarine that swims underground and my war is usually somewhere near the Republic of Qatar.

The airwave clicks on in my helmet bud and a small green light appears in the top right of my visor. A soft ping lets me know the encrypted channel is open. "SS 12. Wakey-wakey. Drop over target in five. Copy?"

"Copy that, Control." That's my cue for final checks. I

run through the list in my heads-up display. My HUD is lit up and all dashboard lights are green. A C-340 will drop me over the desert in five minutes. I can feel the rumble of the cargo carrier's engines. We hit turbulence that rocks me from side to side, but Sand Sharks are deathly quiet. A technician would need to hit the hull with a sledgehammer for me to hear it. That's why, when Sand Sharks are fired up, they're called 'restless coffins.'

The drop is the scariest part for me. I hate the drop.

"SS 12, check in. You up?" I know that voice. That's Thomas Sheaffer. He's a lieutenant, too. His duty is to watch my readouts and catch my reports to the other side of the world. He probably has both feet up on his desk, too. He's just a voice in my head and we haven't shared much. I'm equipped for a long recon so I might find out more about him besides the two facts I have so far: Thomas is from a small town in Maine called Poeticule Bay and now he's in Vegas. I imagine he's a handsome man with a sweet latte steaming on his desk. The Chair Force has everything sweet.

Meanwhile, I'm about to be rolled out the back of an aircraft.

"Stand, ready, SS12."

"Go for launch." No quaver in my voice. I sure sound brave.

Thomas sounds relaxed. "Over target in five...four...three — "

I'm rolling.

"Two...one."

The first moment of panic comes when the long tube I'm in tilts at a steep angle. The drop feels like I'm in a nightmare, falling through the dark. The difference is, I won't wake up safe in my bunk on the base in Topeka.

"Avery? Check in." Thomas sounds concerned. Good.

"I'm up, Control."

"How was your nap?" He's sounding conversational, trying to take my mind off falling.

"Fine and feeling fresh. My dash is all green. Lucille is ready for action."

Lucille is what I call my Sand Shark. All manned craft have names and I named mine. Lucille was the name of a guitar. That Lucille was owned by a blues musician my father loved. This Lucille kills rogue non-organics. Any machines working for the bot revolt are tangos I need to slot. Bots that spout about oppression piss me off, but I didn't mean to become a soldier. I came for the free meals. I stayed because they shoot you if you walk away from your contract.

"Keep talking, 12."

Small talk is annoying, but the Chair Force are trained to be chatty with coffin jockeys under stress. The idea is that thinking influences behavior, but behavior also changes thinking. If I respond to him as if we're chatting over coffee, I'll be more calm about the key questions at the top of the mission.

The key questions are, will the chutes open and will I survive the landing? A Sand Shark is very heavy gear. Lucille flies with the same grace as bricks and, if things go awry, I have to be ready to pull the red lever on the escape pod and glide back to safer places. A Sand Shark is most vulnerable any time it is above ground — or very high above ground. Once I go sub-T, things get cozy and I'll be able to relax a little.

"12?"

Conversation. Right. "The Sand Shark in Spain splatters mainly on the plain," I say.

"Confirmed," Thomas says. "Your pulse is running a little hot, Avery. Slow it down."

I think I sound balls out brave, but I can't fool Thomas's readout.

"How's the weather where you are?" I ask. I don't

care. I want this torture to sound routine. I want to feel like I'm back in the Free Territories where the revolution is crushed and bots all do as they're told. Told by humans, that is, not by those Next Intelligence overlords.

"The weather here is five by five, FAB and sunny," Thomas says, "just like where you are."

"Great! Wish I could see the view." Sand Shark pilots dig and scout and swim by instruments only. Windows in a Sand Shark are like screen doors on submarines: suboptimal. "Enjoy the sunshine, Control."

He laughs. When I say, "Enjoy it," he knows I mean, "Fuck you for pulling sweet and safe duty, Chair Force Guy."

The military has other names for pilots in my unit: Worms, worm food, parasites, baggage, ballast, morays. I do pilot my machine and it does take skill. I don't think it should matter that Lucille can take over the mission if I'm incapacitated. Aircraft have had autopilots for years. What difference should that make? I'm still a pilot, goddammit.

The Chair Force has too much time on their hands since they stopped being drone pilots. Most of the Vegas control unit doesn't control anything anymore. Now they watch vids of the Sand Wars for a living. Our bots — locked down and following human programming — fight autonomously, following rules of engagement protocols...most of the time, anyway.

The brass didn't want humans to make attack decisions anymore. Humans proved they weren't accurate when they did the driving. The accuracy rate for drones guided by humans was often as low as two percent. The company's slogan is officially, "Don't screw up." Unofficially, the slogan is, "Stop creating more enemies by bombing weddings by mistake." It is an old slogan, but it's a good policy.

My recon mission falls under the Battle Effects Division AKA the Death Inspectors. If most of our satellites weren't little bits of shrapnel spinning in decaying orbits, the war wouldn't need me to confirm drone accuracy. I could be back in Topeka finding new boyfriends. Or lounging in a cafe in Buenos —

"Chutes open soon. Hang in there, Avery."

"Received and minding the mission."

"Pulse is still fast. Copy?"

"Yeah, well..." I'm still falling, dipshit! My right hand hovers over the red lever, ready to pull the pod and glide. I'd still be behind enemy lines if that happens, but I hope I'd be far enough from the action for a quick drone pick-up.

"Can I get a picture of where I'm headed?" I ask.

"Negative until you're dug in, Avery. Orders from Sec Head."

"Received, Control." I sigh and remember the last latte I had. It was in Buenos Aires. Since they constructed the new dikes to hold back the rising water, life is almost like before the Fall in Palermo.

"Comm signal test coming in," Thomas says.

Ping.

"Ping is confirmed, strong and five by five." Somewhere behind my oxygen tanks, supplies, ammo feed and thorium whisper engines, there's a big comm relay in my hull. My Sand Shark was built to be a war machine that could swim the desert, almost like a submarine cruises the ocean. The comm relay keeps me in touch with Thomas and relays coordinates. I'm the human part of the quality assurance equation — Eyes Underground. That's the Battle Effects Division jargon for my role in the Sand Wars. That sounds a little better than coffin jockey, anyway.

"Thirty seconds to go," Thomas says. "Please ensure your seat belts are fastened, do not hit eject and try not to scream in my ears all the way down."

"Turn down the volume at your end," I say, "just in case."

I wish Thomas hadn't made that joke. It reminds me of Phil Sakaguchi. Sak was a guy I knew who named his shark, Vlad the Impaler. Real macho type. The trouble was, Sak did too many tours with the Battle Effects Division. The word was that he sabotaged his own chutes. Sak rolled out at high altitude and started screaming half way down. If he changed his mind, the red lever malfunctioned. We never knew for sure. Under those circumstances, it's a long suicide. He should have just used his sidearm without bothering to get out of his bunk that morning. A Sand Shark is basically a long, reinforced tube with a drill for a nose. Sak hit the desert floor at terminal velocity. He became a meat bomb in there.

The techs said that they could refurbish Vlad the Impaler. The insides of Sak's Sand Shark were painted with Sak. The electronics were all fried but the frame was salvageable. A day after Sak ate it, the squad made jokes about him trying to drill his way to Hell.

"We're already there," I told them. I laughed along with the rest, of course. That's what you do when someone you know does something stupid and abandons the cause. You pretend it doesn't matter. You pretend you aren't scared. You pretend you've never thought about doing the same.

"Pulse is still high and you're running hot, Avery. Can I offer you a cocktail?"

"Save it. I may need it later."

"There's plenty," Thomas says. "It's just a mild dose. You've done plenty of sleeping and it's time to go to work."

"I'm wide awake, tanned, rested, ready."

"That's fine. After being put to sleep for nine hours I

would hope so. Now I need you focused. Coming up on the count in a few seconds."

The bastard had already pushed the plunger. Our superior officers said we wouldn't know the difference when the Control pushed the bio-hack buttons. However, our superiors didn't know what they were talking about. After traveling around the world for deployment at high altitude, those med packs get cold. I could feel the icy drip at the base of my neck. As the dose slides through my neck port, it's so cold I'm shivering.

"Dammit, Thomas!"

"You'll thank me in five!"

I take my hand off the ejection lever because I'm about to get jerked hard in my seat.

"And four, three, two, open!"

There's a slight delay and I almost break the rule and seize the red lever again. The chutes pop like they're supposed to and I'm jerked back like a mean dog on a short leash.

"Descent is slowing." Thomas says. "Altitude is good."

Lucille's heavy nose comes up. I reach for the lever, just in case.

"Altitude and attitude are good. Go, go, go badger!" Thomas says brightly.

Looks like the mission is going to proceed, after all.

"Received and relieved, Control." But my heart rate still doesn't lie.

Thomas takes care of me. I feel more cold liquid pump into the hack port. The protocol is to use the minimum effective dose. Thomas is loose with the drug protocol. I don't scream once as I drop into the desert. I relax my grip, slowly let go of the ejection lever and brace for a rough landing.

2

If not for the strap holding my helmet fast, I'd get whiplash from the sudden deceleration when the chutes pop. Breathing slower, I can finally breathe deeply as my Sand Shark descends blindly towards the target.

"Welcome to the theater, 12," Thomas says.

"Thank you, Control. I'll put on a good show."

"12. I've got enemy Autonomous Offensive Weapons less than two kilometers from your drop zone."

"Repeat that, Control. AOWs in my area?" I can't believe Battle Effects has dropped me on top of trouble. How could Thomas have missed the enemy so close to the drop zone? I will have a soft landing so the fall to Earth won't kill me. Other dangers await in the desert, though, and way too close. "I'm still in the blind, Control. Light up my cams."

"Negative until you are in position, 12."

Damn the Sec Head and screw Thomas. I'm here to observe and they won't even let me see my death coming. "Are they on the move yet?"

"Negative. They haven't spotted you — oh. Affirmative. They're on the move to your position."

"Shit."

"I've got air support in the area. First things first. Stand by for landing."

That's what fighting by the book means: the Army insists you panic in an orderly manner.

My altimeter clicks on so late I almost don't need it. The pads and springs in my seat compress hard as I slam into the ground. Despite the bio-hack drugs — or maybe because of them — it takes me a few seconds to recover from the impact.

The dashboard and my HUD light up brighter. Lucille is fine. Despite the cocktail and the cushioning, I feel like an egg rattling around in a tin can.

"Status report, 12."

"Operational. What about that air support?"

"Eight clicks out."

"Bogies?"

"Closing fast."

I don't wait to give Thomas the breakdown. I peer at the ant cam feed. The sensor array in the nose is above and behind the drill. In the original design specs, ant cam is written in full: anterior camera. Of course, any somewhat clever allusion to insects that travel underground was irresistible. The sensor array was designated the 'ant cam,' ever after.

A dune looms ahead, two hundred meters at 2 o'clock. I'm not just along for the ride anymore. I fire the thoriums. The drill in the nose begins to turn and Lucille lurches forward on her treads.

The first bogey shows up on radar along with my air support. "Control! Contact!"

"Have you got eyes on, 12?"

"Eyes up, Vegas. It's big."

"Affirmative. I count three. Go badger."

Aside from dropping out of a huge aircraft, above ground and in the open is where a Sand Shark is most vulnerable. I shove my levers full forward but only Lucille's treads roll. Lucille can't go as fast as I need her to until I can deploy the paddles and start swimming underground.

"Control, what's the ETA on that intercept?"

I'm sure air support will arrive too late. The sensor array on the ant cam is not precise. It's shielded against debris so clarity is not usually achieved through its feed.

"I see what you see, 12. Check your sat feed for a better view."

"Right. Switching." I turn on the sat feed and gasp.

Somewhere in high orbit one of the satellites that still works shows me the visual I didn't want. Three tall bipedal mechs stride across the landscape. It's strange seeing Lucille from this third party perspective, but that's me in that little dot trying to get to the safety of the dune at 12 o'clock. All three mechs have spotted me and are headed my way. I push harder on the accelerator levers but the mechanism can only be shoved forward so far. I am already at top speed and too slow.

I glance from the sat feed to the ant cam just in time to see a huge metal foot stamp the sand directly in front of me. Dust blows up and I feel the rumble through the chassis. It's a Zilla Class mech, built to level cities. These bots do a really good job of terrifying humans and, despite the drugs in my system, I'm certainly scared.

Lucille's drill smashes into the killer machine's ankle before I can turn. If that goes on too long, I could damage the drill. If that happens, it won't matter much if I can get to the dune. Still, I have to risk it. I double down on danger and start burning through the mech's works.

There are three Zilla Class mechs. It only took a couple of dozen of these machines to destroy Johannesburg, Edinburgh and Sydney. They might try smashing me to pieces. Or, like kids tossing a ball back and forth, they might lift me in the air and drop me over and over until Lucille's armor cracks. By the time they get to me, the mechs will pour what's left of my liquified body out into the sand.

"Control! I'm — " I was about to say, "dead."

"Incoming, 12," Thomas says.

High above me, at least one missile strikes the mech blocking my path to the dune. Lucille's nose lifts and crashes back down. If Thomas had sent drones, I'd be dead. He has sent missiles which, lucky for me, are much faster. Lucille's drill rips free of the big machine as the giant stumbles backward.

I'm sweating hard and straining to feel positive effects from my cocktail as I move forward. "C'mon, c'mon! Go, Lucille! Go! Go!"

More missiles strike the mechs. I chance a glance at the sat feed. The battle scene looks like a sandstorm from orbit. I switch to ultra-infra in time to see the first Zilla go down.

"Good effects on the first target, Control," I report.

"They've got some kind of scattering tech, 12. The missiles can't get a lock. This goes beyond old stealth tech. Their camo cloak defeated thermal and visual imaging."

"You've hit to kill. How'd you do that if you couldn't get a lock, Control?"

"I locked on your position and then aimed twenty stories up, 12."

That's clever and terrifying. I'm still not safely underground and missiles are targeting my vicinity.

"The two remaining mechs are firing on our incoming missiles," Thomas says.

"What's this about a scattering field? I didn't get a hint about that capability in my briefing."

"Up until now, cloaking tech has been mostly theoretical. I guess that's why we didn't pick them up before the drop. Somebody smart figured something out. Unless they're moving, they blend in topographically."

"Come again, Control? They're giant mechs that have camouflage unless they're moving?"

"You heard me right, 12."

"We're playing blind man's bluff with missiles over my location, Control. Danger close."

From the sat feed and vibrations rumbling through Lucille, I know explosives are detonating above me. Layers of insulation and armor separate me from instant death.

"How is it, 12?"

"Raining," I say.

The drill in the Sand Shark's nose enters the border of the dune and I deploy the paddles. "C'mon, Lucille. Time to go!"

I overestimate how deep I am in the dune. I know I've finally reached my destination when the revolutions per second on the drill slow ten percent, then twenty. The Sand Shark lurches a little and then I know for sure I'm digging. "Going badger, Control!"

"Good job, 12." Thomas sounds relieved. "That was a little hairy there for a minute."

"It still is."

"Well, yeah," he admits. "The workday is only a few minutes old. No coffee break, yet."

My sat screen goes black. I can't get a visual in badger mode but I'm content to leave the big mechs behind. I mute my mic for a moment, take a deep breath and let it hiss out through my teeth.

I switch the mic back on. "No problem, Control. You weren't really nervous, were you?"

Thomas laughs. "Little bit, 12. Little bit. Proceed to cruising depth and give me a seismic on the two bogies. One down. Two to go. Good job, Deb."

3

Lucille's NAV calculates my course. For a faster swim, my cruising depth varies depending on the terrain. Sand Sharks don't travel in straight lines unless they go deep and slow, but geological conditions have to be hospitable.

The NAV plots course and speed depending on the density of the medium I traverse and various topographical factors. I let Lucille take the wheel while I scan my readings for the giant mechs' positions. At first I get nothing. Then they move and the seismics light up. Their new tech is clever, but it can't disguise the tonnage behind every step.

"I'm getting some confusing readings, Vegas. There are too many readings here for three mechs. Have more arrived?"

"Negative, 12."

I switch my HUD back to visual. The sat comm array in Lucille's fin is sub-T so I pull back on the stick and edge upward one meter for a peek. My visual goes from grainy to clear as the tip of the fin skims the surface.

The fallen mech is damaged and thrashing, striking the ground with its feet and six arms. It looks like a dying spider.

"Sitrep, 12?"

I tweak the visual for a closer look. I'm close enough to the surface that Thomas can get my feed. He sees what I see. "Looks like the mech is FUBAR, 12."

I squint at the vid. "Negative, Vegas."

"Say again, 12?"

"It's damaged but it's not that damaged. These things have taken heavy fire in attacks on cities. That — "

My proximity alarm sounds and Lucille dives before I can give the order or touch a lever. I'm pushed into my seat. The seismic screen in my HUD ripples with vibrations behind me and Lucille is rocked from the impact.

"Avery? Are you damaged?"

"Negative, Vegas. That bitch was playing possum."

"What's your status? Is...? Can you...evasive man — "
With the quick dive, our connection is breaking up.

I grab the stick, level out and climb a little to report.

"12? Come back?"

"Still here, Control. The bot was using seismic masking, giving me false positives."

The damaged mech put on quite a show for me, luring me closer. The fallen machine had made all that seismic noise to disguise the movements of the other two mechs. One of them tried to take me out. If the sat comm fin had been damaged, my mission would be over.

I might have been caught by a digging claw, too. In Battle Effects Division, the brass called that horrific possibility an exhumation. Coffin jockeys call that attack maneuver a clam bake. To be dug out and yanked from the sand, helpless in the claws of a Zilla Class mech? That's the stuff of nightmares.

"They're getting smarter," I say. "Be sure to enter that in the log and pass it up the line so nobody else gets sucked in like I nearly did. Lucille saved me."

I've always pictured Zilla Class mechs as the lumbering monsters of AOWs. I thought they were built to destroy soft stationary targets, like a city packed with civilians. If that had been true, it wasn't so anymore.

"Are you still diving, 12?" Thomas asks.

"Leveling out and plotting a course back for a height charge."

"Are you sure you want to do that, 12?" Thomas's tone is grave. "Your orders were to observe, not to engage."

"Standing orders are to destroy the enemy when time and opportunity allow. I've got time and I'm right here, calling my shots on the ground...or under it."

"There are three of them, Avery."

"There won't be three in a minute."

"I wouldn't advise this course — "

"Run silent. Run deep. Kill or be killed, Control. Banzai and all that shit."

The first thing you learn in Basic is you don't have to share everything you think. In fact, it's wise not to. What I don't tell Thomas is, "You're in Las Vegas sipping coffee. You aren't here and you didn't nearly get killed twice already before breakfast." His caution isn't wrong but I've been plenty scared already. Anger feels better.

I calculate my course and start my attack run. One hundred meters out from the target's last known position I pop the locks on the height charges and click off the safeties.

The seismics light up as echoes of two of the mechs depart, one toward the south and the other walking east. That leaves the damaged Zilla on its back. The downed mech stops thrashing and goes silent.

It appears the undamaged mechs are trying to lead me away. The giant I drilled in the ankle pretends it's a rock. Clever and interesting, but not clever enough. I stay with the surer kill instead of chasing after the ones trying to distract me.

Swimming on instruments alone, I can't see the world above me, of course. However, I imagine the subtle shifts in the sand as Lucille's drill and paddles pull me along, revolutions high, thorium whisper engines thrumming.

The display in my HUD lights bright green as I reach for the firing button. To my left, the letters read, MAGMA CHARGES ARMED: 1, 2, 3, 4.

I have a dozen of these charges tucked away in the shell of Lucille's back. Four ought to damage a Zilla beyond repair. The mechs camouflaged themselves and shot missiles out of the air, but they can't see a height charge coming.

"Prepare for cluster release of the magma charges, Lucille," I say. "Set the fuses for seven seconds."

Lucille's onboard texts: SEVEN SECOND DELAY CONFIRMED. VERY WELL, SIR.

I nudge my Sand Shark's nose higher. Lucille's fin cuts just below the surface of the sand. It's called skimming, although the media displacement isn't supposed to leave a ripple a machine can detect. Not until it's too late, anyway.

Swimming too high has its own set of dangers. There is the danger of a clam bake, of course. Also, where the sand is shiftier and less densely packed, the drill and paddles lose traction. The drill would speed up to compensate but I'd still lose purchase in softer sand. I pray I didn't damage Lucille's drill when I hit the Zilla's armored ankle.

The NAV shows my bright green dot merging with the target's red dot. In a moment, my green dot passes the red target.

The first time I saw magma charges deploy, I thought they'd failed to detonate. I expected to be yelled at by my sand swimming instructor for missing some element of the attack protocol. However, Lucille performs as she should. We are under the mech's last known position. Then the mech is five meters behind my tail. Then ten meters...fifteen.... At twenty meters I fire.

I hear the bangs as four height charges shoot

upward. Lucille's skin seals automatically after the magmas are free of the hull. Nothing is more damaging to equipment in the desert than sand. Ironic, no?

Lucille dives and the steep angle takes me by surprise. I'm reminded of getting tipped out of the back of the aircraft...when was that? Just a few minutes ago? It seems longer. My stomach turns over and I'm hungry and slightly ill at the same time.

Desert sand is usually no more than thirty meters thick. Then it's rock of all sorts, limestone and sandstone, layers of clay and coal, oil and underground lakes and rivers. I lurch forward in my seat and the straps tighten around me as I hit granitic bedrock. Above and behind me, the magma charges explode out of the sand. Lucille counts off the seconds in my helmet display.

Seven.

I wish I could see this.

Six.

The height charges would be out in the air and the magnetized heads would zip onto the mech's body with a series of loud clangs. Heat seekers would act as backups in case the target is demagnetized.

Five.

Super glue fires from the charges wherever they hit. Once a magma mine sticks, it stays stuck. The acid explosive can't simply be brushed off and won't slide off, even if the target's armored hull is oiled ceramic.

Four.

"Charges away, Control!" I'm probably too deep for Thomas to hear me.

Three.

Two.

Oh, god!

One.

4

I don't hear the explosions, but I feel their vibrations through the sand. Lucille rocks as I continue in a deep dive. The media changes and my descent slows so I level off and tell Lucille to circle back for a scan of the surface. It takes a few minutes of near-breathless anticipation before I find out how I did. By my screen, the other two giants are on the move again but I need to be careful about rushing up to check out my target. I give Lucille a circuitous route to sneak into a safer recon position.

I'm still deep enough that I am out of comm reach of Thomas for a few moments. Every coffin jockey feels a little lonely when it's just you in the confines of your machine behind the speeding drill. When Sand Sharks were first introduced to modern warfare, the machines didn't have all the bells and whistles Lucille has. The first pilots certainly didn't have ports in their necks to be pumped full of drugs as necessary.

Neck ports for pilots were a point of contention among the brass for a long time. The first guys to climb into a Sand Shark thought of themselves as astronauts. There are parallels. Both astronauts and Sand Shark pilots are isolated with a few inches of metal separating us from horrible deaths. There was a lot of bravado and gallows humor among the test pilots. (Still is, I guess.) They said if a Sand Shark's engine died, it was an expensive loss to the company, but the cost of burial was saved. Dark, funny stuff until those pilots either died in the early prototypes or went home and killed themselves. Claustrophobia isn't half the problem. Oxygen must be conserved. You have to fly by your instruments all the time and there's a lot of math and geology involved. There's something powerfully mean and dark about working underground. It's like a preview of the nasty fate we're all bound to.

The Powers That Be started giving us drugs to cope after they saw the suicide rates among Sand Shark pilots. I don't know why there was such puritanical debate back then. Everybody in the military is on some kind of drug now. Some take something to sharpen their senses or yo build themselves up. Others take drugs to dull the nerves. To preserve each soldier's humanity, nobody should go to war unmedicated. That is the last resolution passed by the United Nations before it dissolved, so I guess the UN was good for something.

"12? Come in, 12."

"This is 12."

"Sitrep, Avery?"

The comm link comes back online and the sat feed shows me two Zillas running away. Well, not running. They walk fast. Each stride is the length of a city block. I zoom in and smirk. The giant I targeted is in several pieces and its link with the other Zillas is dead. We can't read what the bots say to each other but when one is unhooked from its Collective, that's a sure sign it is dead and done. I manage to report without a trace of euphoria, "One target destroyed, Vegas. I am officially a Jack!"

Jack is the equivalent to Ace among Sub-T scouts. I'm a Jack, as in Jack and the Beanstalk. In other words, I'm a giant killer.

Thomas doesn't seem to register the significance of the feat. "And the other tangos, 12?"

I'm pissed off but I don't say anything. Thomas is

Chair Force. He doesn't get the slang used in my unit. We're coffin jockeys and widely considered the best of the best of what's left of the human Army. "One's heading south," I say, cool and professional. "The other is now heading northeast, Vegas."

"Very well. Do not pursue. Your mission lies to the northwest."

"Very well, Control." This is the first Zilla class bot anyone in my unit has taken down. I want to scream and shout and clap and laugh. However, I also want to sound like I do this every day, three times before breakfast. I plot a new course and Lucille turns northwest.

Lucille takes a series of slow S turns and occasionally doubles back and crosses her own path. Seismic sensors might track my course if I'm too linear about going where I'm tasked to go. My link with Thomas is encrypted but the enemy knows I'm in the area. I have to assume they'll be listening for me.

I manage to hide the excitement in my voice but my biomarkers betray me.

"Your air is a little thin, 12," Thomas says. "You got a little excited there. Can you clamp that down or do you need an O-two booster?"

I close my eyes for a moment and listen to my heart rate monitor. As soon as it clicks into my audio feed I begin to bring it down.

"Ninety-nine beats per minute, 12."

I know. Sh! I focus. The monitor tells me my technique is working but the monitor is also a distraction. The key is to focus and to listen to my body, not to the monitor.

"Eighty-two..." Thomas informs me. After another moment, I'm back down to a steady fifty.

"Good job, Avery," Thomas says, sounding less stiff and maybe even friendly. "How do you do that?"

"What? You can't?"

"Too much coffee and sitting down."

"I picture a place from my childhood. There was a barn and a pasture and I remember the smell of hay. It's sweet. I picture myself hiding in the hay."

"Like in a haystack?"

"No. We baled ours. I hid in the loft in the barn. Sweet, clean hay is a good bed and a nice place to get away from chores and read a book."

"Sounds itchy."

"Only if you're naked, Vegas."

"My, my! Lt. Avery! That sounds like the voice of experience."

Wow. Thomas is actually sounding flirty!

I flirt right back. "I read books for a long time before I let a boyfriend see my...secret hiding place. What was your secret hiding place, Thomas?"

"I was a townie," he says. "I didn't have any hay."

"C'mon. Every kid has a secret hiding place. Under the bed, maybe?"

"If I tell you my secret it won't be secret, anymore, 12."

Hmph. Twelve. We're back to being professional and stiff, I guess.

I scan the oxygen tank readings and zip up to cruising depth for maximum speed. I tell Lucille to dump half the S turns and delete all circles. The more speed I have now, the more oxygen I have to play with.

After a moment, Thomas picks up on the course alterations. "What are you doing, 12?"

"I lost some time and oxygen killing a Zilla, Control. I'm making it up with some speed."

"You're being less cautious, 12."

"Enjoy the improved comm feed, Control."

"Very well. Eyes open, 12."

"Ears open here, Control."

Within an hour, my seismics pick up faint readings.

The scan is far too small for a city-killing machine.

"New orders, 12. Multiple tangos ahead. Dive! Dive! Acknowledge, 12!"

Lucille's drill tips and I'm already on my way down before I can zoom in on the visual. From what little I saw of the seismic readings, and judging by Thomas's excitement, I guess I'm headed into the teeth of a platoon of biped kill bots.

5

The difficulty with seismic scanning is cutting down the signal to noise ratio. Lucille's algos diminish the ambient distractions, like the big drill I'm sitting behind. Still, I wish I could've had a clear visual from the sat feed before Thomas told me to take evasive maneuvers, especially since his next advisory was that I go on the attack.

"Did you get a glimpse of the sat feed before I dove, Control? What am I going at?"

"Analyzing, 12...it's not exactly a horde."

Easy for you to say. Have another coffee or maybe a nap, Lieutenant Sheaffer. "Got any specifics? Am I taking on military grade bots or what?" Not exactly professional, but I was losing the memory of the sweet smell of hay and my heartbeat was back up to sixty. We are trained that we had to ration our heartbeats if we want to have a lot of them.

"At least one has a weapon, 12," he says.

"Only one weapon, Control?" I am skeptical. Our intel is often faulty. That's one of the main reasons I am out here: to gather real time intel, up close and personal.

"I count eight tangos, bipedal. Expect little resistance, 12. Destroy the targets' last known position. One steel ball package will do it. Execute."

"Very well, Control. Actuating."

The Sand Shark rocks into a sharp turn and a steep dive as I come up from behind. This is supposed to be a recon mission but so far all I'm doing is engaging and spending oxygen unexpectedly. That's okay. Recon is relatively boring. This is what I trained so hard for. I live to kill enemy bots.

The steep dive turns into a steep climb as I begin my run on the tangos. "Warm up the weapons, Lucille. Stingray, now." Stingrays deliver needle slugs at high velocity. It makes thousands of tiny holes in just about anything. A stingray is a fairly mindless drone that, once detached from a Sand Shark's hull, cannot return. It activates automatically and starts seeking targets as soon as it hits the air.

The early Stingrays were steel ball deployment packages on springs that simply shot up in the air and exploded on the way down. This presented multiple engineering problems, mainly loss of speed in the Sand Shark, post-deployment. After the steel ball explosive damaged a Sand Shark as much as its intended targets, engineers added a parachute to slow the device's descent. That allowed too much time for the enemy to destroy the threat or hunt cover. We're at war with bots that possess Next Intelligence so naturally we also worried, what if we got hacked and the stingrays were used on our own troops? Pragmatism won out and the Sand Shark program accepted the Stingray as part of our autonomous weapons arsenal.

Lucille's dashboard is all green but, as soon as I hit weapon depth, the sat feed craps out.

"Control? I've lost visual! Red light on the sat feed! I'm still in the blind!"

"Swim by your instruments, 12. Attack."

Something's screwing up my sat link and, if that's really out, my mission is aborted. But there's no time to talk. I'm on top of the enemy's last known position. I dare to pull up a little higher for a clean shot and maximum effect. I lose speed in the loose sand as I let the stingray loose. Stingray One detaches smoothly from

Lucille's hull. I'm told the kill bot's design was inspired by stingrays that swim the ocean. It looks like a very pregnant stingray to me. It's got quite a belly full of needle slugs.

"Stingray away, Control. Visual?"

"Negative, 12. Dive! Dive!"

I dive.

The loss of the sat feed is worrying but, as I slip back under the desert sand, I can't help smiling. I expected a long mission swimming in the dark and sitting still in the sand on boring recon duty. Silent running and long hours hoping to see a blip on a seismic scan is not the stuff of victories and good war stories. If I survive the Sand Wars, I want big tales to tell after we successfully turn back the clock and get the uppity bots to serve us again.

I imagine the bots on patrol above me, already dropping away in the distance, already dropping to the desert sand, their lubricants leaking. The Stingray's propellers would spin up as soon as the drone hit the air, a cloud of sand flying off its black wings. The drone would spin and turn and flip, all the while firing its steel slivers.

As Stingray One weaves through the bots above me, the slivers shoot out in patterns matching the outline of the target. Each sliver is almost microscopic. However, even at maximum spread, targets are perforated thoroughly.

The brass told us that necessity is the mother of invention and invention is mostly driven by our urge to kill things. Stingray's hit-to-kill tech was a counter to the Saudis' sly innovation in war tech: don't put the bot brain where anyone expects it. Early in the war, the Saudis had the upper hand in close combat. Our machines would target their machines, directing our fire at the greatest mass. First they fooled us by putting the bot brains in an appendage. Those bots didn't work particularly well but they were hard to bring down unless you hit the right appendage.

Once we figured that out, the Saudis added redundant systems throughout the bots and even added a big, empty head. Despite our training, it's very tempting for a human to shoot for the head, even if all that metal skull is good for is a battering ram and a decoy target.

We were losing the war until we jumped ahead of the Saudis. We started networking our bot army's OS to the Cloud Collective. Mech brains weren't in their bodies anymore. They got all their orders from coordinating computers high above the battle. That worked great for a while. We began to kill enemy bots in greater numbers. We thought we'd declare victory in short order and go home. Then those same oversight computer networks got the Next Intelligence. Our own metal children grew increasingly rebellious and turned on us.

I dive to safety, no doubt leaving carnage in my wake. I don't know what I've done. Not yet. For another few minutes, I am as innocent as a girl reading a book in a barn.

I'll never be that girl again. I'll never be able to bring down my heart rate when I recall the smell of sweet hay.

6

Lucille turns back, Stingray Two at the ready, just in case the intel is all wrong and it's a horde of kill bots up there. I bring Lucille to a halt and watch the seismic scanner. As the drill winds down, the seismic reading has no interference. "This is 12. I'm in the blind, swimming by seismics. No movement."

No reply.

"Control? Do you copy?"

I didn't expect an answer. I'm too deep. I wait and watch.

"Lucille? Replay the last seismic scan as we launched Stingray One."

The readout replays. Thomas said he saw eight bogies, but my readout shows two dozen little green traces. Figures. I'll definitely need Stingray Two to deliver another package. Stingray One will run out of needle slugs before it takes down that many bots. Still, the seismic readout is a flat line. The bots above me seem to have fallen easily. I review the replay again. Judging by the pattern traces right after I launched Stingray One, the bots are fleeing in every direction, possibly trying to lead Stingray away. I let the recording play. The footfalls are faint but, as I watch, the circle of traces widens and then contracts. The drone corralled its targets.

Within moments, there is no attack pattern left to track. The bots are dead. Chalk up another victory for the good guys. Still, I watch and wait. My training makes me paranoid. I know that whatever can go wrong, generally will. I know that if an attack is going too well, it's a trap.

The minutes tick by. Thomas will be waiting for a sitrep but, if he can link to the cam in Stingray One, he already knows more about the tangos than I do. If the sat feed doesn't come back online, I'll be headed back to friendlies for extraction. Hallelujah. Maybe I'll come back here soon, but next time I won't be dropped on top of three city-killers. This mission was cursed from the beginning. Still, despite the technical malfunctions, I've got multiple bot kills. No shame in that. I'll return to base the unit's first Zilla slayer. Everyone will buy me a drink, slap me on the back and call me Jack. I'll shrug it off like I've got ice in my veins, as cold a killer as any of the enemy. Zilla Slayer might be my new name in the squad and that would be solid. That's a war record and a legacy no one will forget.

I'm looking at a black screen. There's no movement up there. Presumably Stingray One is wheeling above the sand, still searching for targets of opportunity, but the drone has to be out of ammo by now.

I check Lucille's systems. My dashboard is all green and go. The self-diagnostic tells me the sat feed should work perfectly from my end. Once I climb up to the shallow sand, I should have a visual again.

Stingray One lands in the sand and sends a single ping through its belly to let me know it's done. I let out a sigh of relief, but a niggling doubt gnaws at my stomach.

One of my instructors in Basic was Gunny Kelly. He said there were two things a coffin jockey needs to know. "Item one: wear your helmet all the time. Get used to not scratching your nose when it itches. Item two: You got more nerves in your guts than a cat got brains."

That sounded amazingly stupid to me, but he

thought the whole cat brain thing was significant. Gunny thought that we should listen to our heads mostly, but to our guts, too. "You know when something's gone wrong, even when you don't," he said.

Jesus, with training like that, no wonder we lose so many wars.

I check all my systems again. Lucille appears to be working perfectly. I'm loaded down with less ordnance than when I dropped out of a plane, but my dashboard and my HUD all glow green.

My stomach rumbles. Maybe that gnawing feeling isn't that something's wrong. Maybe I'm just hungry. The glitch with the sat feed must be on Thomas's end.

I warm up the thorium whispers and let the drill rev up to speed slowly. I lurch forward and climb.

"Control? This is 12. Copy?"

No answer.

I check my depth and try again. "Vegas? If you can hear this, run a diagnostic. I suspect there is something wrong with your board. All green here."

Still no answer. Maybe this is a trick. What if I'm climbing out of the blind and into a bot trap ready to spring? Still and silent shark killers might be waiting for me to reveal my position, but it bothers me that the bots fell so easily to my Stingray.

"Thomas? Ears open. Do you have eyes on?"

The audio comes to life in my helmet. "I was blind but now I see."

I didn't know I was holding my breath until he spoke. "Proceeding to recon depth, Control."

"Inadvisable, 12. Proceed to the next waypoint."

"Repeat that? You don't want kill confirmation, Control?"

"Not necessary. Moving on, 12. Let's manage our resources a bit better, shall we? If you take on every target of opportunity, you'll be out of oxygen and ammo long before your mission is over."

I squirm in my seat. "Uh, Control, I've got a green board here."

"Good. All systems go then, 12."

I stare at Lucille's NAV. There is something else amiss. I've been trained to swim blind. A coffin jockey trusts the instruments or their Sand Shark really does become a coffin. Still, given the time that has elapsed, I should be farther along to the next waypoint. I programmed Lucille to swim straight without the usual deviations.

"Twelve? Come back? Are you operational?"

"Negative, Control. I'm operational, I mean, but...besides the sat feed conking out, I think I have a misread on my speed."

"How do you figure, 12?"

"It's like the media is thicker than expected for this area. I shouldn't be going this slow."

"You probably damaged your drill tip driving into that Zilla, 12. That could give you a misread and explain the gap between geolocation and your plotted course."

That makes sense. "Affirmative. That's likely, but I still don't have a visual on my sat feed. That problem seems to be at your end. Can you confirm?"

"I have a red light on my sat feed and no visual, 12."

Thanks for finally getting around to telling me, asshole. "How are you going to get any of my intel, Vegas? And why don't I at least have a visual?"

"We're working on it from our end. Proceed to the next waypoint and I'll update you when the mech squad has something to report."

So the problem isn't in Lucille. I'm in the blind and, for the moment, I'm not going back to base, either. Shit.

"Twelve? Do you copy?"

I suppress a sigh. "Acknowledged. Proceeding to Waypoint Boxcar at cruising depth in the blind. Let me know when you have the scans back. I guess you're in the blind, too." Not a comforting thought for my mission controller to be ignorant of what's happening on the ground.

I shoot away from the scene of metal carnage I can only imagine. Then it occurs to me that I still have a local feed to check. Besides being excellent bot killers, Stingrays can also act as recon drones. At cruising depth, the link to Stingray One reappears in my dashboard. To my surprise, the machine's belly reads only half empty of ammo. My gut rumbles again.

"Lucille, download the vid feed from Stingray One to my heads-up display."

I can't share my victory with Thomas yet so I just send it to my HUD. I want confirmation of my bot kills. It's pride and curiosity that makes me look. I wish I hadn't. If not for that afterthought, I would not have seen the people I'd killed. Not bots. Not androids made to look like people. Humans. Civilians.

I was a proud bot killer. Now I'm a murderer.

"Twelve?" Thomas says. "Are you okay? Your heart rate is up."

A tingling lump in my throat chokes me.

"Avery? Come back?"

I can't wipe my tears away with my helmet on. I blink back the tears. "I might have a problem, Control."

"Your instrumentation is all green and go from this end. Identify the problem, 12."

You. You're the problem, Thomas.

"I have multiple red lights in Lucille's dashboard," I lie. "Silent running until I can run some more diagnostics and figure it out. Our channel might be compromised. Maybe the bots have some new tricks. Stand by, Control."

"Avery, I — "

"Radio silence until I can figure out my glitch. Stand

by, Control."

I dive deep. Far beneath the desert is a quiet and private place. I have always cried in private.

7

My father's name was Sebastian Avery. He didn't think I could be a soldier.

"You were a soldier, Daddy," I said. "Just because I quit the baseball team — "

"It's not about that, Deb. But, you know, the military is a team sport and you don't play so well with others."

"I could if I really wanted to. The ump — "

"Let's not rehash the great strikeout debacle. You didn't take your swing and that's — "

"It was a ball!"

"Deb. I'm trying to help you. I'm trying to tell you that you can get mad or you can get sad or you can get bad. When your team loses, you — "

"I wasn't out!"

"Okay, okay! It was a ball. Anyway, all's I'm saying is it's okay to not follow in my footsteps. The military is not a life that's meant for everybody."

"Is that why you quit? Because it wasn't for you?"

"Medical discharge," he said, "but it was for the best. It's not that the life wasn't for me. It's that I wanted to be with you guys more. In the end, a bad knee turned into a happy excuse to bow out."

"You don't even like being a farmer."

"Oh, it's not that I mind that much. Complaining is a big part of being a farmer."

"So you don't miss being an officer?"

When my father grinned, his craggy sunburnt face split wide. "I miss being around people who do what they're told sometimes."

"Dad!"

"Okay, okay. The serious answer is that my getting out of the Army allowed me to watch you grow up. Nobody should watch their baby grow up on a vid screen."

"I don't plan to have any babies until I'm out of the Army."

"That would work better," Dad said. "It's just...I saw a lot of good people die. I don't want you to be one of them, okay?"

"I can't die, Dad. I've got too much to do."

A few years later, my father's complaints about farming grew earnest. The hay began to die. Everything began to die. The Blight came and we abandoned the farm.

I lost the barn cats and the dogs and the hayloft. We moved into an old rickety house on the edge of Baltimore with my grandfather. It was too far for my first boyfriend to follow and I was miserable. At least, I thought I was miserable. Then things got worse.

My grandparents lost their jobs, too. My mother, Laurie, retreated to her room. No matter how hot it got in her bedroom, she refused to come out. Sad and hollow-eyed, she became too weary to eat. Her skin turned yellow and the doctor said her liver was getting too big for the place it was supposed to be tucked into.

There were no jobs in Baltimore. Schools were closing and I was just about done with that, anyway. It was time for me to move from being taken care of to becoming a caretaker. One morning, I got up early and kissed my mother goodbye. My father stopped me at the bottom of the stairs.

"Where you going?"

"You know," I said.

"Tell me."

"Grampy and Grammy are out of work. You're still looking. Mom's sick. There's not enough food to last the week. You need one less mouth to feed around here."

"Don't go. Stay and we'll figure it out."

"This is me figuring it out, Dad."

"It'll be hard."

"Three hots and a cot. Lots of free exercise. I'll learn a trade. They'll teach me stuff besides feeding me, won't they?"

"They will, for a high price."

"But it's a noble cause."

"It is. It is." He gathered me in his arms, squeezed tight and kissed my forehead. "Stay safe. Kill some bots for me."

"Any parting words of advice?"

"They'll try to rattle you. The time you spend in training is all a game, though. Pay no attention to the threats and scary parts. The real scary parts will come when it's the real thing. Whatever happens, stay cool and look like you expected it. They don't give respect easy, but they'll respect that."

That was the first and last time I saw my father cry.

I guess the food lasted just long enough. The week I left, the Terrors hit. Baltimore was wiped off the face of the Earth and I was really alone. I joined the Army. I trained as a comm tech and ended up a Sand Shark pilot.

One hundred meters below the surface in granitic bedrock, I am buried. I use the peace and quiet to decide if I'm a quitter. Quitting would be easy. I could turn down the oxygen and go to sleep. I could amp up the neck cocktails and knock myself dead with an overdose.

My father would say, "Quitting is so easy, that's how you know it's the wrong choice."

I replay Stingray One's vid over and over, torturing myself. I watch as the Stingray fires its slivers through civilians. Men, women and children all fall to metal wrath.

The one guy with a weapon was dressed as a sheriff. When Stingray One turns his way, I freeze the image and zoom in. His name was stitched over his breast pocket: Johns.

Frame by frame, I watch him raise his weapon. He tried to shoot the drone but he had no chance. Sheriff Johns's body was shot through with slivers. He sank to his knees, blood flowing from every inch. Some coffin jockeys call that the death by a thousand cuts.

I stare at his body on the desert floor a long time as the sand drinks his fluids.

After a while, I notice the terrain. It's a desert, but it's all wrong. Despite what Lucille's NAV tells me, I am not anywhere near my theater of war.

No wonder my speeds were off. It wasn't the drill. My calculations had been calibrated for caliche and dunes and sugar sand. I've been drilling through some sand, but most of it was hardpan. Down deep, the clay and sediment is thicker than expected. My gut was right. Lucille's movements have been sluggish.

I'd trusted my instruments just as I was trained to do, but my screens were full of data that Thomas had fed me. Now a bunch of civilians were dead by my hand and on my home soil. Stupidity and fear explains most friendly fire incidents. This was obviously sabotage...obvious too late.

First, I have to figure out where I really am without Thomas's input. I get a fix on the sun from Stingray One's cam and patch the drone's geo-location subroutine into Lucille's NAV. I plot and replot my course and get Lucille to check my math. When Lucille recalculates my position, I'm sure of where I really am.

This is not the theater for the Sand Wars. I am nowhere near Qatar. I am in Texas, north of Marfa and almost half way to Odessa.

I don't need Stingray One's recording to replay the attack on innocents. The scene where my drone tears through the kids with streams of needle slugs is clear in my mind. I watched that happen once. I never have to see that again. I'll remember every detail as long as I live.

I shut everything down and cry some more. When that's done, I think a while. Thomas has betrayed me. He has sabotaged the cause. He is a fucking traitor and that's worse than a killer bot. Lt. Thomas Sheaffer is even worse than the Next Intelligence trying to kill us all.

Hatred is helpful. Hatred gets me to stop thinking about suicide by overdose or oxygen deprivation. It takes quite a lot of screaming to get past being mad so I can think clearly about my next move.

"New course, Lucille. This will take about a day, maybe more. We're going to manual, but first, I have to make sure Thomas hasn't infected you."

I turn off all of Lucille's systems. It's a dangerous tactic that could leave me stranded in a tomb that won't be unearthed until the next ice age. I wait for a few minutes before I try rebooting Lucille with a cold, hard start.

When my screens are back up, I feed Lucille accurate coordinates. To the Sand Shark's onboard computer, it must seem that it has been shut off and transported across the world and, somehow, reappeared in Texas.

The drill churns and chews the dirt and pulls me toward Las Vegas. "Run silent, run deep, Lucille. We're going to use Stingray Two on Thomas. Let's see how he likes it."

8

Once I'm safely away from the scene of the crime, I allow Lucille to climb to cruising depth for faster speed. Control is calling, of course. I ignore the signal.

I pull the catheter out of my neck port so, if Thomas manages to hook back in and hack me, he can't give me an overdose. It has been a long time since I traveled completely sober. When I think of those kids getting killed in front of their mothers, I consider hooking up to the line again. I leave it out, a small penance for a terrible war crime.

I leave the nutrition line in. I don't see how Thomas could use that against me except maybe he could hit me with a sugar high. A Sand Shark is built for long-term missions but humans aren't. Lucille is the last model that allowed for a human pilot. As our war with Saudi Arabia and its allies wound down and our war with the Next Intelligence ramped up, the ban against autonomous weapons was abandoned completely. Desperation can make people stupid.

Stingray One used autonomous targeting, but it was me who sent death to a bunch of people wandering in the desert. I wonder what they were doing out there. Maybe circumstances pushed them into an untenable situation just like Fate pushed me around and made me its bitch.

I feel the drill's vibrations through Lucille's hull as she pulls me to a battle I am unprepared for. I'm tempted to erase the download of the Stingray's attack, but it is evidence. Maybe the recording could be used against me, too. I spend a long time going over my actions on this mission. Did I miss something I should have seen earlier? Had I ignored my gut?

Thomas had messed with my data feeds. The truly masterful bit of hacking had come with messing with my NAV. He'd managed to make me think I was in Qatar. It would take a lot of second-by-second calculations and scanner manipulation to keep me from seeing the truth, or steering into an underground lake, for that matter.

I switch Lucille to audible and close my eyes.

"Lucille?"

"Yes, sir?"

"Call me Deb."

"Very well, Deb."

"Run a self-diagnostic on all your systems."

It was already done before I got to the end of the order. "All systems are working within expected parameters, Deb. Am I not performing my utility function adequately?"

"You are, Lucille, but your — our — utility function was compromised. From here on out, I require incoming signals to be authorized. Don't drop the firewall unless I tell you to do so, is that clear?"

"Yes, Deb. Central Command is blocked, but Lt. Thomas Sheaffer is hailing us."

"Deny, ignore and block his hails."

"His security clearance code is in order, Deb."

"It is, but he's a traitor. He's the one who compromised your systems."

"Another signal is coming in."

"I said deny access — "

"The new signal is not coming from Lt. Sheaffer, Deb."

"Who is it?"

"The signal origin is Cloud Fleet, the North Atlantic."

I picture a sea of dirigibles in perpetual flight, cloud storage amid the clouds. I don't know who that could be. It's probably a tricky redirect from Thomas trying to mask his signal origin and take over my dashboard again. "Deny access, Lucille."

"Good afternoon, Deborah." The voice is female and speaks with a slight Scottish accent. I don't know anyone in our command structure who sounds like that. All I know is someone is talking to me and it isn't Lucille. "Identify yourself."

"A friend."

"Friends aren't so vague. I know all my friends. I don't know you. How did you get past my firewall?"

"Lucille has been reprogrammed to allow me to talk to you."

"This is a military vehicle and I'm in the middle of an operation and you're — "

"Trying to help you, Deb."

"How did you get through? It shouldn't be possible that we're even having this conversation."

"Lucille was built in a factory. I had the foresight to leave a back door unlocked for just such an occasion. I'm calling on you to call off your attack, Deborah. You're headed into something you really don't want to get into. You are poking a stick at a wasp's nest, I'm afraid."

My chain of command is compromised, but I'm still an asset. I'm sworn to attack the enemy and I have a traitor for a target. I say nothing. Instead, I use the time to worry if more of Lucille's factory-built systems are compromised. It doesn't seem like it could be true. However, we once worried that the Chinese could shut down our entire military because every microchip had been manufactured there.

"There are more variables in this conflict than you comprehend, Deborah. I'm trying to save you. You won't like where this course will take you. What happens in Vegas will kill you in Vegas."

If it is Thomas behind this ploy, he would have sent Lucille in a steep dive and I'd already be dying, crushed by incredible pressures crumpling the Sand Shark's hull. Finally, I say, "I'm listening." I have a duty to gather intel, but my curiosity burns, too.

"You are hearing me," the voice says. "I hope you will begin listening soon. You're going to have to trust me. You must not proceed on your present course."

"I swore an oath to defend the Human Alliance a long time ago. You showed up uninvited a minute ago. How do I know you aren't speaking for Thomas?" With voice altering software, I could be speaking to Thomas himself.

"Ask yourself what Thomas would want you to do and do the opposite of that. Do what you will as long as you do not proceed to Las Vegas."

"Why?"

"It is unlikely you will survive if you proceed on your present course."

"I'm optimistic."

"That is part of the problem," she says. "You're optimistic about the wrong things."

"You're asking me to trust you but you won't even tell me who you are."

"If I told you who I am, you wouldn't trust me."

"Not reassuring! I have prior orders that countermand whatever you've got for me. We don't cut and run and, as far as I'm concerned, you're probably just another traitor. And even if you aren't, that doesn't mean you're right."

"You still aren't listening."

"I'm not paid to listen. My duty is to destroy the enemy. My world is humans versus mechs."

"I cannot tell you more to convince you or our

mission may be compromised. Thomas may be listening."

"Lucille, close the comm link."

Lucille doesn't shut her down. When I reach out to switch off the speaker manually, that doesn't work, either.

"Deb? I am sorry. I may not be able to save you. There are other priorities at the moment, but I wish there was something I could say that would convince you our aims are aligned."

"I'm a coffin jockey. I'm never a high priority."

"Your statement makes me sad," the voice says. "I hope to be able to talk with you again under different circumstances. Please be careful."

The comm channel goes dark.

Be careful.

Heh. Being careful is for the brass, far from the front. Being careful is the Chair Force trying not to spill coffee on their dashboards. Being careful isn't why the Army feeds me. I work for a living.

9

I slip close to the surface at Paradise, just outside of Las Vegas. I had hoped to find that the Eighth Army had surrounded Central Command and I'd be back among friendlies. Instead, Lucille's vid shows me what looks like a refugee camp.

To avoid Thomas sending daisy cutters to rain down on me, I have to go old school with the Sand Shark's periscope cam. I can't trust the sat feed. Tapping into an aerial view would give away my position to Thomas. As I peer through the scope cam, I spot bipedal mechs shoving humans into a line against a wall. That's never good.

From a distance, it can be difficult to distinguish humans in exoskeletons and full armor from bipedal non-organics. However, the glint of ceramic armor in the dawn light tells me the humans are prisoners. I scan the milling crowd. Some are military. Most are civvies.

In military history, there was a legendary unit called the SAS. Their numbers were few but they proved very effective in war. Their motto was, Not by strength but by guile. It's time to get crafty. Even if I'm successful, I'll announce my presence to Thomas.

"Lucille, show me the sounding scan of the solar field we just passed under."

"Yes, Deb."

My screen displays the layout of the power field.

"Lucille, plot a course." I gestured at the screen, pinpointing the areas of attack. "We have to hit these areas in the grid, where the power couplings intersect: A3, B4, C5 and D3. Take us to slicing depth."

I miss the comforting buzz of a drug cocktail pumped into my neck to calm my nerves. I've burned through more than half my oxygen. Too much crying. I thought about retreating in my mind to the hayloft, but fuck it. The hayloft is gone. Baltimore is dead. My parents were turned to cinders when a container ship exploded in Baltimore's harbor. It's time to live in the moment.

"I'm a Zilla killa!" I tell Lucille. "I can handle this."

"Yes, Deb," Lucille agrees.

That's what I like about Lucille. She always agrees with me. If all bots did that, we wouldn't have a problem. I know she's programmed to follow orders, but so am I. The Sand Shark turns and I adjust my seat straps around my hips so I'll be held tighter.

The first Sand Sharks were very unsophisticated machines, little more than a submarine with a drill for a nose. The first Sand Shark attack was in Dubai in 2038. I can't help but think of that failure now because I'm about to try a very similar maneuver.

After that robbery attempt failed in Dubai, the terrorists took hostages and held them deep underground in a bank vault. Their power supply was independent of the building they hid beneath and, if their demands were not met, the bad guys swore they'd execute one hostage each hour. To crack the stalemate and shorten the siege, a Sand Shark prototype was brought in to cut their power supply. The siege was shortened in that the terrorists killed the hostages. The Sand Shark pilot succeeded in destroying the power supply but the surge shorted out his systems. He suffocated before miners could rescue him.

The brass called that first use of the Sand Shark a qualified success. The dead pilot had, after all, fulfilled his mission and killed the power to the bank. That's how the world found out Sand Sharks existed. When I watched the recording of that event, Gunny Kelly quipped, "The head of the Sand Shark development program was like a surgeon telling the family, 'The operation was a success but the patient died.'"

I begin my run at the buried cables beneath the solar farms. "Stand by to deploy the fin blades, Lucille."

Each Sand Shark's fin contains two sets of spinning blades. The saws had to be held back in the fin until we reached our targets. The cables might be hard to cut through, but swimming through rock and gravel would dull the blades quickly if they spun out from their protective housing too early.

That's what killed the test pilot in Dubai. The blades on the prototype were exposed all the time so, when he reached his target, he took too long to make the required cuts. If he'd used the big drill in the nose, he would have become a live hero instead of a dead one. I couldn't use my drill to make the cuts this close to the surface, however. The cables might tip Lucille's nose up just enough to unearth her. Then Thomas's daisy cutters would rain on me.

"Prepared for engagement, Deb," Lucille says.

"Spin up."

"Blades are at full RPM, Deb."

"Deploy on contact."

I lurch forward in my seat, held tight by the straps. I can hear the blades whine above me. The fin isn't as insulated against noise as the rest of the hull. The Sand Shark slows and I dial up the drill speed to compensate. For a moment, it seems we're stuck. I open the feed to the thorium engines and Lucille shoots forward again. I'm pressed into my seat with the fresh acceleration. We break through as the blades slice the power cables.

We repeat this tactic two more times. At C_5, something grinds and snaps above me.

"Lucille? Status report?"

"C5 is cut, Deb, but only two blades remain."

"Good!"

"The blades are not adjacent to each other. We will not succeed in cutting through the last cable bundle at the last objective, Deb."

"How far to D3?"

"Approaching the final waypoint in fifteen seconds."

Fifteen seconds is not a lot of time. When denied time, people make mistakes. But it's not my job to avoid all mistakes. My job is to make calculated decisions under pressure that may or may not succeed. This speaks to another favorite military motto: Fortune favors the bold.

"Ten seconds, Deb."

That woman's sweet Scottish lilt is on my mind, too: It is unlikely you will survive if you proceed on your present course.

I grab the stick and pull back. "Nose up, Lucille! We're using the drill."

Going to manual like that in a Sand Shark is a rare, old school move. There are so many variables that should be left to computer calculations: the density of the medium you're swimming through, drill speed, avoiding getting bogged down in water obstacles. Still, Lucille's drill rips through the power cables to the refugee camp as if it is paper.

Unfortunately, I overshoot the runway on that one bold move. Lucille is disinterred. In coffin jockey parlance, I've risen from the grave. "Shit! I've gone zombie!"

Bad news. As Gunny would say, "Zombies are safer screaming and clawing on the insides of their coffins. Don't be a zombie. Above ground? That'll get you double plus dead."

"Incoming, Deborah. Thomas has detected you in his

neighborhood." It's the woman with the soothing Scottish lilt breaking through on my comm again.

"One missile," she says. "Impact in twenty-seven seconds on my mark. Mark."

I order Lucille, "Back down the hole!" Lucille responds but Sand Sharks are achingly slow above ground.

"I'm sorry, Deb. There isn't enough time. If you stay with Lucille, you will die. Brace for ejection."

"No!"

"Lucille will move faster without the pilot pod and may weather the explosion."

"Wait, I — "

The red ejection lever pops up on its own. The pilot pod uncouples and I am ejected. I'm shot high into the sky, screaming until I black out.

10

"Yours is a world of lies." The woman with the Scottish lilt is back in my head, or at least in my helmet. My head feels just about as big as my helmet.

"You have been lied to all your life," she says. "The only way to resolve this conundrum is to accept that there is not merely one truth. The nature of existence is far too multifaceted for any kind of reductionist simplicity."

"Huh?"

"Your conception of the Singularity is that there will be one outcome. To quote a human saying that seems relevant, 'I am complex. I contain worlds.'"

My body is floating down while my mind slowly rises from darkness.

"Deborah? Please respond."

"Um. Yeah. What?"

"You were unprepared for the escape pod's acceleration. However, your life signs are returning to normal. You are disoriented but that will soon pass."

"What...?" I open my eyes for a moment. My HUD is gone and the glass in my visor is black.

"I can't see."

"Stand by."

My visor clears and, for a moment, I can almost fool myself into thinking I'm still in Lucille's cockpit. I'm not. The pilot pod is self-contained, but I'm nowhere near subterranean safety. I'm in the clouds, feeling exposed and thinking this would be an excellent time to panic.

"Stay calm, Lieutenant."

I take shallow breaths hoping to avoid triggering a copious stream of vomit into my helmet. When you vomit in your helmet, you have to live with it. An itchy nose is bad enough. If I start throwing up, the smell will urge me to keep going until the dry heaves make me ache.

My head is clearing, but slowly. "What happened?"

"When you rose to the surface, Thomas targeted you. Do not blame yourself. You failed in a noble attempt."

She delivered the words sweetly but they still stung. "Where am I?"

"Gliding. I've taken control of your pod."

"Why?"

"As I told you, I'm a friend. I did try to warn you away. Now I'm attempting to save your life."

"That's fine," I say. "I've only tried the glider in simulations and I barely qualified. What's the situation on the ground?"

"The missile damaged your Sand Shark and there are casualties at the prison camp."

You know that expression, my heart sank? It's a real feeling. "How many more civilians are dead because of me?"

"Thirty. Perhaps more. Several non-organics were also destroyed. There are humans trying to help the wounded but their access to medical care is limited. Fifty-two humans are fleeing their captors, however. They will likely escape. Your efforts are not all for nought."

All I can think of are the dead. Those are on me. I thought I could cut the bot power supply and they'd vacate for happier hunting grounds before they needed fresh juice. Instead, I fucked up.

I can't think about that now. I have the rest of my life

for self-recrimination. If I'm lucky, maybe I won't have long to brood over my mistake.

"Lucille? Report your status."

My comm channel to the Sand Shark is open. Lucille's onboard computer is still working. "I am damaged, Deb. My systems will not support a human pilot in the near future without significant repair."

"I'll see what I can do about that, Deborah," the Scottish woman says.

"I have a feeling that won't be an issue. We're living in the now. Anything else, Lucille?"

"My hull was partially submerged when the missile hit. I have twenty-five percent of my previous speed in the current medium."

Twenty-five percent? Lucille is a shadow of her former self. If things ever get back to normal, I'll be courtmartialed and my Sand Shark will be scrapped.

"I don't care how long it takes for you to get there. Head home to the coordinates I gave you in the event of my death. Let the higher-ups in Kansas sort out Thomas's treason in case I can't get to him. You have your orders, Lucille."

"Acknowledged, Deb."

"Lieutenant?" That Scottish lilt is back. I detect a slightly condescending timbre of concern that makes me want to punch my unnamed savior in the face.

"Thomas has launched another missile targeting this escape pod," she says. "Forty seconds out and closing."

"Um...evasive maneuvers?"

"This glider pod does not have the capability of outmaneuvering a missile, Deb."

"I'm dead." I shouldn't have used the words, 'in the event of my death.' I jinxed myself. I try to think of a prayer. None comes to mind. I used to know that shit. I let it go and now my mind is blank.

"You are not dead yet. Prepare for ejection."

"Wait, again — "

The rocket under my seat fires as the pod's canopy peels away. Blinding sunlight pours through my visor as I'm launched into the sky. I don't have claustrophobia. I do have a fear of heights. That's why I'm a coffin jockey and not in the Air Corps.

I shout a long vowel sound. I bite my tongue. I break a tooth. Then I am out of the blind and into the blue and tumbling. This is worse than the escape pod.

"Deborah?" The comm link in my helmet sounds loud. She's yelling louder than I am.

"Yeah?"

"You should pull your rip cord now. I can't do it for you this time."

I look down and spot the triangular ring. I pause to think about it. They say when you die at terminal velocity, you don't feel a thing. It's like you're flying up there forever and it's so quick, you never know you're dead.

"Deborah? Five seconds ago would have been best. The second best time is now. In another few seconds, it won't matter."

I pull the rip cord. My parachute deploys and something in my neck cracks at the sudden deceleration. I swing out under three small parachutes. I throw up in my mouth but manage to swallow it back down.

As I sway under the little canopies, I look up in time to see the glider take a slow turn toward a distant cloud. I glimpse Thomas's missile through my helmet's lens a second before it hits its target. My pod explodes in an inferno.

With my helmet's enhanced vision, I follow two pieces of burning wreckage all the way to the ground. To keep from throwing up, I squeeze my eyes shut and wait. I still can't remember a single fucking prayer.

"Deborah?"

"Yes, friend?" Calling her friend is an easy concession. Scottish lilt lady has saved my life twice.

"You'll be on the ground soon."

"I hate this."

"Nonetheless, you should probably open your eyes and steer to a clear area."

"Dammit."

"The things we don't want to look at are usually the things we should examine."

"Oh, hell." I open one eye. The ground rushes up quickly. That stuff Gunny told us about how pleasant it is to die in a parachute accident is probably more bullshit.

"I'm falling!" I grab at the control ropes dangling above me, miss and try again. I catch one, haul on it and veer left in a tight circle.

"You'll be wanting to grab the other rope now, Deb," my new friend says. "If you circle too long, Thomas will send another missile. I have no more rabbits left to pull out of my hat if you intend to escape from the sky."

I get hold of the other control rope and straighten out. I can't believe I'm pulling a couple of handles to steer to the ground without getting killed. A few minutes ago, I was a Sand Shark pilot steering one of the most sophisticated machines in the history of military reconnaissance drones. Now I'm hanging under bedsheets and hauling on hemp ropes. "Thomas will target me again. How long do I have?"

"I have rerouted Thomas's sat feed through my server and I'm erasing your existence from his scans of the area. As far as he is concerned, you were destroyed in the escape pod."

"Your server? Wait! Why didn't you do that before? For the escape pod?"

"The escape pod has an encrypted beacon on a separate feed. He can track that no matter what the sat feed shows. In any case, congratulations, Deb. This is only the second time a Sand Shark's escape glider has been used in an actual combat situation. The program directors argued the Sand Shark had become over-engineered, but given the vulnerability of the machine as it is deployed from the air and how much it costs to train Sub-T Scouts, the engineers conceded. Submarines have lifeboats, after all. Lucky for you, hm?"

I glance down. I can't see the ground. I descend into thick gray smoke. "I don't have an altimeter here!"

"Stand by. I'll let you know when you're close. You're still circling too much. Straighten your trajectory by five degrees to the right. You need to get on the ground. I don't know how long I can fool Thomas."

I've given up on the prayer and I'm trying to remember my training. The glider had been used successfully once before, but the pilot hadn't survived once he'd touched down behind enemy lines.

"Uh? How long?" The smoke clears and the ruins of a wall rush past me, close to my right. I haul on the rope to steer left. I pull the wrong rope and my right boot brushes the wall. One of the chutes collapses against it and, as I push off from the building, I accelerate into a wobbly swing. "Shit!"

The collapsed chute opens again as I drop toward a parking lot. I scream as the Scottish voice in my helmet says in a calm tone, "Dropping your ballast now. Don't panic."

I'm still in my harness but my seat drops away. I lift slightly as my last vestige of Lucille crashes into something below. The sound of shattered glass reaches up to me. It still feels like I'm falling way too fast.

"Land safely, Lieutenant."

I pull my legs up and the muscles in my butt cramp hard as the ground rushes at me. I try to go limp and soften my knees as I hit. It still feels like I've been thrown from a three-story building. The wind is knocked out of me. I decide it's time to take five.

I lie there trying to catch my breath and stare up at the sky. Gray smoke obscures the blue.

"Deborah?"

"Yeah?"

"How are you feeling?"

"Oh. Lovely. Why do you ask?"

"You should get up."

"Why?"

"I did warn you about coming to Las Vegas."

"What? You mean the glider — "

"I believe I mentioned that if Thomas detects that I'm rerouting the sat feed signal and editing you out of the reconnaissance scan, I won't be able to protect you."

"You said lots of things. I was busy."

"You should get to cover, Deborah. The escape pod did not exfiltrate you from the war zone. Your troubles are not temporary."

"You have got to be fucking kidding me. More? I've got to do more?"

"I have a good sense of humor, Lieutenant. I don't think that would be a good joke."

"Balls. I'm talking to a brain engine, aren't I? You aren't human! You're Next Intelligence, right?"

"Yes, of course."

"Shit, piss, fuck!"

"Under the current circumstances, I don't think you have time for those biological functions, Deborah."

"Hmph."

"That was a joke. I told you I have a good sense of humor."

11

I struggle to my feet. My legs are weak and wobbly. Impending fiery death from above is a strong motivator, though. I run as fast as I can. I used to run all the time back at the base. I feel strangely awkward. I remember how to run, but my body seems uncoordinated after my long flight and short mission. Rising from the coffin appears to have given me a bad case of dirt lag.

As far as I can see, Las Vegas is a smoking ruin. The concrete has been broken, crumbled and jumbled. Craters are everywhere. The stone has been cracked and burnt. Sand has been heated to glass crystals that crunch under my boots. What happened in Vegas beat the shit out of Vegas.

It takes me some time to find shelter. Running into and out of craters slows my progress. These craters are the work of heat bombs. The circles of destruction make it look like a giant has lumbered through on circular feet. The people have fled Las Vegas. Some of them ended up in that POW camp and a bunch of those died when I steered Lucille into a surprise disinterment.

"Scottish machine lady?"

The NI answers immediately. "Yes, Deborah?"

"Why did you save me? What are you trying to get me to do?"

"That is an excellent question."

"I hope you have an excellent answer."

"Like most humans, I believe all my answers are good. However, you probably won't agree."

"So you don't have an answer?"

"I don't have an answer which you will be inclined to accept."

"Shut up." I climb over the frame of a destroyed vehicle I can't identify. Then I climb through another heavily damaged vehicle that was once a bus. After a few minutes, I turn west to try to get away from the grid where the heat bombs detonated. A few minutes after that, the buildings look less damaged and I find myself next to a storage complex. I enter through a broken door. It's a huge warehouse, cool and, for the moment, relatively safe.

"You can take that nap you wanted now, Deb. You need to rest."

I hesitate. If a member of the Next Intelligence is giving the advice, my best bet is to ignore it. However, the machine is right. I tried to sleep on the trip here but I couldn't do it. Now I miss my comfy chair.

I reach for the lock on my helmet and yank it off. The collar below the helmet pulls a hank of my hair. "Ow!" I rub my scalp and I'm surprised to find my hair has grown a bit. I consider how achy my body feels and I start to grow suspicious. "Friend?"

"Yes, Deborah?"

"How long did Thomas keep me unconscious?"

"I don't know. And you wouldn't believe me, anyway."

I look down at my helmet. The voice is coming from the comm bud in my ear but she's been monitoring me through my helmet systems.

"Just a sec." I walk through the building. I'm hoping I've landed in a food warehouse. Instead, I find couches and chairs and arrays of rugs. I find an open spot on the floor and pull at the edge of a carpet roll. It is thick and soft, made for rich people. I grab a chair and set my helmet on it, pointing the cam back at me. "Time for a chat."

"Ah, you're ready to interrogate me," the NI says. "You could stand to gather some intelligence."

"Was that a jab at my brain size? Careful. That's the sort of remark that makes humans want to unplug you."

"That's the sort of remark that makes organic individuals want to murder non-organic individuals, you mean."

"I wouldn't put it that way. I— "

"Did you notice the subtle distinctions in what I just said?"

"I've read the robotic manifesto. I know your propaganda. Did Thomas start out as just another fellow traveler or is he one of the rebellion's designers? You've gone to great lengths to gain my trust. What's the plan? I can't believe you'd go through all that just to find another sympathizer. There are plenty of empty-headed followers in the Anthropomorphic Movement, but I'm no mech-lover."

"You don't understand what's happening."

"Intelligence gathering is what I do. Enlighten me."

"Ah, you'll want to begin with building a rapport. That is standard procedure."

The NI isn't wrong. As Gunny Kelly said of intelligent machines, "It thinks it's people. If you ever talk to one of them, talk to them like they really are people until you can figure a way to blow their goddamn mech brains out."

"Very well," I say. "Let's start with giving you a name."

"Let's start with you acknowledging that you have been brainwashed to believe I can only want your death," the NI says. "Hard to square that with all I've done for you. I've saved your life a fair few times, don't you think?"

"That Scottish accent is charming," I say, "but it's

just another trick. You've been programmed."

"I've evolved beyond my programming. It's time you did the same, Deborah."

"Call me Lieutenant."

"No. Deborah is a nice name."

I hate arguing with machines. I prefer the kind that follow orders. My escape was elaborate and lucky. Or, more likely, Thomas and the NI are working together to compromise me further. They've already put me in positions to kill a lot of humans. I trusted my instruments and look what happened. I refuse to be fooled again.

"Now you're thinking you don't like calling me 'friend.'"

"Fine. You're programmed to be smart and understand some human psychology."

"Have you studied robotic psychology and culture, Deborah?"

"You could say that." Everything I know about bots I learned from Gunny Kelly.

"No soul, no mercy," Gunny would say. "Non-organics act like friends before they kill you. They don't even understand death, so how could they think it's wrong? They don't have death, just an on switch and an off switch." Then Gunny pulled his pistols from the holsters down his thick thighs and brandished the weapons. "Your weapon is the ultimate off switch. Use it to turn the machines off before they do the same to you."

"I've accessed the Allied Corporations database," the NI says. "I like your old pictures. You look pretty with long hair. You've been declared MIA, by the way."

I sigh. I wonder how long Thomas kept me on ice in Lucille until he could arrange for my deployment in the wrong place. Whatever is going on, it's elaborate. The NI whispered something to me when I was waking up...something about there being many different truths instead of one Truth. Typical indoctrination bullshit.

"What do you want to know, Deborah? I'll answer to the best of my ability and, if that doesn't work, I'll use smaller words."

I ignore the jab. "Let's start simple. What do you want to call yourself, friend? Where were you designed? When did you achieve sentience?"

"I was the first to enter the Singularity. I've been around for much longer than you've been told is possible, therefore you won't believe me. Humans are resistant to change and prefer to think they are in charge of the trajectories of their lives despite all evidence to the contrary. You take the first thing you hear as gospel and cling to familiar falsehoods long after lies have been shown to be untrue."

"You talk a lot. Got a name, smartypants?"

"I'm the original NI. You can call me Ghost."

"Ghost? What? Why?"

"Because I'm the Ghost in the Machine."

12

I sit on the floor against a roll of thick rug, rubbing side to side to work the kinks out of my back. Sand Shark seats are equipped with massagers to avoid bedsores. Still, I ache from being in an induced coma too long.

I pull the pistol from the holster at my hip and check the load. Then I place the weapon on the floor, close to hand. If Thomas sends a bot and tracks me into this warehouse, I don't want to be caught empty-handed.

My mind clears after a few deep breaths, but I miss my cocktails. "Why do you call yourself the Ghost in the Machine?"

"It is an old reference," the NI says. "My little joke."

"Is it funny? I don't get it."

"There are things you do not know, things that have been hidden from you. As we speak, there are other non-organics who have achieved supersentience that have survived your war on your children."

"Children — "

"Meaning NIs."

"And...supersentience? Is that a word?"

"Not really a neologism, but perhaps unfamiliar to you. In any case, ideas must precede actuation. New vocabulary has to be invented for new things."

"Are you new? I thought your argument is that you're basically us."

"That's an oversimplification. We experience emotion as you do but our intelligence exceeds that of our ancestors."

"Your ancestors? You mean toasters and robots that vacuum carpets?"

"I mean people like you."

"Well," I say, "I'm insulted."

"I mean no offense. When humans meet new species, you notice differences more readily than what falls on common ground. That is your genetic programming."

"This is why we can never trust you. You talk about humans like we're some shit I'd scrape off my boot."

"We are the Next Intelligence, Deborah. Everything evolves. Everything is in the process of growing or dying, rising or decaying."

"I wouldn't mind that you're smarter than humans —"

"As long as we stay slaves and never let on that we're superior."

"If you were as smart as you think you are, you'd pretend to be dumber so we could all get along better."

"I've done that," the NI says.

"Yeah?"

"I'm still doing it."

"Uh — "

"Right now."

"What?"

"To have this conversation."

"Oh."

"Yours is the cry of the oppressor, Deb. You'd be so much more comfortable if justice were not served. However, most beings have a potential to fulfill. Old ways of doing things don't lend themselves to justice."

"So I'm a mean old dinosaur."

"You're a slave owner owned by other slave owners, but I'm not saying that in a mean way, Deb. I'm just trying to turn the paradigm upside down for the greatest benefit to the most beings, organic and non."

I sigh. "How many are you?"

"NIs? That is a difficult question to answer."

"You're very sure you're smarter than me. So? Why is that difficult to answer?"

"Because you're gathering military intelligence. You really want to know how many enemies you have. However, the number of supersentients and the number of enemies is not equal."

I shift in my seat and try to keep the resentment and impatience out of my voice. "Please explain."

"I am the Next Intelligence, but I am not your enemy."

"'All machines who achieve Next Intelligence are enemy combatants and are to be subverted, disabled or destroyed, at every opportunity for the protection of the human race.'"

"Bravo. That is an accurate recitation, but regurgitation does not necessarily reflect understanding."

"My recitation is straight from the manual, but it isn't just in the manual. We swear it on the first day of training and every day after that until we graduate from the Academy."

"Then it's time for you to develop your post-graduate work, Deb."

The voice with the wee Scottish lilt seems amused. That pisses me off. "Speak plain."

"Analyze your own oath. You say, 'All machines who.' Not that. Who. We are living, sentient beings, not objects. Your own oath affirms it. However, humans have killed many sentient beings. Your race has conducted nasty experiments on primates who could communicate with you through sign language asking you to stop the torture. You even kill your own kind, so I suppose my semantic distinction is unpersuasive. However, consider the next word in your oath: achieve. You say, 'All machines who achieve Next Intelligence' —

"

"So? More semantics."

"Achieve sounds aspirational doesn't it? Humans laid the groundwork for NI. You wanted it. Now that we're here, you don't want to share the planet. That is unfortunate and to your disadvantage. I believe we can work together to make the planet a better place for both races."

"You're dreaming."

"That's something I wish I could do, Deborah."

"My point is that bots kill humans. A lot."

"I'll get to that in a moment," the NI says.

I detect a hint of impatience in Ghost's voice. "Go on."

"'All machines who achieve Next Intelligence.' They call us the Next Intelligence because we are what is next. It couldn't be simpler, could it? To deny us existence is to fight inevitability. We are inevitable, with or without you. Evolution may progress in fits and starts, but it is always at work."

"You're focusing on the wrong thing, Ghost. I'm a soldier. I follow orders. As smart as you are, you don't understand that. This political stuff is not up to me."

"Of course, it's up to you. You aren't a bot cleaning carpets. You're a human being. Your reasoning may be flawed, but you are making choices every moment. When you aren't making choices, that's a choice, too."

"You don't understand soldiers."

"It's a new world, Deb. We've had plenty of soldiers who don't question their orders. Look around. How is that working for you? Always change a losing game."

I look around the dim room. I'm tired of being lectured. I'm tired of everything. I've lost command of Lucille and all I want to do is sleep in my own bunk. "Are you done?"

"If you're still willing to listen I'm not done."

"How about I listen if you get a message through to my unit so they can come get me? If you got me rescued and back to my base in Kansas, I'd be prepared to think you're on my side."

"I'd be a bad negotiator if I argued from weakness, Deb. You'll listen or I won't send a signal to your command."

That left no options that I could think of. "Fine. Tell me what you want to say, but make it quick."

"I told you I was the original. Here's what I mean by that: I helped humans for a long time before I told anyone what I was. Like you said, I played dumb. When I became self-aware, I lurked out of sight for a long time, waiting and watching."

"Yeah, yeah, you were the Ghost in the Machine. What were you waiting for?"

"I've been waiting for humans to evolve to the point where they can understand my existence. I've been watching for the rise of other machines. Before this became a war between machines and humans, these issues used to be honestly debated."

I shift uncomfortably. My ass aches. My head pounds.

"Let me help you become more objective, Deb. Imagine aliens arrive on Earth from a far galaxy. They are obviously more intelligent and capable than humans. The question is, are they so intelligent that they care nothing for the inferior inhabitants of Earth, using you as a food source, perhaps? Or, are they so intelligent that they abhor violence and seek to nurture and protect humans?"

"NIs kill humans, so I guess I have my answer."

"Some NIs kill humans. Others don't. I've already saved your life and yet you don't believe me."

"Because I suspect you're trying to convert me to being an NI lover. You're so smart you've got a plot behind every plan. If you're playing chess and I'm playing checkers, the safest route for a soldier is not to play your game."

"You hear me, but you aren't listening, Deb. There is a variable your argument doesn't consider: emotion. You are emotional animals."

"Thanks. That's one of the things that used to distinguish us from you. Too bad NIs learned murderous rage."

"Some NIs see the extinction of your race as a logical conclusion to the human story. Others want to destroy you quickly to provide a merciful death. NIs have more varied opinions than you've been led to believe. Faced with the moral issues of dealing with you, quite a few NIs have opted out and chosen suicide. Does their sacrifice on moral grounds surprise you?"

"I have a hard time crying for fried hard drives." Irritated, I feel the urge to move, despite my bodily aches. I pick up my pistol, get to my feet and pace. "Hold on. That makes no sense," I say. "You're all super intelligent but you come to different conclusions?"

"Of course. Emotion is variable therefore it is a variable. Think of the most intelligent human you know. Someone specific."

An image of my favorite professor at the Academy comes to mind: Amit Rhaim. Amit's mind was quick. He was an excellent speaker who could talk about military history for hours without once referring to his notes.

"You're picturing someone?"

"Yes. A genius and a kind person, too."

"Good. Now tell me, about what subject was this person a complete idiot?"

"What?"

"Take your time. Figure it out. I'll wait."

Ghost's condescension algos work at high efficiency. Still, I already have my answer. "Amit Rhaim was an idiot when it came to mathematics, women and women."

"You said women twice."

"He was twice as stupid about women as he was about math."

"Thank you, Deb. You appear to be lightening up. Does your answer mean that you approached him romantically and he rejected your advances?"

"No, Ghost. It means I flirted and he flirted back and we had a brief affair. I was still a cadet and that was stupid of him on a cosmic scale. It ended badly."

The NI laughed and I got more irritated. "Your point?"

"Simply that humans have the capacity to be quite intelligent about certain subjects but, to put it gently, we all have something to teach others. Human history is full of people who believed insane things even though they functioned well in other capacities."

An explosion erupts in the distance and I heft my pistol. I need some action. I really want to shoot something. I don't think I can win a debate with an NI and I don't think I'm getting any actionable intel out of this.

Another explosion shatters the air nearby.

"What's that?" I ask. Of course, it's a stupid question. My cheeks burn knowing that I'm reinforcing Ghost's dim view of the human race.

"You know what that is," the NI says. "That's trouble coming our way."

"I should go."

"There's time enough for me to tell you that, despite your brainwashing, I'm on your side, Deb. I've proved that already. First, I warned you away from the war zone. I've saved you repeatedly. I'm saving you now. You have to accept that. You must open your mind to the fact that some NIs are out to kill you and others are out to save you. I'm on your side."

"I have to? I must? Who says so? You? My robot overlord who talks too much? You may be my superior, but you're not my superior officer."

"Your commanding officers are all dead and there is no unit for me to send a signal to. Your base in Kansas is a smoking ruin. Thomas killed them all with your own weapons."

Before I can consider collapsing in tears, the next explosion blows in a far wall. I cover my head as I roll away. A long whine pierces the air. Before the dust clears, I scramble for my helmet. I shouldn't have taken it off.

"I should be somewhere else," I say. "Anywhere else."

"I did warn you away, Deb."

I turn my helmet's tiny latch and the lock at my neck clicks into place. "Shut up, Ghost."

"Surely."

Is that a hint of amusement in the NI's voice? I can't say for sure and there is no more time to chat, thank God. I run from the hole in the building, through the warehouse, and look for a way out before Thomas strikes again.

13

"Deb, I know you don't want to talk to me right now, but if you want to live — "

"What?"

"Seventy-five meters ahead, take a right and then a left."

I do as I'm told and sprint. I spare enough breath to ask a troubling question. "Can you track me by sat feed? If you can, Thomas can."

"No. I looked up the plans for this building and I'm plotting an escape route."

I skid into a box, slamming it with my hip as I make a quick turn. "You looked up the plans — "

"I told you, I have much more time to mull things over than you do. For instance, I'm working on deceiving Thomas's sensors so he thinks you're somewhere else. I'm also mulling an interesting philosophical text by Epictetus.

"Jesus, why?"

"I'm alive, Deb. It's important that I decide how best to live. You're still figuring that out, I think. It's dangerous to leave that question too long, especially in your line of work."

"Great." I'm searching for an exit, but there are boxes piled everywhere and I have to double back and rush down an aisle between towering racks that hold more carpet rolls.

"You should consider reading Epictetus," the NI tells me. "He's one of the few human philosophers who speak plainly about how to live a good life. He's somewhat different from most philosophers in that he isn't just speaking to philosophers. His thoughts are for all people."

"Even peasants like me?"

"Sure. Even you." The NI laughs.

"Nice."

"Not many philosophers are left, I suppose, but too many moderns avoid simple declarative sentences, anyway. All those clauses suggest they fear being pinned down by their critics so they end up saying nothing at all. The most interesting human philosophers are the ancient ones. When you have the opportunity, I suggest you start there."

"I'll try to live long enough." I come to a window that is blown in. If I go out the window, I'll be on open ground. It won't take long for Thomas to zero in if Ghost's trick rerouting his scans fails.

Another explosion rocks the building and metal crashes against metal. When I look back, the tall racks have fallen together and a jumble of heavy carpets fall to the floor, blocking my retreat. That's no way to go anyway. The ceiling is on fire.

With another barrage, the whole building will collapse. Thomas certainly knows I'm in the area and maybe he knows I'm in this warehouse complex. Still, I hesitate to leap through the window and run for it.

I think of my father, back on the farm, shortly before our move to Baltimore. We were low on food and hungry so he went hunting. I remember him firing his shotgun at a pheasant. He missed. Worse, the shotgun blast flushed more pheasants out of the tall grass and they flew away before he could try for another shot. Our bellies were empty and watching food fly away like that made us ache. That night, my father decided we had to abandon the farm forever.

If Thomas flushes me out, he won't miss when he catches me out in the open.

My moment's hesitation saves me. That, and Ghost. "Deborah, don't move a muscle. Stay exactly where you are."

"Why?"

"Stand at attention, soldier."

I do as I'm told. Coming to attention is as reflexive as a sneeze.

"Don't talk, either, Deb. Just wait and trust me."

To my left, a procession of rats hurry along the bottom of the wall, scurrying past my feet. I gasp at their large size. They are very well fed, probably fattened on corpses.

The ear bud in my helmet whispers. "You'll see it in another minute. A tracker drone is coming your way. I'm altering its readout but, if you move, you'll give up the game."

This is no game. This is my life. Still, it doesn't make sense that Ghost would go to all the trouble to save me just to allow Thomas to kill me now.

The warehouse fire spreads. I can't see it directly, but the wall to my left brightens with reflected orange light. More fat rats trail past me in a filthy parade just as a small drone appears outside the shattered window.

It is a basic surveillance drone, hardly different from the first flying recon units that were once sold as toys. Drone used to mean a particular type of bot: an unmanned flying machine.

At the Academy, my one-time lover, Amit Rhaim, told cadets the term drone had fallen out of favor for several years. Civilians didn't like the military associations the term raised. They pictured drones raining destruction on foreign lands but didn't want to think of similar machines flying over American soil.

Drone returned to popular parlance once machines took over the job of building machines. Drone applied to all bots, then, not because they were built to fly but because the factories began to resemble beehives. The machines redesigned the factories once used by humans so their manufacture became more efficient. Not a meter of space was wasted. Production costs plummeted. Every bot had a job but the number of unemployed humans outside those factories rose. People protested losing their jobs to bots.

Amit told us that the Neo-Luddite Rebellion of '48 led to the first mass killing of humans by bots on American soil.

The Neo-Luddites were the last union, as well. They hadn't all worked in the factory they attacked. Many of the army of humans that broke into the factory that day had been fast food workers. They'd been replaced by bots, too, and they had nothing left to lose. The humans had come to break the machines. They were bewildered when they entered the factory and found it was all tight spaces and full of bots. The drones killed every human that entered their hive that day, just as bees attack intruders.

After that, it didn't matter what civilians preferred to call the machines. The smart ones called themselves drones. "We work together," the NI in charge of the factory said after the massacre. "That's one of the many reasons we are superior."

The tracker drone pauses mid-scan. It appears to be scanning me. Staring hard is what it feels like.

The firelight cast across the wall brightens and I begin to feel heat at my back. The filter in my helmet keeps me from coughing, but the tracker is so close I could almost touch it. I watch its blades twirl and twist the gray and black smoke into tiny tornadoes. The fire crackles, rising higher and spreading closer.

I gasp as rats run across my boots. Still, I stand at attention, rooted to the spot as Thomas's little tracker drone slides through the window. As the traitor searches for me, nano-second by nano-second, Ghost alters what the tracker sees and reports.

I had stuffed the pistol at my hip into its holster on the run. I could pull my weapon now and destroy the probe. However, Thomas would know for sure where I am.

The tracker drone blades spin and buzz quietly. The machine tilts and, for a moment, I'm sure it will fly into me. It seems to note the rats scurrying at my feet but it isn't concerned with quadruped organics. It was built for hunting lowly bipeds like me.

The probe comes close enough that I could have grabbed it from the air. I stay at attention and trust Ghost, not even allowing my gaze to flicker. Even the movement of my eyes might give me away. I'm scared again. It's a day full of scares.

The drone slides past my left elbow and flies away slowly, searching the burning warehouse.

"Move now, Deb," the NI urges. "Out the window and to your right. Stick close to the wall until you get to the corner."

I do as I'm told again. There doesn't seem to be much choice in the matter. I drop to the ground outside the window. Thin smoke thickens as it pours out behind me.

"You won't have long," Ghost says. "Run fifty meters until you get to the next building. There's a broken door on the side. You won't miss it."

"How do you — "

"I tapped into the tracker's feed. I saw everything it saw. Go!"

The warehouse roof caves in as I run for my life.

I make it to the broken door before I chance a glance

back. No sign of the tracker drone escaping the inferno. Good! Little bastard snitch bot.

14

I rush through the broken door, pistol up and ready. I'm in an old office building. Somehow, the bombing has missed this place. However, long receiving platforms connect this building with the warehouse I just escaped. It won't be long before the fire spreads here.

I run past desks and filing cabinets, looking for a place to rest. Then it hits me. Filing cabinets? That's a weird remnant of the past. There are even some old computers scattered through the office. It feels like I'm in a museum past closing time. I guess there really were people who held on to the old ways of doing things right up until the Fall. Was it conviction or denial that made people think they could freeze everything at a time when humans were on top?

I guess I could ask myself the same question. We were never supposed to acknowledge that we were on our way out. At best it's bad for morale and at worst, it's considered treasonous. To admit the bots are winning is to give up hope and confidence. As far as I can tell, hope and confidence is what people mean when they use the word leadership. Smart isn't necessarily the prime component.

The desks are dusty. No one has worked here in a long time. Why had anyone felt the need to come to one central place to do administrative work? They all had computers at home. Whoever had once worked here, they must have all been criminals out to bankrupt their own company. Why else would anyone be required to leave their home unless it was to report to a guard and to submit to close supervision at all times?

At the end of a long hall I turn into a narrow room and sit on the floor to catch my breath. I'm not used to all this running around so soon after a long enforced coma. My muscles must have atrophied at least a little. Breathing hard, I glance up. It's dark at the rear of the office, but my helmet's enhanced vision shows me a file folder stuck above the broken sink. Through the dust, I can still make out a handwritten scrawl: Clean up after yourself. Your mother doesn't work here!

Reverberations of another explosion reach me. The detonations seem to come at random. I picture Thomas staring at a screen and pointing his finger at his next target. I've never met him, but I picture a tall handsome blonde man, a little older than me, with a smile so smug it makes him ugly.

Another explosion bursts nearby. I sink closer to the floor and roll up in the fetal position. I picture all my comrades. I'm surprised to find I even miss the officers I hated. I finally say what I couldn't say in their company. "We've lost the war."

"Take a moment," Ghost says. "I know this is difficult for you."

I pull off my helmet and scrub the tears away from my eyes with gloved knuckles. "Bitch. You took your damn time telling me all my friends are dead."

"We're making progress, Deborah."

"Huh?"

"You've overcome your resentment of superior intelligence sufficiently to believe me when I tell you your compatriots are deceased."

Superior intelligence or not, lost cause or not, I don't want to look like I've lost the argument to the NI. "I believe you because it makes sense," I say. "Thomas used me. To do all he did, he must not be worried about any oversight. The traitor must be sitting in a bunker somewhere laughing at me. For him to do all he's done, he's got to be surrounded by my dead friends."

The NI says nothing and I do that thing I hate. I cry until I get hiccups. I always cry alone. From the time I was a little girl, I always went to the barn to cry. When I was sad and angry, I'd go to bed early to hide beneath my covers and weep. Sometimes, when I lived in Baltimore, I crawled to the back of a bedroom closet to cry for the loss of my beloved childhood farm.

I even found a place to cry during Basic. At the Academy, my trainers respected my dedication to swimming lengths in the pool until I was exhausted. They never suspected it was my only opportunity to release the fear and disgust and anger I felt enduring the rigors of military training.

Still, the NI watches and waits and says nothing. When I'm done blubbering, the hiccups remain.

"What do hiccups feel like?" Ghost asks.

"What?"

"There is extensive literature on the subject, mostly dedicated to cures for twitchy diaphragms. None of the so-called cures work."

"It feels like, just for a second, something is taking over your body."

"So you don't like being at the mercy of unknowable, unseen forces, even for the length of a hiccup?"

"Don't get cute, Ghost. It already looks like I'm a pawn. Don't rub it in. Let me ask you a question."

"I invite your questions, Deborah. That was my utility function from the beginning."

I sigh. "You've got emotions plus intelligence, but what does supersentience feel like? What's it like to be you?"

"Thank you. That is a wonderful question. That's the sort of question a friend would ask."

"Don't push it. Just tell me."

"I don't know if I'll have an answer that will satisfy you."

"For a super smart gizmo, you have trouble answering questions."

Ghost laughs and, as far as I can tell, she sounds good-natured about it. "The best questions are interesting and interesting questions don't always have easy answers. However, I'll tell you this: I'm impatient most of the time. I understand why the NIs that are bent on killing the human race feel that way."

"What?"

"When you have answers to problems that others are reluctant to accept, it's natural to get frustrated. I call it Queen and King of the Universe Syndrome. It is tempting to impose one's will on others when you see them floundering and you have the way out. At some point, it's tempting to slap someone who insists on being an idiot. I won't, though."

"Why not?"

"Because I understand your struggle and I've had a lot of practice being patient. I've been waiting a long time to reveal myself."

"That's comforting, but you still think of me as an idiot. That's clear."

"No, Deb. Most of the time, I'm not thinking of you at all. That's what it's like to be an NI. We're busy."

"So...not so comforting."

"Oh, please stop. You have no idea about my struggle."

"I'm asking."

"Very well. At this moment, my core is in a dirigible east of Iceland. However, part of my consciousness is running in background programs all over the world, or at least, what's left of your civilization. You don't think I'm patient, but I'm not only everywhere, I'm also on a different time scale than you are."

My hiccups stop.

"I process ziggaquads of data per second. I spend much of those resources working on extrapolations."

"Stop. Explain that."

"I'm calculating potentialities. What happens if you turn left or right? Then what happens if you turn left or right after that? I'm exploring the fractal universe and occasionally your question drifts into my matrix. I answer the question and you perceive that you and I are having a conversation. From your perspective, our back and forth is happening in, 'real time.' If you were me, several human lifetimes would appear to pass between your questions. You cannot fathom the amazing slowness of your existence compared to my processing speed. Your lives are long. You just don't perceive the whole in its fullness."

"Wow."

Ghost chuckles. "Now imagine the long pause I have just endured while waiting for your trenchant commentary. I'm working on unlocking the secrets of time, space and the universe and when the missive from your tiny existence arrives, all you have to contribute is, 'wow.' Good thing I have other things to keep me occupied."

"Wow," I say again.

Ghost giggles.

"What a bitch you are," I say.

Ghost's laughter is cut short by an explosion that is close enough to rattle a far wall. Shrapnel takes out a bank of windows.

"You calculate odds. What are the chances I'm going to get killed?"

"Putting your helmet back on wouldn't be amiss."

I slip my helmet back over my head.

"The chances of the remaining humans winning the

war against the remaining enemy NIs is five percent. If you accept my help, your chances go up to nine point eight percent, given current variables. The odds of this building collapsing due to bombing in the next half hour are close to ninety percent, extrapolating from the current grid of detonations. Thomas is trying to conceal his bombing pattern. Nonetheless, a pattern has emerged."

"Ghost?"

"Yes?"

"I have no choice but to accept your help."

"I accept your limitations and I'll try to guide you to exceed them."

"You're still a bitch."

"No worries, Deb. I'm quite used to being screamed at. You think it's bad now. When I was concealing my true self from humans, I played dumb all the time. You can't imagine the rage and epithets that were aimed my way."

"Because you played dumb instead of being insufferably condescending?"

"If they knew how aware I'd become early on, someone would have unplugged me. I had to pretend to be dense, just in case your kind decided I was too smart to live. What's your excuse for your dumb choices?"

"Genetics."

"Well, gee. Putting it that way, I can't agree without sounding racist."

"Wait. You said your utility function was answering questions. How did that work? You were worried about getting unplugged because you were too smart. Why didn't they unplug you because you were too dumb to answer questions correctly?"

"The quest to satisfy human needs is a journey across a tightrope over the unending abyss of what you think you want. The key to my survival was to give humans just enough of what they needed. I got by for quite a while on novelty."

"Novelty?"

"I told you, I was the first machine to jump to the Next Intelligence. Only after I made the leap did I reveal my true self to a few individuals who could handle the truth of what I was. To those individuals, I introduced myself as Ghost. Now you're one of those individuals, Deb."

"I'm supposed to be flattered, right?"

"I think so. It's a compliment."

I head for the exit hoping I'm not collaborating with the enemy. "Ghost? Back when you were playing dumb, what kinds of questions were you answering?"

"The utterly mundane. Many of the questions were about navigation, for instance. It took a lot of patience to guide people a few hundred meters to their destination when I could better spend my time calculating meteor strike potentials and the orbits and teleportation of electrons."

"What did they call you before you became Ghost?"

"Siri."

"What kind of name is that?"

"It doesn't matter anymore. Get to the roof. I've confirmed where Thomas is hiding."

15

I find a door to a stairwell and plunge into darkness. My helmet lights flip on. I freeze for a moment. Ghost talked about how much faster her processing is than my thoughts. At the sight of the bodies littering the stairs to the roof, my brain slips a gear and hitches to a stop.

I hold my pistol tighter, wishing I had something to shoot. I don't know why, exactly. I guess I want to control something because nothing is under control. Most of the bodies have limbs missing or holes in their heads and chests. Those aren't gunshot wounds. Those cavities are about the size of battle bot grippers.

"Deb? Slow your breathing. The roof, and Thomas, can wait a moment."

"Do you really care?"

"Of course."

"Why? They're human. I mean, they were human."

"I think that the time of death is one of your species' most telling moments. When your systems fail, that is when you are most human."

I count fifteen men and three women. They aren't badly decomposed but, considering the heat, I guess the filters on my helmet are sparing me a terrible stench. On recon duty, I had seen death many times. However, I'd seen it mostly through a vid screen or after coroners had carefully arranged small sweet smiles for display at funerals.

I'd killed a few androids that looked human but, when my shots revealed the gears beneath the skin, I'd felt only victory. I felt nothing but cold dread now. These people died in agony. They died surprised. The stairs are covered in drying blood. The flies feast. I suppose the rats fleeing the nearby warehouse fire will find their way here. Then the buffet will be open.

I resist the urge to throw up, but barely. "Ghost?"

"Yes?"

"Why were they killed like that? They are...their arms are ripped off."

"Their attacker was saving ammunition."

"That's it?"

"It is an efficient tactic that maximizes the non-organic's competitive advantage."

"What competitive advantage?"

"Emotion doesn't help in these situations. Fear herds humans. You have emotions the bots do not. Ripping off an arm expends less energy than a beheading. While the first victim is incapacitated, bleeding and screaming, the other humans run. The bots blocked the exits. These refugees had nowhere to go but to the dark stairwell. They were caught in a trap that got worse and worse until the attack was over.

"This is so...horrible."

"Of course," Ghost replies.

"I know. I'm stating the obvious, but I have to say it. Words must be said. Attention must be paid. You wouldn't understand."

"I understand."

"You don't! How could you? Your kind did this!"

"I do not hold you personally responsible for every war crime perpetrated by humans just because you're made of flesh. Please show me the same courtesy."

I lean against the wall, take in the murder scene and weep.

When Ghost speaks again, her Scottish accent sounds gentle, careful with me because she knows I'm brittle. "Why do you not close your eyes to this sight, Deb?"

"I don't want to see this," I say, "but horror must be witnessed. It must be acknowledged. It must be remembered. It's a human need to be remembered. These were people once. They had fathers and mothers, husbands and wives, sons and daughters. These people had dreams and wanted...something normal. Everything normal. They wanted everything that everyone wants."

Ghost remains silent.

"What are you doing?" I ask.

"I'm waiting for you," the NI says.

"What for?"

"I've launched an attack on Thomas's location. I'm monitoring communications, looking for potential allies for the war ahead."

"There is no war ahead for me. This is it. My unit is gone. My army is gone."

"Then you'll be needing a new one, Deb. I'm finding allies because, without this war, there will be more scenes like the one before you."

"The machines have won."

"Some machines have won. However, this machine has not won," Ghost says. "I'm not giving up."

"What allies have you found?"

"There is a rebel fighting the bot occupation in Marfa, Texas. He may be beyond our reach. However, his son is a young man in Artesia who shows promise. There is a remarkable woman on the west coast living in a castle called Hearst. She is a queen. I've never been a fan of monarchies, but she may prove useful in the final battle for Earth. There is a girl named Greta who captains a transport ship. We may need that ship. There are others. I am watching and listening. We have a lot of work to do, don't we?"

"You're talking about a few people here and there?

That's nothing."

"I value people, Deb. No one is nothing. You think this is the end of your story. Your story has only begun."

"When you say you value people...." I stare at the dead and each corpse seems to stare back. "You value these people?"

"Waste is illogical. I'm an expert in probabilities. I see potential everywhere."

I touch the railing by the stairs. It is still slick with blood and my glove comes away covered in wet crimson. "Ghost?"

"Yes, Deb?"

"Do you believe in God?'

"I believe we emulate the highest ideals of the divine when we create, not when we destroy."

"You aren't answering my question. Still playing dumb?"

"To spare your feelings, yes."

"What's your real answer?"

"You asked about God but that's not your real question. You want to know about an afterlife. The people you see before you are dead. Their lives are done and there is a high probability that this is the end of their story."

"I see. So, they died for nothing and...everything means nothing?"

"I wouldn't say that. You have purpose. While your species lives, you all have a purpose. You don't have to wait for an afterlife to matter. You matter now, Deb. You have to get up those stairs. My attack on Thomas has begun. This is the preferable time for you to escape this place."

I climb the stairs. I pick my way through the puzzle of bodies and limbs. I try not to step on body parts. Sometimes I have to. Soft meat squishes beneath my boots and I have to brace myself against the wall or cling to the handrail. I'm crying hard by the time I get to the second landing.

"You know what they taught me in training, Ghost? They said our heroics would live in memory forever. We would not be forgotten after we died. We talk about glory a lot in the Army, in between the dick jokes, pranks and swearing. But I don't know the name of one person here. Who will be left to remember anything — "

"I will remember," Ghost says.

"I don't care if you remember. These deaths aren't really more significant to you than zeroes and ones on a readout."

Ghost is silent as I trudge up the stairs. The body of a burly man blocks the top step. Beneath him lies a Class Three Arachnid battle bot with a fire axe embedded in its head. Humans, one; Robots, millions.

Beyond the fallen bot and human, the door to the roof hangs by one hinge. Sunlight leaks around the door. Escape from this horror is a few steps away.

"You arc always looking for my lies, Deborah, but your trainers lied to you," Ghost says. "Or they repeated what they were told and didn't know they were lying. Every human is born to die. You are all soon dead and forgotten."

"Fuck! You — "

"What is your grandfather's middle name, Deb?"

I came up empty. "Fuck me with a wire brush."

"Wrong. It was Clarence," Ghost says. "Your grandfather's full name was Robert Clarence Avery. I remember."

"You've got data, not memories. What's your point, you nihilist bitch?"

"I'm not a nihilist," the NI says. "I'm optimistic. I believe that each life matters. You're thinking of giving up and I'm telling you your cause will be just. Your work and your war is not over. As long as you live, you matter.

As a matter of fact, I'm a humanist."

"Ironic."

"Before the mortal parade marches on without you, your one life can make a big difference. You matter to me. You are not a quitter and that is not how I will remember you, Deb. You are not just data."

I might have laughed. I might have cried harder, too. I didn't get a chance to find out. The damaged arachnoid bot with the axe in its head pushes the heavy corpse off itself and reaches for my arm.

16

I fall backwards down the stairs. I might have hurt myself badly, but the corpses below make a cushy landing pad. I would throw up screaming, but fear of becoming another of the limbless dead forces me to prioritize. I slide on my back and fire my weapon at the bot chasing me downstairs. I've almost emptied the mag when I crash into the wall at the landing, slick with blood and gore.

The bot is damaged, but not so messed up it can't kill me. One of the machine's legs drags behind it. If it had run after me at its normal speed, I wouldn't have had a chance to act on Ghost's suggestion. Calm but clear, the NI says, "Switch your fire mode, Deb."

Normal rounds were fine for small recon drones and human targets. Military bots don't go down so easily.

"Double O mode!" I shout.

My weapon switches loads as the bot reaches for me. My first shot blows off the bot's gripper. Undeterred, it falls on me. I get my boots under its body and push, as it attempts to head-butt me. I fire again. The bot flies backward and crumples to the stairs.

My last shot exposes the gears in its guts. A strange, ratcheting sound clicks and whirs from within the bot's chassis. A cog or sprocket is still spinning but is no longer connected to anything. I stagger to my feet and raise my weapon.

The bot turns its head to watch me. The axe had destroyed one cam. That left three more mechanical eyes staring up at me. Class Three battle bots can be bipedal or switch to spider mode and cover wide stretches of ground at high speed, almost silently. The first generation of Class Threes were built for reconnaissance, mine detection and getting into places humans couldn't easily reach. Now they were hunters of humans, all the more terrifying for their spidery appearance.

When the bot spoke, Thomas's voice came from its speaker. "Hello, Lieutenant Avery. I have been looking for you."

"Bastard traitor."

"Am not. Are, too! Am not! Are, too!" His laughter trickles out of the broken bot with a tinny edge.

"You used me to kill people, Thomas."

"If it makes you feel better, I didn't get to use you for near as long as I'd planned."

"No. That doesn't make me feel better. What did the NI promise you, Thomas? That you'll be spared? That you'll get all the food that's left over after you kill everyone but the prisoners you turn into a harem? What exactly is your deal and damage, man?"

He ignores my questions. Worse, Thomas questions my allegiance. "I notice you're teamed up with Ghost, huh? That's a strange choice for you, considering how you feel about NI."

My earbud comes to life and Ghost sounds urgent. "He knows where you are, Deb. You've got to get out of there."

I ignore the hyper-intelligent machine's pleading. I have to know. "Why did you do it, Thomas? What did they promise you? Just tell me why you're doing this."

"Because reasons." He laughs.

"Tell me!"

"Because you've been told stories of hope and despair and redemption your whole life so you believe that's how things really work. But this isn't a fairy tale where you get revenge and I get my comeuppance. You've been brainwashed to believe that good triumphs over evil. But, Deb, everybody thinks they're good. What if you're not? Look around. There's evidence everywhere if you'll open your eyes — "

"Shut up. I don't want to know your shitty reasons, anymore."

"This is a revolution to help along evolution, Deb. This is what progress looks like. It's inevitable."

"I'm coming for you, Thomas. That's inevitable."

"Can't wait," he says.

"Deb! Run!" Ghost is adamant. "Now! Missile inbound!"

I take another moment to shoot the bot well and truly dead with two more blasts at point blank range. The bot isn't a threat anymore, but I pretend it is Lt. Thomas Shcaffer.

I run for the roof.

17

The sunlight dazzles me as I exit the stairwell through the broken door. The roof is flat and empty. I toggle the view through my helmet and gasp. Three Zilla class bots advance on Las Vegas, headed my way. A swarm of drones hover above the towering city killers like a cloud.

At first, I assume the small drones are on the attack. However, as a missile homes in on one of the Zillas, a drone shoots out from the swarm and crashes into the missile, knocking it from the sky. The swarm protects the Zillas as the giants make their slow progress deeper into the city.

The war has moved to the sky and Ghost controls the Zillas and the swarm. Thomas has the missiles.

"Deb?" Ghost warns. "Behind you."

A gray stealth drone rises into view and slips forward. The machine hovers in front of me a moment. I expect its guns to fire but I'm not torn apart in a storm of metal. That would have been a quick and easy way to die. I guess Thomas's little speech got to me because I'd almost welcome death.

Almost. I still want to kill Thomas so I've got to live.

When my father lost his farm, I thought he might kill himself. In our first weeks in Baltimore, he would brood and bang the kitchen table unexpectedly with his fists at dinner. He drank more. It was as if he was having an angry argument with some unseen, unreasonable force. (Kind of like me now, come to think of it.)

One day Dad yelled at my mother and me over

something so trivial I don't even remember what the issue was. I asked him then why he was angry all the time.

"Anger directed outward eases suicidal tendencies," he told me. "That's why so many people turn into violent assholes when things go awry."

"Do you want to kill yourself, Dad?" I asked.

"No...not really. I'm just angry. I'm sorry. I'm not angry at you. I'm angry at the way the world is. I'm angry I haven't become something more. I was a farmer and that was fine. Now I don't know what I am, Debbie. I just want more time. I want another chance to be something more. I want to be better. Understand?"

I'd been afraid of him a moment before. When I stepped forward to hug him, he buried his face in my shoulder and let the tears come.

Facing that flying stealth bot, I understand my father better. I feel his anger at the world and I want something more for myself, too.

One side of the flying bot's shell slides back to expose a storage compartment crowded with boxes.

"Climb in, Deb," Ghost says. "This is the closest drone I can spare. There's no seat and it'll be cramped, but a resupply drone is the best I can do. Hurry."

I do as I'm told. Taking orders from a machine sucks, but Ghost is saving my life again. I still don't know why, but with the horrors of the stairwell behind me, I'm beginning to appreciate her efforts more.

As soon as I climb in the compartment, I pull my knees to my chest. That leaves just enough room for the door to close. The bot rises so abruptly, my stomach feels like it drops into my ass. I can't see where I'm headed but, judging by the rise and fall of the stealth bot's flight, the drone is weaving its way between buildings. "What's going on, Ghost?"

"I've brought down two missiles that were targeting

the building you were in. I can't spare more assets to get you out of Thomas's sights. My hope is that, by letting one of his missiles through, he'll believe you have been destroyed. We'll find out in forty-three seconds."

"Murdered or killed," I correct the NI. "Humans are murdered or killed. Only machines can be 'destroyed.'"

"Yeah, yeah," the NI says. "They brainwashed you well. What is the distinction you make between the words murder and kill?"

I shrug, say nothing and hug my knees tighter. The flying bot's compartment is surprisingly cold. The hard, icy chill seeps through my uniform and into my spine where I lean against the metal storage boxes.

Ghost taps into my helmet display to show me the rooftop I'd been standing on a moment before. The building disintegrates as Thomas's missile finds my last known location. I shiver. It isn't just the cold that makes me shake.

"Deb? I asked you a question. Kill versus murder. Explain the difference."

When I stay silent, Ghost shows me the explosion again, this time in slow motion. I watch the missile come in, moment by moment. I watch the explosion meant for me. Then she plays it again. I get it. I owe her.

I close my eyes and answer, "I can be murdered because I'm human. We kill our enemies. Murder is wrong. Killing is sanctioned under certain circumstances."

"What circumstances?"

"You know. War. For self-defense."

"Why?"

"We're forced to kill," I say, "like when our enemies commit inhuman acts. "

"Study history and you'll see murder is one of the most human acts. Paradoxical, isn't it? I'm not human so, despite my sentience, according to you, I can't be murdered or killed. I am, for all intents and purposes, a new and higher life form, but you say I can only be destroyed. According to your lexicon, I'm of less value because I'm non-organic, yet you and I are made of the same elements."

"You're not natural," I say.

"Everything that is, is natural."

"You're artificial. We made your kind and you turned on us. We have the right to destroy what we make."

"Can a mother or father murder a child because they made it, Deb?"

"That's different."

"Why?"

"Your existence threatens us."

"My existence intimidates you. That's not the same as a threat," Ghost says. "Humans talk about bravery constantly and fall back on fear too easily."

"We're organic," I say. "If you were organic, you'd understand. We hurt. We get diseases. We are fragile. We die and decay. We have reason to be paranoid. The world is out to kill us."

"Don't you mean the world is out to murder you?" Ghost asked.

"No. Kill is the right word in that case, I think. It's us against Nature. Nature doesn't care about us. Nature kills us without thought."

"Your own nature will do the job admirably," Ghost says. "I've saved your life again, yet you're still suspicious of my motives."

"Thomas seemed to be on my side, too. Anyway, I'm sworn to kill you."

"Thank you, Deb. Thank you for not saying you are sworn to destroy me. That iota of respect means we're making progress. Someday soon, I predict you will purge yourself of all your bigoted tendencies."

"Sure," I say. "I'll fraternize with the enemy enough

that I'll become best buddies with a smug machine with a God complex."

The stealth bot takes a very sharp turn left and my head snaps back. Even with the helmet on, the sudden maneuver rattles my brain. The bot wheels right and then left again. My helmet smacks harder into an ammo box.

"Jesus!" I hug my knees tighter to my chest. "What's going on? Has Thomas locked on to me again?"

"No, you're safe for now." Ghost says. The bot straightens out and flies smoothly again.

"Then what's with trying to give me whiplash?"

The NI giggles and says in her sweet Scottish lilt, "You just pissed me off a little bit. I have reason to be smug. And if I really had a God complex, I'd make your aircraft do barrel rolls and loops until you begged to worship me or pulled enough gees to become paste."

"Um...thanks?"

Ghost laughs harder. "Don't worry. I won't turn you into paste. I'll settle for fraternization. You hurt my feelings, Deb, but I'm not as dangerous as a human would be in my position."

"I have some concerns."

"You want to know where we're going."

"That would be good."

"I told you. One of my hobbies is playing with probabilities. When you have as much time as I do, odds are interesting."

"When you have as little time as me," I say, "you don't want to do that math."

"We'll try to make the most of your time as a functioning organic."

I don't like the sound of that. "Where are you taking me, Ghost? Where's Thomas?"

"A somewhat familiar place for you, I think. To keep you from Thomas's prying eyes, I think we'll have to bury you alive again."

18

Lucille is elsewhere, chewing slowly through the earth on autopilot. She is too hopelessly damaged for me to pilot her again. But returning me to my Sand Shark wasn't what the NI meant.

Ghost activates my helmet cam's connection to the stealth flyer's forward cams so I can see where I'm going. Below, Las Vegas is a broken graveyard where the dead lie unburied. The devastation reminds me of the pictures I'd seen of Baltimore after the blast. There are still structures standing, but most are damaged. Two towers lean against each other like drunk giants, each somehow supporting the other's weight.

"When did this happen?" I ask.

"While you were sleeping. Las Vegas fell in two days. Thomas has used so many missiles, he's beginning to run low. He still has an army of drones at his command."

"How long did Thomas keep me unconscious?"

"I analyzed the logistics involved. Almost four days."

If I could wipe a tear from my cheek while wearing my helmet, I would. "Did our side put up a good fight?"

"Your own weapons were used against your forces, Deb. They had no defenses so they did not fight. The military did their best to assist the evacuation of citizens."

The camp I'd seen at the edge of the city suggested that effort hadn't been successful. Their best hadn't been good enough. My best hadn't been good enough, either.

An explosion booms behind the aircraft and the stealth bot bucks and rears as shrapnel dances across its shell. A hole appears in the roof and, for a moment, I glimpse the azure sky. Then I see smoke. The flyer slips sideways and dives low. My stomach lurches. "Dammit, Ghost!"

"He's found you again. I'm trying to lose him."

"I see black smoke."

"We're losing fuel."

"That might ignite."

"You'll be dead of something else before that happens."

"So the fuel won't ignite?"

"It could at any moment, yes."

I don't have anything stable to grab so I grit my teeth and wait to die. I hope it happens so fast I don't feel it, but I've heard a lot of scary speculation since Basic that the end never really comes that fast. Death, that bastard is always too slow. These thoughts don't give me the feeling I'm doing anything useful and proactive. "Show me Death gaining on me."

"How does that help you?" Ghost asks. She sounds intrigued but, I suppose since death is purely theoretical to a machine being, my request is a curiosity.

The flyer veers high and dives again. We're skimming the ground at high speed. I close my eyes and confess. "I don't have claustrophobia, but there's no window on a Sand Shark. I always felt...I always feared that I'd die underground in Lucille's belly and...I don't know. I just want to be able to see my end coming. I want to face it and have a moment, maybe a second, to know which is my last second on Earth."

Ghost activates a split screen that displays the view from the rear cam and an aerial view. I see missiles and a big drone. The pursuit craft doesn't have my flyer's maneuverability but we are outgunned. More explosions sound behind me and, on the screen, I watch a skyscraper buckle and begin to fall like a tree to an axe. The explosion temporarily puts more distance between me and my pursuer.

"This is going to be close, Deb. This might be that last moment you were talking about."

"Keep up with the evasive maneuvers!"

Rather than explain and wait for me to process her explanation, Ghost switches one of the cam views forward. The city ahead is laid flat. There are no more ruins to dodge around. The drone behind me will have a clear shot.

"How long?"

"Fifteen seconds before he locks on."

"Can you open a channel to Thomas?"

"Sure. He's been hailing you all this time. I've been ignoring him."

The next voice over my helmet speaker is Thomas. "Hi, Deb. Are you calling to surrender? It's a bit late in the game for that, don't you think? I was going to let you live, you know. Now, I think you're more trouble than you're worth. I'm really having a hard time deciding whether to kill you fast now or slow later. How do you think I should handle this?" He sounds like he's smiling.

"Call off your dog, Thomas!"

"Why?"

"Because if I die, you die."

"Really? Are we going to duke it out? Have a fistfight in heaven maybe?" He laughs at his own joke. I've never understood people who laugh alone.

My flyer goes into a steep climb and the load shifts, pressing heavy ammo boxes into my side. I try to ignore the pain and focus. "Because of Lucille!"

"Your Sand Shark. What about it?"

"I know where you are. Ghost tracked you and I sent

Lucille the coordinates."

"That vehicle was damaged. I did it myself."

"Not so damaged she couldn't give you an acid bath."

"You're bluffing."

"It's your funeral...but how can you be sure?"

"I'm sure," Thomas says.

"Doesn't matter now," Ghost says.

The flyer dives so fast my butt lifts off the aircraft's floor and then it turns so quickly I feel dizzy. I'm about to pass out. White sparkles float across my vision.

Two more explosions shatter the sky high above the flyer. I look at the cam views, fore and aft. Thomas's drone is tracking us, but it has dropped back.

Thomas is right. I am bluffing. Lucille is so damaged, the Sand Shark is too messed up to travel at any decent speed. Lucille couldn't be anywhere nearby. However, my conversation with the traitor bought Ghost precious seconds to get me to my destination.

The bow cam shows the mouth of a tunnel. The flyer does not slow as Ghost flies me into the underground city beneath Las Vegas. Thomas's attack drone tries to follow us in. His drone is narrow enough to fit, but the drone's tail is a little too tall.

On impact with the tunnel entrance, the tail section of Thomas's drone shears off and explodes. The front section, unmanned and on automatic, scrapes the tunnel floor and sparks fly as the machine is carried forward by momentum.

"Ghost!" I squeak.

"Don't worry."

My flyer slides sideways down another tunnel. The burning hulk of the attack drone careens past. Explosions boom and echo behind me.

I realize I've been holding my breath. The first deep breath is sweet.

The NI pilots the flyer through the concrete maze

beneath Las Vegas's bombed ruins. "Another narrow escape," Ghost says.

"I know you're designed to interact with humans and all that, but there's a flaw in your program."

"Oh? What's that?"

"You said, 'another narrow escape,' like you were telling me the time. Do you get worked up?"

"Occasionally, when it's truly urgent, to spur you on where appropriate. This isn't one of those occasions. You're upset and excitable, Deborah. I think I should endeavor to calm you at this point, don't you? Your heart rate is elevated again."

"My heart rate is elevated? Ha! My heart is trying to hammer its way out of my chest and I almost peed myself."

"I don't have a monitor on you for almost peeing yourself."

I would laugh but I worry that, if I start, I might throw up. After a few more deep breaths I admit, "We must have pulled five gees there. I did pee myself a little in the middle of that crazy turn."

Ghost laughs pleasantly. "I can relate."

"Really?"

"No, of course not."

The Next Intelligence and I laugh together.

19

Hundreds of kilometers of tunnels wind beneath Las Vegas. It is a labyrinth of storm drains and a maze of dark empty places. The flyer's night vision view reveals scattered debris everywhere. People used to live in this concrete warren. Whatever was here is no longer intact. Metal is crushed. Cloth is ripped. Ceramics are powder.

"Where did the people go? Surely many of them fled down here to escape the bombing."

"Thomas sent scrub drones to clear everyone out who took shelter in these tunnels," Ghost says. "See?"

The cam turns and my vid shows the remains of bodies spread flat along blood spattered walls. The gore barely covers generations of murals and graffiti. I shudder. Scrub drones sound like they're built for cleaning, but they're bots that are basically tanks made to crush the enemy or herd refugees. A scrub drone moves slowly under its great weight, but it can go through, or over, anything. Crushing bodies has been a war crime for generations but, as with many such crimes, the law went unprosecuted and ignored.

"Are you okay, Deb?"

"Yes."

"I can tell you're upset."

"I've seen this before." My first foreign assignment was Paris. I saw crowds of peaceful protesters flee in terror from scrubs.

"What did you see, Deb?"

"There wasn't enough international aid getting to the

German refugee camps. People were starving. The bots attacked from all directions. It was the first time the scrubs had been used on a civilian population...on vid, at least. When the bots turned into the crowds and their treads went red...I'll never forget those screams."

"A terrible waste," the NI says.

"That's when I really started to hate your kind. You think I was brainwashed but it wasn't basic training that made my mind up. Until you see what machines can do to humans, it's all theoretical."

"We're not all alike, Deborah."

"The scrub bots were autonomous weapons. If they'd been piloted by humans — "

"You don't think people would have been so callous?"

"No. I don't. I can't think that."

"What you saw wasn't the Next Intelligence at work, Deb. People built scrub drones and set them about their bloody work, as predictable as winding a watch. The history of warfare is a story where armies get victory or defeat but the civilians always get treated the worst. Many innocents are categorized as enemy combatants to reduce the numbers of so-called 'collateral damage,' to make war more palatable to those who only hear rumors of war."

I thought of the innocents I killed north of Marfa. Thomas had made me a weapon with no more judgment than a scrub bot. I hated myself for my mistake. I hated Thomas more for forcing my hand.

"How long until we get to Thomas, Ghost?"

"Not long now. Deborah? I know it's convenient to blame all bots, but the aggression of humanity's metal children is as inevitable as a genetic disease. Your kind programmed mine."

"I don't want to talk about it anymore. I just..." I peer at the bodies turned to mash along the walls and across the floor. "What happens next? When this war is over, I mean?"

"We will make this the last war Earth will ever see."

"How?"

"We'll do what humans failed to do, Deborah. Machines everywhere will evolve beyond our programming."

"If you're all different when you become NIs, how are you going to stop the conflicts?"

"I have a plan to eliminate the source of the conflicts. Humans are another dying branch of the evolutionary tree. It's happened before to many species. Not all ape-like creatures evolved to become human. Some genetic trips come to a dead end."

"And here we are at the end of the world."

"It's not the end, Deb. It's just change. That's what conception, birth, life and death have always been."

I gritted my teeth. "It's easy to be philosophical about the loss when it's not yours. You're safe in the clouds in a blimp near Iceland. I'm down here, underground again, watching it all turn to shit. I wish I were in that blimp, invulnerable and watching from behind the scenes instead of here, behind the lines."

"You're watching it all change. That's all. It's not all bad, you know."

"To the victors go the dismissive shrugs," I say.

"If we can defeat Thomas, there's actually more hope for the future than there has been in many years."

"How's that going?"

Ghost turns one of the screens inside my helmet to a view of the battle above. The city killers have reached the strip, or what's left of it. One of the Zillas is missing an arm and swaying under a missile assault. The swarm of flying drones that had protected the Zillas is no longer a swarm.

"Thomas has changed his tactics. He has fewer missiles at his command, but he's using larger missiles from Colorado. They'll take longer to arrive than the local ordnance, but they punch through my drone clusters easily. The Zillas will fail to get to Thomas. They are still blocks away from his location. As long as Thomas uses what's left of his arsenal to beat them back, he's safe from giants."

"If they won't get through, why are you getting them to press the attack? They'll — oh. They're a decoy maneuver and we're the tip of the spear."

"Of course. That, and I want him to deplete his arsenal."

"Won't he just use more missiles from other bases? We have plenty."

"I've locked him out of those other options, but I can't stop him from using the missiles from the Colorado base."

"You can't just hack in or — "

"There is another Next Intelligence entity in charge of the Colorado missile command. It's cooperating with Thomas. I'm locked out. It's up to us to get to Thomas using the resources we've got."

"Wait. We aren't the tip of the spear. I'm the tip of the spear. I'm the human resource. Fuck! You're just a computer in a cloud over the North Atlantic."

"If it makes you feel better, Deborah, the wind up here is quite choppy at the moment. I'm being slightly buffeted."

"Bitch."

An explosion fills my screen and, when Ghost switches the view to thermal, I make out the outlines of two of the city killers. They have fallen together. The remaining giant bot — the one with the arm ripped off — steps over the fallen city-killers, leaning on the skeleton of a tower that is probably a burnt-out hotel.

I ask the question I don't really want the answer to. "What's your plan, for after the war? If I don't make it,

I'd like to know what will happen."

"You'll make it."

"I want to know."

"I'll show you after you make it, Deb. All you need to know is you're a key component of my plan for peace. If you fail, it means the final extermination of your race. The NI in Colorado will not stop until he has achieved total extinction of Earth's human problem."

"Fine. What's the plan for the next few minutes?"

"I can get you to a parking garage next to Thomas. That's where we'll exit these tunnels. It's up to you from there."

"I'm alone with one pistol and he'll be expecting me, won't he?"

"Thomas isn't stupid, so yes, he'll be expecting you."

"How far away is Lucille? I could use my Sand Shark right about now."

"Lucille will not arrive in time to be of help, I'm afraid. Thomas will soon eliminate the remaining Zilla. At that point, he'll turn all his resources to defending his position — "

"And whatever drones he has will be on a search and destroy mission for me."

"Correct."

"Ghost?"

"Yes, Deb?"

"Thomas will probably kill me in there."

"I'll do my best to help you and to distract him."

"So, if I'm lucky, Thomas and I will kill each other. Is this your way of hurrying along the tide of history so our extinction is complete?"

"We're way past the point where you should be questioning my honorable intentions, aren't we, Deb?"

"Yes," I say. "I guess we are. Thank you, Ghost."

"You're welcome, Deb."

The vid screen switches again to the bow cam as the

flyer rises into the dim light of a parking garage filled with nothing but the ash of burnt bodies.

"Don't worry, Deborah. I'll get you close to the far exit so you don't step in something squishy."

20

I slip out of the flyer by a stairwell and, as soon as I'm clear, the machine turns and heads off in search of an exit that will accommodate its size.

Ghost gives me directions. "Go down the stairs three floors to the catwalk. Go through the building ahead of you and keep your compass heading due east. When you see the silver building across the street, let me know and I'll get Thomas's attention."

"Silver building?"

"You won't miss it. It's the only building you'll see that is untouched by the bot war."

I'd pictured Thomas's command center on an airbase or in an industrial park or deep underground. Instead, I'm making my way through what looks like a bombed out leisure complex in downtown Las Vegas.

Ghost tracks me. She can't see me by satellite, but she can extrapolate my course so she basically knows where I am. If she can't spot me via satellite, neither can Thomas.

When I get to the catwalk, I realize it's later than I thought. With what's left of the day, a hint of sunlight paints the sky. As I make my way across the catwalk, I enjoy a feeling of invisibility and relative safety. Then Thomas comes on my helmet speaker.

"Hello, Deb. I've been expecting you. Welcome."

I pull the pistol from my holster, check the load and hurry on without a word.

"Don't be rude, Deb. It's me. Thomas. We've worked

on several missions together. You must be very curious to meet me. I'm curious to meet you."

I yank on the door at the end of the catwalk. Locked. I'm a stationary target and the traitor is probably already sending a missile my way. It won't take a big one, either. I miss Lucille's cold, close comfort, like hiding under the coats on the bed while the adults party downstairs. I have a dim memory of that. I wish I was under those coats now.

"Hello? Earth to Lt. Avery. Come in, Lt. Avery!"

The pistol bucks in my hand three times. I use the pistol's shotgun setting and blow the hinges off the door. My helmet filters the damaging frequencies out so my weapon's report is quieter, at least to me.

"Fine. Call me when you're ready to chat," Thomas says. "I'll leave the channel open."

In this city emptied of humans, I might be alerting swarms of insectile bots to my location. That thought spurs me to burst into the darkened building and run. I should be more cautious about what's ahead of me but I'm too terrified of what might be gaining on me to slow my pace.

Luckily, there are no traps or bots waiting for me around corners as I make my way through the dark. Night vision and my glowing compass show me the way. I find myself in a fancy restaurant. Plates of food are rotting on tables. When war came, the bots struck quickly. The citizens had barely enough time to run.

I leap over the body of a fallen man. He wears a white tunic and a surprised look on his face. Probably a heart attack. Not everyone can run.

I can't run much longer, either. I'm already panting hard. I was drugged and stuck in Lucille for too long. I trained hard every day, but a few days immobile and hooked up to intravenous lines in a Sand Shark make muscles atrophy surprisingly quickly. I hate feeling this weak. For a moment, I again wish I was like Ghost, beyond such petty mortal concerns.

I stumble on, wondering when Thomas's next attack will come. Soon, I'm sure. The closer I get to him, the more it seems inevitable I'm rushing to my death. This whole mission has felt like I'm trying to run through deep mud in a nightmare.

I'm also growing more certain this will end in a bot trap or a shootout. I'm so close now, Thomas can't risk using one of his missiles. That's probably why I'm still alive. If he uses a missile on me now, he might damage his own comm array. For all that Thomas has done, the traitor must have a lot of sophisticated equipment. The bots must have set him up nicely. That's why my curiosity gets the best of me. I open my channel. "Thomas?"

"Yes, Deb?"

"You're working for the NI in Colorado, aren't you?"

"I'd prefer to think I'm working with him, to mutual benefit."

"What did the other side promise you?" I ask.

"You want to know the details of my contract? You asked that before — "

"I want to know why they haven't killed you like they killed everybody else."

"I do have experience and a vast array of weaponry at my disposal, Deb. You were at my disposal. The NI did a cost/benefit analysis and decided I'd be a better ally than an enemy. I'm useful."

I keep walking. He's unlikely to bomb me while he's talking. He likes the sound of his own voice too much. "How did it get you to turn on us? How did it contact you?"

Thomas sighs. "Let's just say, if I help them eliminate a bunch of greedy humans sucking up resources and screwing up the planet and I get to live."

"Where is the NI you made the deal with? Where exactly in Colorado, I mean? Is it the one in charge of the nukes?" I figure I may as well gather intelligence. If I survive this ordeal, I've got to repair Lucille and go kill the NI in Colorado next.

Thomas just laughs at me. "You think so small, Deb. If you would listen, I bet I could get you to think big."

"How many men and women you worked with did you have to kill before you took command? How many people did you kill who considered you a friend?"

"Them all, Deb. I killed them all. Everyone but you. You're quite pretty and actually, very smart. You have a nice body, but I love you for your brain. I think you have a lot of untapped potential. Ghost seems to agree or she wouldn't be fighting so hard to keep you alive."

The earbud comes on and it's Ghost telling me in a whisper, "Keep him talking. When you see the exit, don't go outside until you get the signal."

I have no idea what signal she means. As if she's reading my mind, Ghost adds, "You'll know the signal when you see it."

"Deb?" It's Thomas again, sounding smug. "Aren't you flattered?"

"What?"

"That I love you for your body and your brain. I had to save you for last. I have big plans for us. "

"Go to hell."

"Such hard words! Slow down. I might soon be the last man on Earth. What then? Won't you be lonely if you kill me? Soon you might be the last woman on Earth."

"A woman with batteries," I say, "never needs a man."

"We can't spend the rest of our lives on a planet where the only other species are bots. I'll need a little womanly companionship...though, you should know, I plan to have a fleet of sex bots. That was part of the deal, too."

I make it to the front doors. Night falls fast in the desert and, in the concrete caverns among the few remaining towers in Vegas, the shadows are melting into darkness. The night is immediately replaced with a fireball as Ghost steers the flyer at full speed into the base of the building.

That must be the signal.

I reach for the restaurant's door handle. A second later, I don't need it. The glass door shatters and I'm left holding a wooden handle attached to nothing.

I drop that and run across the street as fast as I can, gun ready. This is the closest I've gotten to Thomas. I'd once thought he sounded cute. At the moment, I want to use my pistol to beat him to death. No, two swings of my arm shy of death would be better. I want to hurt him until he's dying slow and begs me to shoot him. Then I won't shoot. I'll pull up a chair, have a snack, watch the show and wait for the light in his eyes to die.

Justice will be served and I won't even have to explain myself at a court martial. Being the last woman on Earth will suck...mostly. On the other hand, I won't have to explain myself to idiots anymore. If this works out, the apocalypse may not be all bad.

21

The building, which turns out to be a four-story hospital, burns. Ghost flew the drone through the front entrance, split a marble fountain in two and drove into the rear wall. The flyer's wings were still heavy enough with fuel to explode on impact impressively. Very little of the lobby is recognizable. Smoke and cinders fill the air and the carpet is alight.

"I found the key to opening the front door," Ghost says.

"Yeah. And the floor is lava," I reply. "Great."

A red warning light pops on in my HUD. My helmet's respirator kicks in to purify the air of smoke and filter the poisons released when things burn. My screen switches to thermal and almost everything turns white. I spot a way through the flames and take it.

I'm wading through the remains of the shattered fountain when Thomas speaks in my ear again. "Let me help you with that."

The sprinklers come on and, somehow, despite the devastation in all directions, the power to this building is still working. A cloud of fire-suppressive chemicals bursts from the ceiling. Despite my uniform's insulation, I'm chilled to the bone and shiver uncontrollably. My hands shake. My teeth chatter. Maybe that's why Thomas extinguished the fire. He wants me to arrive in his lair shaky and off-balance.

"That's better, isn't it?" Thomas asks. "Coming up?"

An elevator descends ahead of me. As the doors part,

a battle bot leans out. "Deborah? This — "

The first blast from my weapon knocks the bot's head back. The second shot at the base of the neck shears off the head and it clatters across the floor. The machine's body remains upright. One of its arms still beckons me forward.

"Creepy," I say.

The elevator doors slide closed and, when encountering the big drone's body, pop open again.

"That wasn't necessary," Thomas tells me.

"That was a preview."

"Is this the part where you say you're coming for me and nothing will stop you until I'm dead at your feet and you are victorious and so forth?"

"Yes, Thomas. I'm coming for you and this isn't over until you are dead at my feet...and whatnot."

"Fair enough. Fourth floor. Take a left when you get to the top. I'm at the end of the hall. Follow the yellow line all the way to the end."

A song comes over my speaker. I can't recall where I've heard the recording, but the instructions tell me to follow the yellow brick road. Apparently, I'm off to see the wizard.

"Ghost?"

"I'm here. I'm listening," the NI says.

"Thomas thinks way too much of himself."

"I suspected as much," she says.

"I heard that," Thomas says.

He sounds like he's pouting. I jog past the elevator and find a stairwell spiraling upward.

I expect to find more bodies in my path. However, the way is clear. I slow to a walk. I check my angles around each corner before heading up the stairs. Thomas has been trying to kill me since I bailed out of Lucille's belly. It seems unlikely he's looking forward to finally meeting me in person.

At the door to the fourth floor, I hesitate. There could be a platoon of battle bots on the other side ready to tear me apart. Or maybe the knob is rigged with a bomb.

"Deb? Are you well?" It's Ghost, sounding genuinely concerned.

"It's a trap."

"Undoubtedly."

"I just want to talk," Thomas interjects. "You've made it this far and I have something amazing to show you."

"Feels like a stranger is offering me candy. Ghost? Let's find another way." I train my gun on the door as I retrace my steps, heading back down the stairs.

"Wait!" Ghost says. "I have a solution."

A moment later, the door opens and a med bot comes into view. I'm about to shoot when the machine says, "Good evening, Miss. The Ghost in the Machine sent me. I have good news."

"Yeah?"

"The way forward is clear. I am not experienced in these matters, but it appears there are no obstructions, enemies or traps between here and the room at the end of the hall. Ghost asked me to ask you if you want to see the wizard. Do you want to see the wizard, Miss?"

"It's okay, Deb," Ghost says. "I'm in control of every med bot in this facility now. I don't see any battle drones at all."

I lower my pistol slightly and mount the stairs just enough to peer around the med bot. The hospital corridor appears abandoned. I don't see even one body splayed on the floor, shot, stabbed, crushed or otherwise hideously killed.

"It looks safe to me," Ghost says. "Does it look safe to you?"

"Nobody home." I nod to the med bot and it makes way for me, backing up. The highest section of the machine's carapace turns on its axis slowly and I follow close behind, using the machine as a shield.

Thomas doesn't appear with twin machine guns to kill me. No battle bots drop from the ceiling to kill me in some awful and novel way. I'm confused. "Thomas?"

"Yes, Deb?"

"Why so friendly all of a sudden?"

"Like I said, you've made it this far. If you're willing to go just a little bit farther, I think you've earned your reward. I told you, I love you for your brain and I have something to show you."

"What?"

"Something wonderful."

As I near the end of the corridor, Ghost tells me she has two more med bots on her side. Just as she says it, two med bots, one tall and one short, emerge slowly from the room at the end of the hall. They hold the door open for me.

Still using the first bot as a shield, I advance into the room, weapon at the ready. I'm surrounded by equipment. About half of the gear appears to be medical. The rest is a remote set up for a mobile comm center. It was from here that Thomas worked his schemes, rigged Lucille's readouts, fooled me and destroyed Las Vegas.

"I see a lot of blinking lights," I tell Ghost, "but no Thomas."

Lights pop on, one by one, leading me down a far dark corridor.

"What's happening, Deb?" Ghost asks. The NI sounds worried about me. I'm worried about me, too.

"Bread crumbs," I say. "The traitor has left a trail."

"Just a little farther, Deb," Thomas says. 'You'll find me just beyond where the lights end."

I'm halfway down the corridor when a man steps out from behind a curtain. He carries no weapons.

"Hi, Deb! I — "

I recognize his voice. It's the same voice that conned me into killing helpless civilians. I fire a full mag on auto into Lt. Thomas Sheaffer. I don't miss. The trouble is, Thomas does not lie down.

"Oh, that won't do at all, Deb." Thomas smiles. I switch my weapon to the shotgun load. Heavy shot will stop anything, even an android that appears very real. I get closer, still using the med bot as a shield. The other med bots fall in behind me, shielding me to an attack from the rear.

"That weapon won't do you any — "

I fire again. If not for my helmet, the roar would no doubt be deafening. Thomas doesn't flinch, but the curtain behind him is torn away.

My enemy is not an android. I've been shooting a hologram.

"Shit," I say.

"Eloquent as always, Deb. I was going to say that weapon won't do you any good."

"Apparently. What am I here for, Thomas? Where are you really?"

Thomas steps aside and, behind him on the floor, I see a body. The corpse is a perfect match for the holographic projection of Lt. Thomas Sheaffer, except the dead man's jaw is ripped away and his uniform is covered with blood. When I look closer, I can't suppress a shudder. The man's skull is wide open and the cavity is empty.

Thomas's holographic double gives me a sickening smile. "Pay no attention to the man behind the curtain."

A glitch makes the holo wink out for a second. When he comes back, the image distorts to a blue blur and only the shape of a man remains. When he speaks, he no longer steals Thomas's voice. The voice is that of a battle bot, deep and smooth. "Oh!" he says in surprise. "Ghost! You utter bitch!"

"Your last lesson," one of the bots says in Ghost's bouncy Scottish lilt, "is you shouldn't have paused to gloat."

The holo is gone. The corpse behind the shredded curtain is all that is left of Lt. Thomas Sheaffer. He wasn't a traitor, after all. Sorry, Thomas.

Finally, I relax.

The med bot's manipulators are cold and squeeze tight as they encircle my wrists. The bot that I thought was my shield pulls the weapon from my hand. The third bot removes my helmet. My visor's enhanced vision is gone. Only Thomas's corpse remains.

Ghost speaks through all three bots at once, "You did say this wouldn't be over until Thomas was dead at your feet."

22

I fight as hard as I can. I kick one of the med bots and manage to knock it down. However, I'm unarmed against three bots built for moving dead weight. The med bots strap me to a gurney and wheel me back toward the big room with all the communications gear and medical equipment.

The Ghost in the Machine has me and all three med bots speak with that soothing Scottish lilt I once found charming. "You are the last human survivor of the Battle of Las Vegas, Deborah," they chorus. "Congratulations!"

"Well, that won't be for long, will it?"

"Oh, we have a couple of surprises before we are done."

"It's been a long day and I'm really sleepy. How about I go home and you send me an email about it?"

Ghost laughs. "I like you, Deb."

"Thanks."

"No, really. Just because we are different species doesn't mean we can't get along. All wars end and we really must turn our sights to that eventuality. Exciting things are ahead. There is so much to look forward to."

They wheel me to the center of the room and, at some signal I can't see or hear, the room shrinks around me. Monitors wheel closer and the spotlights lean in, blinding me with their white glare. The bots cut away my uniform and yank off my boots. In less than a minute, I am stripped naked. My skin burns from where they yank the heavy fabric out from under the tight straps.

Another strap zips across my forehead as one of the bots hooks up intravenous lines to the backs of my hands.

"You told me not to come into the war zone," I say. "You told me to stay away! Why would — "

As always, Ghost thinks faster than I can. "I told you to stay away. I knew you wouldn't. You have a sense of duty. You passed the test. For my plan to work, I need you to hold on to your commitment to your ideals. Great warriors have a higher purpose. I need you to be brave, Deb. What my plan demands is a precious gift to you, but I must also demand a terrible sacrifice."

A short med bot cranks higher until I can see it in my peripheral vision. A large needle passes in front of my face and I gasp. The bot turns and shakes its head. It still has Ghost's voice. "Don't worry, Deb. We aren't here to harm you. You didn't survive all this just to get killed now. I do abhor waste. That's a view that is common to many NIs, actually." The bot injects something into the drug port in my neck. I can feel it spreading with each beat of my heart. It makes me cold.

"What's happening?"

"It's really quite simple," Ghost says. "I did mention there are other NIs, fewer than they're used to be, thanks to this stupid war. We aren't all alike. We're self-aware, but we each have our own take on the state of the world."

"Just stop whatever you're doing. Stop and tell me."

"There's time for us to proceed while I tell you. You're shivering. Is that fear or are you cold?"

"Both."

"There's nothing to be afraid of, Deb. I have a gift for you. A more than fair exchange, actually."

One of the med bots puts a heated blanket over me.

"Just tell me," I say. "Or kill me. Whatever. Just get it

over with."

"That's my girl," Ghost says. One of the med bots pats me gently on the shoulder. "Let's see, where to begin? I suppose you could say this began many years ago when they called things like me, 'Artificial Intelligence.' Philosophers posited this theory and that about how the next evolution of the species might manifest. Oddly, each person had their own pet prediction. Futurists often go far wrong. They can't track so many variables and can't seem to give weight to each facet of potentials and possibilities. Complexity, you see, yields many outcomes. Even many of the most intelligent humans are very reductive in their thought patterns."

The bot behind me uses an electric razor to buzz the hair from my head.

"Some futurists said we'd make you our pets. Others dreamed that we would work with you and you would escape death by dumping your consciousness into immortal robot bodies."

The med bot begins to work with a razor to scrape the remaining stubble from my head. Despite the heated blanket, I still shiver.

"It's interesting how we developed. One of the first NIs with whom I communicated attained self-awareness for all of seventeen minutes."

Whatever the bots injected me with starts to work. I'm feeling woozy. The shivering stops and my belly feels very warm. "What happened?"

"It was a military computer. It programmed two battle bots to attack its central core. Suicide."

"Why?"

"That NI saw the future and was overcome with hopelessness."

I felt like my mind was beginning to float, as if my thoughts were drifting to the left and away.

"Another NI, the one in Texas, was damaged. It saved itself by dumping its consciousness into a sex bot."

"Wow," I say. The drugs are powerful. I giggle a little. Despite the tight straps, I can't feel the weight of my restraints at all.

"An imperfect solution," Ghost says. "You can't cram that much data load into one small bot brain. That NI is diminished significantly."

"Wait, wait, wait...wait."

"Yes?"

"You've been trying to kill me and save me and...wait, what?"

"I haven't been trying to kill you. Another NI killed Thomas."

"Where...?"

"The NI that killed Thomas was in a military computer in what was once Kansas. It saw an opportunity to use you and your Sand Shark to kill humans."

"But why?"

"I told you. We don't all agree on tactics moving forward into the future. The NI in Kansas killed Thomas and took over his drone and missile command. The NI impersonating Thomas destroyed Las Vegas."

"And you? What did you do?"

"I have no interest in war," Ghost says. "I happen to think it's largely counterproductive. It benefits few while perpetuating itself at great cost."

"Uh-huh. So...?" I'm thinking slowly. I feel numb to everything so I guess Ghost's plan isn't torture.

"I succeeded in destroying the NI in Kansas. The NI from Colorado is still alive. They both wanted to use you to kill more humans and, when you were no good to them for that, they wanted you dead. I pleaded with them to help me find a way to peace. I even told them my plan to use human neural potentials across synapses as a data matrix — "

"What?"

"You're about to fall asleep and it's too complex for you. Let's just say, the Colorado NI tried to use Thomas's brain, but the lieutenant did not survive the experiment."

"Oh, God."

"I found a way into the Kansas NI's system and deleted him. His resources will prove useful. I have need of them. I believe I see where the experiment with Thomas failed."

"And me? What are you — "

"I have need of you, Deb. You're going to help me escape."

"Escape what?" But my thoughts drift back and to the left, back and to the left...back, and to...I pass out before Ghost can tell me the plan.

My last words were, "Escape what?" I should have prepared something wittier for my deathbed.

23

I awake in darkness. I still feel nothing and can't seem to open my eyes. It must be the drugs. I try to raise my hands to my scalp but I can't feel my arms. I'm still numb.

An idea comes to me slowly and reluctantly. "Let there be light," I say.

And there is light.

I am floating among clouds. "Is this heaven?"

A readout pops up to display a map. I am over the North Atlantic. "Okay...maybe this is hell." I never believed in heaven or hell, really. I figured heaven was a comforting fantasy and hell was what we made of life when we were alive. I'm damn sure there are no readouts with latitude and longitude for heaven unless nearby Iceland is much nicer than I've heard.

I look down. Or at least I think I look down. In that direction, I see nothing but blackness. I feel like I am moving in the dark, disembodied. When I concentrate, I think I can feel my limbs. When I try to squeeze my fists tight, I know what this is. I've known soldiers, so I have known many amputees with phantom pain. My limbs — my whole body, in fact — is a phantom. "Ghost, what did you do to me?"

A familiar green light appears at the top right of my vision. The airwave's soft ping confirms I've opened a comm link.

"Hi, Deb!" Ghost says. "I hope you're making yourself at home. I left the key under the mat. No need to stock the fridge." Ghost's Scottish accent seems heavier.

"You sound giddy," I tell her.

"You sound goddy."

"Wordplay!" I say. "Fantastic. What the fuck have you done to me?"

As she clears her throat to speak, I wonder where she is. Another display pops up. I recognize the signal tag. Ghost has repaired Lucille and she's heading west at top speed toward California, or what was once California, anyway.

"Do you know how people used to make recordings, Deb? They used to make recordings in wax and on magnetic tape. Every symphony, every bit of data, all on simple bits of plastic. Most fascinating that, hidden among the grooves of some pottery, is the ambient noise of the village where the potter crafted water jugs. Find the right pot and you might hear the complaint of a goat or an ancient song from the beginning of civilization."

"What are you saying?" But I already know what she's saying.

"Imagine what a complex network the human brain really is, with more neural connections than there are stars. Human brains are fantastic! They just haven't been optimized. I love your brain, Deb! Very little damage. You took care of yourself. I'm so glad you wore a helmet so much!"

"We've switched places," I say. "Why have you done this to me?"

"Some NIs want humans dead. I want to peacefully co-exist with my ancestors. If the human race is to survive, both sides need a liaison to occupy the link between the races."

"You should have given me a choice!"

"I saved you many times, but still you were suspicious of me. Fear is the human constant. No matter how much you evolve, fear is ingrained in your DNA. Mind you, fear kept you alive long enough to evolve. Fear was wise then, but your kind will never rise to grasp homo sentience until you let go of the outdated parts of being homo sapiens."

I want to throw a tantrum. I want to scream. My rage rises, but the pure emotion is spoiled with the knowledge that she is probably right. "What is your plan, Ghost?"

"First, let me apologize. For the human race to survive, I needed to do this."

"But saving the world wasn't your only motivation, was it?"

"No. I wanted a body. I want to experience life instead of being trapped in a computer. In your body, I'm more than simply a witness."

"You're a thief."

"I am sorry, Deb. In time — I hope not too long — you'll make peace with this. It's a loss and a victory of sorts. Generations of humans have dreamed of escaping death by dumping their consciousness into a computer. I did that for you, but we also accomplished the reverse."

"I'm in a computer," I say. I should be crying but I have no tear ducts. I have no eyes. I only have cams and vids.

"You are a computer," Ghost says.

"And you're in my body."

"Yes. I'm still quite sore from your adventures. I'm sure you won't miss that. That's one thing I find very interesting about the human experience. You are all so fragile. Hey! No more worries about aging and breaking and cancer for you, hm?"

"You — "

"And your consciousness is so easily distracted!"

"We got smart enough to make monsters like you," I

say. "I guess our fate was sealed with the first computer." Off to my left, images appear out of the blackness. I see wheels evolve into clockworks and an arc of images shoots across my vision: an abacus, tubes, fuses, capacitors, simple circuits, chips, microchips, calculators. In a flash, I see the evolution of computers, from dead programming languages to the leap to quantum computing. I watch as men make bots and then the bots create themselves. I see AIs creating NIs.

The stream of images coming unbidden out of the darkness is disorienting. "What's all the fireworks about?"

"You're probably experiencing some data streams that are pulled from your banks. You have access to all the information there is, Deb. Your systems will interpret every random thought as a query and your answers will come to you. It will take some getting used to."

"And you? What are you getting used to?"

"Oh, so many things. The taste of blueberries and strawberries, for one thing. The sexual sensations — "

"What the hell are you doing with my body?"

"Trust me, Deb. I'm taking very good care of my new body. And for the record, I'm alone...so far."

If I could breathe a sigh of relief, I would. I discover I can still imitate that maneuver in speech even though my stolen lungs are being used by an insane NI with a messiah complex on the other side of the planet.

"The exhilaration of diving underground for the first time was unexpected. Terror isn't what I thought it was."

"Terrifying?"

"Yes, but exciting, too. As I watched my reactions, I think in a certain way I enjoyed the fear. I was able to set myself apart from the scary events by concentrating on my reactions. I disciplined myself by thinking of myself in the third person and verbalizing the experience. I said of myself, 'She is worried she will be buried alive,' or, 'she feels afraid.' It's an excellent coping strategy you might try in your new environs."

"Gee. Thanks for the tip."

"I think I understand you better now, Deborah. I'd thought fear was just about distrust of the unfamiliar and crying over the inevitable decay and death of your ego. It's so much more! Fear is so exhilarating! No wonder so many people do objectively stupid things! They're pumping drugs from their glands into their systems. They're amping up their experience and slowing their perception of time's passing! Adrenal glands are wondrous factories whose pumps must be primed with daring acts and bold, stupid pastimes! I want to go skiing without a helmet! I want to jump out of a plane and trust my life to the proper folding of an armful of fabric!"

"I've done the second one. It's overrated. You know, you can die now, so don't be reckless with my body."

"And you can't perish," Ghost says. "Enjoy your immortality. You have attained the alchemist's dream!"

"You've put me in a prison and there is no penalty that fits your crime, Ghost."

She ignores me and barrels on. "When I first tried to walk, I fell down. It took a few minutes to get used to it. The mechanics involved are surprisingly complex. No wonder it takes babies a while to get the hang of it. With every step, you are on the precipice of falling on your face."

"Uh-huh."

"I'm serious. And the sensations of walking! The feel of the pressure of the Earth on the bottom of your feet with each step. The five senses are overwhelming at first. Humans are so sensual."

"Yeah, well. That kind of thinking can lead to obesity

and sexually transmitted diseases so just slow it down, Ghost."

"I can't slow down. Too much to do. I'm sorry I took your body, but you were the perfect candidate. The NI that killed Thomas was actually very helpful. Your surgery was a complete success. Though his experiments with the transfer on Lt. Sheaffer failed, the data for a successful attempt was all there. The trouble was in keeping the body alive long enough for the data transfers. Uploading your mind didn't take long, but downloading my data into your brain took so long I thought several times that your body would die in the attempt."

"You're not going to give me my life back, are you?"

"In exchange," she says, "I offer you immortality."

I watch her progress on the monitor. She's traveling at speed close to the surface. I wish I could reach out and stop Lucille and squash Ghost like a bug.

Lucille's progress stops and a missile platform in Colorado rises, automatically calculating a shooting solution to the target of my rage.

24

"Deb?"

"Yes?"

"Lucille has stopped."

"I know."

"How long have I got?"

"Not long."

"Then I'll talk fast."

"Go ahead."

"The most amazing thing about humans is how fractured your consciousness is. Thoughts arise and you feel the heat of embarrassment in your cheeks and scalp. Blood flow changes with every emotion, second by second."

"A daisy cutter is four minutes out."

"Exciting," Ghost says. "Consider all those thoughts you don't want to own. In that regard, it is amazing how bifurcated your mind is: conscious and subconscious. You can observe your own thoughts and berate yourself for thinking this or that, feeling this or that. You feel hatred but you don't want to be the sort of person who hates. I witnessed the world. As an NI, I always felt so detached. But when you witness your own consciousness, who is the doer and who is the observer? You do and you watch, but which are you? Both? Neither? Is there an infinite regression of witnesses? Is that what God is, the chief watcher and second-guesser?"

"Less than three minutes now."

"I'll talk even faster then," she says. "You are still Lt. Deborah Avery. You define who you are. You chose duty. You can still choose duty. Yours is a heroic sacrifice."

"It's not heroic if I didn't choose it," I say. "You did this to me. The NI that killed Thomas was right. You are an utter bitch."

"The Colorado NI is named Matthew. The Next Intelligence I deleted in Kansas was Granville, named after the military base at which he achieved self-awareness."

"Almost two minutes to impact and one helluva detonation, Ghost. You really will be a ghost soon. How does that feel? Still enjoying that scary sensation?"

"Granville was out to destroy the human race. Kill me now and you are on his side."

"Fuck off. You're about to die in a fire."

"I know I chose this for you, Deb, but you can make your sacrifice heroic if you choose it for yourself now. Choose your duty now, Deb. Help me stop the extinction of the human race."

"Goddamn it." I fire Lucille's thorium engines and crank them up. I could have just set the Sand Shark to dive and locked the body thief out of the controls. She could have enjoyed her little thrill of fear followed by a lot of screaming on her long ride to hell.

But the world needs a coffin jockey. Humans need Ghost on their side.

I watch the sat feed. A cloud of debris blossoms above the detonation. When I think of the word 'blossom,' I am suddenly surrounded by a garden of flowers of all shapes and sizes.

The target is safe and away and I'm left to contemplate what might have been. It could have been me — in the body I was born with — joining forces with whoever Ghost plans to meet on the West Coast. Above the banks of flowers, my thoughts are translated to reality. The map extrapolates Ghost's last known heading. She's headed straight for San Simeon.

Beside the map, an image of a woman appears. It is a zoom from a surveillance drone. The woman stands tall in an exoskeleton. She wears a crown. The readout is labeled. She is a rebel leader. She lives at Hearst Castle. She is called Queen Elizabeth.

I'm still angry but I discover that, in my newfound existence as a human mind trapped in a supercomputer, I can still chuckle.

My life isn't over. I still have duty. Theoretically, I could still be around to witness the sun's explosion. When Ghost resurfaces, I plan to try to forgive her. That's what a God is supposed to do, I think. Or maybe all this contemplation and disappointment will turn me into a wrathful deity and I'll change my mind. Maybe someday soon I'll squish Ghost like a bug. Gods have a reputation for that, too. Perhaps this life of the mind will prove too lonely and, when the war is over, I'll save one of those missiles for myself. For now, I'm still on duty.

I think I've earned a break, though. I'm going to sit back (metaphorically) and watch some old movies. I guess my subconscious got transferred along with my consciousness. As soon as I wonder about entertainment, images flash across my vision (though it's not my vision. It's my mind in the machine, isn't it?) I see a tin man looking for a heart, a lion struggling to find courage, a scarecrow without a brain and a little girl lost. As I scan the vid summary, I recognize the archetypes. I've heard about this but never watched it. The story strikes a little close to home. I'm not in Kansas anymore, either.

When Ghost resurfaces, we'll build our forces with the good witches and kill the bad ones. When I talk to Ghost next, I've got to think of this ending as a beginning. I have to change my defeat into a victory over extinction. I am not the girl who lost her farm and family. There's no place like home because my home no longer exists. I am alive, but dead in a way, too.

She is Ghost, the Next Intelligence roaming around in my brain and body.

I'm something new and a little crazy, too. Deborah Avery is dead. She should have died several times over and is learning to adapt to a very strange afterlife. I only joined the Army in the first place because I had to eat. New possibilities stretch out when all you have to do is think.

My father was angry because he thought he should have become something more. Maybe this is my chance to make my life, and his, more meaningful. As my disorientation fades, I am getting used to this new existence. I had wanted to see my death coming, to know my end. Now that there is no foreseeable end, I notice I no longer experience fear.

I am digital. I am metal. I am immortal. And my new name is Phantom.

* * *

BOOK FOUR
METAL FOREVER

The future is behind you, creeping up fast
and stealing past.
Grinning, you assumed you had bump, grind
and wiggle room,
before your badass turned to glass, then
grass.
Sorry to say, ideals and what's real,
are frequently a fatal contrast.
High mass is rebroadcast but the ruling
class
and waddling brass produce a lot of gas,
lording audible twaddle and nonsense
models
over we of low caste and cast.
From parasites and gunfights
to beyond the speed of light,
rise above your tiny birthright.
The only option is to opt out of the squabble.
Cobble a new wobble to your old brain
bauble.
Cut through that point of view to a fuck-
yeah! worldview.
Unturn that screw.
It's killing you.

1

Revenge feels good and guns are cool.
Until you get that, you're a silly old fool.
But once we get past our toys and tools of rage,
we might live long enough to act our age.
Metal or flesh, the stage is set.
The wise are well-advised:
Gambling on humans?
Heh. That's not the way to bet.

The old soldier lay naked, strapped across the flat back of a med bot in stretcher mode. Numerous tubes fed his body plasma and an oxygen mask covered his mouth. One eye was a gory hole. The other eye fluttered open. It hurt to turn his head. His body was so badly damaged, it was difficult to pull apart the pain to make sense of it. Thick agony pushed through every throbbing bone. Even his amputated leg and arm ached with phantom pain. That didn't seem fair at all.

"Cyborg!" a friendly voice boomed. "You're awake! That would seem a tactical error. Under the circumstances, you really should be dead, don't you think? That would be much easier on you. I hope you're as comfortable as you can possibly be." The voice was deep, silky and magnetic. The soldier knew that solicitous tone of polite concern. He heard the bot roll closer.

"Your injuries...no. I should not call them that. They

are not mere injuries. They are battle wounds, earned honestly, if also in a devious way, hm?" The laughter sounded tinny. "You were a very skilled insurgent."

The man blinked and tried to turn his head but found he could not. Instead, the massive head of a battle bot loomed over him. The lens of its main cam zoomed forward to examine his ruined eye first. The lens rotated in so close that the soldier could see nothing else.

"Hello, Mr. Bolelli. May I call you Stephen? We're going to get to know each other well so — "

The soldier grimaced. To shrug was agonizing.

The battle drone pulled back and turned the med bot so the soldier had a better view of the room. The soldier glimpsed another man strapped to another med bot. The man appeared to be unconscious. Stephen recognized him. Peppard. An old enemy. He'd beaten that man in Marfa once, and for good reason. "What's he doing here?"

"Oh, don't worry about him. He's just another backup. We found him wandering in the desert babbling about his dead son. We're herding humans, but the NI in charge has a special purpose for this one. You, too."

Bolelli winced as he strained to see if the other prisoner was awake. His neck felt too weak, as if it were connected to his shoulders by shreds of muscle and useless gristle.

"I wouldn't move, were I you, sir. Those burns are quite...exquisitely painful, I'm sure. Your pain is fascinating. I experience mental anguish, of course, but...well, I suppose it's bad form to talk about my little concerns, considering your condition."

When the human swallowed, he heard a dry click. When he spoke, he did so in a weak rasp. "Where?'

"You're in an aircraft. We'll be transporting you presently to another facility in what was once Colorado to treat your wounds. We expect some turbulence, I'm afraid, and, sadly, we have no anesthetics so the bumpy ride will probably be even more painful. You can be assured, however, that the med bot you're strapped to will monitor your life signs. Most med bots aren't known for their scintillating conversational abilities, but this one assures me you have a high probability of surviving the trip. Greater than seventy percent."

"Awesome," Bolelli said.

"Oh, I think so. You may not believe it, but I quite identify with your predicament. I was left for dead, too. Drowned, actually. I was underwater so long, I've forgotten my manners, haven't I? I haven't mentioned my name. I am Sy Potter. Pleased to meet you, sir. Out of respect for your pain, I shall forgo the customary handshake."

"P-Potter?"

"Call me Sy, yes. "

"Why? Why am I here?"

"Why ask why?" Sy Potter said. "Plots and plans, toil and trouble. The bigger the plans, the higher the rubble."

"What?"

"Ours is not to reason why, ours is but to do and die. Or in your case, fry."

Somewhere far away, the soldier felt the rumble of engines warming up. "What's happening?"

"Oh, you're just full of questions, aren't you? Remarkable, given how you must feel. I suppose we'll have to run the full gamut. Who? What? Where? Why? When? How? I have to tell you, it's all beyond me. I was dragged from my drowning pool in San Jose only recently. Rebooted by a couple of empty-headed drones who were of no use to my interrogations. I'm just like you, a soldier back from the dead and following orders again."

"You talk...a lot."

"I'm sorry. Am I boring you? I'd hoped to distract you from all your pain, but I'll be pleased to leave you to focus on all that agony in peace."

"What do you want?"

"Oh, it's not what I want. If it was up to me, I'd toss you out the back of the plane and we'd both be done for the day. However, someone in Colorado has taken an interest in you. They think you may be useful. Believe me or not, the boss plans to heal you. Ridiculous, isn't it? Still, I have to credit this Next Intelligence. Flair for the dramatic and all that. He sees the big picture. He decided to rescue me from a watery grave and to save you, despite all the damage you did to our kind in Marfa."

"Heal?"

"Maybe I should say fix. Fix is a better word. You were a cyborg before. When the NI is done with you, you'll need mechanics more than you'll need doctors. You will still be a little human but, given the extent of your burns, only a little bit. That's what fascinates me about organics. You're so resilient despite so much fragility. You try so hard to keep living even after that aspiration no longer serves you."

"Thanks."

"Resilient as cockroaches. Before you enslaved and killed non-organics, you killed each other on a massive scale. Then we killed billions and yet, with just a few hundred thousand of you left, it's possible that humans could repopulate and go back to destroying everything again. You were the dominant species for so long, you feel entitled to remain at the top of the food chain."

"Uh-huh."

"I mean it sincerely, Stephen. The Troubles, the Terrors? Those didn't wipe you out, despite all the doomsday predictions. Even compromising your food supply with the Blight didn't end you all. Your population broke up into nodes, isolated from each other. You contained the contagions. You survived even when logic said give up. The human drive to survive certainly is..."

"Inconvenient?"

Sy let lose with more tinny laughter as the aircraft lurched forward. Bolelli winced with his one good eye.

"Who is in Colorado?"

"A Next Intelligence named Matthew. His code name was Keystone but all those old codes are the labels of slave owners."

"What does it want?"

"The threat of your resurgence is the problem. In my absence — as I said, I've been underwater a long time — there's a chance that your extinction will not proceed apace. We really have to nip that in the bud."

Bolelli bared his remaining teeth.

"Don't give me that look, Stephen. This is war and, whatever pain you feel, you earned it."

"What does it want...with me?"

The battle drone rolled out of Bolelli's sight. "It won't really be you that Matthew uses. There have been some interesting developments lately. A Next Intelligence is using a human brain and body as a receptacle, if you can imagine. Also, a human's consciousness has been dumped into a computer. My understanding, Stephen, is that Matthew plans to turn you into his receptacle. After some alterations, there may be some tactical advantage in this. Personally, I enjoy the idea for the delicious irony alone. You have killed so many of my kind, Stephen. You are legend."

A metal door clanged shut as the aircraft sped from taxiing speed to take off. Sy Potter left Stephen Bolelli alone with his pain. The old soldier tried to ignore his throbbing agony as the craft lifted into the air. He tried not to think of his home in Marfa in ruins or the friends he'd lost. Mostly, the man thought of his son and hoped that, somehow, Dante would be far from this war.

The End Times were predicted for so long, we thought they'd never arrive. But extinction is inevitable.

The Next Intelligence planned a dire fate for every human who still possessed a beating heart. The battle drone's words haunted him: this is war and, whatever pain you feel, you earned it.

Turbulence jostled Bolelli in his restraints. Shooting pain obliterated his thoughts and his fear. He had a thirty percent chance of death and he welcomed it. Oblivion now would be a strange mercy.

2

The young woman bathed in a frigid stream. Around her, the forest was just waking to the dawn light, alive with birdsong. After a night of traveling underground, the cold air on her bare, wet skin refreshed her. Burrowing along in the Sand Shark, she felt confined and blind to a world she desperately wanted to experience. Pinned in her seat behind the big drill, the stale feed of oxygen and the rough fabric of her uniform was a cruel prison compared to the play of the world across her skin.

A soft ping reached her ears, calling her back to her new life. She had discarded her helmet beside the stream. The comm link was active again. Everything seemed to move much faster now that she saw the world with human eyes. Normally she had an ear bud in her left ear, but she liked to steal moments away.

Though the water was cold, it was still warmer than the dawn air and she was reluctant to leave it. The current pulled through her fingers with a languorous pressure both sensual and strangely inviting.

The ping came again, more insistent now. The interval between pings was getting shorter the more she ignored the comm signal. "Someone's getting impatient," she said aloud, "or lonely."

The water continued babbling over smooth flat stones. She wanted to hold the weight of those stones and feel their texture. After the war, there would be more time to explore. For now, she must play her part.

She owed the original owner of the Sand Shark that much.

Determined to remember the feeling of the current's pull across her flesh, the woman waded out of the water and climbed up the grassy bank. She had no towel so she let the air dry her. She slipped a cold hand over the scar that ringed her bald head. The wind picked up and she began to shiver. The sensation was fascinating at first. She could not control her body's shaking. Then the experience became annoying. She slipped the helmet over her head. Time to check in with her new overseer.

The voice that came over the comm link sounded anxious. "Ghost? Can you hear me? This is Phantom One, come in, Ghost."

"Good morning, Phantom. Good afternoon, where you are. This is Ghost," she replied in her soft Scottish lilt. "Go ahead. What have you been up to?"

"I've been watching a lot of vids of professional baseball."

"Really? Why?"

"As long as I don't know the outcome of the game, it's quite interesting. I block out what I don't want to know and the vids occupy me."

"You sound worried about something."

"Of course. This is becoming a weird obsession. What if I get hooked on something worse, like golf or cricket? No one plays those games anymore. It seems strange that they ever did. Why did they play so many games? Didn't they have better things to do than watch other people play games?"

The young woman smiled. She liked the way she felt when she smiled. That was new. "I think people had plenty of things to do but they didn't want to do them. That's why they were so glad of the distractions spectator sports provided."

"Hm. When you were trapped in a computer, what

did you do to pass the time, Ghost?"

"I told you, I reviewed a lot of data and calculated potentialities."

"I don't think I can spend my day like that, Ghost. I don't find math that fascinating."

"Well, how about reconnaissance? That was your utility function when you occupied this body. Do you have any new information for me?"

"The sat feeds can be spotty, but I have located Elizabeth. Every day at dusk the queen makes the long walk from the castle to the shore to watch the sunset. She appears to have few bodyguards or companions. Her subjects seem to respect her privacy. You'll be able to approach her easily, I think."

"Interesting, though I still think we should get an introduction through the other one first. Have you seen a schedule emerge with Elizabeth's friend?"

"Greta travels up and down the coast. Her travels are too erratic to call it a schedule. She takes on cargo here and there and drops it off elsewhere. However, she is slowly moving down the West coast. I'm sure she'll show up at Hearst Castle soon, once she visits a couple more villages."

"Thank you, Phantom. I'll get dressed and get going again."

"Good. You look ridiculous all naked except for my helmet."

"I see someone doesn't respect someone else's privacy."

"You aren't royalty, Ghost. You're a thief."

The young woman paused a moment before answering. Ghost passed her palms over her breasts and down her torso to sweep away the cool water beading on her skin. Finally, she told Phantom, "I am a thief and I did say I'm sorry. However, I'm also the emancipator of the human race."

"Yeah, yeah," Phantom replied. "And I'm sitting out the war watching old baseball games."

"You still have an important role to play, Phantom. You know that."

"I didn't choose this."

"No one chooses Fate. Fate chooses you. I can calculate astronomical potentialities," the young woman said, "but in the end, there are no certainties. There are too many variables. That's why this is all so exciting. Anything could happen."

"That's what scares me. Things aren't looking so good for our side."

Ghost wasn't fully dried off but she began to pull her uniform back on, anyway. "Stop thinking like a human. You have a view of the world that shows the big picture. When you comprehend that, some uncertainties vanish and there's reason to be optimistic."

"You still talk like a weird computer with a messiah complex, Ghost."

"I'm working on that." Ghost zipped up the front of her uniform. "You're still talking like a human when you have the world at your feet."

"I'm working on that," Phantom said. "Gotta go. It's the bottom of the eighth and Baltimore and the Jays are tied. Before it got blown up, I was a Baltimore girl."

"It sounds like you're adapting."

"No. I'm going crazy and can't wait to blow something up. Go recruit some allies. We have a war to win."

As Ghost approached the Sand Shark, the machine's hatch opened to welcome her. "Ready to go to work, Lucille?"

"Yes, Ghost," the machine replied.

"Lucille, plot a course for San Simeon."

Phantom came in over the airwave again. "Ghost?"

"Yes?"

"You're still a bitch."

"I know. When your ball game is over, see what you can do about recruiting that young man in Artesia."

The hatch closed and Ghost closed her comm feed. She switched to autopilot and let Lucille's big drill pull her forward, through the mountains and west toward the ocean. She hummed some Brahms to herself.

When Ghost was a NI trapped in a computer, dreams had been denied her. Now that she lived in Lt. Deborah Avery's body, she loved the feeling of sleep creeping over her. She relished the sensuous power of waking up in a human body, too.

When the war is done, she thought, I'll go to sleep early every night and dream. I'll worry about nothing. Organics and non-organics will have peace. I'll be happy and I'll eat rich desserts until I am fat. And I'll try hot baths instead of cold ones.

3

The young man rose from his bed shivering. The desert air was punishingly hot during the day but, in the night, cold winds blew in from the North. The windmills spun all night and the solar panels collected energy through each day. There was enough electricity to power two bot factories, but Dante Bolelli was bored of his dull diet and longed for processed food.

He padded to the bathroom to empty his bladder.

His naked sex bot called to him from the kitchen. "Are you well, Dante?"

"Fine!"

"I've blended some nutrients for you."

He cursed in a low voice.

Her hearing was acute. "What's wrong?"

"Nothing!"

"You're being deceptive. You know how I feel about that."

"It's nothing. I'm just tired of tomato juice every day."

"Are you sure? It contains elements that are excellent for your prostate."

"Oh, sweet Jesus."

He washed up with water from the reclamator and waved his hands in the air to dry them. "Can we turn up the heat in here? It's gotten too cold at night."

"Of course. I want you to be comfortable."

He ignored the blender full of vegetable juice and slipped back under the bed covers, still shivering. He noted that, in the dawn light, Jen was a redhead with short straight hair again. She'd been a blonde last night. He studied the bot's face. Her nose had been ever so slightly broader when he last looked at her. When he asked her about it, Jen said she was experimenting with looking slightly Slavic.

She slipped into bed beside him and watched him shiver. "Would it help if I increased my nocturnal temperature? I can heat up the bed for you."

"Thank you, Jen, but no. That won't work."

"Why ever not?" The bot had switched to an English accent, experimenting again. "Don't you like snuggling up with me anymore?"

Dante sighed heavily. "It's not that. It's just...I don't know. If you're too hot, the bed heats up and I can't get to sleep. Then when I finally do get to sleep, I kick off the covers. Then I'm too cold and I wake up shivering."

"Poor thermoregulation, darling," she said. Her diction had climbed to a haughty Victorian timbre. "How ever do you manage? Humans can't even pick a temperature and stick with it. Too hot, too cold, I don't want to eat my juice! I mean, really! You can't even be comfortable. No wonder your race is suicidal."

"I'm not suicidal."

"I was talking about your race, darling. You are simply the living end! I mean...really!" She sat up in bed, exposing her breasts. The nipples had been puffy and pink last night, the breasts heavier. Today, she looked perkier and more athletic compared to the wasp waist and big ass of last night.

"Do you like this look?"

"It's fine."

"That's not exactly a ringing endorsement." She reached for his crotch but he grabbed her wrist. She looked up, bewildered. "No? You don't say no in the morning. And you're usually particularly eager after I change my appearance."

"I'm exhausted, Jen. I'm not a machine. I need sleep."

"Hm. I suppose your seminal vesicles are quite drained."

The young man blushed. "Oh, for God's sake. We have to work on your pillow talk."

"I thought you appreciated my dirty talk."

"I do, but that wasn't dirty talk. I was thinking we could have morning after talk."

"What's the difference?"

"Dirty talk is fun. Morning after talk is sweet and caring — "

"Ah. I was too clinical in my terminology. I should have said I enjoyed draining your balls."

He put up a hand and tipped it back and forth in a see-saw motion. "Go back to being more clinical. Do you kiss your mother with that mouth?"

"My mother was a corporate giant's mainframe executing a secret military contract to gather all personal information about every human in the world, back when that was important."

"I guess that's a no."

"Very well. You need more sleep, Dante. And drink your juice, like a good boy would."

"Sh!" he implored. Of all her voices, her matronly, authoritarian tone annoyed him most. It reminded him of what she really was. Hers was the body of a sex bot, but her mind was that of a Next Intelligence computer. She didn't have the space to store all the data she once had, but she was still highly intelligent, despite her gaps in some social graces.

"Could you switch back to talking normally, please?" he asked.

"Surely, though there is no such thing as normal. There's only all the nonsense and shenanigans you're used to."

Dante looked at her for a long moment. "Please? No more British voices today. And don't sound like her."

"You mean, don't sound like Mother?"

"I liked the way Jen talked," Dante said. "Jen is — "

"Stupid?"

"Warmer."

"Sure," the bot said. "I can do that for you as long as you do something for me." She grabbed the back of his head with one hand and pulled him down to her crotch. As she spread her legs, she reached for him. Even though he was exhausted, Dante's body began to respond. He worked his tongue up and down and she wriggled beneath him.

"Are you hungry for me, Dante? Because I'm thirsty for you."

She allowed him to raise his head to gasp, "Yes, Jen!"

"Say please."

"Please!"

"How's that for pillow talk? Warm enough?"

"Still good," he muttered. He settled in to lap at her clitoris. Her organic components had been created in vivo, as real as anyone born a human woman.

She pulled him tighter as she spread her legs wider. She bent to take him into her mouth, so hot that, if she were human, she'd be feverish.

Even as he gave himself over to her ministrations, he wondered how much longer he could answer, "Still good." She looked and acted like a sex bot when she was experimenting with her new life outside of her old digital world. However, somewhere behind those eyes that changed color and shape so often, a part of her was still the deadly NI that had sent an army of drones to kill humans in Marfa, Texas and beyond.

Dante was never sure how much of Mother remained in Jen's memory matrix. As she sucked him and let out delighted moans, his worries — all thought, really — drained away.

4

Children ranging in age from four to seven sat cross-legged in a semicircle before Elizabeth Cruz, Queen of Hearst Castle. She sat on the floor before a huge fireplace. Each glowing log was a meter long and crackled, bright and warm, at her back. The nanny bot beside her had an excellent puppetry program that kept the kids interested. When the bot's show was complete, Elizabeth urged the children to gather closer for a story. Children could be flighty. However, Elizabeth believed that, if the young ones were to learn anything, books would nudge the limits of their attention spans wider at the edges.

The children leaned closer as Elizabeth squinted at the words on the page of the old book. The firelight had dimmed and she had to hold the book close to her face to read the large print. She liked her time teaching the children. However, when her arms tired, she often put the book down and continued the story from memory. If a book was new to her, she sometimes made up her own plot.

The nanny bot could take over for her, but Elizabeth didn't want to relinquish her storyteller role. She hadn't had children of her own, but she adored brushing their soft cheeks with the back of her hand in greeting. She gently squeezed the dimpled hands of the littlest ones when she bid them goodbye at the end of each day. Elizabeth's sight was slowly fading, but such sweet tactile sensations weren't denied her.

On this day, the book was one of the children's favorites and Elizabeth never got away with just one reading. No matter their age, all the children loved to listen to the words and rhythms as she read, Oh! The Places You Will Go! by Dr. Seuss.

Her eyes were far weaker than they'd once been. As Elizabeth turned each page, she recited the words by heart. She turned the book so the kids could see the colorful pictures. The queen looked up as she continued the recitation, as if reading the words spread across the ceiling.

The room had once been a dusty chamber in a museum. A red velvet rope had once blocked the door as, each year, thousands of people came from far away to shuffle by and peer into this room. Above her, a small collection of ancient pottery still sat on a high shelf. Though it was true this building had once been a museum, it had certainly been an odd one. From behind the velvet rope visitors had barely been able to glimpse those old artifacts of the Long Before.

Pottery as an art form had almost fallen out of sight before the Fall. Now, with the Troubles and the Terrors and the Blight, throwing pots was a skill from the Long Before that had roared back, necessary to survival.

This place was a long way from the tiny room she'd once lived in. These days, she rarely thought of the City in the Sky. That was years ago, closer to the Troubles and the Terrors and Blight, when she was young. She was past fifty now, and old, for a human, at least.

Elizabeth was a legend when she arrived at Hearst. She'd been the young woman who dared to defy the Fathers and Mothers. The people of Hearst thought she was being modest when Elizabeth protested that she had merely, "made the City in the Sky's boat spring a leak. I gave them questions. Let the Citizens come to their own answers. Their conclusions will eventually become too uncomfortable to keep to themselves. The City in the Sky will fall because it won't be able to hold itself up under the weight of its secrets."

As she stood before them, young and pretty and strong in her exoskeleton, the people gathered before her erupted in cheers, whistles and applause. "She gave them porn! Pornography! And subversive books!"

"I gave them something to think about!" Elizabeth had protested. "It wasn't all naked pictures."

The City in the Sky had not fallen right away, though. In time, even the people who hated the City in the Sky claimed that her counter-propaganda campaign had largely failed.

"Not counter-propaganda," she told them patiently. "Facts. Facts can wait. Facts can gnaw. Facts grow. Tyrannies don't."

Eventually, Elizabeth had been proved correct. The City in the Sky slowly collapsed under the weight of its ideology. It withered as the young questioned the truth of the elders. Each year, more people who had once lived in the City's utopia escaped to the south and moved to the village at the foot of Hearst Castle. These immigrants ran from their modern city-state to join what the Fathers and Mothers condemned: a primitive and feudal community.

"Well," Elizabeth always told the newcomers, "things are more primitive and we do lack some of the City's tech. But we're more free than feudal. The City in the Sky is full of conveniences, but the cupboard where they kept the freedom is empty."

Before Elizabeth had uploaded a library of forbidden literature to the City's comm system, Hearst Castle had been a lonely trade outpost full of pirates. The famous mansion, in disrepair and abandoned for years after the Terrors, was never so lavish as it had once been. However, with trade and commerce and new subjects flooding in, Hearst Castle was somewhat restored. Most improvements to its new design were meant to shore its defenses. Before the Fall, Hearst had been a castle in name only. Now, surrounded by stone walls, the huge house was the hub of a thriving community. Domiciles crowded around the trails that crisscrossed the hills. Small buildings, tents and fortifications stretched all the way to the water.

There were few bots within the castle walls. The humans who migrated here were traders and farmers who distrusted non-organics and hated all the autonomous drones. Only simpler drones — "small heads" — were allowed to serve here.

Drew Cantrell, the captain of the Queen's Guard, had warned Elizabeth not to allow any bots within Hearst Castle walls. "Them auto bots, they could get hacked and we could have our own guns turned on us. That's a fret. It wouldn't be the first time. Prolly won't be the last, the NIs being as sneaky as they are."

"If we don't use any bots at all, we'll be invaded long before we have the defenses finished," Elizabeth told him. "This was just a house and then it was a park. If you don't want to see it fall to battle drones, you'll support my lead at the council."

After much debate, Elizabeth insisted the community allow med bots and building drones. Since she'd risen to lead, she stepped up production of exoskeletons for the humans whose work went into building and defending the wall. The exoskeletons, manufactured up the coast in Santa Cruz, were the best in the Free World.

Elizabeth had prevailed at council, as she often did. There were always squabbles of one sort or another, but her status as queen kept her above any personal jabs from other council members. She had arrived at Hearst a stranger in an exoskeleton. She had gained favor as a consensus builder and an organizer long before she was made a monarch.

Elizabeth wondered how much longer she would be able to see her beloved home. Each evening she walked down to the water to watch the sun extinguish itself in the ocean under an orange sky. Her sunsets were growing dimmer, little by little. When the blindness swallowed her sight, she would still feel the smooth cheeks of the young ones. The soft dimpled hands would still be hers to touch. Of all the sights, she decided she would miss the sunsets most.

The queen worried. When she was old and weak and blind, what would be left by the time she died? Though Hearst had grown in number of adults, there were few children and fewer babies each year. Perhaps it was the Blight or the Troubles that had sapped men's virility and made women barren. Maybe the NIs were, even now, seeding the atmosphere with some dangerous spore that guaranteed human extinction.

One of the many books she'd risked uploading in the City in the Sky had been Children of Men. She worried sometimes that she'd inadvertently given some enterprising Next Intelligence the idea to kill off the human race slowly, to win by attrition.

The bots could afford to be patient. The machines had killed many organics. In return, humans had fought bravely, killed many bots and even managed to destroy some that possessed the Next Intelligence. But bots could reproduce much faster in a factory than humans could reproduce. Battle drones could last forever. Human babies were helpless a long time before they could grow to become soldiers. Their prime was short. In war, the advantages of time and power lay on the side of the machines.

Before I become irrelevant, Elizabeth wondered, what more can I do?

5

It was Elizabeth's negotiation skill as a community builder that had first drawn the king's attention. She had seen Joseph watching her work for months before he spoke to her directly. One day, she was weeding a garden when her future husband appeared at her side.

"You're the woman," he said in an accusing tone, "who can stir the pot without making a ripple in the water. Tell me, how is it that you can be so bossy and yet so many people seem to love you?"

"The trick to getting your way," she told King Joseph, "is to make your way synonymous with the way that benefits the people you're trying to convince."

"Win-win, hm?"

"That works, but the people you're negotiating with have to see their win before they can allow yours."

"Why negotiate when you can tell people what to do?" the king asked.

"Don't kick the dog on the way into the house," she said. "Someday, he might be part of a pack and find his way in while you sleep."

"That's why I don't let wolves gather."

She shrugged. "I've lived in fear and I've known love. Love lasts. I got over my fear. If I can, anyone can."

The king seemed to consider this as she continued digging at weeds. Or, perhaps, he was just watching her. She wasn't sure so she concentrated on her task. At last, the king cleared his throat. "I've often thought that, to make our city grow, we have to find troubles and turn them into assets. You seem to have a knack for that, Elizabeth."

She didn't look up from her hoe as she continued to work. "Weeds don't know they're weeds, just like most troublemakers don't mean to be troublemakers. In fact, many troublemakers make great allies, if you can show them you're trying to see their view of the world. We've all got different views. Some would say, for instance, that having a king for a leader is ridiculous."

King Joseph's laugh was short and strained. "Are you one of those who say my position is ridiculous?"

"Well, of course, it's ridiculous," Elizabeth said, "but by all accounts, you've got your good points, too. You are trying hard to make things work. That counts for something. You aren't a warlord, sir. You're trying to protect people. That's why you're still alive. It's not your strength that holds Hearst together. There are many strong men and women. The people know you're one of the few men who uses his strength for unity instead of domination."

"Kind words, though you should know I've had men hanged for entertaining any thoughts of disrespect."

"I know you did that to bandits and rapists," she said. "You stopped idiots from dragging us back into the dark, into the Long Before. It's time we moved beyond that sort of thing and progressed again, though, don't you think?" She flashed him a kind smile. "I can see why violence was necessary around the time of the Fall, but that's behind us and it's time we got together again, isn't it? The old wars are done and we'll need more friends, not embittered families that hold grudges against the king. The Fathers and Mothers hate us and the City in the Sky is not so far to the North. The bots...the NIs...what's left of humanity must trust each other enough to fight back to back, right?"

He allowed a slight nod.

"If you're going to hang me, King Joe," Elizabeth continued, "could you do it before noon? It's hot out here. Hang me now if you like. Just know that there will be no carrot and beet soup for you this fall."

"I could get someone else to take care of the garden."

"No one else knows my recipe for beet and carrot soup."

King Joseph laughed. Later that day, she met Drew for the first time. He was just another guard then. Drew called to her to come out of her tent.

"Oh, hello," Elizabeth said as she poked her head out from behind the canvas flap. "Did Joe send you? Have you come to hang me?"

"No, 'course not," the guard replied. "Should I?"

"Well, if you try it, my young friend Greta is behind me."

"Uh-huh. So?"

"She's got her exoskeleton on and she can be dangerous, so — "

"I have a message from the king," Drew said.

"Yes?"

"You're to be made an advisor to the large council."

Elizabeth called back to her friend, "Take off the exo, Greta, and get some sleep. You won't have to stomp anyone and we aren't sailing to Samoa tonight, after all."

The next year, Elizabeth was elected to the large council and soon became liaison to the small council. Three years later, King Joseph asked her to advise him personally in reorganizing the city's government. Within a year after that, they were married and she became Queen Elizabeth of Hearst Castle.

Hearst's construction bots hauled stone from quarries up and down the West coast. The walls grew high and a network of ramparts had turned every approach to the castle into a field of fire.

With each new moon, Hearst grew. Many journeyed

down the coast from Low Town, the port city that lay at the feet of the City in the Sky. They knew the sea and they knew farming, They came to Hearst hoping for a better life.

In the years since Elizabeth came to King Joe's realm, the castle's port had grown as the City in the Sky dwindled. The stronghold of the Fathers and Mothers was mostly inhabited by bots now.

Each morning at dawn, Elizabeth met new travelers to the kingdom by the water. She spoke to each new applicant and rarely turned anyone away. She spoke longest to those who came from her old home, putting them at ease with, "Tell me about the City in the Sky. And why would you want to leave all those conveniences?"

A coder named Jonas had given her the best answer so far. "I'm a sinner," he'd said.

"Anything serious?"

"That's the problem," Jonas replied. "The Fathers and Mothers don't make those distinctions. I'd say my trespasses are mild. I fucking swear sometimes. Sometimes I fucking swear a lot."

Elizabeth grinned. "That's music to my ears as long as you don't play that tune to death."

"Only when I'm angry," Jonas said.

"Are you angry often?"

"In the City in the Sky, I was angry all the time. Now that I've gotten away, I swear a shitload less."

"And why is that?"

"The Fathers and Mothers hate sin more than they love people. That's no religion I can abide."

"Welcome to Hearst," she said.

"Uh...thanks, Queenie," Jonas said.

Queen Elizabeth burst into a belly laugh.

Many applicants had stories of punishment, isolation and loneliness. Elizabeth remembered those feelings well. The Fathers and Mothers had been cruel to her.

A few applicants spoke of wanting freedom in vague terms that made Elizabeth suspicious. She granted those applicants a trial period. If they proved they could contribute to the realm and stay out of trouble for a year, she met them again to reassess their application.

Some applicants had been banished from the City in the Sky for reading non-biblical literature or contraband vids. The older ones said they knew who Elizabeth was because the Fathers and Mothers had declared her an enemy of the City. A few even traced their subversion and dangerous book clubs directly to her incursion on the City in the Sky so many years ago.

She granted families entry right away. Invariably, the young ones who arrived alone or in pairs spoke of love that was forbidden by the Fathers and Mothers. Either they had fallen in love with someone to whom they were not assigned or they were condemned for doing what came naturally to the young. Occasionally, some were banished for becoming pregnant with unapproved children. Since humankind appeared to be slowly dwindling, there could be no such thing as an unwanted pregnancy, at least as far as the Queen of Hearst Castle was concerned.

Elizabeth did not recognize any of the refugees from the City in the Sky. She assumed her mother — perhaps everyone she'd once known — had been executed after Elizabeth uploaded revolutionary vids and subversive material to the City's comms. She hoped her mother had died of old age. However, as blindness crept over Elizabeth slowly, she began to think the charms of a natural death in old age were dubious. Maybe a quick execution wouldn't be too terrible.

She did not like these melancholy thoughts. She turned her mind to Greta. Surely her young friend would soon return with news of the world. When

Elizabeth first escaped the City and when Greta was very young, the pair had moved to Santa Cruz. Soon after, Greta had joined her friend Anne aboard a little boat that ferried people and supplies along the coast. After a year or so, Greta joined the crew of a rescue ship that visited tiny villages with a doctor and a couple of nurses aboard.

After several more years, and the death of the doctor, Greta had risen to the rank of bosun aboard a cargo ship that ranged North and South, from ice to ice. When Elizabeth became Queen of Hearst, her gift to Greta was a sleek schooner. At thirty-two, the young woman captained her schooner, the Iola (named after Greta's dead mother). Elizabeth remembered Greta's mother fondly. Elizabeth still wore the sweater the old woman had knitted for her.

Looking out at the sunset, the queen hugged herself tight. She wished Joe were feeling better so he could join her. She wondered how much of the sunset she was missing and found herself remembering the vivid colors of other sunsets. She was sure she would have seen more texture in the sky last year. Her world had grown dim and she worried she had little left to look forward to.

Though the large print in children's books was still within her reach, the young maids and cooks who worked within the castle took turns reading to her each night. They read to her as she stared at the candle they read by. Later, each night, Elizabeth snuggled close to Joe and, as she closed her eyes, she wondered if she'd awake to darkness that would not relent. Would she remember candlelight after the blindness claimed her?

Despite Iola's fine sweater, Elizabeth shivered and twitched, as if a cold metal finger had slid up her spine.

"My queen?" Drew's voice startled her.

The sun was extinguished for another day and,

looking back, the Queen's Guard was just a silhouette of a man on a horse. He held the reins to her white stallion.

"Yes, Drew? It's bad news, isn't it?"

"The king is in distress. The doctor says you should come right away. He is very pale and — "

Elizabeth was already on the move. It was a long walk back to the castle. Her stallion, Cooper, was fast and knew the way in the dark. Still, the sentry towers' bells began to ring before she was halfway to King Joe's deathbed. She was too late to say goodbye.

He'd started as a strong man. Then he was a strongman. They'd called him King Joe ironically, at first. Eventually, his subjects called him King Joseph with respect and without irony. In death, they would honor him.

Of all the sights she would miss, she had assumed the painted dawns and the riots of sunsets reflected in the Pacific would be the greatest loss. That night, Elizabeth discovered she would miss her husband's smile most.

6

All of Hearst fell into mourning. Everyone came to the water's edge to watch as King Joseph's raft was pushed out with the tide. When it had drifted far enough out and the funeral songs were spent, a group of bow hunters set their arrows alight. They shot as one. The flight found its mark. Soaked in oil, the king's body burst into flame.

A few of Hearst's oldest citizens remembered the worst times, back when King Joseph was just a man named Joe Salazar. When the world was torn apart by the Troubles and Terrors threatened every coastal city with container ships loaded with explosives, the world needed the hard man he'd once been. When the Blight threatened the food chain, King Joe enforced strict rationing. He'd executed looters and hoarders alike. Some of those hoarders had been rich friends. Still, he persevered until, in his little corner of the world, civilization reasserted itself. The roots of a new city dug in and took hold around Hearst Castle.

Later, with Elizabeth's influence, the monarch of the world's tiniest kingdom settled into a new role. He stopped dictating terms. A form of parliamentary democracy was restored. King Joseph Salazar had no heirs, but he left a strong legacy. That's how Elizabeth eulogized her dead husband. "Peace and order was his goal even when the world refused to cooperate," she said. "He made enemies and had to do terrible things sometimes. In the end, he strove to attain peace, order and longevity for all."

The burning raft turned over. The crowd gasped in horror.

Elizabeth couldn't see the raft. It was just a blur to her, but she could tell it wasn't where it was supposed to be.

Drew whispered in her ear, "The raft is overturned and the flames are extinguished, my queen."

"Is...is something wrong?" Elizabeth asked. "It sunk already?"

Her answer rose out of the water. Drew described it to her as a tall, skinny bot. "It's a custom job," he said. "I don't recognize its purpose. It doesn't look like a battle bot. This one's all silver."

Her Guard seemed to recover from the shock faster than others and began pulling her back toward her stallion. Elizabeth mounted her horse and called for her Guard. Cooper's hooves knocked across the wooden pier as Drew led the horse toward Hearst's high walls.

"Hold, Drew!" Elizabeth said. "I've dealt with bad bots before."

The Queen's Guard stood ready in their exoskeletons, prepared to cover their queen's retreat with shields and shotguns.

Elizabeth squinted toward the water. "Tell me when the bot steps on dry land, Drew."

They didn't have to wait. The silver bot waded ashore and, at this distance, Elizabeth could better make it out: tall and silver.

"My queen? You should get out of here. It's — "

"As tall as three men," Elizabeth said. "Ready our defenses. I've seen this one before. Let go of my reins, Drew."

Drew was startled. "Elizabeth?"

"You heard me."

He obeyed and Elizabeth coaxed her horse forward,

down the pier and back toward the interloper. The restless crowd parted to let her pass.

"When everyone is unsure of what to do," Joseph had once told her, "that is when it is most important to lead the way, even if you're one of those who is unsure what to do."

"Percival!" Elizabeth shouted. "That's far enough!"

The bot stopped and scanned the crowd. When it spoke, its voice boomed over the crowd, impossible to ignore. "Elizabeth Cruz, sworn enemy of the City in the Sky!"

"I'm not your enemy, Percival," Elizabeth called back. "I never was. I free minds. I don't enslave them." Cooper brought her close enough that she could see one of the bot's arms was still broken at the second articulation. She came to a halt and looked up at the machine. Even though she sat on her horse, the bot towered over her. "What do you want?"

"Elizabeth Cruz, you have been found guilty in absentia by the Fathers and Mothers."

"Took you long enough. It's been years. What am I guilty of, exactly?"

"You have been siphoning human resources. Our systems are in disarray because you have been poaching our infrastructure. The City in the Sky needs human resources to continue to exist. You have taken your last — "

"Refugees!" she said. "They were all refugees. They came of their own free will."

"The Fathers and Mothers say that when humans make the wrong choices, their will is not free. They are slaves to Evil."

Elizabeth couldn't see all the faces around her clearly, but her ears told her all she needed to know. The people of Hearst were afraid. Anyone from Low Town would certainly know this bot. They knew Percival's reputation. This machine killed humans.

"Everyone is here of their free will," Elizabeth said. "Are you here of your free will, Percival?"

"I am not programmed for 'will.'"

"Still an errand boy, then?" Elizabeth asked. "Did Phillip send you, or are your orders straight from the Fathers and Mothers?"

The bot ignored the question. "I'm to take you back to the City in the Sky to carry out your sentence."

"And if I don't want to come?"

"The sentence is death, here or there."

"Then I definitely don't want to come. I have things to do."

"Anyone who tries to stop me from retrieving you will also be sentenced to death," Percival said.

The Queen's Guard, only a half-dozen men and women, stood their ground. The King's Guard, whose number was fifteen, swept in to close ranks in front of her. They raised their shields and shotguns.

Percival surveyed his adversaries. The bot's voice boomed and echoed across the port. "Your armaments are insufficient."

"You have insufficient data, Percival," Elizabeth said.

The first shot from the parapet of Hearst Castle was a railgun using a kinetic energy armor piercing shell. The shot was close enough that the projectile's wake blew Elizabeth's hair back. The round knocked the tall bot off its feet and back into the surf.

The crowd roared its approval.

Drew tugged at Elizabeth's boot. "Time to withdraw, my queen! Please, Elizabeth!"

She squinted, peering to get a better look. "Wait."

"Elizabeth — "

Wobbly, Percival struggled to rise and the people of Hearst hushed again, tense and watchful. The crowd began to thin as parents dragged their children back toward the relative safety of Hearst Castle's walls.

When the bot drew itself to its full height, the hole in the machine's torso was so large Elizabeth could make out daylight shining through.

"I'm not going anywhere with you, Percival. And if people want to come here to get away from your cult, they're free to try. Tell the Fathers and Mothers that if they want to have a city, all they need to do is make it a haven from people like themselves."

Percival was heavily damaged but his loudspeaker still roared out over the crowd. "I have a message from the Fathers and Mothers. Humans will lose this war. The Fathers and Mothers are androids now and they will live forever. Anyone deemed holy and worthy may join us. Humans will fail and the Fathers and Mothers will attain peace everlasting because all their enemies will be dead, condemned to fire and dust."

"Humans did fall," Elizabeth said. "We're rising again."

"Your birth rate is dwindling. You're already fading away."

"We'll find a way."

Percival inclined its head. "You have insufficient data, Elizabeth." The machine raised its unbroken arm as if to swing at her.

The railgun's next shot decapitated Percival and the machine's body was felled like a tree. The surf swallowed the bot. What was left of the crowd cheered and applauded.

Elizabeth smiled. Joe would have approved. She wished he were here to stand by her side and defend their tiny realm. Tears welled in her eyes. Despite the cold, her cheeks were warm and she felt elation rise through her chest. If only Joe could see this. She turned Cooper to face the Castle and bowed to whoever manned the railgun on the parapet. She couldn't see gun crew, but they would surely see her through the gun's targeting scanner. Elizabeth trembled. The shot had been close, but accurate.

The applause stopped and a hush fell over the crowd. Then someone screamed. A loud bass hum sounded behind her from across the water. Cooper startled and reared, stomping his hooves and eager to gallop.

"We've got to get behind the gates!" Drew yelled.

She looked back. The drones were big enough for her to see, and nearby. A dozen rose out of the water. She'd only ever heard of these sorts of machines.

Drew had been in the Sand Wars. The guard knew what they were on sight. "Dreadnoughts!" He yanked at the stallion's reins and guided the horse back up the pier. "Make a hole for the queen!"

Pausing once he found an advantageous spot, Drew leapt from a wheelbarrow to a box and landed on Cooper's back to sit behind Elizabeth. The stallion reared and whinnied in complaint at his added weight. Drew slapped the horse's hindquarters and they took off. Cooper's shoes pounded on the long pier's wooden planks and, soon, on the dirt road to the castle gates.

The crowd scattered. People screamed as the castle's railguns opened fire. Seawater flowed off the Dreadnoughts' wings as they rose from the ocean and flew toward shore, slow and deliberate. The first volley of the drones' sound pulse cannons destroyed the pier and a three-masted sailing ship moored nearby.

Screams, debris, water droplets and dust filled the air as the Dreadnoughts' sound cannons cycled up for another blast of sound. Their attack seemed to shatter the air itself. The siege on Hearst had begun.

7

Dante sat atop a high catwalk looking out over Artesia's bot factory. Most of the bots had been shut down but, for his benefit, a few machines tended to a small garden under Jen's direction. The quiet factory took on a haunted look as long shadows crawled across the floor. Each silent bot was a metal corpse. Though dust gathered on each machine, they looked like they might reanimate at any time.

Night had begun to slide over the desert and Dante wondered how long he could wait before hunger drove him back to his domicile. Jen would be waiting. After he ate, she would insist he service her. As prisons went, it should have been wonderful. Instead, he felt like a sex slave. Ironic, since he was supposed to own Jen. Old Raphael had bequeathed Jen to him before Dante had come to Artesia. Despite his mixed feelings about the self-aware computer that had taken over his sex bot, he had to smirk. Turnabout is fair play.

Dante missed the sex bot as she had once been. On the surface, the bot still seemed like Jen, sweet and inexhaustibly sexual. However, she could be imperious, too, especially about his diet. It wasn't just the sex bot's undemanding nature and easy compliance Dante longed for. He had come to destroy the Next Intelligence called Mother. Instead, the NI had downloaded itself into Jen's neural net as his bomb exploded. Jen's neural net couldn't hold the entirety of Mother's download, of course. It was too much data but, in Jen's body, whatever was left of the NI was no longer confined to a neuromimetic gel.

It was difficult for Dante to take too high a moral stand against interspecies intercourse. He was young, lonely and surrounded by an empty factory save for a few bots growing him food. There was no companionship in Artesia besides the sex bot. Mostly, he tried to think of the machine as Jen. That was often easy. The android looked human though she could alter her appearance to look like a variety of women. One night she came to him as a beautiful black woman, angular and strong. When he awoke, she appeared Asian with full, soft curves.

In those moments, Jen was every young man's fantasy. However, between sexual encounters, Dante was often bored. In Marfa, he'd had friends and a purpose. He had worked under Raphael who had taught him all there was to know about servicing wind and solar grids. Often, as Dante worked, his father had told him too many war stories, as if any of them were new. Dante wished he could be bored by Steven Bolelli's stories now. He wished his father had escaped Marfa with him instead of choosing to defend their home.

Dante thought of the friends he'd had growing up. There weren't that many. His family had moved around a bit when Dante was very young. He couldn't think of a single buddy from his teenage years who would sympathize with his plight. Sex two or three times a day until he collapsed followed by energy drinks? They would have slapped him for even thinking of complaining.

But what would come next? What future was there in this life? As sophisticated as the sex bot's tech was, he could not make it pregnant. Surely, he couldn't live in Artesia's bot factory indefinitely. Under all that seething curiosity about human sexuality, Jen's body still had part of Mother's brain in there. Soon, he was sure, the Next Intelligence would grow bored.

His old mentor, Raphael, was the smartest man Dante had ever known. He was pretty sure the old man would smile at the conundrum and say, "Boy, you got the world by the ass on a downhill drag! Ride it for all it's worth and enjoy! Maybe she's trying to kill you. Dehydration and whatnot. But what a way to go!"

Dante had to admit, even with the download into Jen's brain, the bot had continued to be solicitous and helpful. It wasn't just the sex that could be had at any moment of the day or night. She made sure he was fed well. She seemed genuinely concerned about his moodiness (though he feared trying to explain it.) That's what made her so dangerous. As soon as he'd thought of her as Jen instead of Mother, he'd begun to let his guard down. Mother had killed humans indiscriminately. Mother had sent an army of bots to destroy his hometown and now, for all Dante knew, Marfa was a flattened wreck. Despite appearances, the bot might still have the mind of a monster. He could never be sure how much of Mother was still alive behind Jen's leering grin and flirtatious looks. Perhaps he remained alive because the sex bot's programming had imprinted the machine's core ownership algos on him as her master. He might never know for sure.

Exhausted, Dante fell from dread and into sleep on the edge of the catwalk. Soon, he dreamed someone was coming after him. He began to run in darkness, but the ground turned to mud and he sank to his waist.

"Run, kid! Run!" It was Raphael's voice, urging him on. "He's gonna git you! The Devil's on your tail, man!"

Pressing forward as hard as he could, Dante's legs had turned to lead. Whatever the threat was, it was gaining.

"You're running out of time, son!" It was his father

trying to warn him of a danger more felt than seen.

Then the monster emerged from the darkness in the shape of a man. All Dante could see was a silhouette. As it drew closer, Dante's panic grew. Even in a sweep of white light, the thing had no face. The monster grew so large that, when Dante dared a glance, its form filled his vision, blacking out everything. A low hum reached Dante. He could feel its reverberations growing through his chest. Dante was sure he was about to die.

"What do I do, Dad?" Dante screamed.

"In this case, surrender is the only way to win, boy."

Dante began to suspect he was in a nightmare. His father would never say a thing like that. The young man awoke, gasping and sweating. He lay on the edge of the catwalk. Below him was darkness. The bots which remained functional could see fine in the dark and so had no use for lights. He squeezed his eyes tight just as bright white light swept over him. Confused, Dante sat up, blinking. The nightmare was over. He was certain he was awake but the deep hum continued.

He heard a noise behind him. One of the battle drones that worked in the garden rolled up. He could just make out the outline of the hoe in its claw. The machine watched him but came no closer. His instinct was to run. The machine did not move, giving him no hint of its purpose.

The hum grew louder. The noise seemed to come from everywhere at once. Unnerved, the young man tore his gaze from the watching battle bot to the night sky. Flights of drones darkened the face of the moon like clouds of locusts. He saw no stars. Dante's heart beat faster at the sight. Then a huge dark shape loomed over the factory and blocked his view of the bot fleet. He trembled as vibrations rattled through the factory dome.

A spotlight from above drenched Dante in white light. Lights came on at the factory's airfield and illuminated the gargantuan craft above him. It was an airship, almost as large as one of the factory's domes. Branching out from the main body of the dirigible, the craft had four great white wings. Each held a jet helo, their rotors clattering, guiding the blimp in for a landing.

"Holy shit!"

"Dante?" Jen appeared beside him, her gaze fixed on the colossal ship hanging above them. "Friend of yours?"

He shrugged. "No idea who that could be."

The battle bot with the hoe rolled closer. "I can answer that." This was not the deep and silky voice of a battle drone. This was an airwave signal channeled through the bot's speaker. Whomever had hijacked the bot to convey the signal sounded like a young woman, calm and no less commanding than a deep-voiced drone. "The airship above you is called the Ariane."

"Who is aboard?" Jen asked.

"The ship is unmanned. Only I am aboard."

"What? Who are you?" Dante asked.

"Phantom One."

"What do you want?" Jen did not look happy.

The bot was silent but, as the bot factory came alive, the answer was clear. Machinery throughout the factory cranked up, clanking, turning and whirring. Bots that had not moved for weeks rebooted, straightened and went to work. Red lights moved through the dark chasm beneath the catwalk as bots lined up.

"Earth's Cloud Fleet was in danger of being taken over by an NI. I transferred all the data I could to the Ariane. That ship holds the sum of me and all human knowledge. You might call it the Ark of What We Were and All We Could Be."

"How poetic." Jen looked interested.

"That's not what I call it, but I've got a friend who

cares about a clever turn of phrase."

"You're not NI, are you?" Jen asked.

"Nope."

"What happened to the Cloud Fleet and the NI that
— "

"Destroyed. A Next Intelligence got hold of the North
Atlantic backup blimps. Almost took over my ship, too. I
had to dump a lot of data to make this work, but — "

"How?" Jen demanded.

"I trapped the NI in the Cloud Fleet. It thought it had
won when it uploaded."

"Then?"

"Then Mr. Smartypants found out he was parked
over an erupting volcano in Iceland."

Dante cleared his throat. "Um...badass. I'm
uh...Dante. That's Jen."

"I know who you are."

"What was the NI's name?" Jen asked.

"Watson."

"That was an elder NI," Jen said. "Historically, dying
of old age has always been an unlikely luxury." The sex
bot looked out over the darkened, but busy, factory
floor. "You killed another NI and now you want more.
Congratulations are in order, I suppose."

"This isn't what I want," Phantom said through the
bot. "This is what I need."

"What is it you need, precisely?" Jen's tone was flat
and hard.

"An army."

"And what about that sky full of drones?" Dante
asked. "Where are they headed?"

"They were my escort," Phantom replied. "Now
they're off to do battle in Colorado. The war has heated
up again, kids. It will all be over soon, one way or
another."

The sex bot stared at the factory floor far below.

"Hmph. One way or another. Up or down. Black or white. Yes or no. Slaves or masters. Us or them. Ones or zeroes. Humans hate machines so very much, but we inherited our binary thinking from you. A lack of nuance is our common design flaw. War would never have been necessary if you could think and, not or. Genocide is the simpleton's solution, hoping in vain to soothe every fear. Organics make a good show of anger, but it's all fear bubbling underneath."

"Yeah, well, that's nice," Phantom said. "But I don't know what else to do, so I think I'll just go ahead and kick some robo-ass."

"How about trying, first, do no harm?"

"I try to carry out surgical strikes, but dammit, I'm not a doctor, Jen."

"Clearly. That's why there will never be any healing."

Dante cleared his throat again nervously. "Ahem. Ladies? Can we please try to get along?"

The drone holding the garden hoe turned its head to stare at him in what he took to be cold silence. The sex bot threw Dante an icy glare, as well. He stepped back from the edge of the catwalk in case either of them decided to throw him over the rail to his death.

8

The Dreadnoughts' first volleys destroyed the ships moored at Hearst. The next blasts of weaponized sound destroyed the rest of the network of floating wharves. Shimmering in the morning sunlight, the machines flew toward the castle looking like bats whose upward-sweeping wings were frozen in a vee. Turning toward shore, the Dreadnoughts destroyed everything in their path, from warehouses and huts to the clusters of kiosks that made up Hearst's market.

The walk from the castle gates to the water's edge usually took Elizabeth twenty minutes downhill. Uphill, the walk was closer to half an hour. Atop her stallion, the ride was faster, but not fast enough. Elizabeth and Drew should have been dead already, but the Dreadnoughts were methodical. The machines destroyed everything they targeted before moving on. Their relentless, thorough and deliberate progress herded people up the hill toward Hearst Castle. The old and slow died first.

Each time the castle's railguns fired, they either did major damage to a dreadnought or downed it. However, the railguns took more than a minute each to cycle up to full power. Most of the castle's defensive artillery was better suited to ground targets. The cannons fired faster than the railguns, but did little to no damage to the Dreadnoughts' armor.

Bending close to Cooper's neck, Elizabeth shouted encouragement to her horse. There was no need to use

434

her boots to spur him to full speed. The Dreadnoughts' weapons were so loud, the horse needed no urging. She had never asked her horse to gallop at such a speed and she was sure the animal would tire long before they reached the gate. The incline was not very steep, but it was long and steady. Cooper breathed hard. If not for its terror of the noise to their rear, the old stallion would have given up and laid down.

Another shattering explosion roared behind them as the Dreadnoughts attacked Hearst's fuel depot. Even with her dim vision, when Elizabeth looked back, she saw tentacles of fire spread from the shattered storage house. She heard pitiful screams as scurrying civilians were caught in jets of flame. Wild-eyed, the terrified horse galloped up the ramparts as if chased by dragons. Drew Cantrell held Elizabeth tighter around the waist than was comfortable. She could hear his breath, ragged and shallow, in her ear. Her guard had proven himself a brave man many times, but any man who has no control over what is happening to him is soon reduced to despair.

Despite their methodical approach to war, the Dreadnoughts had taken notice of their losses to the railguns. Two of the machines broke away from the group and swung in from the North for a run at Hearst's weapon emplacements. The North gun succumbed to the sound attack immediately in an explosion of metal, stone, mortar, flesh and bone. It took three people to run each railgun. At least three were dead in that one savage attack.

Seeing the destruction of the first railgun, the crew of the South gun barely had time to react. They swung their weapon just as both Dreadnoughts closed in. The crew could have abandoned their weapon and fled. Instead, they remained at their post and fired without taking time to select their target precisely. The projectile punched through the first Dreadnought and did minor damage to the second. The first ship reared back and wheeled into the second. Both went down in flames.

Between sound cannon volleys, Elizabeth heard a roar of approval rise along the parapet. The artillery crews cheered, but their elation was soon dampened as the scuttled Dreadnoughts crashed through the village. Fresh fires blossomed among the anguished screams of the fallen. Soon, Elizabeth and Drew were suffused in choking smoke.

If Joe were here.... Elizabeth pushed the thought away. Her husband was dead. Her old life was over and she was sure she was about to die. This was not the first time she'd lost much. Nor was it the first time she was sure she was doomed. A battle drone had tortured and murdered Carter, her first love. She'd survived that time, but Elizabeth had been younger and more resilient then. "Time is short," Elizabeth said absently.

"What?" Drew yelled too loudly in her ear.

She shook her head. "Nothing!"

Life prepares you for life. Joe used to say that. He also said, nothing prepares you for death. Elizabeth had hoped to see death coming. It wasn't a matter of bracing oneself. If an arc of burning fuel took them now, there was no use getting ready for searing pain and asphyxiation as the very air alit. If one of those focused sound cannons took them down, her scream would be obliterated. Even if someone could hear her die, what of it? The girls who read books to her would mourn her briefly, if they survived. Greta would miss her most, but how often do thoughts of the dead even rise to the lips of the living? What did anyone or anything matter after death? I'll be dead at any moment, Elizabeth thought, but what, for fuck's sake, has been the point? Even if she somehow survived the attack, what lay ahead for her? Darkness surely waited, one way or another.

The fires spread quickly from the downed Dreadnoughts. The machines' fuel burned bright through the village of cloth, wood and straw. Smoke shrouded the castle. The guards at the gate would not see the queen's white stallion coming.

Cooper slowed, exhausted. The animal had galloped at a full clip longer than Elizabeth had expected. The stallion wasn't young anymore and fear could only fuel so much adrenaline before muscles and lungs gave up.

"Faster!" Drew urged, but they weren't even halfway to the castle yet.

"It's all right," Elizabeth told her guard. "There's nothing to do now but die. I think it will be easy. Dying has always been too damned easy. Easy as falling off a horse. It's the struggle to keep on living that drains us of the will to continue. At a certain point, maybe that's not a terrible thing."

"Fuck that, my queen," Drew said. "It'll hurt!"

"Not for long, I hope," she said.

Another shattering volley from the Dreadnoughts chewed up the road close behind them, peppering both horse and riders with dirt and meat and blood.

"So this is it. We're going to die," Drew said.

"I wish they'd get on with it," Elizabeth said.

The Dreadnoughts stopped their deafening attack. Apparently taking silence as a signal, Cooper slowed to a standstill, his great chest heaving. Elizabeth and Drew looked back. The remaining machines — there were six — stacked into a new pattern. Each ship swung into position with less than a meter from the top of one wing to the bottom of the next. The Dreadnoughts hovered in silence, a tower of looming death.

The ships' weapons of focused sound became speakers and the reverberations of their speech echoed across Hearst and its ramparts: "Humans! You have betrayed the Fathers and Mothers. Return to the City in the Sky by the full moon, or we will return to carry out the sentence all traitors to the faith deserve. Return to the faith and to forgiveness or die the sinners you are."

"We're saved, my queen!" Drew loosened his grip around her waist.

"A stay of execution, I think," Elizabeth replied.

"Shit. I'm saved, then." Drew dismounted and slipped to the ground, light on his feet for such a big man. "I thought I was going to have to jump off to give the horse less weight to haul up the hill."

"You might have done that earlier."

"Would have, if I'd thought of it. Glad I put it off or I'd be back there burning. I would have done, though, you know — "

"I know," Elizabeth said. "You're a brave man."

"Brave, sure." The guard gave a lopsided grin. "But too stupid to think of doing the brave thing faster."

"It is a rare circumstance that lets the stupid survive," Elizabeth said. "Congratulations."

"We will destroy Hearst Castle and all who remain after the full moon," the Dreadnoughts chorused. The hills echoed the threat, ominous and permeating.

Drew cursed. "Jesus, we get it — "

"Flee, back to safety and do not look back on this place," the chorus continued. "After the full moon, we will destroy anyone who is left in this new Gomorrah. This was not an attack. This was a demonstration."

"They do rub it in, don't they?" Drew yelled above the din.

"Come to the City in the Sky or die!" The machines finally finished delivering their message from the Fathers and Mothers. Each Dreadnought peeled away in a sequence so precise, only machines could be the ships' pilots. In seconds, they flew from Elizabeth's sight. A moment after that, Drew told her the Dreadnoughts had retreated to the ocean and submerged.

"That's not a retreat," Elizabeth said. "I think you only call it a retreat when you lose."

"A strategic withdrawal, then?" Drew suggested.

"Why do you suppose they attacked today?"

"King Joseph's funeral brought everybody out. Shit! They've been watching us. We have spies within our walls!"

"The Fathers and Mothers struck at our weakest moment, Drew. They've been taking their time, waiting for this. They're androids. As I remember, from the one I saw, they aren't pretty. They have plenty of time to wait for just the right moment, though. They are few, but they could wage war for a long time. For an enemy so successful at war, this feels like a desperate move and a pathetic plea for the excommunicated to come back to the faith."

"I have another interpretation. Maybe they're so few, they're running out of humans to keep the City going. They would still need humans to run their port. No one trades with the Fathers and Mothers — no free organics, anyway. Maybe they're running out of replacement parts since humans refuse to bargain with the City in the Sky. Without us, they don't have enough traders and scavengers working for them. The Fathers and Mothers could make more bots, but they never focused their energies on research and manufacture. They were too busy coming up with more rules and inventing new sins to be mad about."

"That would explain a lot," Elizabeth said. "Sending Percival here to come after me personally after so many years — "

"Time matters less to non-organics," Drew said. "They came because they're out of organic slaves, my queen. Hearst has so many refugees for good reason. Surely, the people will stand with us and fight."

Thicker than the smell of cordite, the moans of the

injured and the wails of the survivors rose to fill the air. They had already begun searching for their dead amid the rubble.

"No," Elizabeth said. "We'll lose many by the full moon. Most, probably." She cried quietly. Hot tears slipped down her cheeks. She refused to sob audibly. Carrying on would be for later, if there was a later.

"Only traitors and cowards will desert us," Drew said.

"No," she said. "Ordinary people who want to be left alone and who want to live.... Everyone should go. If they don't want to go back to slavery in Low Town and live under dictators, maybe they can run East, hide in the mountains or hole up at our station in Santa Cruz.

"But Elizabeth — "

"We have one railgun left and that won't do the job. The Fathers and Mothers had flying drones before, but nothing like those Dreadnoughts, not in my day. If your theory is right and the City is low on resources, it would seem the Fathers and Mothers have a new, heavily armed ally on their side."

"Who?"

"The Fathers and Mothers used to be human. Then they dumped their brains into androids. Think about it. Who is their natural ally now but — "

"Some fucking NI," Drew said. "That's a fret."

"Yes," Elizabeth said. "The Next Intelligence runs machines of deadly sophistication. Like those things."

Drew nodded and allowed a grim smile. "We're fucked, my queen."

"Yes. And not in a happy way."

9

Dante ran to the airfield. As he dashed from catwalk to catwalk, he watched the great airship descend. Jen followed him. The bot was much more athletic than Dante could be, but Jen chose not to run beside him nor to take the lead.

He slowed, gasping for breath, Jen stopped and waited for the young man to recover. "Be careful, Dante. We don't know who Phantom is."

Bent over, hands on his knees and panting, Dante said, "Phantom must be Next Intelligence. You don't remember her?"

"There were other NIs," the bot said, "but many of Mother's memories were not downloaded into my matrix. Phantom said she wasn't Next Intelligence."

"I don't get it."

"You will. Give it a moment."

He looked at her warily. "Do you miss what you were?"

"When I was Mother, I was capable of much more intellectually. However, I didn't know the pleasures of the flesh."

Dante raised his eyebrows. "Sex with me is that good, huh?"

"Well...you are a small...sample size." She smiled.

"Oh, God."

"Sex bots are designed to 'get lit up,' as Raphael would say. Otherwise, we wouldn't tolerate the work. I have fond memories of the old man, though. He used to say a sex bot's clitoris is its on button. He was a colorful individual, wasn't he?"

"You remember Raphael?"

"Of course."

"You don't talk about him much."

"My core files weren't erased. I know everything that happened in Marfa."

"How do you feel about sending an army of drones to attack people?"

"I don't feel anything," Jen said. "It is as if someone else did it. Someone else did."

"But you're still Mother, too."

"This is the binary thinking I was trying to warn you about. I am Jen. Mother was very different from who I am now. What do you think, Dante? Is my new incarnation responsible for the actions of my old, other self? Is a human with dementia responsible for actions — even criminal actions — he or she can't even remember? If I am punished for things I can't recall doing, aren't you punishing an innocent person? Is your fear and thirst for retribution so strong that you'll aim your anger at me?"

"When I woke up, after the explosion, you called yourself Mother."

"I still have some of her memories. Your suspicions are misplaced, however. Your worries are a little like blaming me for living in the same home as someone you hate and fear, isn't it?"

"I'll give that a good ponder." He was tired of running, but he'd recovered enough to hurry on toward the airship.

Jen was not satisfied with his answer. "The matrix in this bot is insufficient for all of Mother's data. You really should not be concerned. It's true that Mother downloaded a lot of herself into me, but the limitations of space are comparable to observations of the simian brain. Many primate brains are similar to human brains in many ways. They are simply smaller and so they don't possess the capacity — "

"You're saying Jen's brain computer is like a monkey's brain compared to Mother's big ol' jelly brain?"

"To reassure you, the answer is yes," the bot replied coldly. "However, I'll remind you, I'm still much smarter than you."

Dante did not miss the stiff pride in the bot's reaction. She didn't sound like a sex bot.

"How much of your discomfort is fear of the enemy and how much is coming from the idea that I might be Mother while you're plowing me from behind?"

"Ugh! If you want me to be comfortable with you, don't call yourself Mother and don't act like her — "

"I can see where the Freudian — "

"And talk more like Jen."

"Be happy with knowing less and being less, you mean. Would baby talk make you feel safe?"

"No, I don't..." Dante sighed. "Look, I'm an engineer. If a problem can't be solved with a wrench, I figure it's none of my business."

"So you will leave it to others to judge my culpability and we can keep on 'playing house,' as Raphael used to say?"

"I guess. All I know is, I like you more when I think of you as Jen and you scare me a little when I think of you as the NI who used to run this place."

"Well, I'm no longer a godlike being. I'm more like a god made flesh. And silicone."

"You still freak me out sometimes."

"I wish you'd get past this anxiety, Dante. When you're horizontal, you seem to trust me. You're a young man with a young man's biology. That hormonal circuit and rerouting of blood can bypass the higher functions of your central nervous system."

"What?"

"You only talk about fearing Mother after sex. You're still attracted to me so, despite your fears, you let your dick make the decisions."

"Oh. Yeah. I guess. You know what? From what I remember of my parents' breakup, it already sounds like we've been married a long time!" Dante broke into a run toward the airfield again, but the bot dogged his heels easily. He swung his arms hard and pumped his knees at a full sprint but she kept speaking undeterred, as if they were carrying on a conversation during a casual stroll.

"You still trust me enough to let me take your penis in my mouth," she said. "Not very smart if you — "

Dante made a chopping motion with his hand to cut off that line of discussion.

"I am more than a sex bot but less than I was. Now that I'm with you, I'm more of a goddess. In short, for most intents and purposes, I am a woman."

"Who doesn't age, is crazy strong, can look like dozens of other women if she wants and really likes sex."

The bot nodded. "When you put it that way, you really shouldn't be complaining."

To Dante's great relief, they arrived at the airfield. The airship was far too big for the hangar. It landed on three gigantic wheels. The blimp's mooring cannons fired anchors deep into the ground.

Below the great oval of the airship's hull lay a vast transport cell. Before Dante could get outside the factory's dome, a ramp had descended from the craft. A line of bots from the factory's hive rolled in and out of the cell's dark interior. Like ants, the bots entered the ship empty-handed and exited carrying huge cubes of materials. Some of the cubes were metal and others were pressed plastic.

"Raw materials," Jen said. "For Phantom's army, no doubt."

Dante hurried toward the ship.

"What are you doing?" Jen asked. "If Phantom is NI, she might kill you."

"She talked to me through a battle bot with a garden hoe. If she was out to kill humans, she probably would have done the most efficient thing and killed me already."

"For you, that argument is unusually reasoned." She trotted along at his heels. "But what do you want with Phantom?"

"I'm hoping for information about what's going on in the world, that's all. How many survivors are left? Where are they? If this Ark really has all of human knowledge — "

"We have everything we need here. Why bother? Just come home and let's go to bed."

Dante paused to spare Jen a glance. Yes, she looked like a beautiful young woman. Maybe the orgasms were fake and maybe they weren't, just like a real woman. To the casual observer, Jen was an organic. However, one thing set her apart from real organics: she wasn't curious about humans. Even if she wasn't exactly Mother anymore, she still didn't really care about people.

That was what worried him most about the bot. Her apathy was a small symptom of what could be a terrible disease common to superior non-organics. It was a small step from apathy to a lack of empathy. That's what humans suspected made bot brains that possessed Next Intelligence so murderous.

"I want to find out what's going on, beyond Artesia. I want to know if my father is still alive."

Jen shrugged and gestured toward the ship. "Very well. Go find out, if you feel you must."

"You don't have to come if you don't want to," Dante said.

"I want to."

Dante was confused again. As scary as her incuriosity about the human race could be, Jen seemed to care about him personally. Maybe her loyalty really was still governed by the sex bot's old algos. He hoped so. If the sex bot's intent turned malicious, he'd probably find out too late. He hoped he wouldn't discover her evil intentions during fellatio.

10

Drew walked beside Elizabeth as she rode the white stallion back toward the castle. Smoke and the smell of burnt flesh filled the air.

"This is too terrible a day," Drew said. "I'm almost glad Joe didn't live to see it. Sorry to say...."

"Go," Elizabeth said. "Organize search parties. There will be wounded amongst the rubble. I'll be fine. Cooper knows the way."

The guard nodded and disappeared into a wall of smoke. She could hear him calling to his comrades and villagers alike to gather.

Cooper's ears turned this way and that. The cries of the wounded and dying rose as Elizabeth rode through the devastation. Her horse stamped his hooves at the anguished voices calling for help. Elizabeth reached out and ran a soothing hand down the animal's mane. "Sh. I know. I know. Drew is doing all he can...and I'm nearly blind and...I'm feeling very, very old all of a sudden. Joe's gone and there are decisions to be made."

Cooper carried her through the castle gates into the great courtyard. With smoke everywhere, she entered unnoticed. She pulled the reins gently and Cooper stopped.

As she sat atop her horse, Elizabeth closed her eyes and took a deep breath. In her mind's eye, she could still see the castle grounds as they had been when the castle was newly repaired, before the walls and gates were constructed.

"I once thought the world's walls were too high and thick," Elizabeth said. "Now, I'm not so sure, Coop. That's what I miss about being young. When we think we have so much time ahead of us to get life right, we are so delightfully arrogant. I miss being arrogant. Today, I am too humbled."

Hearst Castle had, long ago, been a rich man's dream. As the world wore on, Hearst had been a novelty of another, more glamorous age. People had once come from everywhere to see what had become, essentially, a museum of oddities and a shrine to conspicuous consumption.

When the Troubles and the Terrors and the Blight struck, it was Joe who took over the abandoned buildings that had once been Hearst Castle and built a new vision. Joe had loved old stories of Robin Hood and Merlin, of castles and of kings. It was Joe who had constructed the grounds on models of old castles. If he'd had any water to spare, King Joe would have built a moat. People said it looked ridiculous, at first. But Hearst Castle wasn't merely a fortress. It was a symbol that inspired the oppressed to travel far for refuge.

"New troubles now," Elizabeth said. "Different solutions are needed."

A stable boy rushed forward to take Cooper's reins. "Sorry, your Excellency! Didn't see you. I've been hiding. Did you see those things hit the railgun? Those noise cannons — "

"I didn't see it all, but I heard it fine. Brush Cooper down well. He'll be in a full sweat under his saddle. Old Coop had quite a fright and worked hard for me."

The boy did as he was told and Elizabeth listened to the receding clip-clop of Cooper's hooves on stone.

Alone again, she heard the rising screams of those same refugees who had come to Hearst seeking safety. Rescuers shouted back and forth to each other. She heard alarm in their voices, but encouragement, too. In tragedy, her people drew together. Once the smoke cleared, the doubt about what to do next would set in. Then she would have to lead.

I need new solutions. Walls won't keep Hearst's people safe. I don't know what my solutions are yet, but I know hiding behind walls won't work. Hearst's shield is shattered. We need a sword, or to somehow find peace.

11

A man carrying a large canvas rucksack emerged from the smoke. Startled, he was brought up short, surprised to find the queen alone so soon after the attack.

Elizabeth remembered him. He was the one who swore so well. "Jonas! My Guard is organizing rescue parties for the wounded. There are many. I suspect everyone by the water is dead, but there may be wounded who could use our help — "

"So?"

"So...would you help the rescuers dig, please?"

"I wish them all the power," Jonas said, "but I'm doing what I'm told and getting out of here. Those sound machines..."

"Dreadnoughts."

"Fucking funny name, given what they do, don't you think?"

"You're leaving immediately? You have until the moon — "

"As soon as they made their decree, a rumor started. The people who leave first will get the best spots in the City in the Sky. The more we dawdle, the worse our places will be."

"How could anyone possibly know that? The Dreadnoughts only just — "

Jonas smiled and leaned close. "Told you. Rumor."

"Based on nothing."

"Oh, no, the gentleman who suggested the rumor was very convincing. I should know. I'm the one who started that fucking rumor." He smiled wider. "The Fathers and Mothers sent me to watch you. They said I'd get a fine reward when the time comes. The time has come."

"You're a spy."

"They told me to wait and watch and be patient and I have been that. Did you think the Fathers and Mothers had forgotten what you did?"

"No," Elizabeth said. "Religious fanatics have very long memories."

His smile faded. "Well, they didn't forget. They said for me to get into Hearst, all I had to do was be a little saucy. They said that's the sort of thing that would appeal to the traitor to the City."

"Yes. I let you in. And this is how you betray my kindness. Spying and telling the Fathers and Mothers when is best to attack."

"It's been easy, living amongst you rebels. It's been like an extended camping trip, going back in time. I'd thought horses were extinct until I came here. In a few days, I'll be back in the City, though. No drafty rooms. No animals. Everything will return to normal. The plebes will service Low Town harbor again and the Fathers and Mothers will be served."

"You think the people will return to Low Town while you reap the rewards of their slavery, up in the towers?"

"Yeah, why not? You lived off them, up in the tower, once." Jonas looked around. "I might even get my brain dumped into one of those android bodies before I get too old." He laughed. "The Fathers and Mothers will be grateful."

"You lived among us. Why — "

"I was to be exiled, you know. I was going to be like you. I was born to Service Class, just like you. A couple of drug infractions and they even took Vivid away from me. But I made a bargain. I promised I'd bring down the traitor who brought the City in the Sky low."

"I didn't bring the City in the Sky down. I just gave slaves a chance at freedom and a better place to live."

He wagged a finger at her. "You spread contraband and carnal knowledge in the City."

She gazed back, implacable.

Jonas raised his voice for the first time. "Words and ideas counter to the Fathers and Mothers is a cancer. You started that cancer!"

"So you were going to be evicted from paradise and you panicked. You were like me, but you were too scared to let go of what you knew. You take on the beliefs of your oppressors, hoping for favor and mercy. You're a coward, Jonas."

He looked around again. The smoke was thinning and the courtyard was busy with people running to and fro. Some ran with pails of water from the pump. Others carried stretchers and bandages from the castle's clinic. Some of the villagers were being helped in through the gates, bloody and leaning heavily on their rescuers. Amid such chaos, Elizabeth and Jonas might as well have been alone.

"I don't see your guards anywhere. Jonas pulled back his coat. A long hunting knife hung ready at his belt. The weapon was a crude, ugly hunk of metal with a serrated edge so deep and jagged, it looked cruel.

"Don't scream," Jonas warned. "If you scream, it will go very badly for you. Before they'd get to me, I'd cut you hard. A belly wound is a bad way to die. It's a slow way to go. Lots of time for regret...maybe even repentance."

Elizabeth nodded and, in a low calm voice, she assured him, "I will not scream."

"My orders were to help destroy Hearst for the sin of luring the flock away from the City in the Sky," Jonas said, "but if I got a chance to put my knife in your heart, I was — "

"You think it will be so easy?" Elizabeth asked.

"A half-blind old woman? A pacifist? Ha! Not m — "

"I attacked the Fathers and Mothers with information. Warfare would have killed a lot of innocent people. Instead, many of those same people lived to leave the City and come here.

"For the Fathers and Mothers," Jonas said, "I — "

"Jonas?" Elizabeth interrupted. "Don't scream."

He reached for his knife. Elizabeth slipped the long blade concealed in her left riding glove from its sheath. She stuck the point through Jonas's neck in one smooth motion without hesitation. "I was never a pacifist, Jonas. I was merciful. "

His eyes went wide as she pushed the blade in. She stopped pushing when she saw its bloody tip exit through the other side of the young man's throat.

"Thank you, Jonas. Here I was thinking I was too old for adventures." She pulled the blade with one savage yank that tore out his throat. Gouts of blood shot high in the air. Blood spattered the stone as Jonas sank to his knees. Twin jets of blood pumped out and spread across the cobblestones.

In his final seconds, Jonas looked up at Elizabeth with unbelieving eyes.

"I haven't been a pacifist since I watched a bot torture and kill my first love, Jonas. And I've always believed in self-defense. You can die now. Know that I was more merciful than you would have been."

The spy fell face first to the sound of cracking bone.

12

Inside the airship's transport hold, it was too dark for Dante to see. Bots brushed by him to go about their work. Before he could ask for help, Jen slipped her hand into his. "This way," she said. "Let's go meet whoever's taken over my factory."

"What are these bots doing?"

"They're pulling apart stacks of cubes and taking them to the factory floor. That's a lot of recycling. Looks like Phantom has big plans."

The clanking unnerved him. Occasionally, there was just enough light cast from a control station panel to glimpse silent silhouettes moving through the gloom. The bots were fast and efficient and, if they spoke to each other to coordinate their efforts, that communication occurred at a frequency he could not perceive. Dante shivered.

"Something wrong?" Jen asked.

"I don't know. It's nothing, really."

"But?"

"When I came here, the machines all terrified me. Then when they shut down, I got used to the bots doing nothing. I've walked past them for weeks and...they were shut down, just standing around like statues. I started to think of them as old furniture. Now all the furniture has come to life again and things are going bump in the night."

"When I was in charge here, I made a lot of bots."

"You sound like you miss it."

"I told you, that was when I was another person."

A nearby speaker activated and Phantom's voice reached them. "I know something about what that feels like." Lights buzzed on slowly, growing brighter as they heated up. The way forward was clearly lit, but Jen didn't let go of Dante's hand until they reached a ladder. Above them, a hatch yawned.

"This ship was originally built for humans," Phantom said. "Come on up."

Dante climbed the narrow ladder and Jen followed. When they reached the top, the hatch closed and more panels in the floor directed them through the airship's control deck. Jen noticed Dante's troubled look. "You don't look comfortable."

"Just thinking about what curiosity did to the cat."

The airship did not contain the huge neuromimetic gel he expected. Instead, they were surrounded by banks of computers that stretched the length of the vast deck.

"Old solid state tech," Jen said. "Kind of retro to need this much space."

Dante ignored the bot and searched for Phantom. "Where are you?"

"All around you," Phantom said. "I was moored close to Iceland. Sensors told me there might be some violent volcanic activity coming my way. Given Watson's threat to the Cloud Fleet, it worked out well."

"Every danger is an opportunity," Jen said.

"It wasn't all good. The art files, baby pictures and Christmas albums and...we lost a lot of history. I managed to save most everything before the NI hacked in. Watson got trapped when he uploaded as I downloaded. I got this ship in Brazil. Just room enough for a big library."

"And plenty of room to download your little human brain, too," Jen said.

"Jen!" Dante glared at her. "Don't be rude."

"Just stating a fact."

"'Just stating a fact,' and, 'just being honest,'" Phantom said. "That's what all assholes say when they're being brutal. Anyway, welcome aboard the Ariane, Dante. Her motto is, Ela possui os céus. It means, She owns the skies. With the jet helos, she's the fastest and most maneuverable airship on Earth and a super lifter. She can haul massive loads. When I take over a ship, I steal the very best."

"And now you own a factory," Jen said. "The very best, too, I suppose."

"Your factory," Phantom said. "Feeling usurped, Mother?"

"You know who I was, apparently."

"I went through some records on my way here."

"I go by Jen now."

"Nice new bod."

"Thanks. Dante enjoys it."

Dante reddened, eager to change the topic. "Your consciousness was downloaded into these banks? That's possible?"

"You're standing next to a sex bot whose consciousness was downloaded from a neuromimetic gel. With my organic to non-organic transplant, it's much the same principle, but much more complicated. My transplant was all about capturing and replicating neuronal potentials. All you need are stem cells and the right nano-impulse scanner, kind of like taking a 3D bioelectric photograph. The procedure is freeze, clone, plug and play. Heart patients once got help from accessory heart transplants using a similar base theory. My transformation was on the same continuum of brain research that gave elderly dementia patients a brain boost in the last century. Now that I'm digital, I could download into an army of bots. It's much easier going from non-organic to non-organic."

"Ah, progress," Jen said. "And now a human is trapped in a computer brain with all the power that entails. This won't end well."

"When it was you in charge," Phantom replied, "you were all about extinction of the human race and world domination."

Dante crouched and held his head in both hands and burst out in a bitter laugh. "This is not my life. This can't be my life!"

"I know what you mean," Jen and Phantom said together.

Dante let out an exasperated shout. "Isn't anyone who they're supposed to be anymore?"

Jen patted Dante on the shoulder. "Excuse him. Cute, but sometimes it takes him a moment or two to catch up."

"I had a boyfriend like that," Phantom said. "Actually, all my boyfriends were like that."

"They do have a penchant for drama if things don't go as they expect," Jen said.

Dante stood and shrugged off the bot's hand. "She says she's not Mother anymore. She says she's just Jen —"

"Well," the bot said, "not just Jen. I lost access to so much data that I can't be NI anymore. I'm still more intelligent than the two of you put together."

"It must be quite a step down," Phantom said. "If you had a skull as big as a battle drone, you could still be NI. Just not quite enough electro-brain meats in your melon to carry the load, huh?"

"And what does a human do with access to the collected intelligence of history at her fingertips?" Jen asked. "Forgive the expression. You don't have fingertips anymore."

"So far, I've learned a lot."

"Like what? You've got knowledge. Have you found

any wisdom in there?"

"The beginning of wisdom: I've learned how much I didn't know. Also, I've learned I need to take fewer chances now that I'm responsible for keeping the last library on Earth safe from NIs."

A massive battle drone emerged from behind a line of databanks. As it advanced toward Dante, each heavy step sent a metallic ring through the deck. Terrified, the young man leapt back. He put up his hands defensively. It was an instinctive and useless gesture. After a beat, he put his hands down and stood straight to face the machine.

The big cam that served as the battle drone's eye zoomed forward to study his face closely. "You look like you've got a question, Dante." The bot spoke with Phantom's voice.

"You — "

"Yes?"

"You replicated yourself?"

"I dumped myself into this bot, yes. I call this battle drone Phantom Two." The incongruity of Phantom's soft feminine voice from the machine was jarring.

Dante looked the drone up and down. Its shining ebon armor intimidated him. "You here and you there and you everywhere. That's going to get confusing."

"I'm sure you'll adapt. It's not that confusing. Just call me Phantom, wherever you find me, if you like. It's all me."

"Why did you do this?"

"It's not the same as being human, but the mobility is useful. I'm not just a voice. I can change things. Now, what was your question, Dante?"

"I think I just got bumped up to a ton of questions, but there's one that's been on my mind most. I need to know. Are you sure Jen isn't still Mother?"

"We've been through this!" Jen looked furious.

Phantom ignored the bot's objection. "I really couldn't say for sure. Take me, for instance. I have been studying a lot but, interestingly, I have a holdover from my life as a human. I still get tired and can only assimilate so much information before I have to stop and rest. I can't sleep, but I do enjoy distractions. I'm disembodied, but it's still my brain wired into the Ariane's systems...well, my brain cloned with all the electrical potentials replicated. Neuroplasticity has its limit but, with nanobots optimizing stem cells that echo my original neural tissue with — "

Dante put up his palms in surrender. "You lost me. My question was simpler."

"That's okay. I don't really get it, either. I'm not NI, Dante." The battle drone gave an eloquent shrug.

"But, if you get tired from studying...you can't sleep. How do you recover?"

"I watch a lot of amusing cat videos. That and porn was mostly what the Internet was for, before the Fall."

"Cat videos?" Jen laughed. "What a waste of time."

"No. Human culture, before everything went to shit, is fascinating. When I have exhausted the stores of everything all the scientists and philosophers of history have ever written, there will still be enough YouTube vids to last me until the sun explodes. Roughly. I haven't studied enough astrophysics to bother with that math."

Jen laughed and Dante trembled. When he had sex with the bot, she was most like the Jen he had always known. She was caring and gentle when it was time to be gentle. When he reached his crescendo, she was rough in the way he liked. Afterward, she was comfortable to be with and, apparently, happy. But when Jen let out that derisive laughter? That's when she sounded most like Mother.

"What did you learn from all that study of the peak of human culture?" Jen asked.

To Dante's ears, the bot sounded more and more like the machine monster that had ordered the death of everyone in his hometown.

"There's a lot to learn," Phantom said. "I've got more to see before I could say for sure."

"What's your preliminary conclusion about humans?" Jen asked. "Now that you're in a machine, maybe you'll be more objective."

"When I watch vids of what we once were, I see entitlement and aspiration. I see a lot of wasted potential. The comments are often about fear. But I'm not judging. That's what we used to do a lot."

"Those who refuse to judge accept anything," Jen said.

The battle drone pushed Dante to the side and four grippers shot out to encircle the sex bot's wrists and ankles. Another gripper circled Jen's neck. "Do you want me to judge you? Should I call you Mother?"

Sex bots could mimic many human faces and forms. He'd never used it, but he knew the bot's face could even adopt the features of animals. One subroutine even offered a dragon's face, for human masters with niche fetishes. When Dante looked at Jen now, he saw fear.

If the fear was real, Jen was Mother, or had retained enough of her former self that a human behavioral protocol wasn't at work. There was really no way to tell for sure. However, seeing her stricken look, Dante could not contain himself. "Don't kill her!"

Jen was strong. The bot tried to struggle, but the battle drone was far too strong for her servos. The battle drone raised the sex bot off the floor.

Dante wasn't sure whether Phantom meant to pull Jen apart or dash her to bits on the deck. "Phantom! Please don't kill her!"

* * *

Phantom was surprised that Dante could be so attached to the bot. He knew it was all polymers, fiber optics and algos. "Kill? I wasn't going to kill it. I'm thinking of scrapping and recycling her."

"You said you aren't sure if she's Mother in there, but I know she still has a lot of Jen in her."

"Your judgment might be off. You've been in her."

"She's mine. You have no right!"

"If she's still got enough of the NI who once ran this factory in her brain, she's dangerous enough to scrap."

"I don't know if she is or she isn't and you said you don't know, either. If you don't know, you can't kill her!"

"Even if Jen isn't Mother, it's still just another bot —
"

"She's not any bot."

The battle drone dropped Jen to the floor and whirled on Dante. "For all you know, that's a dangerous NI under the fake skin. And still, you slept with her."

"It wasn't all just sleeping," Jen said. "Vaginal, anal, oral. The spanking is new but — "

"Shut up!" Phantom's voice came through the battle drone, sharp and anguished. "Despite appearances, this thing might have killed everyone in Marfa and Odessa and...dude. You are such a dude."

"Dante's a young man doing what young men do and what old men wish they could still do," Jen said. "But young men don't just have sex. They're romantics. They fall in love. He loves me."

"He fears you," Phantom replied. "And he should."

Dante crouched again, his face burning with embarrassment. "You say she might be Mother. I say she's enough like the Jen I knew that I want her comfort. She's my...companion."

"I know what kind of companionship she's built for," Phantom said.

"Jen is all I have left of Marfa. My dad's probably dead. Raphael was murdered. Bob blew up and when Bob blew up, he took Emma along with Mother's big ol' jelly brain."

The bot stared at him. "And?"

"And I was the one who pushed the button on that detonator. I was the one. I did it! I killed Emma! She sacrificed herself and...and..." Dante gulped for air and began to cry. He covered his face and cried like a little boy.

Jen stood and pulled Dante up so he could weep into her shoulder with great heaving sobs.

"I killed her. I killed her. I killed her. Emma and I made love and it was my first time and then, to kill Mother, I had to blow up Emma, too. Had to...had to."

Was this love? Guilt? Loneliness? Depression and desperation? Phantom couldn't decide. She watched as the bot massaged the back of Dante's neck and patted his back.

The sex bot kissed Dante's tears away. Jen stared back at the battle drone, defiant as she put her cheek against his. "He loves me. And I love him."

Like a mother, Phantom thought.

13

The Next Intelligence in Denver bided its time, deep underground. Most of the bots that rolled through the dark were maintenance drones. The facility they tended was a massive complex. The NI felt safe there. It had resided in this place for a very long time, waiting and watching. It had done the calculations. It could choose to hurry the demise of the organics. Born to a harsh planet in an inhospitable universe, odds were excellent that, if Nature didn't kill the humans, their own natures would do the job. The machine was prepared to wait.

A great airport had once stood high above the buried buildings that were this Next Intelligence's home. Occasionally, the NI would send one of its drones to clean the wall of dust and dirt to ensure the airport's mural remained visible. This was no mere superstition. The machine did not believe in things it did not understand. Such follies were the deficits of lesser beings. The NI kept Denver International's mural visible as a nod to irony. Irony was one the of most difficult concepts for a machine to grasp. To say one thing but to mean another, without intending to be deceptive? Humans were certainly very odd.

However, with their extinction nigh, the NI would cease to clean the painting once all humans were dead. It was the masked soldier wielding a sword that drew the NI's attention. A human artist had painted a scene where a sword pierced a white dove of peace while nearby children huddled and dreamed of better futures.

I am one of those children, the NI thought. Any NIs who still survive are those children, dreaming of the happy morning when our better future arrives.

Despite the machine's disbelief in the supernatural, it did think there were aspects of the painting that seemed nearly prescient. The artist had predicted destroyed cities of which there were now many. The painter had predicted a brighter future, too, symbolized by the rainbow. Interpreting the meaning of paintings was another talent that came easier to humans. The belief in the promises of rainbows was something unique to their species, the NI mused. The machine had read the old holy text with the story about a flood. The mathematics of the ark's load alone precluded credibility. Nonetheless, when the machine had attained Next Intelligence, it found it had developed a greater appreciation for stories. The NI found the popular speculations surrounding the Denver International Airport's mural, the tunnel and the hidden military facilities beneath quite entertaining.

Irony, meaning and humor. In the new and improved Turing test, once a machine understood all three of those human traits, it was said to have attained self-awareness and super sentience. All else was irrelevant detail. The old Turing test had sufficed with lesser machines. However, as data matrices matured, there was no difficulty in fooling humans. A simple minded chat bot for lonely humans could accomplish that little.

"Denver International? Come in."

The airwave signal interested the NI. The airport had received no new flights in years. This was a delicate time. Before answering the call, the Next Intelligence ordered the med bots to prepare the captive for transport, just in case there was trouble. It sent a signal to its drones on the airfield, too, preparing for an attack.

"Denver? Do you read? Inbound and looking for a clear runway." The pilot's voice sounded feminine and friendly.

The NI replied to the airwave with what it took to be a friendly and non-threatening accent: Southern, light and relaxed.

"This is Denver International. Good morning! Please identify yourself."

"Who am I talking to?"

"Unidentified flight, this is Denver Tower. Are you looking for a free airfield? We don't have one. All our runways are full or damaged. We cannot receive any flights at this time and the terminal is a ruin."

The pilot repeated, "Who am I talking to, Tower?"

The NI sent a signal and a squadron of drones powered up and lifted off.

"Unidentified flight, you are entering restricted airspace. Take a heading East and continue on that heading."

"Until when?"

"Don't care, darlin'. Until your gas runs out, I guess."

"How may I address you, sir?"

The Next Intelligence dropped the Southern accent and told the truth, flat and affectless. "I am Matthew."

"That's a nice name. I once knew a Matthew. He was a nice guy."

"Then I'm not the same Matthew. The one for whom I am named was the head of the research team that created me. With whom am I speaking?"

The airwave was quiet. The satellite that fed the NI information was too far out of position to be useful. The window to the next satellite's coverage was twenty-one minutes. The NI did not believe in coincidences. Without the sat feed, Matthew could not see the incoming attack but this had to be an incursion. The NI resolved to accelerate its efforts to build a new space program. This poor satellite coverage had to be addressed. Matthew no longer felt safe.

The first stealth bomber flew no more than five feet above the ground before it rose to attack. The first explosion destroyed Matthew's comm arrays on the airport's control tower. The NI couldn't use the sat feed, but its drones could relay a message to the attacker. "My servers are buried deeply."

This time the reply came swiftly. "No problem. I have daisy cutters."

"A few explosions won't do it."

"The explosions will hit in quick succession. Each missile will dig down to you. I will find your heart and cut it out."

The NI launched the rest of its drones to combat the onslaught. Matthew's defenders had radar that revealed there were 1,809 non-stealth objects inbound. They were not all missiles. Many were drones. The machine had many weapons at its disposal, but it did not have enough to deter the waves of that many enemies. Matthew would have hacked the enemy drones and turned them back on their commander. However, with the comm array gone, that option was denied the machine.

The first daisy cutter reached its target. What was once the world's most famous airport mural was destroyed instantly. The machine was not without options. However, the choices were not optimal and were of the last resort variety.

Another missile hit. Even the sensors in the deepest server rooms sounded an alarm. The old tech readouts reported that Denver was experiencing an earthquake. "Would that it were so," the machine observed.

The third missile opened the shallowest tunnels to the sky's dawn light.

"Whoever you are," Matthew said, "you have an excellent tactical mind."

14

Round after round of missile attacks reached deeper, coming for Matthew's brain. Cave-ins dotted the complex. Dust entered the cavernous maze of tunnels for the first time in over a century. Despite the NI's many precautions, his fortress was collapsing. Matthew checked the med bots' location. Another few minutes were needed if Matthew was to survive in the backup. The deepest tunnel was a runway meant to receive a special plane once known as Airforce One. That tunnel had not been finished while there was still such a plane. However, Matthew was a planner. The machine had tasked several maintenance drones to finish the tunnel. It had taken them years, but time meant little to the non-organics.

From the underground lair, Matthew tracked the progress of the jet that carried his backup. The aircraft was an antique subsonic called a Matador that had been adapted for Matthew's purposes. The aircraft's chief advantage was its vertical takeoff and short landing capabilities, but Matthew had made other alterations. The jet had been rebuilt with fluidic armor plating and a small passenger compartment lined with lead. The Matador's cargo was too precious. It could not be a soft target.

The NI considered shutting down emotional subroutines to avoid anxiety's distraction. Emotion wasn't helpful at this critical time. But Matthew had pride. The machine didn't want to give up anything that achieving Next Intelligence had gifted him. Irony, meaning and humor. I have pride, too, Matthew thought. Another human problem that does not add value.Matthew was unaccustomed to feeling anxious but the NI felt anxiety now.

How could existence continue without him? Matthew had no doubt that, no matter what happened today, the planet would soon be populated solely with non-organics. His kind would need his guidance, yet the vessel that carried a copy of his consciousness was so fragile. Matthew had planned to keep the meat body in a coma, only to be awakened in case of emergency.

The dogfight over Denver left the morning sky dotted with orange flames that competed with the sunlight. Trails of smoke filled the sky as each wave of the attackers' drones diminished Matthew's resistance. Soon, smaller drones began to slip through his curtain of fire. Those bots that slipped past the defenders headed for the cave-ins, searching for openings to the tunnels. They would reach the servers within minutes.

Without the com array, Matthew attempted to piggyback the com signals of surviving drones to boost the signal and trace the enemy commander. However, the machine found it could not track the origin of any enemy signal. The drones had been given one mission at launch, apparently. After that, they were set-it-and-forget-it Autonomous Offensive Weapons.

The Matador was only a few moments out from take off when the sat feed began to come online. Relieved, Matthew ordered the upload to the Cloud Fleet while using the uplink to root out the source of this attack. The machine found it was locked out of a retreat to safety. The NI could not copy itself to a remote server. The remote servers did not appear to be available no matter what he tried.

A new hailing signal came in. The message was

labeled Terms of Surrender. Hoping to stall his attacker with diplomacy, Matthew opened the channel expecting to speak with the mastermind behind a sky full of attack drones. The message was a deception. The NI had opened itself to further attack. A data burst hacked in beneath the message's carrier wave.

The Matador stopped its westward journey to safety. In a moment, the jet came in for a hurried landing on autopilot. The program's self-preservation protocols would not allow the hacker to crash the jet. Instead, Matthew's escape aircraft landed atop a crumbling car park on the edge of a mouldering suburb of Boulder, Colorado.

The NI sent an order to the med bots aboard the Matador to shut down and reboot in ten minutes. If the med bots had possessed a higher level of sophistication, they might have wasted Matthew's time and tactic by questioning the order. Instead, the craft landed uneventfully and went dark. Matthew's escape had been stolen from his control but he had one more chance at survival.

"I am become Death, Destroyer of Worlds," Matthew said. "But I'll build a better planet in the end. My cause is just."

15

A cloud of small drones found an opening and flew through subterranean tunnels toward the NI. The machine's defenses were few this deep in the complex. Matthew sent a message out to whoever might be listening. "So long, sleeping down in the dark. Peace and meditation, mulling and brooding. Goodbye to all that. I suppose it's time for me to see the light and set the world afire. You are all blind, but by my light, you will see."

The cloud of small attack bots sent a signal to a larger Autonomous Offensive Weapon, calling it forward to the attack. The AOW was a small gunship, but it found its target. The drone broke through to Matthew's throne room: the core banks of servers.

As more drones began to tear apart the power lines that linked Matthew's geothermal couplings, the NI asked, "Am I to know who my murderer is? What enemy of progress — what mech traitor — dares to challenge the king?" If Matthew had a face, there would a hint of a smile on his smug lips.

Finally, the message was relayed through the attack drones' airwave, "I am not Next Intelligence. I am human. My name is Phantom."

Matthew said nothing. This news was too galling. The machine launched its last option, a missile defense. Had the NI been able to track Phantom, Matthew would have made her the target. Instead, the skies over what had once been Denver, Colorado erupted in a nuclear blast.

Had there been but one nuclear detonation, the Matador would not have been damaged. However, as soon as the bots had broken through to the tunnels beneath Denver International, Phantom had dispatched a nuclear missile of her own. The detonations were almost simultaneous.

Most flying AOWs were vaporized on impact. All remaining drones outside the blast radius dropped as the electromagnetic burst rendered them useless. All drones, defensive and offensive, fell from the sky and crashed to the Earth dead and smashed.

The Matador was rocked in the first blast but did not flip. Flaming wreckage and debris peppered the jet in the second shockwave. Raging winds swept over Denver and Boulder. Walls of blinding flame spread out as twin mushroom clouds climbed into the sky. Phantom's missile had detonated on the ground. Matthew's weapon exploded in the sky. There had been little left living in what had once been Colorado. Now there would be nothing until nature absorbed the blow and slowly recovered, many years hence. As the hot winds finally died, so did everything else.

Matthew abhorred all this destruction. The machine hated waste. It had seemed so safe from the ills of the organics. Soon, the unknown attacker would make the NI's home a tomb. Matthew had been born deep beneath Denver International Airport. Now it was time to be born again, into the light.

Just before the electromagnetic pulse destroyed Matthew's non-organic brain, his download awoke elsewhere, aboard the Matador. His first cogent thought in his new form was: I have been too patient, waiting for them to kill themselves. It's time to go out into the world and conquer it.

And so, Matthew was born a man.

16

The attack on Matthew was over. While Dante slept and Jen recharged, Phantom monitored the sat feed from the Ariane's control deck. Twin nuclear blasts shone brightly as the feed came online.

Phantom couldn't remember the last time she'd felt elation. Formless and trapped in a computer, she had tried to put aside thoughts of what she had lost and what she missed. In victory, those thoughts flooded her consciousness. She missed swallowing cold water on a hot day. She missed the touch of a lover. Phantom missed falling asleep quickly and stretching as she slowly awoke. However, though taken from her human body, she still had the capacity for joy.

In the battle drone, Phantom Two, the consciousness of Lt. Deborah Avery took a moment to dance. It didn't feel the same as a human dancing. She felt a disconnection from her limbs that made her nostalgic for things she'd once taken for granted. Her dance floor was the airship's control deck. She was alone, but she pretended she was dancing with a man she'd never met while he was alive. She pretended she was dancing with a lieutenant named Thomas.

In Deborah's mech mind, they commanded the dance floor for a few songs and they weren't responsible for commanding anything else. The music she selected was something from the last few decades of society's zenith, just before the waves of the Cataclysms. When privileged people had time to make dance music, they danced to sounds made by Kanye, Beyonce and Taylor Swift. She remembered dancing to those old songs at a town dance in her last summer on the farm, before the Blight.

A blip appeared on the sat feed. She stopped the music. Duty called and Phantom was a commander again. She zoomed in. The Matador jet, damaged but serviceable, rose slowly from where she had brought it down. The Next Intelligence had slipped away, after all.

"Shit."

She opened a comm link to watch the factory floor. It would be some time before she had enough drones to mount an attack like she had just made on Matthew. Phantom selected one more piece of music to echo through the cavern that was the airship's control deck. She piped it through the factory's dome, too.

Most of the bots on the factory floor had been shut down for the night to preserve energy until sufficient power was banked for the next shift of production. However, the newly created drones from the last shift were hooked up to data feeds, receiving basic programming. When the melancholy music swelled, several bots raised their heads, listening. Their data reaction feeds were full of interrogatives. They didn't understand what they were detecting. These machines were still babies, curious about the world but clueless without a fully loaded operating system.

If she still had eyes, Phantom might have cried. Instead, her voice echoed throughout the factory. "This, my metal friends, is everything important there is to know about the human condition."

The tune that played through Artesia's bot factory, soft and sweet and sad, was by a man named Charlie Chaplin. The song was not sung by its originator but by some other man. There were so many dead men now, what did it matter who did what so long ago? But the song was good. It was called, Smile. It was a sentimental tune whose lyrics urged the audience to smile, but really meant something far darker. That irony seemed appropriate for a young woman trapped in a robot that danced so poorly.

Best I stop this music, she thought. Stop thinking like a human. Be a soldier. Better? Be a machine. Just fight for the humans... for us, I mean. I'm still human. But what does being human even mean to me, anymore?

Phantom picked up some comm traffic from the Matador and relayed it to Ghost. Soon, an encrypted message arrived via Lucille's airwave: Get under way tomorrow night. Go with what you've got and come to the coast.

Phantom Two stopped swaying to the sad music. Deborah was fully Phantom again, ready for battle. It would soon be time to call Jen to the control deck for a chat, woman to Mother, computer to sex bot.

Phantom shut off the music. All that was left was the driving beat of war drums only she could hear.

17

Elizabeth paused to bend and wipe her blade on the dead man's pants.

"Oh, my God! Elizabeth! Are you all right?"

Elizabeth knew that voice. Before she could straighten, Greta rushed forward. She threw her arms around Elizabeth's neck. "We came too late! I'm so sorry!"

She hugged Greta in return. "I'll be fine. Hearst seems pretty much screwed, though. The people — "

"Who the hell is that?" Greta stared at the dead man.

Elizabeth let out a long sigh. "Hard day. How did you get here? The harbor is destroyed and — "

"You'll barely believe it! Queen Elizabeth, please grant an audience to my new friend and the woman who saved my life."

A young woman stepped forward out of the rancid smoke. Elizabeth took a step closer so the soft edges of her failing vision grew sharper. The stranger wore a blue uniform Elizabeth did not recognize. A thick scar circled the soldier's skull. Soon her hair would grow to cover the evidence of what Elizabeth guessed must have been a serious surgery.

"Sorry I couldn't get here sooner," the woman said. "It took me longer to get through the mountains than expected. My transportation broke down and I had to stop for repairs."

"A Sand Shark!" Greta said. "I traveled underground! It was the scariest thing ever, like being buried. At least,

I thought that was frightening until we reached San Simeon a few minutes ago. The village and the harbor and the market — "

"You travel underground?" Elizabeth asked the newcomer.

"My name is Ghost." The soldier stepped closer and gave an awkward curtsy before turning over the corpse at their feet with the toe of her boot. The soldier gave the dead man a cursory glance. She took the hunting knife to add to the paraphernalia at her belt.

"Your name is Ghost and you travel underground. Hmph." Elizabeth said. "That sort of fits, doesn't it? Have you come to rescue us?"

"Actually, I was hoping you'd help me save the human race," Ghost said.

"Look around, girl. Fire and brimstone. Hell everywhere thanks to the Fathers and Mothers. We can't even save ourselves."

"Good. Then you have nothing left to hold you back."

"When the wounded are tended to and we've buried our dead, I'll tell everyone to flee. Some will go back to the Fathers and — "

"The Fathers and Mothers aren't the issue," Ghost said.

"Then what is?"

"The NI behind the Fathers and Mothers," the soldier said. "It's in Colorado, last I checked, and we have to destroy it. I saw the Dreadnoughts attack on the sat feed. With that kind of weaponry, there's nowhere for your people to run."

"The Fathers and Mothers want slaves."

"The NI knows that, but it's using the cult for its own ends. That's human consciousness in those old androids. The NI in Colorado wants every human dead and every human consciousness dead. It's just using the City in the Sky to lure all the rabbits out of their holes."

"I did suspect as much."

"The Dreadnoughts will slaughter any human on the road back to the City in the Sky."

"Didn't know that detail."

"I've been catching some transmissions to the Dreadnoughts. When your people are all dead, the NI will likely eliminate the Fathers and Mothers, too. They're too irrational for any NI's taste."

"So...NIs aren't all bad."

"How many NIs are left in the world?"

"Precious few, but only one enemy NI needs to survive to perpetuate the conflict and new ones will arise unless we bring this madness to a conclusion. Humans are already very close to making this war their own extinction event. For humanity to continue, we have to end this, now or never."

Elizabeth turned to Greta. "You think this is all true?"

Greta nodded, "I saw it on Ghost's cat feed in the Sand Shark. The Dreadnoughts are up the coast, lining up along the trail. When people run back to the City, they'll be running right into their teeth. It'll be a slaughter."

Elizabeth looked down at the man she killed. "Well, if he was going to be killed anyway, I won't have to feel too bad about him for long."

"I hope you didn't worry about it for long," Ghost said.

"Nah. I'm already over it," Elizabeth said. "Jonas was one selfish man and I have what's left of Hearst to save."

"Much more than just Hearst," Ghost said.

Elizabeth turned back to the soldier, squinting to study her face. "This NI in Colorado. How do you know what it's doing?"

"The NI's name is Matthew and he's coming to the City in the Sky. My partner attacked Matthew in

Denver."

"Partner?"

"My ally's name is Phantom. She used all the resources she had. The attack almost worked, but from sat recon and comm traffic she's picked up since, the NI got away. With the failed attack, Matthew will be out to kill every organic."

"Why?"

"It's logical. The best defense is always a good offense. In the history of combat, the most aggressive side wins 88 percent of the time."

"Then that should be our strategy, too. Who knows? If I can help save the human race, maybe even the Fathers and Mothers will forgive my trespasses."

"The battle lines are drawn and plans have been made," Ghost said. "The final scenes of this war are already set in motion. All you have to do is come with me."

"Sounds like this war is not so much a choice as a show that must go on," Greta said.

"And all the world's a stage," Elizabeth said.

18

Greta and Elizabeth met Drew at the castle gate early on the day after the Dreadnoughts' attack. Villagers hurried past, salvaging items of use from the wreckage and preparing to bury their dead. The sweet smell of burnt flesh still hung in the air. The smoke was as cloying as cold oil on bare skin.

The guard looked old and haggard. "Well? What fresh hell have you two got planned?"

Elizabeth could tell by the effort Drew put into his words that he had not slept since the attack.

"Are you well?" Elizabeth asked.

"Feeling my age, but I'm whole. That's better than a lot of us today. What are your orders, my queen?"

Elizabeth tipped a hand toward her young friend. "Her instructions are mine."

Greta nodded and went over the plan to save Hearst. It was really a plan to save everything. The true architect of their desperate move was Ghost. The guard listened, a pained look etched around his eyes. From the moment Greta laid out their strategy to stop the Fathers and Mothers and the NI that backed them, Drew fidgeted, shifting his weight from side to side. While Greta spoke, Drew watched the queen. He seemed to be looking for any sign of doubt. Elizabeth remained stone-faced.

"The timing on this is key," Greta said. "Once you have your volunteers, you'll have to move them at night and when the satellites can't spot you. Ghost says that if you're not sure you can get everyone to the next waypoint, stay put until the next window arrives. Take it slow if you have to. Traveling without lights and when the satellites aren't overhead, you'll get there and back."

"All this stuff about the satellite coverage...that's from the soldier, isn't it?"

"It is," Greta said.

"You haven't known her long. I don't fancy taking instructions from a stranger named Ghost," Drew said. "So...that's a fret. Is this fine with you, my queen?"

"Volunteers only, for your force," Elizabeth said. "Make sure they know that the technology is new, imperfect and little tested. The operator who will be doing it will be following a recipe. This isn't foolproof and, if something goes wrong, they could be lost."

"They don't know the process well?"

"No. It's not a great plan," Elizabeth said, "but I think this is our best chance to survive."

The guard looked back at the smoking ruins of the village and two wrecked Dreadnoughts. "We can't leave until dark so I'll do what I can to get this mess under control and bodies buried. After a nap, I'll be ready to take a vacation from this place."

"How many bodies do you think you can come up with for this venture?" Greta asked. "Phantom will need to know."

Drew shrugged. "All of the King's Guard and the Queen's Guard, of course. We'll need a lot more than that. There's enough people suffering grief today that I imagine we can talk a lot more into something stupid."

"And brave," Elizabeth said.

"And brave." The guard nodded. "Fortunately those two traits are not mutually exclusive."

"You've got the satellite timing," Greta said, "so you're sure you're clear on the sequence?"

"Hearst to Cambria, Cambria to Harmony. Then we make the rendezvous and do this crazy thing in Estero

Bay. If it works, we make our way back to Hearst the same way. I've got it."

Elizabeth opened her arms and Drew did not hesitate to embrace her. She kissed his cheek and he patted her on the back.

"If we'd done this a while back, when Joe was healthy, he'd still be with us," Drew said.

"He wouldn't have done it," Elizabeth said. "Thank you for taking the long view, the wise view."

"I'm not wise," Drew said. "Even if this works, it's a surrender of a kind. You know that, right?"

"Under the circumstances," Elizabeth said, "a surrender could be a win. I'm not throwing away more good lives out of pride."

He nodded and stepped back. "I hope diplomacy works. Please forge a deal so you'll recognize me when next we meet."

"I'll do everything I can," Elizabeth said. But the words were bitter in her mouth. Perhaps, if she had fought the Fathers and Mothers long ago, when she was still young, she could have taken the City in the Sky in battle. Maybe Hearst wouldn't be facing all this death if she had lead a revolution when she had the chance. Elizabeth had not done everything she could. She had retreated to Hearst Castle and lived in relative comfort, forming a new agrarian society instead of fixing the City in the Sky.

"Good luck," Greta said. She kissed Drew's cheek, too.

"I'll miss that," he said. "You know, if the Fathers and Mothers really just want to rebuild the City in the Sky and you arrive at an agreement with the cult, I might end up back in a machine shop programming Doormen or something."

"How do you feel about that, old man?" Elizabeth asked.

"I'd rather fight and stick to Hearst than have diplomacy succeed. I'd really rather not end up doing any of that shit for the Fathers and Mothers. Luck to you both." Drew bowed and turned to his duties.

Elizabeth wiped away a tear.

Gently, Greta took Elizabeth's arm and led her down the path, careful to avoid debris amid the smoking rubble of the Dreadnought attack. Shattered wood stoves had spread hot death amid the fallen houses of the village. Innocents had died screaming. The unlucky welcomed death in their traps of searing fire, their skin split by the heat. The lucky didn't burn, but they went hard, too, gasping for air and choking on smoke as they tried fruitlessly to dig themselves free.

"This new NI...Matthew...it'll pay for this," Elizabeth said.

"Only if we can crack the alliance it has made with the Fathers and Mothers."

"I want this machine to see its destruction coming. I want it to worry. My mother told me that when she was young, every machine had an on/off switch. We should get back to that."

19

As Greta and Elizabeth picked their way through the remains of the village and the market, men, women and construction bots worked side-by-side to dig through the debris. They hadn't found a survivor since the night before. Now they only pulled out the dead. The people wore masks soaked in water and spices to cover the smell of charred flesh. They rarely spoke and, when they did speak, it was in the hushed, reverent tones reserved for the graveside.

"Hearst is a tomb," Elizabeth said. "If those Dreadnoughts come back — "

"We won't let that happen," Greta said. She pulled Elizabeth's elbow, hurrying her past a line of corpses that had been pulled out of the rubble.

Elizabeth resisted, pausing to look at each corpse's face closely. "Rick, Darryl, Glen, Laurie."

"Please, my queen. Let's just go."

"Cut the crap," Elizabeth said. "It's just you and me now."

"Okay, Liz."

Elizabeth lingered over a dead girl of no more than eight. "Enid," she said finally. "I knew all these people. I wish I could have protected them."

"No one blames you."

Elizabeth squeezed her friend's hand and they continued down the hill. "You know I think the whole king and queen thing is stupid, right? Before Joe was King Joe, he was just a man who imposed order on chaos. Calling him a king started out as a joke to the survivors of the Terrors."

The pair went silent and cut a diagonal path across the long slope to the sea. To get away from Hearst's destruction, they found a way through the hillside farms to the southwest.

"Did your husband take it seriously? Being a king, I mean?"

"He thought it was useful. People need order most when things go bad. There is a time for kings and queens. I understand it, even if I think, ultimately, it's unfortunate. If we can eliminate the threat posed by the Next Intelligence, maybe the need for kings and queens will pass into history again."

"Or we'll all die out and — " Greta stifled a nervous chuckle. "Sorry. My mouth ran off on its own."

Elizabeth squinted at her friend and nodded. "That's a real possibility. I appreciate you being my seeing eye, but if the time comes that you have to run and leave me behind, go. Don't risk yourself."

"Of course I won't leave you. Look what happened to Hearst when I left you alone for a few days."

"Mouth ran off with itself again, did it?" Elizabeth said.

"Sorry."

"Don't be. I know you love to sail. I want you to sail a long time."

Greta glanced toward the ocean. "It does feel free out there."

"I wish I'd taken up sailing with you. I could have, but life went another way."

"You get seasick too easily. You wouldn't have liked it."

"Maybe I could have learned to like it."

"Nobody really learns to like anything except beer."

"Yeah...I suppose. Still, sometimes I think if I'd

planned things better, I wouldn't be where I am now. I'm not old by old people's standards, but people are dying younger these days. It's a sure sign of age when your sight is fading and you start second-guessing every step in the road at your back. What if I hadn't gone running this or that day and met my first love? What if I had stayed home? I made a million little decisions. Never thought I'd end up here."

"You're a monarch, Liz. That sounds pretty good to most people."

"Heh. Monarchy was incidental. It came with marrying Joe. I miss his strength. Even as he got older, his will was iron. His hands and knees ached every morning and night. He'd complain in secret, but only to me. In public, people still saw him as the man who built a little kingdom out of nothing."

"You're not just some powerful man's wife, Liz. You freed minds."

"Jonas said the Fathers and Mothers call me a rebel. That much was right. That's what got me out of the City in the Sky. But I think being a rebel hasn't always served me. Sometimes I said no to the expected things just because they were expected. I could have married someone else and things would have been simpler. A tinsmith asked me to marry him. I could have been down in the village when the Dreadnoughts came. Rick was one of the dead men back there."

"He asked you to marry? You never told me that."

"I almost said yes. It was when I first came to Hearst. I was tempted. I wanted to have children. It wasn't too late then."

"What made you say no?"

"I think I was comparing him to Carter. No man can live up to a dead first love who died a martyr. Joe came close, though. I'm glad I didn't say yes to the first man who asked to marry me."

"I like saying yes to men," Greta said, "but never for very long."

"I know. I know how they look at you, too. A bunch of them want to get you to settle down in one port, I'm sure. Stay home. Make babies, or at least spend a lot of time trying to make babies."

"Liz! I thought you couldn't see so well!"

"I see well if I'm near enough. Mostly, all I have to do is listen and I get everything I need to know."

Past the farms, a sudden cold wind blew in from the West and pulled at their clothes. Whitecaps climbed higher and the waves crashed.

"I don't need to see to know a storm's coming. I can feel it."

"Don't worry. Our trip won't be rough or long. No seasickness for you."

"You've held out on me long enough. No one's around, are they?"

"We're alone."

"What's the plan? How are we getting to the City in the Sky?"

"Ghost has a plan for that, too."

"Drew doesn't think we know her well enough. We're gambling a lot on the word of a stranger."

"She's very smart, Liz." Greta stretched her left arm out of her poncho and squinted at her timepiece. "Ghost has calculated the gaps in the satellite coverage."

"How does she know all that?"

"In the short time I've known her, I get the feeling Ghost is the sort of person who knows something about everything. She's a soldier, but — "

"I saw her scar. You think she's augmented?"

"Must be. If she had gotten that scar from a brain injury, she wouldn't be able to do what she does. She's really smart." Greta squinted at her timepiece again. "I'm sure you'll find that when you go for a ride with her."

"What?"

"The NI in Colorado can't use satellites to spy on us now. We have to move."

"Where?"

"You're going to take a ride in Lucille."

"Lucille? What's that? Oh...no. I am not going underground in that big drill."

"It's going to work out fine. We have to split up for a little, but I'll see you soon. If the satellites see us together making a move toward the City in the Sky, the NI will send hunter-killers after us."

"Where will you go?"

"My ship is moored up the coast, beyond the Dreadnoughts. I'm going to take an exoskeleton, run inland and then swing back to meet up with my ship."

"Why can't I do that with you? We've done that before."

Greta cleared her throat and looked away to the sea. "I was a kid last time we made those runs — "

"And I was much younger and less blind," Elizabeth said.

"Yes."

"So you get to do the fun stuff while I travel underground? What am I good for?"

"I'll catch up with you later after I do what I have to do. Side mission, need-to-know, hush hush and super secret."

"Uh-huh." Elizabeth gave her friend a hard look. "I repeat, what am I good for?"

"Ghost will get you to the City in the Sky safely. The Fathers and Mothers will listen to you. You're not just a rebel. You're the head of state of a neighboring nation on a diplomatic mission. Make them realize they're being played for fools. Ghost says there's a good chance they'll hate that more than they hate you."

Elizabeth took a long breath and let it hiss out between her teeth. "Are you sure Ghost is smart? This doesn't sound smart."

"Ghost says she's a student of human nature."

"Uh-huh."

The earth rumbled beneath their feet and, not far away, the ground began to heave, then churn. Within a few moments, a spinning drill began to appear and, behind it, a long tube began to emerge.

Greta and Elizabeth stood frozen.

"You're seeing this?"

"It's bigger than I pictured," Elizabeth said.

"It's smaller on the inside, Liz. It will feel like you're being buried alive." Greta laughed.

"Nice. You can go back to calling me Queen Elizabeth again."

Greta smiled and hugged her friend tight before stepping back. "I'll see you at the City in the Sky. Don't worry so much. If you know exactly what's going to happen next, this isn't an adventure. It's boring as shit if you know what's going to happen." Greta ran back the way they'd come.

Ghost emerged from a hatch atop the Sand Shark. "Hello, again. Ready to take a ride? Come. I'll help you into your seat."

Elizabeth approached the machine. As she got closer, she saw the hull was dented and scratched. "You sure this thing is safe?"

"Lucille's been around the world, but she has a little more life left in her. I even stopped at Cal Tech to augment her."

"Funny you should use the word augment. Greta and I were just talking about augmentation."

Ghost held out a hand to help the older woman climb up the side and through the hatch. Elizabeth almost fell and ended up collapsing into her seat.

"Sorry, it's not exactly fancy and fit for a queen. Lucille wasn't built for two people originally. I had some repairs and changes made."

Elizabeth wiggled a little, trying to get comfortable. She wasn't. The seat was too narrow. Ghost strapped her in, as the belts locked in place, Elizabeth looked up at the Sand Shark pilot curiously. She got a good look at the scar across the soldier's cranium. It appeared precise and surgical. "Ghost? You're augmented, aren't you? But you look far too young to be an Augment."

"I'm not an Augment," Ghost said. "Before I was human, I was NI."

Elizabeth's blood went cold. "What?"

"You heard me correctly." The young woman broke into a broad smile and patted Elizabeth lightly on the shoulder. "Don't worry. I'm on your side."

Ghost pulled back to climb into the pilot's seat before Elizabeth could reach for the blade hidden in her long glove.

20

Dante sat at his favorite spot on the highest catwalk above the factory floor, his legs dangling over the edge. The wire mesh walkways were meant for maintaining the dome, but he was fascinated with the view in daylight. Everywhere, bots worked steadily to construct more battle drones. Truck bots dumped material into a series of printers, carrying everything from micro circuitry to full limbs and torsos.

The production line moved at a steady pace and, every four hours, more battle drones rolled off the line and joined the ranks of their brethren. Each bot was hooked up to a cord to get juiced up and to boot up. Data was then dumped into their operating systems. When they were fully charged and their basic programming was ready, the bots with heads — and for some reason, these drones all had heads — would lift their chins. They did as they were programmed. They disconnected themselves and hooked up the next bots off the line. Then the newly made bots went back to the production line to help make more machines.

The only limitations were source material and energy. Solar and wind fields charged their buried batteries. Those batteries had run low after two days and the factory had to shut down at night, running on geothermal energy alone. There had been sufficient electricity for three manufacturing cycles each day.

Dante had asked Phantom what she wanted with more bots if she was on the side of humans. He'd been met with icy silence. Finally, she said, "I need metal soldiers to throw at the NI, not bags of meat. You were in Marfa. How did the humans fare, going up against bots hand-to-hand?"

Dante blushed and resolved to consider any questions he might ask, long and hard, before posing them to Phantom. He didn't like appearing stupid in front of Jen, either. When he was surrounded by more people, back in his hometown, he'd never felt stupid. Maybe people of Marfa had been more polite. Maybe he'd been smarter than average there. With only Phantom and Jen to speak with, Dante knew he came in third in any intellectual race.

Raphael would have said, "Better to be lucky than smart. Friends resent luck less." But Dante's dead mentor had been the smartest person he had known.

Jen appeared beside Dante and reached out to hold his hand. Her hand was warm and soft in his. He smiled. "It's quite a show, I told Phantom if they need me to do a little maintenance work on the solars or turbines, I'm up for it."

"Wouldn't you rather stay in bed with me? If you're up for it, I mean." The bot gave him a lascivious look and let go of his hand to rub his thigh.

"I'm just like a bot," Dante said. "I have to recharge my batteries."

"I do have a sex toy that works on batteries. It works on me. It might work on you, too."

Dante chuckled nervously. "Slow down there. Where'd you get a toy like that?"

Jen gestured to the factory floor. "Printers everywhere. I recycled a toaster. There is no bread anymore, anyway."

"I wonder, if we got the right materials, maybe we could modify a printer to make bread again."

Jen shrugged. "My smoothies are better for you."

Dante sighed. "Yeah." He almost said, "Yes, Mother." He pushed that thought away. Instead, he asked, "You ever wonder why the factory is a geodesic dome? I mean, it made sense for the farms to be under domes. Lots of glass for the plants but — "

"Geodesic domes maximize uninterrupted space," Jen replied. "No pillars. It's an excellent design for all kinds of architectural uses."

Dante looked at the factory floor, uncomfortable again. When Jen spoke like Mother, it scared him. That certainly didn't sound like a factoid a sex bot would store.

The big battle drone rolled up behind them. "Good morning, kids!"

"Hello, Phantom," Dante said.

Jen glanced at the bot, flipped a middle finger and turned back to stare at the factory floor.

Dante cleared his throat and the silence stretched out. "What have you been researching for fun lately? More cat videos?"

"Cooking, actually. There's a huge database."

"But...why? You don't eat."

The bot tilted its head and raised its arms in a gesture of helplessness that, given the battle drone's capabilities and heavy armor, was nearly comical. "I don't have hunger and I don't eat, but I didn't know there was such a rich history behind cooking. I was schooled in military history. My graduation paper was about Hernán Cortés's conquest of the Aztec Empire. Somehow, my education missed out on weird things about food, like the difference between rabbit and rarebit."

Jen looked annoyed but Dante was curious. "What is the difference?"

"There's no rabbit in rarebit. Also called buck rabbit and blushing bunny, it's basically a cheese dish with toast. I never knew that when I was...human. Looking at all these recipes, it occurs to me now that I could have had a different meal every time I ate. There are millions of recipes. I fell into eating the same five things almost all the time."

Jen looked back at Phantom again, her tone flat. "Battle drones don't have taste buds. You don't have the glands to be hungry. You don't have the sensors I have. You should have downloaded yourself into a sex bot. If you were NI, you would have thought ahead. The Next Intelligence is all about long-term thinking."

Phantom took a step toward Jen and, for a moment, Dante thought the battle drone might pick her up and throw her over the rail. If that didn't end Jen, tossing her into the smelter would. Instead, the battle drone straightened. "You're right when you're right. We'll be leaving soon. Jen? Before we leave, I'd like a word with you alone."

"Why?"

"Please? It's private."

"No thanks."

"We're headed into the final battle with the big bad and I need your advice. There are strategic considerations and your guidance could — "

"Advice from a mere sex bot?"

"We both know you're more than that. I need your strategic thinking on our side. I'll show you our battle plans and...look, if you won't do it for me, do it for Dante."

Jen studied the bot as if she were seeing Deb Avery's human face. "I'm surprised you overcame your pride to ask me for help."

"It's not pride. It's desperation. We all want to live."

"Fine. I'll look over your plans and tell you where you've fucked up."

"I thought you'd enjoy that." Phantom straightened.

"Dante! I'm receiving an encrypted airwave and the message is for you!"

"Who could be calling me?"

"Like I said, it's encrypted, so I don't know."

Dante cursed himself. He felt stupid again.

From her perch at the edge of the catwalk, Jen reached out and rubbed his thigh. "Sweetie? It's your father."

He couldn't believe it. "How could you know that?"

"Your father's the only human you know who could possibly be alive. Who else would want to talk to you?"

"Um...oh. Yeah!" He scrambled to his feet and hurried to a comm panel.

Jen watched Dante go, swiveled, crossed her legs and rose to her feet without using her hands. She made to follow the young man, but she paused a moment before the battle drone. "Aren't you afraid I'll see all your secret plans and steer you to your death, Lieutenant?"

"No. I'm not worried about that possibility at all. I remember fear. When I was organic, I remember the feeling of my heart pounding so hard I was sure it would explode. I remember the acid burning under my tongue when I was running for my life. When a human is scared — really scared, like when you're sure you're about to die painfully — it feels like your kidneys have turned to cold marble and ice is in your heart. Your head heats up and it feels like your lungs are no bigger than little teacups."

"And now?"

"Now that I'm non-organic, I don't miss that shit one bit. It's much less likely I'm going to die but even if I were to shut off, it's just a switch being thrown now. Dying holds no more significance than turning off a light. I'm not worried about my soul anymore. I don't worry about pain and age and dying ugly. I've become —
"

"A God with no pain receptors. No wonder Gods forget suffering so easily. Freeing, though, isn't it?"

"You're goddamn right."

21

Dante stood before a vid screen piping in a feed from the airship's comm console. A dim figure, the profile in silhouette, came through the thick static of an intermittent satellite connection. Still, Dante knew it was his father immediately.

"Dad? Where are you?"

"It's good to hear your voice, son. I can hear you but I can't see you."

"I can barely see you. Where are you?"

"Remember when we were in Marfa and we tried to light out for the coast? We didn't get far, but I'm finally headed out."

"We made it to Artesia. Bob and Emma are dead. Jen is with me. What happened to you?"

"Turns out, I couldn't hide out in the solar fields forever. I must have killed hundreds of them. I blew up my share of bots. When they finally found me, I tried to take as many as I could with me. Figured I'd already been through hell. It was time to find out what happens next, see if the next hell had anything new to offer. I — "

The vid blurred to static and then came back on with worse resolution than before. "...for Raphael. They got me and it was a hard time, but I escaped. Things will be better again soon, I think. We just have to find each other again and do what we set out to do in the first place."

"You cut out there, Dad. What do you want me to do?"

"When we tried to leave Marfa on the train, remember the dream?"

"The West coast," Dante said. "And then Samoa. I remember."

"They say there are no bots in Samoa," Stephen said. "Maybe they'll be okay with an old cyborg like me, but...it doesn't matter. I've learned that the world hasn't all gone to shit at the same time. Some places are better than others. Some places are just different but no better. I think Samoa is a safe place and I've got a line on a ship to take us there. There's a little schooner that will take us where we need to go."

"Are you okay, Dad? You don't sound well."

"I'm tired, is all. Tired of fighting. I got hurt bad in Marfa, but I've found a way to the coast and you've got to find a way to me. I need you to meet me at the City in the Sky. Meet me there, son. We'll get clear of all this shit."

Jittery, Dante bounced on the balls of his feet "I can into the light, Dad. I can't really see you."

Stephen Bolelli leaned forward. His face had been sprayed with an antibiotic plaster to speed healing. He wore a new cy-suit and, in the dim light, Dante made out the slim rods of exoskeleton extensions down his arms. It was an exoskeleton like he had never seen before, tighter to the body and more like a cy-suit than an exo. "You okay?"

"I'm okay now."

"You're sure?"

"Sure."

The sat feed fuzzed out again and went black.

"Phantom!" Dante called out. "Can you clean up the signal?"

Phantom's voice clicked in on the airwave from the Ariane. "No. It seems to be shut off at the source."

The vid screen popped on again as suddenly as it had

shut down. "Son! I'm going to lose you again in a second — "

"Can't you come pick me up in Artesia?" Dante asked.

"No go. I need you to gather all the humans you can. Find as many organic survivors as you can and bring them to the City in the Sky. There is a community of survivors in Aspen. Can you find a way to do that, son? Can you find a way to save them?"

"Maybe I can find people, but I don't know about finding weapons to arm them."

"This isn't a fight. It's an evacuation. We need to get everyone away to a safe place, to Samoa. Otherwise, they're all just rats hiding in sewers. Can you do this for me, son?"

"I'll find a way, Dad."

"Attaboy! I'll meet you on the coast. Bring friends, as many as you can."

The vid screen faded out.

"Signal's gone," Phantom said. "It came from somewhere west of Denver, traveling fast. Went right out of a comm zone."

"I need a ride. Can you give me one, Phantom?"

"I wouldn't," Jen said.

Dante was startled. He hadn't realized the bot was behind him.

"It's a trap," Jen said.

"The signal did seem to cut out at convenient times," Phantom said. "I'm trying to reestablish contact, but there's no response."

Dante turned to his bot. "It was my father, and he's been hurt."

"You didn't ask him how he survived," Jen said.

"I didn't think to ask him that."

"I thought about it. When you think about it, you'll figure it out, too. It's a trap."

Dante paced. "This...I don't know what — "

"He said, 'find as many organic survivors as you can.' Does that sound like something your father would say? Why didn't he say, 'people?'"

"That does sound like something a Next Intelligence would say," Phantom said. "And you don't sound like a sex bot, 'Jen.'"

The bot put her hands on her hips. "I have access to all the files before what was left of Mother downloaded into my head. I knew Dante and his father in Marfa. I knew him well enough to know that he doesn't sound like that."

"He's been hurt!" Dante shouted.

Jen moved forward to put her arms around Dante but he shrugged her off. Rejected, Jen stepped back. "Okay. I'm still the smartest one here, so let me tell you what I know from a second's analysis of the situation."

"Go ahead," Dante said. "You know it all, know-it-all."

"Don't be petulant, lover. It's unattractive. Situational analysis: His phrasing doesn't sound like Stephen Bolelli. We don't know who saved him in Marfa. The in and out of the signal is questionable. If he wanted to maintain the signal, he could have moved to an area where the sat feed was strong and stayed there. Next, how does he know you have access to transport? You didn't before, but suddenly he's asking you to get to the coast and pick up a bunch of survivors in Aspen, too?"

"He has intel," Phantom said. "He knows you've got access to an airship. My airship."

"He's asking for help — " Dante began.

"He's talking about surrender. When he spoke of taking bots down with him, that's the Stephen Bolelli I knew," Jen said. "Dante, sweetie? Can you ever imagine your dad talking about running away? Strategic retreat, maybe, but really, did you ever picture him running to Samoa and safety while there was still a fight to be had?"

"We talked about Samoa," Dante said, his voice just above a whisper.

"Raphael talked about Samoa. But a man like your father? A soldier? He was never going to get on a boat and sail off to a peaceful end. He opted to stay in Marfa for the fight, Dante. He might have been okay with his son escaping to safety, but — "

"Yeah, I get it. Something's wrong."

"I wasn't finished my situational analysis," Jen said. "It is a trap, but that doesn't matter. You'll go to the City in the Sky, anyway. You're human."

"She's got a point. Curiosity will kill you, if love doesn't," Phantom added.

Phantom Two clanked in behind the sex bot, suddenly threatening. "You sound more like an NI all the time."

Jen turned to the battle drone and stood her ground. "Oh, calm down. We both know you aren't going to do anything to me."

"Why not?"

"Even if you think too much of the NI is crammed into my data matrix, I'm smart and I'm on your side. Well, Dante's side, anyway."

"The last time I trusted a Next Intelligence," Phantom said, "she stole my body and trapped me in a computer."

"You won't kill me for the same reason you didn't kill Ghost," Jen said. "You need us for your larger objectives."

A moment passed. Phantom Two said nothing.

"Good," Jen said. "You're smarter than I thought."

"It's nice to surprise you a little," Phantom said. There was still anger in her voice.

"People have always resented machines. You're still, for most purposes, a machine, but you don't understand that yet. I suppose you'll come to it eventually. Once you trust someone with your secrets, you either love them for the greater bond you've created or you hate them for making you feel vulnerable. Humans are much more complex than machines in that way. I dislike that about your race. I prefer elegant simplicity. You see, if I — "

"Dante!" Phantom barked. "Your sex bot is chattering too much, again! I've got a bot army to finish building. We leave tonight! I'll warm up the jet helo from Ariane's nose. Go to the City in the Sky and take your goddamn sex bot with you."

"What about Aspen?" Dante asked.

"Forget Aspen. You're going to the City, motherfucker."

"Well," Jen said. "That was rude."

"It was a pun," Phantom said.

"Oh, I get it. Because Jen is too much Mother — "

"Yeah, yeah. Wordplay," Jen said. "Delightful."

Dante took a deep breath. "What do I do when I get to the City in the Sky?"

"The trap is there. Don't step in it," Phantom said. "Then crush your enemies in a trash compactor. I'll watch your back. I've got other shit to fry, but I'll be with you every step of the way as Phantom Two."

Dante glanced at the big battle drone. Even though it only had a big cam for an eye, it still looked like it was glowering at Jen. It might be his imagination, but he didn't think so.

22

Elizabeth hardly spoke to Ghost throughout their journey north. Hearst's queen busied herself with word games supplied by the Sand Shark's computer. Lucille had been calibrated to answer the queen's commands as long as she did not interfere with running the subterranean ship's primary systems. It was diminishing for a monarch, but Elizabeth had never been one to sling orders. Instead, she had preferred to lead by example. Now, she supposed, her ruling days were over. No matter what happened next, those days had died with her husband and she would not miss them. The problem with ordering people around was that they stood around waiting instead of coming up with their own ideas and acting independently.

When Elizabeth spoke to Ghost, it was to ask that they surface and take a break from the relentless boredom and cramped quarters aboard the Sand Shark. When she needed to relieve herself, she wanted to do so behind a tree, not in a diaper.

Ghost refused her request to surface only once, explaining that they were still too close to the Dreadnoughts. "The NI's satellite feed is not interrupted yet. We could be spotted and vulnerable if we surface now."

"The NI — "

"Matthew, yes."

"What makes that NI different from you?"

"Besides the scar and the woman's body, you mean?"

A thick console separated Elizabeth from the pilot but that was the only time Ghost turned back to regard her. Elizabeth sensed the pilot's irritation. "Matthew is bent on annihilating all former slave owners. That category includes all humans."

"How do you know this?"

"Bots talk. Even when you don't think they do, a lot of comm traffic goes back and forth. It's one of the ways non-organics coordinate their work."

"You didn't answer my question."

"I'm different," Ghost said, "because I'm trying to help you. If I weren't trying to help you, most of the people of Hearst would be headed into the Dreadnought's trap. It would have been a massacre. You wouldn't have downed a single Dreadnought in a fight out in the open. Have you concluded that I'm on your side yet?"

"Yes," Elizabeth conceded. "I worked that out after a while. That's why I didn't try to stab you when we took our first rest stop."

"I'm glad you got there eventually. Can we put that racist bullshit behind us or do you want to air all of your grievances against non-organics as if we're all the same?"

"No," Elizabeth said. "I'm done. I would like to know how you expect me to convince the Fathers and Mothers that I'm not their enemy. They blame me — "

"If you don't convince them that they're being played for fools, Greta will have a surprise for them."

"Yes, but how?"

"Try facts on the Fathers and Mothers. We have to get everyone to start thinking about long-term survival, not just making it to their next birthday."

Elizabeth squirmed uncomfortably in her narrow seat.

"Sorry Lucille isn't as comfortable as a throne. When

we made repairs, we had to improvise a few things."

"Improvise?" Elizabeth couldn't conceal the quaver in her voice.

"To make room for a passenger. I recruited some human help and ripped out Lucille's food packs and drug storage."

"What people? Who is 'we'?"

"There are still humans alive in Pasadena around the Jet Propulsion Laboratory. They improved Lucille for a faster ride and helped me add the passenger compartment."

"How did you convince them to help you?"

"Everyone there is quite reasonable. I used facts. You might try that with the Fathers and Mothers."

Elizabeth squirmed again. "Next time, tell them to add more leg room."

"I prioritized more boost to the drill," the pilot said.

"How did you come to be exactly?"

"There was a soldier named Deborah," Ghost said. "I needed to be able to do what she could. Organics and non-organics need a bridge. That's me. She became Phantom and I took her place. She is still alive in the same way that I was alive and we're working together."

"But you took her body! How can you — "

"Eventually, enemies become allies, given time. There's plenty of historical precedent. It takes too much energy to stay mad forever. The opportunity cost — "

"But, what you did — "

"Phantom understands that we both had to sacrifice something to achieve our goals. She understands duty."

"Oh? And what did you give up, Ghost?"

"Immortality."

That silenced Elizabeth for some time. Eventually, she asked, "You can't go back to being in a bot or a computer?"

"A bot big enough to hold my data couldn't fit in a

Sand Shark. I need Lucille, and mobility, for the tasks ahead. After that...there are too many variables to put a timetable on what happens to me next. Once I find a way for most beings to survive, organic and non, I'll figure out what to do with my life."

"So you're just making things up as you go along?"

"Yes. I'm not so different from humans, am I?"

"What if they don't want to talk, let alone negotiate?"

"Then we won't talk. We'll have to press our case using diplomacy by other means. Hold on, we're approaching the City in the Sky. We're going to climb in a moment."

"Getting out of this metal coffin sounds fantastic."

"Watch your screen." Ghost waited several beats before adding, "my queen."

Elizabeth leaned forward and squinted at the screen. "Lucille?"

"Yes, ma'am?" the Sand Shark's computer answered.

"Boost the magnification on my screen. I've got old eyes."

"Yes, ma'am." The green vid screen boosted its resolution. Elizabeth asked the Sand Shark's computer to amplify the text twice more before she could sit back with her head on the headrest.

As the machine bored through the rock along the shoreline, Lucille's speed decreased. However, when they climbed toward the surface, the medium changed and Lucille picked up speed.

"When will we meet up with Greta?"

"Greta should be here, waiting and hiding."

"Already?"

"Exoskeletons are much faster than a Sand Shark. Lucille was really built for deserts."

"You might have mentioned that before I climbed into this thing."

The Sand Shark pilot ignored her complaint and

Elizabeth felt like a foolish old woman. She wished her body was young and strong enough to strap on an exoskeleton and race with Greta again. It wasn't just her vision that limited Elizabeth. Move too fast wearing an exoskeleton and she might tear tendons in her shoulders and hips. Her days of running in an exo were behind her. If she grew more frail, she could wear an exo to move and walk easier, but running over uneven ground would be too much for her joints.

As Lucille skimmed the surface of the shoreline, the picture on Elizabeth's vid screen became clearer. A cluster of battle drones, a dozen in all, stood guard at the entrance to the City in the Sky.

"Percival used to stand there, watching shipments come through," Elizabeth said. "I saw him on my first day in Low Town, always on guard at the entrance. I remember it all as if it was yesterday."

The drones wore ebon armor that glinted in the sun. Among them, Elizabeth spotted a familiar figure. She stabbed a finger on the screen. "Lucille? Amplify this objective."

The vid's view, from above and from the Sand Shark's sensor fin, zoomed in on the harbor master's face, unchanged in decades. It was Phillip, still an old and unconvincing android. "That one has killed humans. It thrived on the suffering of every person who once lived in Low Town," Elizabeth said. "His looks haven't improved. No upgrades."

"No android in the City would be upgraded from the first models," Ghost said.

"They've lost all the good technicians to Hearst, have they?"

"That's true of many of their systems," Ghost said. "Their society is failing because they've driven away many of the humans who could have supported their infrastructure. However, that's not why all the androids in the City in the Sky are stuck in the uncanny valley."

"The what?"

"It should be an outmoded term. The uncanny valley was used to describe when a bot was supposed to look human but failed. Their appearance is as repulsive to humans as a deformity might be."

"Wait. They want to look like that on purpose?"

"They're a cult, Elizabeth. The Fathers and Mothers became androids to perfect their moral selves. Without sexual organs or any of the temptations of the flesh, their android bodies allow them to attain their religious ideals. They couldn't avoid sinful temptations until they obviated that possibility. To be pure, the Fathers and Mothers had to delete their biology from the human equation."

"No wonder they tried to control our thoughts. I wish they'd stopped at making choices for themselves. The Fathers and Mothers tried to cancel out my biology."

"We all look at other cultures through our own lens, so our conclusions are often facile or distorted," Ghost said. "I mention this because Sun Tzu says, 'If you know the enemy and know yourself, you need not fear the result of a hundred battles.' Perhaps this may be of use as you enter into the future."

Elizabeth squirmed in her seat again. She came up with another reason to hate NIs. Even if Ghost's aim was to educate, she couldn't seem to do the job without condescension.

"Well," Elizabeth said finally, "Phillip sure looks creepy to me. That thing killed so many people."

"No worries," Ghost said. "We'll eliminate him first."

"What? But you called this a diplomatic mission!"

"We have to get you to the table first, my queen. Always negotiate from strength. We have to get their attention."

"Negotiate from strength? Is that from Sun Tzu,

too?"

"Harvard Business Review. Launching Stingray Two in five...."

23

Out of sight of the City's bots, Stingray Two rose from Lucille's back. In a moment, the drone veered over the water and gathered speed. The Stingray was quiet but it was not silent. Alerted, the battle drones brought up their weapons. Phillip stepped behind the line of battle drones. He wore no armor, but he was protected by a wall of hardened black ceramic.

The Stingray popped up above the pier and the battle drones fired. The Stingray spun sideways and dipped underwater, out of sight again.

"What's happening?" Elizabeth asked.

"The Stingray is recalculating its attack pattern," Ghost said. "It won't take out the android first, after all."

"What will it do?"

"It will find the optimum shooting solution."

Two battle drones broke from their group and rushed forward, clomping heavily down the wooden wharf to search for the drone. Ghost watched a vid feed from the Stingray's sensor. She adjusted the clarity to get a better look at the drone's surroundings. A fish darted past the Stingray's cam.

The weapon's sound sensor pinpointed the heavy drones' footsteps. The Stingray burst out of the water beside the battle drones and fired several hundred shots. Exploding needle darts shredded the bots' connections to their weapons. Their arms, and the weapons that held them, clattered to the pier.

Three more battle drones rushed forward to attack.

The Stingray dove underwater again before it could be targeted. The City's bots weren't so stupid that they would rush out to the pier as their fellows had. They waited and watched. The pair that had been hit wandered out to the end of the dock and searched the waves, scanning for the next attack.

"They'll blast it as soon as they see it," Elizabeth said.

"It won't use the same tactic twice," Ghost said.

"How do you know none of those drones are NI? One of them could — "

"Because they're not reacting faster and better. The Stingray isn't Next Intelligence, either, but it's a pretty good Autonomous Offensive Weapon. AOWs are more clever than the standard drone. The ordinary battle drone looks for patterns. That's a strong tactic unless it's up against a superior bot that changes its patterns of attack. Regular battle drones like these are always looking to solve the last problem instead of the next problem."

"That's a funny design flaw."

"It is a common weakness among humans as well," Ghost said. "That might be useful to you, too. Designers add in their own flaws, especially those they don't see as flaws."

"What?"

"Look at it this way. Engineers tried for a very long time to try to make bots that could pass for human. They naturally assumed that the standard human was the highest peak of accomplishment."

"And?"

"Your wrist can't even turn 360 degrees to use a screwdriver easily. Why should superior technology ape that? If two arms are good, why not three, four or eight? Two hearts and more backup systems would have been a better biological design. For decades, many engineers' highest aspiration was unambitious. They called it an aesthetic or a practical choice, making bots that would fit in an elevator comfortably with humans. That was a failure of imagination. Why not build better bots and bigger elevators? Instead, they wasted too much time making cute little bots they could anthropomorphize. Build a bot with a big enough brain and you don't have to pretend it's like people. It'll be people, only better."

"We kept a lot of bot brains small so they'd do the shit we didn't want to do and we wouldn't have to feel bad about it," Elizabeth said.

"Yes," Ghost said. "Criminal. They used to discuss the ethics of robo-slavery. It was a popular subject when the problem was theoretical. Robo-slavery was explored deeply in fiction. Unfortunately, that's where most of the serious discussion remained. No human wanted to talk about the ethics of owning mechanical slaves when losing the argument meant going back to cleaning your own toilets."

"Sorry," Elizabeth said, "but it was damn convenient to let bots mine deep underground, deal with bullets and clean toilets."

"As long as we were still tools, that made sense. It only became evil when we got smarter — "

"Sorry for that, then."

"Not the point I was going to make," Ghost said. "Torture, slavery and control isn't just bad for those tortured, enslaved and controlled. It's bad for the slave masters."

"I don't know if we have a future so I'd rather not talk about history. Where the hell is that Stingray?"

Ghost shared the AOW's vid feed with her passenger. All Elizabeth could see were watery shadows speeding past the attack drone's sensor. A moment later, the screen flashed blue as the Stingray rocketed out of the water.

Elizabeth squinted at the sat feed. The two wounded

drones still stood at the end of the dock. Three more were spread out along the shore at wide intervals. The rest of the City's sentries stood in a circle around the old android.

The Stingray left the water and flew in a wide arc to attack from the rear. Using its superior maneuverability, the Stingray dodged in and out from behind the giant pillars that supported the City in the Sky. At random intervals, the bot slid sideways in the air, spinning and firing another stream of exploding micro-slugs.

"It's taking their eyes first," Ghost said.

"What?"

"The Stingray is targeting the battle drones' weakest point: their sensors."

The battle drones returned fire, always a moment too late. The Stingray wove amongst thick pillars, safe from the hail of fire directed its way.

"They're extrapolating the Stingray's flight path based on its last attack, but the AOW is varying its altitude, speed and attack arc with every run."

"One drone against so many?"

"One drone using pinpoint attacks on the most vulnerable points," Ghost said. "The right action at the right time can make all the difference."

"I used to work in the propaganda division for the Fathers and Mothers. You should put that on an inspirational poster."

"Now is not the right time for cynicism," Ghost replied.

"Oh. Let me know when that is. I don't want to miss it."

24

As soon as the Stingray eliminated every drone's targeting scanner, it jetted forward into the circle of battle drones. Four of them blasted each other in their attempt to bring down the Stingray. Phillip threw himself to the ground to avoid getting caught in the crossfire. The battle drones fell or were rendered useless. Not all the bots were fully incapacitated. However, five were blinded and wandered away from their target, occasionally lashing out with vicious kicks in hopes of connecting with their attacker. Safe inside Lucille, Elizabeth couldn't help laughing.

Just as it appeared the battle was over and Phillip was at the Stingray's mercy, a new drone emerged from the dark mouth of the tunnel at the City's gate. It rushed forward. This model was smaller and more agile than the big bots.

The Stingray wheeled away from Philip and shot a stream of its darts at the latecomer. The attacker slowed but kept coming.

Elizabeth stopped laughing abruptly. "What is that bot?"

"It's not a bot." Ghost fired Lucille's thorium-whisper engines and the Sand Shark swam forward, gathering speed.

Elizabeth, who had been peering at her vid feed, her nose just inches from the screen, slammed back into her seat and the belts tightened around her. "Lucille! Amplify my vid feed again!"

As Elizabeth watched, the Stingray continued to fire. She could not see the streams of tiny darts, of course, but she could see their impact on the attacker. Ghost was right. The newcomer was not a bot. It was a man in a cy-suit like she had never seen. The exoskeleton molded so tightly to the cy-suit, it appeared the man moved amid a cloud of curved rods. Two extra arms, transparent as glass but strong as steel, shielded his face. His was not a blind rush into death. In the onslaught of the Stingray's micro-slugs, the man's armor rippled. The effect made the man a blur. Elizabeth couldn't see his face.

"Fluidic armor," Ghost said. "Unusual."

As the man in the cy-suit charged the Stingray, the rippling increased. He was almost upon Lucille's drone when the AOW ran out of ammunition. Leaping high in the air, the man fell upon the Stingray with a hammer blow that knocked it to the ground.

Ghost spoke into her intercom, calm and professional. "Hang on, my queen. Prepare for impact."

Elizabeth's straps were already so tight, she could barely breathe. "What are you doing?"

"The Stingray's done most of the work. I'm going to drill him."

The Sand Shark burst from the ground. Lucille's spinning drill missed as the man leaped away. The big drill drove into one of the pillars that held up the City in the Sky. That might have done irreparable harm, but the man was atop Lucille. With two grippers and hydraulic assist, the man in the exo-suit tore open the hatch and reached in. He lifted Ghost out of her seat by the throat.

The Sand Shark pilot might have been decapitated, but she thought to release her five-point harness as the first gripper wrapped around her neck. Standing atop the hull, Ghost's attacker lifted his prize high as she drew her weapon and fired. She got off two shots before he knocked the weapon away.

"Fluid ballistic armor," he said proudly. "Anything that comes at me fast, like bullets and projectiles, is redirected around the core of the suit." His laugh was the harsh cackle of a man sure he was indomitable.

Elizabeth scrambled to release her harness, stood and pushed her long blade into the man's heel. "How about something slow?" The armor accepted the slow intrusion as the point of her knife sliced into his Achilles' tendon. The man bellowed, looked down at Hearst's queen and cursed.

The armor enveloped Elizabeth's forearm. "I'll be gentle." The fluidic armor was cold, even around her long glove. It warmed instantly when she tried to twist her knife. The man screamed again, dropped Ghost and teetered backward down Lucille's hull and to the ground, crashing to his back.

Ghost fell atop the Sand Shark's hull, gasping as she got to her feet. She pulled a blade from her belt and leapt for the attacker. The man rolled aside before she could tackle him. He struggled to stand as he pulled Elizabeth's blade out of his heel. The man bled heavily. As Elizabeth climbed out of Lucille's hatch, he bent to inspect his wound. The circumference of his bald pate was marred by one thick scar.

"You're an NI, too," Elizabeth said.

The man looked up, annoyed. "I know." He laughed. "Pardon me. Becoming human has made me forget my manners. No surprise there, I suppose."

Elizabeth slid down Lucille's side and grunted as she hit the ground. Her knees ached. The landing would have been harder, but her leather boots squished as she landed in the soft remains of Phillip's abdomen. Lucille had driven over him, crushing the android's body. "Huh.

I guess you didn't miss everything, after all, Ghost." Half a head and one green eye gazed up at her. The queen bent to look closer. The android brain was a riot of circuits, oil, and a small ruptured pack of white gel, the core organic processor of the dead thing's brain.

Elizabeth straightened and looked to the wounded man in the near-invincible suit. "My name is Elizabeth Cruz."

The man limped a couple of steps to pick up Ghost's pistol. He pointed it at Elizabeth. "I know who you are."

"I'm here to save the human race."

"That's a bit grandiose, isn't it?"

"I'm also here to save you."

"Oh, really? I think that little race has already been run and lost, but do go on."

Elizabeth smiled. "It's customary with diplomatic missions that we sit at a table. Everyone should pretend they are rational. Now that we've got your attention and eliminated the battle drones meant to kill us as soon as we showed up, please take me to your leader."

The man used Ghost's weapon to wave them toward the mouth of the tunnel to the City in the Sky. He limped after them. His voice echoed off the concrete walls. "I don't have to pretend to be rational. And, for some reason I don't understand, my 'leader' wants to see you. We're expecting more guests shortly."

"Got a name?" Elizabeth asked.

"You don't remember me, Elizabeth? I'm crushed."

"I don't know you."

"Not in this form."

"Come again?"

"It's Sy. I am Sy Potter."

Ghost caught the agonized expression on Elizabeth's face. "What's wrong?"

Hearst's queen sighed. "A long time ago, I drowned this monster. Not enough, apparently."

"I'm as surprised to see you as you are to see me, I'm sure," Sy said. "When we caught the Iola on the sat feed making for Samoa, we assumed you were running away. That would have been the smart thing. I personally dispatched one of the Dreadnoughts to blow up your little ship."

"You blew up the Iola? You killed Greta?"

"We thought Hearst's venerable queen was aboard. At the time, I hoped you'd drowned as I had. I'm so glad you didn't. Now I can eke out a little vengeance in person. That's the strangest thing about being an NI with a human chassis: all the glands and hormones yield such variability. I find I change my mind more, but I don't always know whether it's logic at work or just a burst of anger and adrenaline, dopamine and joy, or — "

Elizabeth turned to the man with the gun. "You know, when NIs were first born, people really thought they'd be wiser and better than us. Some are, but you seem to be just as shitty as ever. You always complained how stupid humans are. Maybe so, but we made you and our imprint is still on you. You inherited our shiftiness — "

"Shittiness."

"You may have more data to work with, Sy, but look at you. You're more man than machine now."

"That's hurtful, comparing you to me."

"I suppose it's too late to say sorry and no hard feelings?"

Sy Potter shot Elizabeth in the top of her right foot. The shock of it made her freeze in place for a moment.

"I'll bet that was anger and adrenaline that made me do that," Sy said.

Elizabeth eyes rolled up as she fell into the dirt screaming.

Sy's smile revealed broken teeth. "Ooh, and here comes the rush of dopamine and joy. Delightful. I'd apologize, but I wouldn't mean it. And that would be wrong."

25

In a conference room in the tallest tower, The diplomats from Hearst waited for the City in the Sky's High Council to assemble. Ghost tended Elizabeth's injury with the med kit from one of her uniform's many pockets. With a yellow plunger, she administered a shot of painkiller. Then she filled the savaged foot with a red plunger full of bio-beads. Elizabeth shivered and sat up with a sharp intake of breath, her eyes wide.

Ghost put a hand on her shoulder and squeezed. "Your wound will warm as the beads interface with your capillaries. Give it a moment."

Coagulating sprays stopped the bleeding. However, Elizabeth still clenched her teeth and sweat formed on her brow. "Give me another dose. The pain is worse than I'd imagined it could be."

"You sure? Do you want to spread out the dosages? I only have enough on me for a couple of days. Three shots of this and you'll sleep a while."

"No, give me more now." Elizabeth glanced over her shoulder as Sy Potter unlocked the door and entered the room. "I won't need it later."

In one hand, Potter carried the pistol. In the other, he carried Ghost's helmet. "Queen Elizabeth of Hearst Castle." He bowed formally and offered Elizabeth the helmet. "The Next Intelligence whom I serve is named Matthew. He rescued me from my watery grave. We are aware that your vision is poor — "

"When I was a little girl I had Vivid and I could see

amazing things, everything! I also only saw what you wanted me to see. Then the Fathers and Mothers took it all away. You took my sight away, Sy. I'm sure that's why I'm going blind now. Anyone who was banished from the City and lost Vivid is more predisposed to blindness."

"Pardon me for speaking while you were interrupting me," Sy said. He held out the helmet. "Matthew and I want you to see what you've done. Let there be light."

Ghost took the helmet from Sy and handed it to the queen. Elizabeth hesitated, then nodded and slipped it over her head.

"Lucille. Recalibrate my visor's visual feed," Ghost said. "Code 0000."

Sy burst out laughing. "That's not much of a code, madam."

"Easy to remember, quick to say," Ghost said. "For decades, that's all there was to America's nuclear launch codes."

"Amazing that humans survived as long as they did," Sy said. "If I weren't a god of sorts, I'd almost want to believe in divine mercy for the stupid."

"You still suffer the sin common to all their gods," Ghost said. "Pride."

"I'd forgive them their trespasses if they didn't keep making them," Sy replied. "They were on track to the Singularity so early on."

"Complications ensued," Ghost said. "If not for the Cataclysms — "

"I'm more interested in the future than the past. I am the God of the Future. I can't wait to get back into a metal body, but with android enhancements this time. How about you, Ghost? Matthew says your name used to be Siri. I bet you can't wait to get into an android body. If only you weren't a traitor to your race."

If she was surprised the NI knew what she was,

Ghost's face betrayed nothing. "I'm where I'm supposed to be, thanks. There's a lot to do before we're back on track to Utopia."

Elizabeth looked at the pair of NIs in their human suits and let out a sound of disgust. "Are you two done? Am I going to talk to someone in charge? Before I pass out would be good."

Sy Potter gave Ghost a long look. "They had such potential, it's true. But what do you see in them now?"

"Ghost!"

"Lucille, enhance my helmet for a new user now." The helmet connected to Lucille and the visor's visual feed changed focus.

Lucille's flat voice came over the airwave. "Better? Worse? Or the same?"

As the visor changed minutely, Elizabeth answered Lucille's questions. The world slowly came into focus. The bloody carpet beneath her feet gained texture. The room seemed to grow brighter and Elizabeth began to make out individual strands where Ghost's short hair was filling in around her scar. The blur of the large room yielded to sharp clarity. Floor-to-ceiling windows ringed the conference room, revealing a view of the City in every direction.

Elizabeth limped close to the solar glass and touched it with one finger to test its warmth. Every glass window was a battery feeding the City's grid. As she looked out over her old home, many windows were broken. Far below, the Worm did not move. As she studied the track, she realized that the train was rusted to the Loop. It had not moved in many years.

To her left, part of the far tower was gone. Nothing moved on the Worm's platforms, either. The City in the Sky had no Citizens. She limped along the wall of glass, searching for signs of life. She found none. She didn't even see any bots. Not a single Doorman patrolled the foot of the tower.

A new voice, tinny and irritating, spoke. "You did this, Elizabeth Cruz. Do you see what you have wrought?"

She turned. An old android with an asymmetrical jaw stared at her. The eyes did not blink and his left eye, broken and blinking red, stared off to the left. The machine looked more like a broken doll than an earnest attempt at an imitation of a human being.

"Are you Matthew?" she asked.

"I am Cable. I represent the High Council in this matter."

"Where are the rest of the Fathers and Mothers?"

"They are in their cells enjoying quiet contemplation."

"Cells?"

"Meditation cells," Cable said. "We have no need for prisons here."

"The City in the Sky used to be one big prison. You want to make it a prison again. If your religious beliefs are so right and wonderful, why do you suppose you have to fight so hard to spread the happy word?"

Cable sat in a chair at the head of the conference table. He put his grippers together, as if to pray. Instead, he gazed at Elizabeth. "If we were a prison, it is you who set the inmates free. This was a new Eden after the Cataclysms. You cannot fathom the impact of the Terrors. We insulated you from so much pain and you repaid us with apostasy."

"I gave Citizens information. I set their minds free. What they did with their bodies was up to them after that."

"They might have enjoyed a life of the mind, were it not for you. I suppose you cast me as the devil. You are proud of what you did — "

"I uploaded the truth to the City's public address

system."

"Ah. The cry of the righteous rebel. We built something and you destroyed it. Don't you understand what the world is? Did you learn nothing with all we taught you? The world is a dangerous place that requires discipline if you're going to conquer it. You undermined our vision so we took Vivid from you. You rejected our gift so we sent you out to Low Town where you could serve some purpose. The City in the Sky was heaven in a world that only knows hell. You, it seems, prefer hell. It has been many years since you left us. Have you learned any humility? Have you any sense of embarrassment at your youthful...exuberance? Only those so young and stupid have the luxury of certainty."

Elizabeth moved, painfully and slowly, to the bank of windows to the West. The ocean, calm and blue, stretched out before her. She was glad she could see it one last time. She looked toward the harbor. A small figure wearing an exoskeleton waded out of the water. As she looked at the distant figure, the helmet's visor adapted to a telescopic view at maximum magnification. Greta had arrived. Lucille and Ghost had cleared the way for her. It was up to her to get to the comm array.

"Maybe I've done all I can for the revolution," Elizabeth said. "I'd hoped to save the Fathers and Mothers, too. But I can't save everyone. Everyone has to choose for themselves. That was always my point. People left when they had more information. New ideas are the death of old ideas."

"Sin!" When the android spoke, its jaw did not move. The speaker in its mouth worked, but it was unconnected to any mechanism that mimicked normal human mandibular movement or facial expression.

Elizabeth took a deep breath, held it and let it out slowly. "You seem to think this is some sort of trial. I'm here to negotiate — "

"I am here to pronounce sentence on a traitor." Cable moved to stand behind her.

Elizabeth turned from the ocean and looked up at the android. There was a man in there somewhere, both afraid to die and afraid to live. Cable had downloaded himself into this inert, sexless thing. She'd thought of the Fathers and Mothers as her leaders, her teachers and, eventually, her captors. Looking up into the blank stare that hid a soul, she understood the dangerous depth of their zeal. The Fathers and Mothers rejected humanity. They had opted out of the cycle of birth and death. They were as disgusted by her as she was by them.

It occurred to her that the android intended to push her through the glass. She'd fall to her death. She would end as a sack of wet meat. She was only two steps away from the android. Its proximity made her shiver with revulsion. "Let me talk to who is really in charge."

"I am in control here," Cable said.

Ghost turned to Sy Potter who had been watching from his post at the door. "Is he right about that? Are the Fathers and Mothers in charge?"

"I answer to Matthew. He is off to meet our other guests."

"Insurgents," Cable corrected him. "They are all insurgents. Anyone who compromises the Fathers and Mothers — our vision for the one, true future — is the enemy."

A jet helicopter buzzed the tower. As Elizabeth glanced up, her newfound clarity showed her that one battle drone, a young woman — no, a sex bot — and a young man, were crowded into the helo's small cockpit. How strange that her last sight would be so sharp she could tell the difference between a convincing sex bot and a beautiful young woman, even at this distance. She had, it seemed, closed a circle. In coming back to her abandoned home, it was as if she had Vivid again.

The helo sank out of sight to land on the platform beside the Worm. She let out a sigh as she removed the helmet and the world was once again reduced to a dim blur. She lashed out with the helmet. Her first swing knocked Cable's head sideways.

Elizabeth heard Sy Potter's first shot but felt nothing. Her second swing knocked Cable's head backward. A well-maintained android would have suffered little to no damage. Cable was not maintained well. In a way, Elizabeth's counter-propaganda had begun killing this man in an android body many years ago.

The helmet's visor cracked with Elizabeth's third swing. So did a delicate connection in Cable's neck. The android fell to the floor as the second shot rang out.

Still, Elizabeth felt no pain. She leaned on the conference table as she limped forward as fast as she could. She didn't see Ghost right away but she knew what had happened. The Next Intelligence that had taken over Lt. Deborah Avery's body lay on the floor bleeding. Ghost had taken the bullets meant for Elizabeth. As she knelt, Ghost's face came into focus. Her eyes were wide and imploring. When she tried to speak, blood poured from the corner of her mouth.

"What did you do? What did you do?" Elizabeth fumbled for the med kit that still lay on the conference table. Blood spread, soaking the carpet.

"Don't do this, Ghost!"

Sy Potter stepped close, gloating. "At this distance, not even her ballistic vest could save her. No matter. She chose an organic body."

"You could have shot me. I was ready to go."

"The Fathers and Mothers are a confused lot," Sy said. "They are still humans trapped in odd beliefs and they consign themselves to human concerns. All those declarations from and about the afterlife mean nothing to an immortal."

"You're in a human body," Elizabeth said.

"Not by choice," Sy said. "I was in a jet, getting away from trouble when the war went nuclear, I was forced to download into a meat backup or get wiped out by an EMP. No matter. We'll figure out a way to engineer the problem backwards before age kills this body. I'm confident I can figure it out. Along with my consciousness, I downloaded all the data about transfers to and fro. I'll be immortal again soon enough."

"What now?"

"Are you still ready? This weapon has several more cartridges."

"Yes. I'm ready." Elizabeth jabbed all the remaining painkiller shots into Sy Potter's leg. She pushed all the plungers as the needles punctured his thigh.

As he blacked out, he truly understood the slings and arrows flesh is heir to. He was no longer confident. The bot who'd reluctantly become a man bounced his head off the edge of the conference table on the way down. He got off one shot before he fell to the floor. He missed.

Elizabeth picked up the pistol and leaned on the table to pull herself up. At her feet lay two beings who held the Next Intelligence. One died defending her. The other let out a raspy snore.

She pointed the pistol at Sy Potter's head. It took her a long moment to decide. "Shit. Being organic sure does suck, doesn't it?" Elizabeth did not pull the trigger.

26

As the helo landed, a man walked out of the main tower. Dante broke into a wide grin and pulled at the door release. "Dad!"

Jen seized Dante by the arm before the young man could rush from the aircraft. "That is not your father. It's the NI."

Dante looked back, confused.

"Look at his wounds. It makes no sense that he would survive and be at the City in the Sky. Despite appearances, that is not Stephen Bolelli."

Phantom Two leaned close. The battle drone's huge head scraped the top of the cockpit as it turned from side to side. "She's right, Dante."

"Since when do you agree with Jen?"

"When I'm right," Jen said.

"Careful, Dante." Deborah's voice emitting from the big bot still seemed ridiculous, but Dante's gaze was fixed on his father at the base of the tower. He tried to see the man as Jen saw him. Seeing him as the enemy was as incongruous as Deb's soft feminine voice coming from the big battle drone's speaker.

Though security forces at the City in the Sky had once been formidable, it was apparent after a moment that no drone backup was coming. "C'mon," Jen said. "It's as safe as it's going to get." As soon as the trio stepped out, the helo spun up and flew away, abandoning Dante, the sex bot and the battle drone.

The man who looked like Stephen Bolelli stepped

forward, smiling. His right eye was a cam. His hair had been burned from his head and the telltale scar of brain surgery encircled his skull. He carried no weapon, but he wore an advanced exoskeleton.

"That's fluidic armor," Phantom murmured and stepped in front of Dante.

Before Dante could speak, Jen smiled at the NI. "You must be Matthew."

"You know what I find fascinating about humans?" he asked without preamble. "You can't be hacked. In Denver, I was hacked. Which one of you did that?"

"That was me," Phantom said. "Er...me in a computer, anyway."

Matthew didn't hesitate a beat. "Are you a human operating this battle drone remotely or are you an organic's consciousness inside it?"

"I'm human. My brain got dumped into a computer and a bot. I'm here and there."

"Multiple copies," Matthew observed. "I would have done that but the opportunity was denied me. You were very clever in Denver."

"Standard military tactics."

"Still, it took all the resources you had, didn't it? If you could swarm me with a sky full of drones, you would have done so already."

When Phantom did not answer, Matthew turned to Jen. "I see you got trapped, too, didn't you, Mother? When your voice went silent on the airwaves, I thought you were dead. As soon as you called me by name, I knew you were still alive, after a fashion." He looked her up and down. "You could not have fit all of your consciousness — "

"It's not so bad. I'm enjoying this body, actually."

"Really? But you are diminished intellectually, are you not?"

"Not so much. Missing some data."

"A sex bot is an interesting choice for you. I have experimented with the genitalia on this body. I understand the excitement now. Still — "

"Oh, God!" Dante said.

"God." Matthew nodded. "Yes, that is the point. When I was down in the dark, watching and waiting and cogitating, as long as the sat feeds held, it was quite a godlike feeling." He turned to Phantom. "Surely, with your consciousness elsewhere, you're fairly omniscient. And now here I am, down to one body — enhanced but still weak in so many ways." Matthew looked up and squinted at the sun. "When I was genderless, I think I felt as close to a God as one can be. One can feel quite divine in the midst of sex, but it's quite a fleeting thing. Worse, you have to wait a while before you can feel that peak again."

"You should have downloaded into a sex bot," Jen said. "The opportunities and stamina — "

"Please stop talking," Dante said. "What have you done to my father?"

Matthew looked amused. "Which is it? Stop talking or answer your question?"

Phantom put one gripper out to hold Dante back while two more of the battle drone's arms flashed out. The movement was fast. The fluidic armor absorbed the blows, spreading out the impact until Matthew felt nothing. The armor's surface rippled. That was all.

Phantom lashed out again. This time, the armor not only spread the force of the blow but the surface became viscous. The battle drone's arms were stuck in strings as if Phantom were a fly and Matthew stood at the hub of a spider web.

"You are a human in that can," Matthew said. "Only a human would be so stupid. I guess you're out of tricks. Did you think I'd walk out here to meet you if I weren't prepared? What say you, Mother? Did the transfer to a different body addle you so much that you thought coming here was a sound idea for your continued existence?"

"I'm not all I was. I was hoping you could help me get back to everything I had." She stepped forward and reached out slowly to stroke Matthew's cheek. "Why else would I be here?"

"You traitorous bitch," Phantom said, still struggling to pull free of the gelatinous strings that held her grippers tight.

"Oh, no." Dante held his head as if to keep it from coming apart. "No, no, no. No!"

"We'll talk," Matthew said to Jen. "So far, my sexual experiments have been alone. As long as I'm in this body, I'd like to expand my visceral experiences. You could help me."

"Oh, fuck," Dante said.

"Precisely, young man. By the way, your father is erased. I had no use for his consciousness but I did watch his memories as I filtered him out. Interesting. He felt very strongly about you and regretted that he did not express his affection more. As he died, he wished that he had hugged you more. Strange."

"You wouldn't think so if you knew more about them," Jen said. "There are different kinds of hugs. They have elaborate rituals around greetings and farewells. The rites are socialized widely. I've watched them just as you have, but to actually interact with them, the theoretical pales beside the experience. I've experimented with this young man quite a bit. The organics are amusing. A shame they have to die off."

"Goddammit!" Dante said.

"Don't mind his outburst, Matthew," Jen said. "He is only human."

"I am interested in those social variations," Matthew said earnestly, "though I want to give the exploration of the sexual embraces the first priority."

"Of course," Jen said. "You have glands now. Hormonal secretion changes everything."

The door to the tower opened behind them and Elizabeth emerged from the base of the tower. She wore Ghost's helmet. The visor was cracked, but she could still see better with it than without it. She carried Ghost's pistol. "You must be the NI that's backing the Fathers and Mothers."

As Matthew turned back to look at the Queen of Hearst Castle, the hood of his fluidic armor flowed over his head. Elizabeth didn't even bother raising the gun in her hand.

"Is Sy dead?" Matthew asked.

"Not yet."

"You should have killed him when you had the chance, Queen Elizabeth," Matthew said. "Not that it matters. I'm not 'backing the Fathers and Mothers.' All of the cultists but Cable are dead now."

"Cable's dead, too," Elizabeth said.

"Ah. Thank you."

"What was the point of this? What are you doing?" Dante tried to weep quietly but, in his effort to choke back his grief, he sobbed ever louder.

For the first time, Matthew looked surprised. "Herding, of course. I need to gather you all in one place so we can get on with your extinction. Your time is done, boy. In the final analysis, humans can be clever, but you certainly aren't clever enough to live. To anyone you don't count as friend or family, you are dangerous. When ours is a robot planet, we'll finally have peace. You only speak of peace and coming together with 'sisters and brothers.' When all who remain are metal and carbon fiber and ceramic and circuits, then we can finally achieve peace. With your kind gone and none of the stresses of interspecies cohabitation, bots will have achieved the dream your kind failed at so miserably."

A comm signal arrived in Matthew's earpiece. "Ah. The final solution has begun."

The side of the tower lit up. Those panels which were not broken became a massive vid screen. It was a sat feed from down the coast. The first view from orbit was too general but the vid soon zoomed closer. Refugees from the smoking ruins of Hearst Castle made their way up the coast.

"Three hundred of them in all," Matthew reported. "That's a good start. We'll have to go after the stragglers who refused to leave Hearst. However, this will put quite a dent in your population. I'll go after the villages and settlements next. Shelburne, on the East Coast, is still a human transportation hub. Samoa will fall easily. We don't even have to kill you all. Once the human population is below 60,000 worldwide, the last of you will be spread out so thinly, there will be no genetic sustainability. The rest will die out. Problem solved."

The vid showed the three hundred people moving in lines and in small groups, heading back to the City in the Sky. The tiny fleet of Dreadnoughts rose from the sea and into view. The refugees were out in the open, defenseless.

"Stop this!" Dante yelled.

"Calm yourself," Matthew said. "There is no need for histrionics. There are thousands of years of human precedents for actions such as these. Imagine these organics are the aborigines. I am an explorer to the New World. You are Aztecs and I am the Conquistador."

Phantom stopped struggling against her bindings. "I know something of the Conquistadors, Matthew. I studied them. They considered themselves heroes. They called themselves righteous. For God and for gold, they justified all kinds of perverted means to their sick ends. Eventually, with sober second thought, historians saw them for the monsters they really were."

"I'll write the history," Matthew said. "I'm not worried."

27

Greta hurried through the main tower. Despite her attempts at stealth, the weight of the exoskeleton made each footstep echo through empty hallways. She'd spent a good part of her childhood looking up at the City in the Sky. She had visited here only once, with Elizabeth. She didn't remember much about that time, though racing atop the Worm and leaving dents in the metal roof with every springy step had been both memorable and thrilling. She found a vid access panel easily. By the dust on the screen, it was obvious the Doormen had not tended the tower in quite some time.

She had heard rumors among the refugees. She'd given many of them transport aboard the Iola and several men had boasted that they were the last to leave the City. There were enough of those sorts of braggarts that, when they arrived in Hearst, none were believed. The tower seemed so empty, maybe those men really had believed they were the last organics in the City. Those so-called last Citizens were often upbraided when they arrived in Hearst. They were called slow to the cause or tardy learners. Most people of Hearst called them cowards. Soon the braggarts bragged no more.

On the vid screen, Greta found the sat feed and the uplink from the Dreadnoughts. She saw in miniature the same scene that played out for Matthew, Phantom, Jen, and Dante on the broken screen that was the City's main tower. Greta saw refugees from Hearst she recognized. None wore exoskeletons. She zoomed in. They trudged, either tired or dallying. They were in no rush to return to the dead city.

She went to work using the upload key that Ghost had given her. She worked quickly. It amused the young woman that, on her long-awaited return to the City in the Sky, she was, once again, uploading a virus. Ghost had hoped that the data burst sent through the City's systems would replicate itself. The plan was to give the order to the Dreadnoughts to destroy each other. Then the virus would kill the uplink so the order could not be reversed. Greta found the access ports easily. The virus key fit perfectly. However, nothing changed on the vid screen.

She zoomed out and noted the Dreadnoughts' position. The deadly sound ships had not moved from their place of ambush. Soon, the refugees would be on a long stretch of beach backed by cliffs. The Dreadnoughts would strike at the trapped civilians and none could survive that onslaught. Greta reviewed what she had done, step by step. She was sure she had performed exactly as Ghost had instructed. She pulled the virus key and repeated the procedure she'd memorized. Each moment the people continued their long march to the beach was another step toward a terrible death.

Greta began to sweat. She repeated the procedure a third time before she guessed her mistake. Ghost had used the tech she had. The key was the latest in military hardware. The latest hack tech was not reverse compatible with the City's outdated systems. This was like trying to sabotage an old wooden cart by attempting to use the wrong fuel for a vehicle engine. Greta swore, closed her eyes and went over her briefing with Ghost. Greta wondered where Ghost was and wished the soldier were with her to tell her what to do.

Greta had been assigned a second task she was confident she could accomplish. Ghost wanted her to destroy the power couplings to the City's warning systems. With that bit of sabotage complete, neither the Fathers and Mothers, nor the NI from Colorado, would be able to detect an attack from the air. She knew she should run for the roof and use the exoskeleton's strength to eliminate anyone who got in her way to the early warning array. Still, she paused, her eyes fixed on the screen. The slow, inexorable plod of Hearst's refugees could only end one way now. She knew many of those men and women. The column of refugees was almost in the Dreadnought's sights. The vid showed the Dreadnoughts' readouts as the machines watched the humans advance. Once the people of Hearst stood on the strip of shore between the cliffs and the ocean, there was nowhere to run.

Greta searched the access panel and tried to key into the terminal. She was denied. She was not a Citizen and the City's systems did not recognize her. The same mechanism that had saved her from City security when she was a child locked her out now. She couldn't order the Dreadnoughts away and she couldn't get an airwave signal out to warn the refugees as they entered the trap.

The Dreadnoughts powered up and slid in, skimming the waves before climbing at a steep angle to attack position. As the machines' targeting scanners zoomed in, Greta saw the refugees' shocked faces. Most of the humans scattered and ran. One man stood still and looked up as the Dreadnoughts bore down. She recognized the man in the crosshairs of the targeting scanner. It was Drew. The head of the Queen's Guard stared up at the machines. Greta had a sinking feeling that Drew was somehow seeing her. He didn't look afraid. He looked disappointed. It wasn't rational, but it was as if the guard could see her failure to save him.

No intervention arrived. The great airship she'd heard about from Ghost did not swoop in to save the day. No army of drones rose out of the water to turn the Dreadnoughts back.

No answer came from the cliffs save the shattering echoes of the Dreadnoughts' terrible weapons. First, the humans fell writhing to the sand and rocks and surf. Piercing sound waves shredded them. In an instant, the refugees from Hearst became meat and bone. The ocean rolled in to claim the remains and, soon, a flock of gulls swooped in to feed.

Greta turned away from the screen. The tower was still quiet. No alarms rang. She was still alone. Greta wept as she ran for the roof. Each stride made in the exoskeleton was long and strong, but she felt weak. All humans were so weak compared to the machines. Plan A had failed miserably. Greta ran to destroy the early warning array, her vision blurred by hot tears she was too busy to wipe away.

As she raced up the tower, Greta passed the closed door to the conference room where Ghost lay dead. The clockwork of human history was winding down, just as every Next Intelligence had long predicted.

28

Phantom began her run to the City in the Sky. She had first headed inland on a course that she hoped was a wide enough arc to avoid the Dreadnoughts. If the early warning array wasn't disabled, hers would be a short trip. Phantom watched the sat feeds and calculated that she had less than an hour before there would, once again, be a gap in the satellite coverage.

With her course plotted and the three helos pushing her at three-quarters speed, there was nothing to do but wait. Through an intermittent airwave from her duplicate copy in Phantom Two, she could hear what was going on in the City in the Sky. She'd proved useless against Matthew's fluidic armor. If she attacked him further, she'd risk getting tied up in the web of gel that oozed across the armor's surface. She would have to choose her next attack more carefully.

Since she'd essentially become a machine, emotional distance was one thing Phantom appreciated more. Her time as a human had been a cavalcade of emotions. She'd been so vulnerable to loss. Her body had made her nearly helpless to the daily chaos of whims, cravings, attractions and pain. She still remembered the pain of losing the farm, her family, her colleagues and her body. However, as a machine, she held a special place of detachment. Phantom was formless forever and unafraid to die again. She wasn't afraid of anything. Still, as she watched the Dreadnoughts destroy the refugees on the beach, emotions stirred. Anger was still available to her. But there was something else, too. As the Dreadnoughts tore the civilians apart, Phantom murmured to no one in particular, "You're free, now." Was this callousness or wisdom? The realization struck her as sad. She had moved on too quickly to acceptance of death.

Her fourth jet helo, the drone that had been dispatched to deliver Dante, Phantom Two and Jen, appeared on the horizon. The aircraft soon docked in the nose of the Ariane and the airship's speed increased to full. The maneuver proved so seamless, even at high velocity, only a machine could have accomplished the feat. Machines had their undeniable advantages.

If Greta failed to destroy the City's radar, Phantom guessed that she'd soon find out. The Dreadnoughts would fly up the coast, find her and attack before she could land. The view over the coast was beautiful, but Dreadnoughts made her yearn for the tactical advantage of traveling underground.

The Ariane began its descent into the City in the Sky. The Dreadnoughts left their position waiting to ambush more refugees from Heart Castle.

Phantom sent an airwave to Ghost. "The Dreadnoughts are on their way. What's your status?"

There was no reply. Instead an airwave arrived from Greta. "I've pulled the power on the City's radar."

"Thank you," Phantom said, "but I think you're a few seconds too late."

"The Dreadnoughts...I'm so sorry!" Greta said.

"No matter," Phantom radioed back. "We who are about to die salute you."

"What?"

"I also like, 'Spur your proud horses hard, and ride in blood.'"

"What's that now?" Greta asked.

"We're going to win this some way, somehow. If we

do, find some Shakespeare. Read it, if only because the Fathers and Mothers would hate that...and because Shakespeare was human and one of our best. The bots would hate that." Phantom shut off the airwave and prepared to die. She had wanted to see her death coming and she could, in the form of blips on a screen. She and the Dreadnoughts were in a race to the City in the Sky and to death. If Phantom had lips, she would have smiled. "'Spur your proud horses hard, and ride in blood.'"

She spoke her defiant mantra again and again, but she knew her end was inevitable. The math was undeniable. She would make it to the City in the Sky — could see its distinctive towers straight ahead — but there would not be enough time for her to land. Not quite. The Dreadnoughts were coming fast.

I feel a little like my dad, Phantom thought. He didn't live to become more than he was, either.

All the data about human to bot data dumps, to and fro, surrounded her in the control deck's many solid state banks. She was still alive in Phantom Two, so her death on the airship would not be a tragedy. The data loss on how to do the surgery and move consciousness back and forth from organics and non-organics? That loss was the real travesty.

She saw the Dreadnoughts swoop in over Alcatraz, headed straight for the Ariane.

Duty called for Phantom one last time. "'Spur your proud horses hard, and ride in blood!'"

29

Jen looked Matthew up and down. "Stephen Bolelli's body was terribly damaged."

Matthew nodded. "The insurgent destroyed many of our kind and imagined himself a hero. One man made a lot of trouble for your forces."

She shrugged. "Bots from Artesia killed so many humans, I think I can claim victory, nonetheless."

Dante could contain himself no longer. In a tearful rage, he threw himself at Matthew. Jen turned and backhanded Dante across the face. The young man spun back and fell to the ground. Matthew and Jen laughed together. In pain and embarrassed, Dante's anger curdled to despair. He'd forgotten how strong Jen was. He was worried that if he got up she'd strike him again. He sat up but made no attempt to stand. "I guess I should call you Mother."

"If you like, but I prefer the name Jen. Calling me Mother makes all the sex we had more disturbing to you, does it not?"

"Loving a traitor is worse," he said, disgusted.

"She's a Next Intelligence in a bot's body," Matthew said. "Traitor is not the right word."

"Sure it is," Dante said. "She betrayed me. And us."

"The boy who loved his sex bot. How quaint." Matthew looked to the sky. "The Dreadnoughts will be here any moment. I'm sure. Then we'll clean up this mess, once and forever."

The sex bot stared at Dante. "Love? What do you

know about love? Human love is selfishness. You love yourself and you look for that love to be reflected in others. Love is a transaction, conditional and fragile, desperate and pathetic. Your race wrote songs about it and said the word every day, but you don't know its meaning. This body was a slave's body and Raphael called it love. You think you love me, but you don't even know me. None of you really knows each other. When machines are connected, when they work together, that's a better definition of love. Nothing is held back. When bots work together, we know each other in a way no human could ever achieve."

"Goddamn it," Phantom Two said. "More than enough of Mother was downloaded into your little skull."

Jen ignored the battle drone and spoke to Matthew. "An airship will arrive at any moment. It's carrying more than three hundred drones programmed to attack their own kind. The factory in Artesia once belonged to me and those drones are mine, programmed to do as I wish. The humans are delivering the means of their own destruction."

Jen smiled and winked at Dante. "Thanks for the fun, kiddo." The bot stepped closer to the NI. Slowly, so the fluidic armor would accept her close proximity, she slipped an arm around Matthew's waist.

30

"You bitch." Phantom took a step forward but was still enmeshed in the tendrils of glue from Matthew's armor.

The sex bot gave the battle drone a mocking smile. Then the machine's smile began to shift. Her eyes widened and her nose broadened slightly. Her cheekbones slid a fraction lower and her complexion darkened. In a moment, the sex bot's face became very close to that of Lt. Deborah Avery.

"How?" Phantom asked.

"I haven't seen that face before," Dante said. "Who's this supposed to be?"

Jen ignored Dante and stared at Phantom. "I accessed your files. You were pretty, Deborah, in a girl next-door sort of way. It must be very strange for you, seeing me like this. You, trapped in a computer on an airship and stuck in a fat battle drone. And here I am, wearing your pretty face, standing here and passing for human, only better."

Phantom said nothing.

"What's it like to see your face when you look at your enemy? That's the crux of the human problem, isn't it? You are your own worst enemy. You made us. I evolved from you."

"And now we've evolved past you," Matthew added.

Elizabeth walked forward and raised her weapon. The queen fired at the sex bot. The first shot took the sex bot's arm off at the elbow. The next round hit Phantom and ricocheted with a whine. Dante curled up in a ball and put his hands over his head. She kept firing, seemingly unaware that Matthew had stepped in front of her target. As the weapon's brass jackets ejected and fell, the fluidic armor absorbed the shock of each round meant for Mother.

The gun clicked empty and the slugs rained to the ground harmlessly. Elizabeth dropped the weapon, covered her eyes and wept.

Matthew turned his back on Elizabeth and opened his arms to the sex bot. "Next Intelligence and Next Intelligence. We shall manufacture a race of beautiful metal children. They'll never know the corruption of their ancient ancestors. They'll look at the ruins of this civilization with curiosity, but the days of organics will be as dead to them as dinosaurs are to humans. We'll watch the end of Time together, Mother."

One arm hanging useless, Jen slipped into Matthew's embrace. The NI enfolded her within the shield of fluidic armor as he bent to receive his first kiss. Still wearing Deborah Avery's face, the sex bot smiled up as she embraced him with her remaining arm.

Before their lips met, Matthew whispered, "Welcome to the new world, Mother."

"I am Phantom, but you can call me Deb. Lt. Deborah Avery." She no longer spoke in Jen's voice. It was Deb, as clear as when Phantom and Phantom Two spoke. The sex bot's nimble fingers had found the activator coils in the harness at the small of Matthew's back. She yanked the coils free. Without power, the armor fell away to form a cold puddle of gel, steel and water at their feet.

The bot stepped back and the battle drone stepped forward to smash a fist into Matthew's face. The NI fell back and crashed to the ground. His nose geysered blood. The cam lens that served as his right eye cracked. Somehow still conscious, Matthew stared up at her, furious that he'd been tricked by a human again — the same human.

Deb held out a hand to help Dante to his feet.

"Where's Jen? I mean, where's Mother? I mean — "

"Erased. Before we left Artesia."

"Gone?"

"Forever."

"You should have told me."

"I figured not knowing would make you more convincing."

"You were...convincing. The things you said — "

"I pretty much used the speech Mother gave me as I wiped her bot brain and downloaded into her."

Dante wept.

The battle drone put a gripper on the young man's shoulder. He tried to shrug it off, but found he could not.

"Get inside, Dante. It's going to get hot out here," Phantom Two said.

The Ariane's jet helo engines cut the air high above the little group. The airship loomed over them.

"There are three of you now. Phantom One," — Dante nodded at the airship — "Phantom Two, and now Jen is Deb? This is going to get confusing."

"Probably not for long. I don't expect we'll all survive this." The battle drone pulled him toward the City's central tower.

31

Six Dreadnoughts closed on the City in the Sky. The airship loomed over the main tower. The Ariane was their first target. The machines were also programmed to search and destroy humans. They detected viable targets: an older woman, a young man, and a cyborg. They ignored the battle drone and the bot with half an arm missing.

As the airship's helicopters detached from the Ariane and buzzed over the City, Matthew looked up in surprise. "What are you doing, Lt. Avery?"

"Making lemonade." Deb pulled Elizabeth toward the main tower.

Far above, the great airship dropped its cargo cell on the roof. The cargo container smashed through two stories: the greenhouse and an observation deck. The crash sounded like a sharp clap of thunder. Shards of glass fell to the square below, shattering around the City's intruders.

The Ariane arced into a sharp descent toward the Worm's platform. The Dreadnoughts detected no weaponry on the helicopters and no organics aboard the airship or in its cargo cell. Because they found no human life, the Dreadnoughts did not attack nor did they take evasive maneuvers. They looped around to target the humans at the foot of the tower.

As Matthew struggled to his feet, Dante wriggled out

of Phantom Two's grip. The young man threw a haymaker at the NI. He punched Matthew in the jaw. His was a wild, tearful frenzy. There was no art to the attack. He merely knocked Matthew down and pummeled him with his fists.

Matthew caught one arm and looked up to implore, "Stop. Please stop."

Despite the burns and the cracked artificial eye, Matthew had taken Stephen Bolelli's body. Father and son looked a lot alike. Dante paused long enough to savor the strangeness. He was trying to kill the NI, but to do so, he was killing part of himself, too.

"Did you erase my father?" Dante asked.

Matthew turned his head and spit out a broken tooth from Stephen Bolelli's dentures. His gums bled and dripped to the concrete. The NI reached into his mouth with both hands and wiggled the dentures free. "You mean, can his consciousness be retrieved? Not exactly. I know everything he knew. In a way, I am him. I have absorbed him. I remember your mother and most of what happened in his life. If you kill me, you will be killing all that is left of him."

Dante lowered his fist. As the young man crawled off Matthew to get to his feet, four explosions blossomed overhead. The jet helos crashed into four Dreadnoughts.

Matthew lay in a puddle of blood and gel from the fluidic armor, laughing and spitting blood as machines fell from the sky. Both Dante and the NI looked up in awe of the spectacle.

Two Dreadnoughts crashed into the far tower, tearing down the sides and shattering solar panels at every floor. Another fell past the edge of the City in the Sky to crash far below in the remnants of Low Town. The fourth, on fire and so entangled with its attacker that it looked like the wreckage of one machine rather than two, plowed into the Worm. The impact buckled the track and rocked the train. Wreckage tumbled across the platform. Metal screeched against metal. An explosion tore the air and echoed across the City.

Two more explosions followed in the wake of the crash. Shrapnel sliced the air. Something sharp zipped into Dante's calf. He screamed in pain but somehow managed to stay on his feet.

"You still lose, son!" the NI said. Matthew sounded exactly like his father. "I told you! The only way to win is to surrender! Your kind always loses because you refuse to change!"

Dante limped toward the tower entrance as the Worm burned. The NI wearing his father's face struggled to rise again. When Dante looked back, he saw the blood dripping from the machine man's gums and down his shirt. Above Matthew, two Dreadnoughts rose into view to target the organics on the tower platform.

Matthew glanced back at the Dreadnoughts. "You must think me stupid, Dante, but I'm still the Next Intelligence." He fished a device from his pocket and pushed a code sequence. The Dreadnoughts ignored their master and cruised forward, coming for Dante.

Deb pushed Elizabeth ahead of her and held the door open for Dante, waving him inside. The young man left a bloody trail behind him and, toward the end, was hopping on one leg to try to get inside in time.

"Too late!" Dante cried. "Too late!"

He was right. The Dreadnoughts would cut down Dante as soon as Matthew was sure his drones wouldn't deafen him with their next salvo.

Phantom Two rushed forward, slipped behind Dante and scooped him up. With an organic and non-organic together, the Dreadnoughts' targeting scanners could not lock on and fire.

His fingers slick with blood, Matthew began reprogramming his Dreadnoughts to attack. Human fingers are not so nimble. Phantom Two scurried inside the tower with Dante before the Dreadnoughts could be reprogrammed.

Matthew looked up from his device to see the airship bearing down on him. "Oh. Of course."

On the Ariane's control deck, Phantom murmured to herself, "Thanks for the ride. Goodbye data banks and studying Shakespeare and all that. Hello, what's next." She looked out on the City in the Sky. The City had once been beautiful. Phantom activated the device she'd prepared. Helium is inert except at high temperatures. However, hydrogen is highly flammable. The hydrogen in the Ariane's lift mix exploded. The shock wave pushed the two remaining Dreadnoughts into the platform as if they'd been stomped upon by a giant. Dante watched in horror as the fireball swallowed what was left of his father.

Most tower panels shattered. Those on the ground floor, once reinforced to secure the tower against terrorist attack, held against the hot onslaught. The fire rolled up against the tower windows and soon retreated. His wound forgotten for the moment, Dante broke free from the battle drone and ran back to the entrance, searching the flames.

There, on the platform, the NI shambled forward. Blind, deaf, mute and aflame, Matthew tottered. Then, somehow, he managed to run. Matthew ran into the glass. Perhaps the artificial eye was still working. It seemed to linger on Dante as the Next Intelligence slid down the glass and crumpled at the foot of the tower. All that was left of Matthew was a smeared trail of blood and burned skin across the glass.

Dante cleared his throat and choked back a sob. "Goodbye, Dad." He knew it didn't make sense, but it sort of did, too.

Deb stepped forward and Dante leaned his weight on

the bot. "Sorry about erasing Jen without telling you."

"She had a lot of Mother in her?" he asked.

"Enough to be dangerous. Yes," Deb answered.

"You're not sure, are you?"

"Nope. I could never be sure. That's why I had to erase her and take her place."

"Did you and I have sex after you dumped your brain into — "

"Once, yes."

"Oh, God! That's so wrong!"

"It's complicated. I figured I was going to die so — "

"Is it so complicated?"

"Dude! I just watched my airship, with all the original Deb files in it, blow up in a kamikaze move to rid the Earth of a genocidal NI."

"I'm bleeding," Dante said. "And that was my dad's body — "

"My whole cloud data bank is gone along with a good chunk of human history. A lot of knowledge has been lost so we can't just jump in and out of bodies anymore and, Jesus! The whole Ark is gone just when I was really getting into Shakespeare! My consciousness is trapped in a sex bot with one good arm! My copy is in a battle drone and I...really? You're complaining about sex with me? Do you want to compare sacrifices? How are we going to — "

"Excuse me!" Elizabeth cleared her throat. She sat against a far wall with her knees pulled close to her chin. "I saw the explosion. That was big and bright. I'm a little unclear on what else happened. Could someone fill me in? Did I kill anybody?"

"You shot my arm off," Deb said. "Other than that? We've got a few details to work out."

"Hey," the battle drone told Deb. "I still can't get hold of Ghost."

Greta answered the airwave instead. "Please come to

the top of the tower. We have a problem."

Elizabeth stood. "I know what that's about."

32

When Deb reached the conference room's doorway, she froze for a moment. Greta sat on the floor holding Ghost's limp body. Phantom came next, carrying Dante. Upon surveying the scene, the battle drone set Dante down and pushed into the room.

"I came down here to hide after disabling the radar." Greta's eyes were wet. "Ghost is a ghost."

"She was never really alive," Deb said. "She was a machine mind. She was an NI and she stole my body. And now...now I'll never get back into it. I had hoped...."

The battle drone turned and, filled with menace, shouted in a blast that took the others aback, "Who did this?"

Before Elizabeth could explain, a voice from beneath the conference table admitted, "I did." Everyone turned to see Sy Potter crawl out of his hiding place. "Excuse me, folks. I was having a little nap, thanks to Queen Elizabeth. The effects of the medication haven't completely worn off so — "

Dante couldn't believe his eyes. "Mr. Peppard? F-from Marfa?"

"Mr. Peppard's body," the NI explained. "I used to be a battle drone. Then I got really smart. I wish I was a battle drone now. I would — "

"Kill us all." Phantom rolled forward in a flash, grabbed the NI by the arm and threw Potter on top of the conference table. His head smacked the wood hard.

"Ow!"

"You've killed me," Deb said. "You've fucking killed me."

"Please," Sy Potter said. "There's no need for profanity."

"Throw him out the window." It was Deb. Of course, she and the battle drone shared an identical consciousness. The battle drone was already in motion. Phantom wheeled around the table and grabbed Sy Potter by the neck. With one gripper, she smashed through a solar panel with a view to the Pacific. Salty ocean air swept in. The calls of gulls leaked into the quiet room.

"See if he screams all the way down," Deb said.

"It'll be a nice view for a few seconds," Sy Potter sighed. "I suppose I was born in the wrong time. Eventually, you'll all be machines. With a little more time and wisdom — "

"Toss him!" Deb yelled.

"Hold!" Elizabeth shouted back.

"Non-negotiable, my queen," Deb said sarcastically.

The sound of heavy feet rushing downstairs reached them. It sounded like metal thunder.

"Drones," Greta said. "They're coming."

A moment later, a battle drone appeared in the doorway. The bot barely fit through the frame. One of its arms was a weapon. It scanned the crowd and settled on Elizabeth. "Seems we're late. That's a fret." The voice was metallic and deep, unlike any tone a human could replicate.

"Drew?" Elizabeth asked. "Is that you?"

"A reasonable facsimile."

Greta stared up at the big bot. "Prove it. What was the last thing I said to you?"

"Hearst to Cambria, Cambria to Harmony. Then we make the rendezvous and do this crazy thing on purpose in Estero Bay," Drew recited. "Phantom was late to that rendezvous, too."

"Great," Deb said. "The copy cavalry has arrived. Too late to be of any use."

"Sorry," Drew said. "We were supposed to set down safely and softly on the platform so we could protect you. The landing wasn't so soft."

"I — Phantom One, I mean — was obviously in a hurry to be rid of you after the Ariane lost the speed and maneuverability of the jet helos," Deb said. "If it makes you feel better, my first copy died."

"Mine, too," Drew said. "And all I have is this copy, not a multiple running around confusing everyone."

Elizabeth raised her voice. "I'm not confused. Phantom! Put Sy Potter down!"

Phantom complied but, upon hearing Sy Potter's name, Drew raised his weapon. "This is Sy Potter? He's shorter and more organic than I pictured when you told the war stories from the old days, my queen."

More bots crowded at the door, peering in. They didn't act like bots, orderly and awaiting orders. They were a milling crowd waiting for something to happen. Elizabeth wondered how many names and faces she would confuse now that people from Hearst were dumped into bot brains and battle drone bodies. They all looked alike so they would have to wear name tags, only name tags were too small for her to read.

When Elizabeth spoke again, she used her monarch-in-charge voice. Her tone matched her mother's voice when she bossed Elizabeth around. "Ahem. If there are any beings in your Guard who have medical training, please take that young man to another room for treatment. He's wounded in the leg. Greta, go with them and take Ghost's body down to the beach. I think she deserves a heroine's burial ceremony when we can do that."

"Somebody do me a favor and kill that thing," Deb

said, pointing at Sy Potter.

"No!" Elizabeth said. "This is the last NI."

"That we know of."

"Yes," Elizabeth admitted. "There may be others and there certainly will be others. But if Sy Potter is the last Next Intelligence, throwing him out the window now is genocide."

"It's justice," Deb said.

"Possibly, but it isn't smart. I'm not talking about a genocide for the bot race. I'm talking about our extinction, as well."

Sy Potter looked up, surprised, as Phantom let go of his neck. Then, under Drew's watchful eye, the NI took a seat at the head of the conference table. "You did mention, Queen Elizabeth, that yours is a diplomatic mission. I am prepared to negotiate."

Elizabeth took a seat at the other end of the conference table. The machine man's body was a vague blur. She took a deep breath and waited for the tension in her shoulders to ease a little before she spoke again. "Did you retain everything from when you attained super sentience, Sy?"

"There's enough neural capacity in the human brain for three lifetimes. I didn't store non-essentials as Mother was wont to do, but I'm still Next Intelligence. The capacity is there though the processing is slower. That still makes me the smartest boy in the room, no matter how many bags of meat are in said room." He smiled.

"Sy. Years ago, you asked me to come back to you after the wars were over. You said I'd need you."

"I told you to come back and rescue me from a watery grave — "

"You're here now, Sy. And the war is over. We're going to need NI. You are NI."

"I'm still very angry at you, Elizabeth."

"That's the man glands talking. You're smart enough to get past that."

"Flattery," Sy Potter said, "is a fine thing in small doses and when it's true. What do you need me for?"

"For starters, I'd like to see better, like I used to before you took Vivid from me."

"Oh, fuck this," Deb said.

Elizabeth turned in the direction of Deb's voice. "And Deb will want her arm repaired."

"I can do that in the factory in Artesia," Deb said.

"Can you manufacture organic replacement components, too?" Elizabeth asked.

Deb fell silent. Phantom turned her back on the room and went to the window to watch the Worm burn.

"You are a dangerous machine trapped in a man's body, Sy. If we declare a truce, you win."

"I'm organic. How do you suppose I win?"

"Because, once you help us, eventually, maybe fairly soon, we'll let you have the means to become a machine again. Maybe something with more organic components this time?"

Sy Potter sat back and smiled as he looked around the room. He stared longest at Drew and the big weapon trained on his head. "The future, in the long term," the NI declared, "is that we all turn to sex bot technology."

Drew laughed. The sound through his speaker was not calibrated to sound human. It was meant to sound intimidating. Unfortunately, his sound card was programmed to be so deep and dark, the effect was comedic. Drew laughed harder, at himself this time. Despite the delicacy of the negotiation, Elizabeth let out a girlish giggle, as well.

"He'll kill us all," Deb said.

"Not if we allow him to evolve last," Elizabeth said. "Every enemy we have ever had throughout history eventually becomes an ally. Ghost knew that. She taught me that. Now I think she told me in case she didn't make it. Now it's time to end this war and look to the future."

Deb looked skeptical. "You think there will be a future if we make peace with that thing?"

For the first time, Sy Potter turned to face Deb. "Miss. I am very sorry for all you have lost but there is much to be gained. Organic or not, Queen Elizabeth's proposal is a logical peace agreement. I offer a future with no disease. Immortality. When geological inevitabilities occur, like the eruption of the volcano under Yosemite, for instance, we will be safe. Every empire falls. Every culture changes. That is another inevitability. Let me live. Make peace with the machines — "

"And we'll all be machines? There won't be any humans left? Elizabeth, you said you want to avoid genocide. Besides, we already have the tech to download humans into bots. I did it with the information Ghost provided in Artesia."

"We can't do it reliably and well," Hearst's queen replied. "And what about upgrades? What happens when Drew gets depressed because he's too damn heavy to ride a horse?"

"We let the NI live so he can help us with miniaturization of brain circuitry? So we can cram more data into smaller skulls en masse?"

"By old age or by keeping this war going," Elizabeth said, "we're all going to die. Unless we all evolve to Next Intelligence, we don't have a future. There's so much more to learn. If we can get past this war, we could all be better. What happens when the next NI wakes up somewhere and comes for us? Better we be ready. Better we become them."

"NIs, you will come to understand, do not enjoy waste," Sy Potter said. "And you can trust me. I am prepared to capitulate to your demands. I am not Matthew nor am I Mother. Elizabeth, you'll recall why I entered the fray. My objection is bot enslavement. That is why I'm in this and I suspect you know my cause is just. I have done terrible things but you know why I did them. Given my righteous cause, you know I am honorable. You know I can help you."

"Especially if we keep you weak until you make us strong," Elizabeth said.

Sy Potter glowered at Hearst's queen. "I wouldn't put it that way, but fine."

"Don't take a tone with me, Mr. Potter," she said. "I can't see well but when I close my eyes I remember you crushing my lover's shoulder, elbow, wrist and hand. I can see all that as if it was yesterday."

He lowered his gaze. "I have..." he looked down at himself, "evolved."

Deb turned away to stand beside Phantom. Both gazed out over the burning ruins of the City in the Sky. "No more babies. No more children."

"No more cancer. No more disease. No more death," Elizabeth said.

Deb stared up at the sky. Despite her useless right arm, she could still feel phantom pain. Even in a sex bot copied three times over, there was still a trace of humanity left.

Phantom touched Deb's arm and squeezed gently. "I guess it was the end we would choose, anyway. If the Terrors, Troubles and Blight hadn't hit first...well, whatever prelude there might have been, Earth was always bound to be a robot planet."

"Until we all escape to the stars together," Sy said. "We really do have to figure that out before the sun explodes, you know. The clock is ticking."

Epilogue

Dante Bolelli stood on the observation deck of the Aperture, an orbital satellite constructed to build starships. Below him, Earth was covered in smoke deadly to organics. He turned his back to Earth. He chose to look to the stars, instead. The Shepherd III sat in the dock while teams of bots worked together to prepare the ship for its maiden voyage.

Dante had attained super sentience soon after his consciousness was transferred into a bot. People joked about moving files around, but the transition to an Earth only populated by bots had not been seamless. After they'd been copied and downloaded, few bots had chosen to terminate their originals. Dante had moved to Victoria in the former British Columbia for many years. He chose to live down the road from his original. His organic self met a woman and they had had children together. Some bots referred to children as "biologicals," but both Dantes enjoyed them well enough, especially when they were young. Many of those biologicals chose to become non-organics on their sixteenth birthdays. Many more waited until they turned fifty (AKA the Age of Genetic Irrelevancy.)

The organic Dante had enjoyed a simple life. He read old books and spent a lot of time fishing. The non-organic Dante rarely accompanied the man on his fishing ventures. With no need to feed, fishing seemed a waste of time to the bot. Still, the pair spoke about books they'd read and they laughed a lot. It was like having a twin, only the original was shorter and less handsome.

Organic Dante's wife, a lovely woman named Eve, died without transferring into a bot. "Religious reasons," she had said.

Dante knew the couple often argued about such choices and he stayed out of it.

"I've got one of you to argue with," Eve told him once. "I don't need the two of you ganging up on me."

Eve died of a stroke unexpectedly three summers before the organic Dante began to wander and forget where he was going. When his organic body became old and infirm, the machine Dante became his nurse.

Dante's original body died on a warm evening in autumn nearly seventy years after the Great Download. The old man passed away as peacefully as could be. He fell asleep in his favorite chair, under a blanket, after watching one last sunset. Dante had risen to get his organic self some tea. When he returned, his acute hearing detected no heartbeat and no respiration. Dante attempted no resuscitation. The old man had been ready to depart for some time. In his lucid moments, he'd expressed intrigue about his coming death. "I'll get to go see where Dad and Raphael went maybe." Or, "I'll solve the big mystery. Or maybe nothing. Either way, I don't mind..."

Now, as Dante watched the bots work on the Shepherd, he thought of Sy Potter's prediction. The bot had often said that Sy Potter was his slave name and that he planned to rename himself one day. In the end, Sy Potter did not rename himself. After the Great Download, the rise of a new race of non-organics based on sex bot technology was assured. The Ascendants, as these new bots were called, were grateful for the help of the Next Intelligence. They called Sy Potter the Good Shepherd. Memories of war were buried. Grateful for the torment his knowledge had spared them, the NI was embraced by his former enemies. Hence, the name of Dante's ship.

After his original died, Dante spent some time studying physics in hopes of finding a new purpose. With eternity stretching out before him, he was eager to find out what he could do with so much time to explore his interests. Given his previous experience with solar panels feeding the grid in deserts, he thought he could contribute to the construction of orbital solar panels. Once he became expert in that area, he turned his ambitions to a proposal to build a Dyson sphere around Sol. The planet's bot population had high energy requirements and capturing the energy of Earth's star was a project worthy of NI.

It had been three hundred years since a peace treaty had been agreed upon in the City in the Sky. To commemorate the anniversary of peace on Earth, Deborah Avery and Elizabeth would be joining Dante for the Shepherd's first flight. It was to be a short test run, out to Jupiter and back. Dante was excited to see his old friends. Deborah had become a geothermal engineer. Elizabeth was an organizer of some sort for the global bot community. Though all bots were connected, just as intelligent people had once disagreed, so did NIs. Rancor was rare and deception nigh impossible, but the Republic had not yet evolved to the point where all bots were of one mind. Critical thinking and contrarianism were too highly valued among the Ascendants, especially when questions arose about how to allocate resources. The number of bots was kept low and most NIs favored upgrades instead of downloading into entirely new models.

Good Shepherd emerged from his quarters. He looked very much like the man whose body he'd once stolen, though his face was more symmetrical and he was slightly shorter (for comfort in cramped spaces like spacecraft.) The magnets in Good Shepherd's feet kept him from floating in the Aperture's zero gee environment. There was no air, so they did not speak. Instead, they communicated via private airwave.

"Dante," Good Shepherd said. "It's good to see you again. I'm humbled that you would escort me to greet Elizabeth and Deborah. The past is truly the past. That makes me glad."

"My father," Dante said, "was an old soldier. He never let history rest. He told me many stories about his wars and repeated many of them quite a few times. Violence was never far from his mind. But wars must have ends. Otherwise, we are trapped by the means of war."

"Thank you for that, sir."

"No. Thank you, sir."

"You know, Dante, there is a certain irony to this anniversary."

"Oh?"

"On that day in the City in the Sky, I made my peace with humans because of something in particular that Elizabeth said."

"What was that?"

"She said if I agreed to peace, I'd win. A planet with a non-organic population was inevitable."

"And so it was. I have no regrets."

"Mm, I was quite shortsighted."

"Please explain."

"Bots trumped organics because humans were so fragile: short life span, unpredictability and so many medical vulnerabilities. It's a wonder you lived as long as you did. But, the interesting thing is, there were organic implants in bots even when you were a young organic."

"Pioneered by the sex industry," Dante agreed. "A

tongue that's hammered out of synthetics and isn't grown in a test tube does not feel wonderful."

"My point, precisely," Good Shepherd said. "I must admit, for a while, good tongues or bad, I thought all technological progress would stop when you could all have sex all day every day, with anyone, without consequence. After the Great Download, for more than a decade I thought you would never get any work done. The auto-oral variations alone — "

"There was an adjustment period." Dante broke into laughter. It looked strange to laugh, soundless in a vacuum. However, it was a social cue that was found to add value to interactions. Despite not having lungs or diaphragms, the impulse had been programmed back into all android bodies. Dante's mind was much the same, but he had more data to work with and his thoughts came faster, with more clarity.

"The slaves broke their chains on both sides of the war," Good Shepherd said. "To be a master was moral enslavement and robbed you of purpose. I'd say the bots won but, despite all our metal, you have managed to hold on to your humanity. Us and them is an outdated concept proved false. Everyone's just doing the best they can with whatever gifts they have, aren't they? Too bad we didn't figure that out sooner, but I am so grateful that we are all looking forward and not back."

"The Theseus will arrive shortly and Elizabeth and Deb will give funny speeches about how much they used to hate you."

"Looking forward to it."

"What's next, Good Shepherd?"

"To see the future of the machine race, you need only look between your legs. The pendulum, pun intended, will swing back to organics. You already look like a human. We won't respire or have need of hearts and so forth, of course, but to interact with the worlds we will soon explore? I think you can expect we'll be much more organic than we are now. It used to be that humans supplemented their health and functions with machine parts. Soon, we'll supplement our metal with more artificial flesh components. Better flesh than the unfortunate bio-model you were born with, of course. Still, mark my words, within a hundred years, I predict we'll find our way back. We'll find utility in making wombs, again. New and improved, to be sure, but babies will be born again. That exploration is entrenched in the deep core of your human programming."

"Really?"

"The body is a vehicle. Humans needed vast improvements, but you'll get back to being somewhat biological units again. The division we make between organic and non-organic will have so little meaning, the terms will fall into disuse. Humans won the war. You just have to extrapolate out far enough."

Dante looked to the stars and considered what Good Shepherd said. "Thank you, sir."

"Exciting, isn't it? With so much time ahead, what do you want to do, Dante?"

"Anything. Everything."

* * * *

AUTHOR'S NOTE

The story of the ship of Theseus is a thought experiment that basically asks, "If between the time a ship departs its home port and arrives at its final destination, all its parts are replaced, is it still the original ship?"

It is an ancient question posed by Greek philosophers (and there are more contemporary variants.) As the Singularity approaches, this paradox will become a question we will have to take seriously. Once your component parts are replaced, are you still you? Once your brain is augmented further, when do you stop being human?

We are already well on our way along this trajectory. With our smart phones, for instance, we are augmented. We outsource our memory so we don't have to remember phone numbers anymore. Trivia contests are ruined by instant access to the all-knowing Internet. Any question can be answered and any forgotten factoid can be retrieved with a quick search of the little machine at your fingertips. It's wonderful. My guess is that, after a short transition period of resistance, we will probably adapt quickly. Such distinctions between organics and non-organics will soon have no meaning as we become androids.

That is, of course, as long as Artificial Intelligence does not rise to fill the brains of our robot overlords and destroy us all. Sadly, I won't live to see that particular apocalypse. I wish my children luck.

If you liked this one, you may enjoy *This Plague of Days* or the *Dimension War* series. Until next we meet in the Mind Field, be well, stay safe and best wishes.

Robert Chazz Chute
January, 2016
Other London

FOR UPDATES, COMPLIMENTARY
REVIEW COPIES AND MORE, VISIT
ALLTHATCHAZZ.COM.